"Loaded with subtle emotions, sizzling chemistry, and some provocative thoughts on the real choices [Grant's] characters are forced to make as they choose their loves for eternity." —*RT Book Reviews* (4 stars)

"Vivid images, intense details, and enchanting characters grab the reader's attention and [don't] let go."
—*Night Owl Reviews* (Top Pick)

Praise for the Dark Warrior series

"The world of the Immortal Warriors is a thoroughly engaging one, blending powerful ancient gods, fiery desire, and touchingly human love, which readers will surely want to revisit." —*RT Book Reviews*

"[Grant] blends ancient gods, love, desire, and evil-doers into a world you will want to revisit over and over again."
—*Night Owl Reviews*

"Sizzling love scenes and engaging characters."
—*Publishers Weekly*

"Ms. Grant mixes adventure, magic, and sweet love to create the perfect romance[s]." —*Single Title Reviews*

Praise for the Dark Sword series

"Grant creates a vivid picture of Britain centuries after the Celts and Druids tried to expel the Romans, deftly merging magic and history. The result is a wonderfully dark, delightfully well-written [series]. Readers will eagerly await the next Dark Sword book."

—*RT Book Reviews*

"Another fantastic series that melds the paranormal with the historical life of the Scottish highlander in this arousing and exciting adventure." —*Bitten By Books*

"These are some of the hottest brothers around in paranormal fiction." — *Nocturne Romance Reads*

"Will keep readers spellbound."

— *Romance Reviews Today*

PASSION IGNITES

DONNA GRANT

St. Martin's Paperbacks

This is a work of fiction. All of the characters, organizations, and events portrayed in this novel are either products of the author's imagination or are used fictitiously.

PASSION IGNITES

For information address St. Martin's Press, 175 Fifth Avenue, New York, NY 10010.

ISBN: 978-1-250-07194-1

Printed in the United States of America

St. Martin's Paperbacks edition / November 2015

St. Martin's Paperbacks are published by St. Martin's Press, 175 Fifth Avenue, New York, NY 10010.

10 9 8 7 6 5 4 3 2 1

To Elizabeth Berry –
Brilliant woman and precious friend.
You're beautiful inside and out.
I'm blessed to have you in my life.

ACKNOWLEDGMENTS

Words can never express how much I love working with my beautiful, gifted editor, Monique Patterson, enough. Our partnership is amazing!

To Alex, Erin, Amy, the truly amazing art department, marketing, and everyone at SMP who was involved in getting this book ready. Y'all rock!

To my agent, Natanya Wheeler, thanks for loving my dragons!

A special thanks to my family and friends for the endless support.

CHAPTER ONE

Edinburgh
October 24

I'm going to find him.

It was an invocation Lexi repeated several times a day. It was the first thing she said upon waking, and the last thing she said before she fell asleep.

She looked at herself in the mirror and shoved her light brown hair out of her face. "I'm getting closer," she told herself. "I'm finding more information every day I search. I will find him, Christina."

Lexi spun away from the mirror and walked out of the bathroom. Her other two friends were sitting at the breakfast table talking in low tones.

What began as a memory making trip with friends had ended in disaster a week ago when Christina, the fourth member of their group, had been brutally murdered.

Lexi had been the one with Christina that night. She had also been the one who found her. The image of Christina's body laying naked in the alley would forever be stamped in her mind.

"I'm going out again," Lexi told them as she took a quick drink of coffee. "I don't know how long I'll be gone today."

They both kept their heads down for a moment. Then Jessica lifted her blue eyes to Lexi. She then quickly looked away. Crystal didn't even bother to do that much. Neither of them had gone looking for Christina's killer with her, but then again, they hadn't seen her in the alley.

Lexi shook her head and turned away—only to stop dead in her tracks when she saw the luggage by the door. Her stomach fell to her feet like lead.

She stared at the luggage and felt the last threads of her life unraveling at an insane rate. Lexi slowly turned back to the table. "You're leaving."

"Yes," Crystal answered. She stood and tucked her dark hair behind her ear. "Christina's body was shipped home yesterday. We want to be there for the funeral."

"So you're giving up here." Lexi didn't understand why neither of them were as worried about finding Christina's killer.

Jessica stood up so fast the chair flew backward. "You're not the only one hurting!" she yelled. "Stop making us feel like we don't care just because we aren't walking the streets following people like you are!"

Lexi was taken aback by Jessica's outburst. The four had been friends since high school and then college roommates. For over five years, they had been as close as sisters. Yet, Lexi couldn't help but feel like she didn't know Jessica or Crystal anymore.

"Come back to Charleston with us," Crystal pleaded. "Christina's parents will be devastated if you aren't at the funeral."

Lexi shook her head. They didn't understand, and she couldn't explain what drove her to follow those with red eyes, looking for the one responsible. "I have to find her killer. If I don't, he'll kill again."

"You gave all the information you had to the police. Let them do their jobs."

"But they aren't doing their jobs." Lexi blinked to chase away the tears. "I was with Christina. I saw the guy she left the bar with. I'm the only one who knows what he looks like."

Jessica walked to her and put her arms around her in a tight hug. "You don't have to do it all, Lex."

For just a moment, Lexi let the grief envelop her. It was so great at times that she couldn't breathe. If she let it take her, she would never be able to recover from it. So, Lexi kept it at bay with thick walls that would never be penetrated. It was the only way she could get through each day until Christina's killer was caught.

"I do," she whispered. Lexi sniffed and stepped out of Jessica's hold. "Please tell Christina's family that I won't rest until the killer is found. He'll pay for what he did to her."

Crystal's forehead furrowed in a deep frown. All her anger was gone, given way to worry. "If you stay, I have a feeling we'll never see you again. You keep tracking this murderer, he's liable to learn about it and go after you."

Lexi knew how he killed. She wasn't going to fall into the same trap as Christina. How could she return to South Carolina knowing she let a predator walk free?

"I'm going to be fine. I check in with Detective Inspector MacDonald often." Lexi forced her lips to turn up at the corners a little.

A horn honked from outside, startling them.

Jessica gave her another hug before she hurried to put on her coat.

Crystal walked to Lexi and took her hands, looking

deep into her eyes. "The flat is paid for another week. Jess and I both knew you would stay. We wanted to make sure you had somewhere safe to sleep."

The kindness of her friends made Lexi realize just how fortunate she was to have such people in her life. "Thank you."

Crystal hugged her before she spun around, but not before Lexi saw the tears. She watched her friends gather their luggage and walk out. With a last wave, the door banged loudly behind them, giving the scene a finality that left Lexi feeling hollow.

She looked out the window and watched Crystal and Jessica get into the cab and then drive away. It wasn't the first time Lexi had been alone, and she doubted it would be the last. It was as if it were her destiny to spend her life by herself.

Lexi turned and put on her jacket. Then she walked out the door. She had hunting to do. Her first stop was with D.I. MacDonald.

That conversation went just like it had the day Lexi said she was going to help them. After Lexi filled him in on where she had been the previous day and what she had seen, MacDonald ordered her to return home and let him do his job.

Lexi stopped herself from rolling her eyes. If he were doing his job, he would know he wasn't looking for just any murderer. Then again, if he was doing his job, he would've believed everything she had to say instead of dismissing half of her statement, citing that she was inebriated.

In all her college years, Lexi had been drunk a total of one time. It sucked. The headache, the awful taste in her mouth, and the fact she had been bent over a toilet for hours. There was no need for her to have a repeat of that. Or to become her mother. Her drink limit was two.

"I can help you," Lexi told MacDonald.

He lifted his tired hazel eyes to her. Then he sat back in his chair and ran a hand through his dark hair liberally laced with gray at the temples. "I like you, lass. It's because I like you that I've no' had you arrested. Your friends are on their way back to America. You should be with them."

"Thank you for your time," Lexi said and rose from the chair. There was no use remaining any longer. "Call me if you find anything."

She walked toward the entrance knowing she would never hear from D.I. MacDonald, because he was looking at the wrong sort.

Just before she exited the homicide division she saw a pretty woman with turquoise eyes and blond hair in a pixie cut staring at her. The woman hastily looked away after a brief smile.

Lexi walked out of the station without a backward glance. She then ambled along the streets, zigzagging her way through the city until she came to the section where she saw the red-eyed men daily.

No matter how long it took, no matter what she had to do, she was going to find the son of a bitch who killed Christina.

For two weeks, Thorn had been in Edinburgh with Darius hunting the Dark Fae. He wasn't exactly thrilled that the Dragon Kings were spread so thin throughout Scotland to kill the bastards.

Then again, he was killing Dark Fae, which made him extremely happy.

He liked Darius, even if he had his own demons to battle. Darius wasn't the issue. It was Con.

Thorn halted his thoughts as he jumped from the roof he had been on and landed silently behind two Dark. He came up to them and smashed their heads together. Then, with his knife, he slashed their throats.

Both Fae fell without a sound. Damn, did he ever like his job. Thorn threw both Dark Fae over his shoulder and hurried to the warehouse where he and Darius were stashing the bodies.

He did most of his killing at night when the Dark came out to prey on the mortals, but Thorn never passed up an opportunity to kill the buggers.

There were half a dozen Dark lying dead in the warehouse. With merely a thought, he shifted, letting his body return to its rightful form—a dragon.

His long talons clicked on the concrete floor as he looked down at the Dark. Thorn inhaled deeply, fire rumbling in his throat. Then he released it, aiming at the bodies.

Dragon fire was the hottest thing on the realm. It disintegrated the Dark Fae bodies instantly. When there was nothing left but ash, Thorn shifted back into his human form.

He clothed himself and returned to the streets that were overrun with Dark. The humans had no idea who they were walking beside or having drinks with. Many mortals he and Darius had saved from being killed by the Dark, but there were so many more that they couldn't reach in time.

With just two Dragon Kings in the city against hundreds of Dark Fae, the odds were stacked against the humans.

Thorn didn't understand why the mortals couldn't sense how dangerous the Dark were. Or perhaps that's exactly what drew them to the Dark—that and their sexual vibes the humans couldn't ignore.

The Dark weren't as confident as they were a few weeks ago. Their ranks were dwindling, and though they suspected Dragon Kings were involved, they had yet to find him or Darius.

If two Dragon Kings could do so much damage, imagine what twelve could do? That brought a smile to Thorn's face. The Dark thought they were being smart, but they had begun the war a second time. And Thorn knew it would be impossible for the humans not to learn just what inhabited their realm with them.

His smile faded when his gaze snagged on a woman he had seen daily for the past week. She kept hidden, but it was obvious she was following the Dark.

She had a determined look on her face, one that had anger and revenge mixed together. Thorn knew that expression. It was the one that got mortals killed.

Her pale brown locks hung thick and straight to her shoulders. She tucked her hair behind her ear and peered around the corner of a store.

Thorn slid his gaze to the three Dark she was trailing. They were toying with her. They knew she was there.

"Damn," Thorn mumbled.

He and the other Dragon Kings vowed to protect the humans millions of years ago. They fought wars and sent their own dragons away to do just that. He couldn't stand there and let the Dark kill her.

Nor could he let them know he was there.

He flattened his lips when she stepped from her hiding spot and followed the Dark down the street. They were leading her to a secluded section.

Thorn didn't waste any time climbing to the roof of the building. He kept to the shadows and jumped from roof to roof as he tracked them.

He let out a thankful sigh when she ducked into an alley. Thorn jumped over the street to the opposite building before landing behind her.

"Not this time," he heard her say.

An American. Southern by her accent. He reached to tap her on the shoulder when his enhanced hearing picked up the Darks' conversation. They were coming for her.

Thorn wrapped a hand around her mouth and dragged her behind a Dumpster. "Be quiet and still if you doona want them to find you," he whispered in her ear.

She was struggling against him, but his words caused her to pause. A second later, she renewed her efforts.

Thorn held her tightly, her thin form easy to detain. The more she struggled, the more he could feel every curve of her body.

It wasn't until the Dark reached the alley that she stilled. He couldn't even feel her breathing.

"There's no one here," one of the Dark said in his Irish brogue.

"She was here."

The third snorted. "Not anymore. Come on."

A full minute passed before the three walked on. The woman's shoulders sagged as she blew out a breath. Thorn released her and held up his hands as she whirled around to face him.

Slate gray eyes glared at him with fury as her full lips pulled back in a scowl. Her cheekbones were high in her oval face.

She wasn't a great beauty, but there was something about her that wouldn't let Thorn look away.

"You're in way over your head," he told her.

CHAPTER
TWO

Thorn wasn't sure if it was the subtle narrowing of her eyes or her arm shifting. Even though he knew she was about to strike, Thorn didn't move.

He felt the blade pierce his left side, sinking through skin and muscle. With a scowl down at her, he grabbed her wrist and pulled the dagger from his body.

"Don't touch me," she said through clenched teeth.

She wasn't worth the trouble. At least that's what Thorn tried to tell himself. He'd saved her from the Dark—today. Tomorrow would be another story, but he couldn't follow her around and ensure she was safe when she was so bent on following them.

He had an entire city to rid of the Dark Fae.

"Then doona attack me," he retorted.

Her gray eyes widened a fraction before a look of annoyance and skepticism contorted her face. "You're the one who grabbed me."

"To save you."

"Whatever," she said with a roll of her pretty gray eyes. "Look, just leave me alone."

Thorn cocked his head to the side. "This might be a

tourist mecca, lass, but it isna a place for you to be alone. You hear an Irish accent, go the other way."

She mumbled low, but he still heard, "I wasn't alone before."

That's when he saw the sadness and grief she was desperately trying to hide with anger and fervor. At first glance, she was able to disguise her true feelings, but Thorn was looking deeper.

And he didn't like what he saw.

He didn't need to ask her to know that the Dark must have killed someone dear to her. That's the only reason a mortal would hunt them.

The fact she continued to get close to bastards and not throw herself at them begging them to ease the desire burning her was enough to make him wonder what made her different.

By the determined set of her jaw, Thorn didn't bother to try and dissuade her from following the Dark. She had been doing it for days, and she wouldn't stop until she found what she was looking for—or they found her.

But it wasn't in his nature to let her go like a lamb to slaughter.

"If you're going to follow someone, watch your back as well," he warned before he walked out of the alley, leaving her and her soulful slate gray eyes behind.

Thorn had learned a very long time ago that he couldn't save everyone. He had tried. Once. If a mortal didn't want to be helped, there was nothing he could do about it. And he certainly wasn't going to stand around and watch her die.

He didn't stay on the sidewalk long. The Dark had spies everywhere, and the key to the Kings gaining an upper hand in this war was to be as invisible as they could.

Thorn ducked into a narrow side street and stopped. He

sighed and slowly turned around. There he waited until he saw the female peer around the side of the building where he'd left her.

He smiled, nodding in approval as she waited for a group of people to pass her. She fell into step with them as if she were a part of them.

That, at least, proved she had brains.

"You just might make it after all, lass."

Two hours later, Lexi stared down at her knife that rested on the kitchen table in her flat. She thought she had stabbed the stranger in the alley, but he hadn't so much as flinched.

Was her aim that bad? If so, she was going to have to practice more. In that close proximity, she should've hit her mark.

In truth, she had no desire to get close to the red-eyed men, but she didn't have a choice. A knife was easier to buy, hide, and use than a gun.

She was still shaken by her near run-in with Red Eyes. That's what she had started calling them. If the stranger hadn't gotten to her, the odds were that she would be as dead as Christina.

Lexi shuddered to think of it. She feared dying like anyone else, but it was the thought of failing her friend that was the real kicker.

She rose and poured herself a glass of wine. Lexi didn't bother turning on the TV or the radio. She sat on the couch and stared out the window.

When they first arrived, she had sat in that very spot looking out over the city. It was Christina who had found the flat. Christina had a knack for discovering such places that were always perfect.

If only Lexi had stopped her from leaving the pub the

night she died. Lexi had stupidly thought it was her imagination or a trick of the lights when she saw the guy's eyes change from blue to red.

But a nagging feeling of something dreadful had Lexi running from the pub to find Christina. In the ten minutes it took Lexi to go after her, and another forty-five looking for her, Christina was murdered.

It was by happenstance that Lexi paused on the street, wondering which way to go to look for her friend, when she glanced over her shoulder.

That's when she saw him. The man Christina had left the pub with walked from an alley with three other men. In the streetlight, she saw that two had black hair while one had blond and another red.

Then, in the blink of an eye, all four had black hair liberally streaked with silver.

She gasped. Lexi remembered that clearly. The shock of it had surprised her so profoundly that she hadn't had time to realize she made any sound until it was too late.

The man who had lured Christina turned his gaze directly at her as he stood beneath a streetlamp. There was no mistaking his red eyes.

Lexi was thankful she had been in shadows and near a parked car so that she could duck behind it. She waited until the four men were gone, then she ran to the alley.

She squeezed her eyes closed as she recalled finding Christina. The memory was one she wished she could wipe away.

Lexi took a long drink of her wine and felt it burn down her throat to her stomach. For the first time in her life she understood why some people could become alcoholics.

She hadn't been able to sleep for more than twenty minutes at a time since finding Christina. Jessica and Crystal had checked in on her often, but Lexi was never asleep. She lay in the dark, the flash of red eyes haunting her.

With her wine finished, she rose and poured some more. Then opted to bring the bottle with her to the couch. She held the bottle in one hand and her glass in the other.

Her eyes felt as if the entire Mojave Desert had been poured into them. No matter how much she blinked, they stung. Yet every time she closed her eyes, she saw Christina.

Lexi finished off the bottle of wine. It wasn't until she was up and opening another that she realized what she was doing. She released the wine bottle as if it were acid and took two quick steps back.

"What am I doing?" she asked herself.

She pivoted and walked to the bedroom. There she stripped down to her panties before she tugged on her nightshirt and crawled into bed.

Maybe that night she would be able to sleep.

"We're being followed."

Gorul slanted Vaurin a threatening look. The stupid Dark Fae could never keep his mouth shut. Gorul's smile was tight as he turned to put his back to the bar and wrapped an arm around Vaurin. He kept the smile in place as he lowered his voice and said, "Keep talking, and I'll kill you right where you stand."

Vaurin was using glamour again. Tonight his eyes were green and his chin-length black and silver hair was brownish blond. He shrugged off Gorul's arm. "You make light of it after so many of our brethren have been slain?"

"If they're stupid enough to get caught, then that's their problem."

It was a brave face Gorul put on. He, like every other Dark Fae in Edinburgh, had been searching for some clue as to how many Dragon Kings were in the city. It was unnerving not to know or see the Kings who had always been so ready to battle.

"Besides," Gorul said. "It wasn't a King following us today. It was a human."

Vaurin downed the last bit of his ale and set the glass on the bar. "Human or King, I don't like being followed."

"The human is easily taken care of. If the female wants to know more about us, I'll be happy to show her."

Vaurin frowned and turned to face the bar. "We were sent to infiltrate the mortals here just as we do in Ireland. Perhaps we should stop killing for a few nights."

"Stop?" Gorul asked with a bark of laughter. "How can you ask that when the humans are so tempting? Just look at them," he said as his gaze roamed the pub. "They sense our sensuality. They know the pleasure we can give them. Why should we deny them that?"

Vaurin looked over his shoulder at two of their comrades who were wooing four females. All it took was a mortal being near a Fae for them to forget who they were. All that mattered to the humans was finding pleasure.

His friends were working the table with ease. A simple touch from a Dark against a female's face, or leaning close to whisper in a female's ear had them literally panting and begging for release.

Their friends stood, the four women quickly following. A moment later, all six were walking out the door.

"That's our cue," Gorul said with a smile.

Vaurin felt need stir deep within him. It was a curse of a Dark. No matter how much sex they had, it was never enough. The mortals were like a drug. After one taste, there was no turning back.

He tried to remain at the pub, but it was useless. Vaurin walked out to find Gorul waiting for him, a knowing smile on his face.

"There's no need to deny what we are, Vaurin. We're Dark. We chose this, and I, for one, don't regret it. This should've been our realm. The Dragon Kings made a serious mistake in not forcing us to leave. Let's show them the power of the Dark."

Vaurin walked with Gorul across the street and down an alley to a door. They went inside where all four women stood naked amid boxes and crates.

They were oblivious to where they were as they ran their hands over their bodies, begging to be touched. Gorul patted him on the back and went to a blonde with short hair and large breasts.

Vaurin's cock was hard. He knew the pleasure that awaited. There was nothing so mind-blowing as having sex with mortals and feeding off their souls. The humans had no idea what was happening, which made it all the more pleasurable to a Dark.

Vaurin walked to the female who sat on a crate with her legs open fondling her clit as she watched the others. As soon as she saw him, the human smiled and slid her fingers deep inside her.

Vaurin took her mouth in a savage kiss while she hurried to unbuckle his pants. How stupid the humans were to so freely give their souls to the Dark. They were mindless cattle, the needs of their flesh outweighing the danger that surrounded them.

Oh, but the decadence of taking souls was one Vaurin couldn't deny himself.

CHAPTER
THREE

Thorn dumped three more Dark Fae bodies in the warehouse. He turned when he heard the door and saw Darius.

"They're like fucking roaches," Darius grumbled. "The more you kill, the more you find."

Thorn chuckled as he moved away for Darius to dump his two bodies. "It's a never-ending job, but someone has to do it."

"So true," Darius said, his dark brown eyes lighting on Thorn as he grinned. "It feels good to kill the evil buggers."

"We're stretched too thin." Thorn looked at the corpses. "Con has us all over the U.K., but it isna enough."

Darius ran a hand through his shoulder-length blond hair. "He's keeping enough of us at Dreagan to hold the magic there."

Thorn pulled out his knife and spun it on his open palm. He caught it before it stopped spinning. Dreagan wasn't just their home. It was sixty thousand acres where they distilled whisky and remained hidden from the world. "The Dark have the numbers, but we have the strength."

"Aye," Darius said, his gaze on the ground.

Thorn knew Darius's thoughts were on Ulrik. All of the

Dragon Kings' thoughts were on him. A Dragon King who had been banished.

For centuries, Thorn had been against Ulrik. All that changed a few weeks ago when Thorn was with Warrick in Edinburgh watching over the Druid who had unbound Ulrik's magic.

The last thing Thorn had expected was to come face-to-face with Ulrik after so many eons. It alarmed Thorn how much Ulrik had changed.

"I doona blame you," Darius said.

Thorn blinked as he was pulled out of his thoughts. "What?"

"What happened with Ulrik here. Warrick was in love with Darcy. You did what any of us would've done for another King."

"No' any of us," Thorn said tightly. "Con would never have joined forces with Ulrik."

Constantine was King of Kings, the one Dragon King who had more magic and power than any of them. He led them, kept them together all these millennia. But things were beginning to unravel.

"Con sees one goal—our survival." Darius shrugged. "Everything else comes in second. He's sacrificed a lot for us."

"We've all sacrificed." Thorn paused and shook his head ruefully. "I wouldna trade places with him for anything."

Darius crossed his arms over his chest. "Neither would I. Ulrik will challenge Con soon."

"Eventually. Right now, our focus is the Dark. The bastards are getting bolder. They're freely showing themselves to humans, and it willna be long before they show them magic as well."

"With more and more bodies piling up, the city is trying to crack down on who's to blame."

Thorn grunted. "It willna take them long to focus on the Dark. And that willna end well."

"It never does." Darius dropped his arms and began to remove his clothes.

Thorn spun on his heel and walked out. They took turns burning the bodies of the Dark. While Darius shifted, Thorn would take watch to make sure no humans took interest in them.

As he stood atop the roof walking the perimeter, Thorn found himself thinking of the female he'd encountered earlier. He had a sinking feeling that he would happen upon her body very soon.

He frowned as that thought angered him. The mortal had spirit and gumption. She recognized the Dark as dangerous and sought to go after them. Despite the silliness of a human against a Dark Fae, the mettle that took kept her in his thoughts.

Thorn touched his side where she had plunged the dagger. She was quick with the blade, and obviously ready to take action against anyone she felt was a threat.

He might not have always agreed with the way humans went about their lives, but they were oblivious to the magic around them. They had no idea that dragons had been around since the beginning of time, and were on the realm long before the humans ever were.

They didn't know of the Fae—Dark and Light—and how they fought to take the realm from the Dragon Kings. So many wars had been waged on the fringes of the humans' awareness that it was laughable.

The mortals were weak against the Fae, and had nothing with which to fight off any magical creature. Yet, time and again the Dragon Kings had saved them.

Perhaps it was their innocence in comprehending that vastness of the universe despite their trips into space. It might be because there had been some truly great mortals who had been friends with the Dragon Kings. Or it might be as simple as the vows the Kings took to always watch over the humans.

Whatever the case, Thorn didn't want the female to die.

The city was disrupted by bells tolling from a church in the distance. Another death, another funeral.

"That's the third time tonight," Darius said as he came to stand beside him.

Thorn squeezed the bridge of his nose with his thumb and forefinger. "Same as last night."

"I asked Con to send another King to help us."

Thorn jerked his head to Darius and raised a brow. "And? What did our fearless leader say?"

"He will as soon as he can."

Thorn knew all he had to do was call Warrick. War would be there in an instant, but Con was already pissed at Thorn.

"I saw you today," Darius said. "With the human female."

Thorn didn't respond, because there was nothing to say.

"I saw her tracking the Dark yesterday," Darius continued.

"I warned her away from them."

Darius grunted, giving his opinion without words.

"Why do they never listen?" Thorn asked.

"Because they think they're invincible. You know she'll end up dead."

Thorn knew that all too well. "She stabbed me."

That had one side of Darius's mouth lifting in a grin. "Did she now? I think I like her. How did she manage that? You're normally much quicker. Or did a pretty face leave you slack jawed?"

"She doesna know she stuck me. She thinks she missed."

Darius's smile vanished. "Why is she following the Dark?"

Thorn took in a deep breath and slowly released it. "I believe the Dark killed someone close to her. She's out for revenge."

"You can no' save them all, Thorn."

He looked at Darius. "I'm no' trying to."

"And I'm no' pretending that the past isna haunting me. Shall we both stop lying now?"

Thorn dropped his chin to his chest. "I'm no' prying."

"Neither am I. I'm pointing out facts. The Dark came after her today. Had you no' been there, she'd be dead."

An image flashed in Thorn's mind of vacant slate gray eyes. It angered him to such a degree that he heard a growl rumble from his throat.

"I thought so," Darius said.

Thorn clenched his teeth. He'd learned his lesson before. He wouldn't get involved. He couldn't. It never ended well for him, and he was tired of it all.

Darius put a hand on his shoulder. "Deny it all you want. When you come to terms with things, come find me. I know where she lives."

It was the worst thing Darius could've said. Thorn squeezed his eyes closed. He had done so well today by letting the female go. He hadn't followed her or asked her name.

He'd then set about trying to forget her.

Which was easier said than done. For those few moments with the mortal had burned into his mind more than any other.

Thorn listened to Darius's steps fade away. There was hunting to do and more Dark to kill. Thorn palmed his dagger and jumped over the side of the roof to land between buildings.

He walked only a block before he encountered a Dark. With ease, he killed the Fae before hiding his body until he could collect it later.

Thorn kept to the shadows, but even then the mortals sensed something angry and vengeful was near. They gave him a wide berth. The Dark, however, had no clue he was close.

He came upon a group of six and merely smiled as they turned to face him. The woman they had been having sex with lay upon the ground naked, moaning for more even as her life drained away.

She was a lost cause, but killing the Dark around her would save others. Thorn stood, eyeing the group as he waited for one to attack.

As soon as they did, he released his fury.

Darius stood on the roof above Thorn and watched him fight. There wasn't a move wasted. Everywhere Thorn placed his feet or hands went against the Dark.

The battle was concluded quickly enough. Thorn stood over the fallen Dark, but Darius knew it wouldn't be enough for Thorn. Because he was trying to be something he wasn't. He wanted to ignore his gut and forget the female.

It was a valiant attempt on Thorn's part, but it wouldn't last. Thorn was strong, but the part of him that took his vows seriously was the same part that made Thorn noble and honest.

Darius wished he could be more like Thorn, but it would never be. Darius accepted who he was—or who he was trying to be.

He followed Thorn from one skirmish to the next. A few times, Darius fought Dark who tried to come up behind Thorn. Both left a trail of dead Fae across the city.

By the time the first rays of the sun broke through the night sky, Darius had carried over twenty dead Fae himself with Thorn bringing in another thirty.

Darius waited outside as lookout as Thorn shifted and

burned the remains. Darius liked killing the Dark Fae scum, but he loved shifting. Neither he nor Thorn could take to the skies since the Dark were looking for a Dragon King, but those few minutes in dragon form restored balance within Darius.

Thorn came to stand beside him, buckling a new pair of jeans. For some reason, Thorn didn't like to remove his clothes before he shifted, which meant he went through clothes quickly.

"You didna need to follow me last night," Thorn said.

Darius lifted one shoulder in a shrug. "I knew you would find the Dark, and I felt the need to kill more."

"I doona want to go to her."

Darius didn't bother to pretend he didn't know who Thorn referred to. "I know."

"I can no' stop thinking about her."

He looked at Thorn and merely waited. Con might question Thorn's loyalty after he worked with Ulrik to help Warrick, but Darius didn't. Neither did Warrick.

"She willna welcome our help."

Darius grinned. "Oh, I doona doubt you can change her mind."

Thorn sighed deeply. "I know I'm going to regret this, but take me to her."

Darius led the way without another word. He wondered if the female would realize how lucky she was to have Thorn looking out for her. If she didn't, Darius would set her straight quick enough.

For better or worse, Darius was making Thorn face his past. But even Darius knew he could never do the same.

CHAPTER
FOUR

Lexi stared at the ceiling, her thoughts as rambling as a rabbit's path. She felt drained, weary, and yet there was a fervent need within her she couldn't deny.

She closed her tired eyes and squeezed them. Nothing stopped the burning. With a sigh, she threw off her covers and rose. A quick shower later, she changed into jeans, boots, and a sweater.

Only then did she pore over a map of the city dotted with the places she had encountered Red Eyes. She ate a piece of buttered toast and had a second cup of coffee before she readied herself to leave the flat.

It wasn't until she picked up her knife to tuck it into the arm strap she wore that she thought of the stranger. Though she comprehended the fact he knew of the Red Eyes, it wasn't until that moment that it fully hit her.

"Stupid, Lexi. Very stupid," she chided herself.

If she hadn't let her anger overcome her, she might have found out more about the Red Eyes. Now, she was no closer than she had been yesterday or the week before. Her money was running out. Even with Jessica and Crystal renting the flat for another week, it didn't help with food or the exorbitant fee imposed on her by the airline to change her flight.

She had just a few days left to find Christina's killer or she would be returning home without her revenge and ass-deep in debt.

For just a second, she contemplated taking the pills the hospital had given her to help her sleep after Christina's death. For that brief moment, she actually considered not following the Red Eyes around looking for her culprit.

But the second passed. She took a deep breath and put on her coat before she walked out of the flat. The blast of cold hit her immediately. As did the spray of rain. Was she so out of it that she hadn't seen it was raining when she glanced out the window?

She got enough sleep to function, but the situation confirmed that she needed to pull her head out of her ass and pay more attention to things. It wasn't just her life on the line and Christina's murder to avenge, there were others at stake.

Lexi pulled her black coat tighter and dug her hands into her pockets. She had figured out the route she would take while looking over the map. Everywhere she went there were Red Eyes, but more were concentrated near where she had been the past three days. There was no reason not to return there. It was, after all, the perfect place to find the murderer.

She had to put her head down against the rain, it was driving so fiercely into her. In moments, her head was soaked. Luckily, her jacket was water repellant, but her jeans weren't.

A shiver took her. After another two blocks, Lexi gave in and hurried into a co-op. She shook off the rain and soaked in the warmth.

It was several minutes after walking the narrow aisles

that she found herself in front of the newspaper section. She frowned and picked up a paper to read the headline.

FIVE MORE MURDERS

It was like being punched in the stomach. Lexi couldn't catch her breath as she scanned the article looking for a description of how the people died. When she found it, the room began to swim. She tilted, bumping into a man.

"Horrible, is it no'?" he asked and nodded to the paper. "Every day it's the same headline, just a different number. How many more of us have to die before the authorities do something?"

She set the paper down, her hands shaking from much more than the cold. There was no doubt in her mind who had done this—Red Eyes. Why didn't anyone else see them? Why did no one else take notice of their look?

Lexi didn't consider herself intuitive by any means, but even she couldn't ignore that feeling of wrongness she had whenever one of the Red Eyes was near.

It was almost as if she were the only person in the world who knew how bad the Red Eyes were. The fact D.I. Mac-Donald or any of the other police didn't believe her only made her feel more adrift.

Lexi wasn't sure what she should do next. Her decision was made when she looked up and saw the clerk's red eyes looking at her.

"Everyone has those contacts," said a twentysomething woman with red hair. She batted her eyes at the clerk with her overdone makeup. "I want to get some. Where did you find them at?"

Red Eyes smiled at her. "It's a secret, but I can show you when I get off work in a few hours."

"I'll be back then," she said with a little wave of her fingers.

Lexi wanted to gag. Here was a young woman flirting

with evil. It was there in his eyes, in his smile, if she would only open her eyes and see it. Sure he might be handsome, but there was something darker, malicious, that no amount of good looks could overcome.

She strode out of the co-op, intending to find the woman and warn her. Lexi ignored the rain and ran after the girl.

"Wait!" Lexi called as the woman hailed a taxi and jumped inside. "Wait! Please!"

Lexi got there just as the taxi pulled away. "Damn," she mumbled.

She squared her shoulders and glanced at the store. Once she was finished with her scouting, she would return and warn the woman then.

After finding a hiding place to watch people, it only took twenty minutes before Lexi spotted her first Red Eyes. He was with a group, and then branched off alone.

His hair was black and laced with silver, and it was cut short like the man who had murdered Christina. Lexi's heart pounded in her chest. Could she have found him?

She remained on the opposite side of the street, slowly following him. Her hands itched to feel the hilt of the knife in her palm. It took every last shred of control for her to walk as if she weren't trailing a murderer.

Her stomach rolled as she watched woman after woman—young to the very old—gaze at him as if he were some god. He was a monster, and it sickened her that no one else knew it.

Someone bumped into her shoulder. It jarred Lexi enough to make her realize she had begun to walk so fast she was nearly jogging. She paused and made herself look away from the killer.

Lexi turned to look in a store window to get control of herself. In the glass, she could see him behind her. He stopped and swiveled his head in her direction.

Her blood turned to ice in her veins as fear took her.

Her breath buffed around her, past her parted lips. She was terrified of getting too close. All of the Red Eyes were pure malevolence. No one in their right mind wanted to get near that.

Except for her. And she just needed to get close enough to see if he was Christina's killer.

He was looking at her. She couldn't blow her cover now, not if she wanted to succeed in bringing him down. If she thought the police would do anything, she would call D.I. MacDonald right now. But she wasn't a fool. She knew they wouldn't be able to do anything.

No, her best course of action was to kill him herself. Lexi had never taken a life before, but she didn't think her soul would go to hell for stopping evil. Then again, it was a chance she would take to save others. Edinburgh had dozens of serial killers and didn't even know it.

How many? She had lost count of the many men and women she spotted with red eyes. There were more men, but since she also knew they could change their look, she couldn't be sure of her count.

Change. She shook her head. How was it possible for someone to switch their eye or hair color in the blink of an eye? That wasn't possible.

Lexi shifted her gaze back to where she had last seen Red Eyes and jerked when she found him gone. She remained where she was and used the window as a mirror to see if he had moved.

She released a sigh when she found him farther up the street. Lexi knew she had to take her time in following him. There was crucial information she needed, like where he lived, who were his accomplices, and how he killed.

The weight of her knife along her inner forearm made her feel safe. At least if she was approached she wasn't without a means to attack.

* * *

"The lass is daft," Darius whispered.

Thorn pressed his lips together. She was certainly insane. "At least she's keeping her wits about her."

"She thinks there's only one Dark, but there are three others watching her."

Thorn clenched his right hand into a fist. "We doona have to keep hidden from the Dark, but I also doona want the mortal to know we're helping her."

Darius jerked his head around to spear Thorn with a confused look. "She's already met you."

"Aye, and I was here just a few weeks ago protecting a Druid. Look how that turned out."

"You mean because Warrick fell for Darcy?"

Thorn cut him a scathing look. "I doona fear falling for a human, because I know it willna happen."

"Then what is it?"

"I doona want her to know of us."

Darius grinned knowingly. "Riiiight. And it has nothing to do with the fact that every time a King comes in close contact with a mortal recently that they end up as mates?"

"That female knows there's something different about the Dark. If she learns about them from us, we'll have to tell her who and what we are. I'd rather no'."

Darius looked back at her. "She's attractive."

"I suppose."

"If you like stubborn, courageous women with stormy gray eyes and long hair."

Thorn blew out a breath, hoping Darius would shut up.

"She's smart, too."

"Then go for her." Thorn didn't know why he said it. The words just came out of nowhere.

Darius shrugged. "I just might."

"And find a mate?" This time Thorn cringed. He knew

better than to bring up mates around Darius, but he had been thrown so off-kilter at the thought of Darius pursuing the mortal that he hadn't thought about his words.

Darius didn't say a word, but the stiffening of his body relayed more than his words ever could.

"Plenty of us share our beds with humans and doona fall in love," Darius said, his voice low and raw. He glanced at Thorn. "Besides, I'm no' the one who feels obligated to watch over this mortal."

Thorn looked back at her. Her black coat kept the rain from her, but the rest of her was soaked. If she wasn't careful, she could end up sick. By her pale skin and dark circles under her eyes yesterday, she was already weakened.

"We're going to have to kill these four Dark," Thorn said.

Darius's smile was eager. "You doona hear me complaining, do you?"

"The leader of this group is playing the female. He knows she's following him."

"Too bad for him he's about to die."

"Aye. I'm all broken up about it," Thorn said as he stepped from around the building and went to the Dark who was following the mortal.

Thorn slammed his hand into the Dark's chest, sending the Fae flying back into an alley.

CHAPTER
FIVE

It was over too quickly. Thorn stared down at the dead Dark as he braced a hand on the Fae's chest and pulled back the dagger that had ended the Dark's life.

The Fae were immortal, as were the Dragon Kings. But just like the Kings, there was a way to kill the Fae. Weapons forged in the Fires of Erwar could end a Fae's life. Thorn had gotten his dagger during the Fae Wars after killing a Dark commander.

Thorn straightened and turned to look around the corner in time to catch sight of the female. He found her easily enough, but there were two more Dark focused on her.

He saw movement out of the corner of his eye. Thorn spotted Darius making his way to the Dark from atop the roofs.

Thorn looked around for more Fae and then slipped out of the alley. He kept his head down as he walked with the crowds who didn't seem to care that the rain had begun to fall in a steady drizzle again.

He kept his strides long, eating up the pavement without drawing attention to himself. It wasn't until he saw the

Dark begin to close in on the female that he ducked between buildings and took to the roofs.

If he didn't get to her, the human would die. Thorn bent low on the rooftops, just in case the Dark happened to be watching. He and Darius were risking a lot by both being out in the open to save the woman.

Thorn cursed when the Dark she was following led her down a quiet street. He crept silently and peered over the side of the roof just as the female halted. She turned on her heel and started to return the way she had come, but three Fae stood in her path.

"You've been watching us," said the Dark leading the small group. "What do you want with us?"

The woman's entire attitude shifted. She softened her body and smiled as she faced him. "You're gorgeous. All of you. It's not every day that I get so close to such . . . perfection."

"Oh, you're good, lass," Thorn whispered in approval.

The leader preened. "You're American."

"And you're not Scottish." She lowered her gaze and then looked up at him with seduction in her gray depths.

"Irish," he responded.

Her brows raised in interest. "All of you?"

"Aye."

"Why the red eyes?"

His smile was slow, like a wolf about to pounce on a kitten. "Do you like them?"

"I . . . shouldn't, but I do."

Her flirting skills were impressive. But it was all a game the Dark were playing with her. Thorn had seen it before. She was looking death in the face.

The leader took a step closer to her. Thorn waited to hear her moan as all humans did at the nearness of a Fae, but this female was different.

Thorn watched her carefully, as did the leader. She was

affected. She tried not to show it, but her breathing had quickened and her lips were parted.

"You feel that, don't you?" the leader asked as he leaned in and inhaled her scent. "Unimaginable pleasure awaits you."

Thorn refused to wait a moment longer. It was enough that the female was feeling the effects of the Dark. He didn't want her so drugged by their sexuality that she couldn't remember she was fighting against them.

He was about to vault from the roof when Darius turned the corner. With a smile of anticipation, Darius waited for the Dark to notice him.

The leader saw him first and hissed as he pointed. The three Dark turned as one to Darius.

"I'm thinking more like death awaits *you*," Darius told the Dark.

While Darius fought the three, Thorn landed behind the leader. The Dark had his hands on the human, who valiantly tried to shake them off. She was also fighting the effects the Dark had on the mortals.

Good, Thorn thought. The more she fought, the better.

The leader turned and tried to drag her away. The woman planted her feet and tugged against him. The Dark then saw Thorn and instantly released her. With the woman falling to the ground, Thorn prepared for the Dark to attack.

He stared in wonder for a moment when the coward ran away. But he couldn't allow that. None of the Dark could know how many or which Kings were in the city.

Thorn pulled out his dagger and threw it. It flew end over end, embedding with a thud in the spine of the Dark who collapsed without moving again.

Just as Thorn was about to retrieve his dagger, he heard the woman groan. Thorn went to her and began to reach out for her.

In the next heartbeat, she was on her feet, her blade once again breaking through his flesh as she pushed him against the building before pulling the weapon out quickly. "Stay away," she said. Then she blinked, as if just recognizing. "You again."

"I warned you the city wasna a safe place." He tried to move around her, but she held up her weapon to stop him.

"Are you following me?"

Thorn certainly didn't want to admit to that. If he did, it would lead to all sorts of questions he didn't want to answer. "I just happened to be near and saw them."

"The Red Eyes."

He raised a brow, glancing over as Darius was still fighting one of the Dark. She followed his gaze and watched the scene with interest for a second.

Then she turned her eyes back to him. "Who are you?"

"Nobody. I was near and thought I'd help."

"You're lying."

Lexi wasn't sure how she knew, she just did. It was a dead end street, and no one had been on it when she followed the Red Eyes. Where had the stranger come from? And was the other man with him?

She was still shaking off the effects of whatever Red Eyes had done to her. It infuriated her that she had been unable to control the need pulsing within her. That had to be the reason she had missed—again—when trying to stab the stranger.

Granted, she hadn't recognized him when she defended herself, but it didn't help her self-confidence any.

She looked at the stranger with his dark hair that hung to his shoulders and his brown eyes that were so dark they were nearly black.

He wasn't as pretty as the Red Eyes, but his ruggedness, the sheer masculinity he exuded was hard to dismiss. In fact, it was difficult for her to look away.

How could a man appear sensitive and ferocious at the same time? And yet, he did. Lexi had the insane urge to rest her head on his chest. A chest on which a black shirt was stretched tight over hard muscles.

She had to look up at him, he was so tall. Lexi frowned as she noticed his incredibly long, dark eyelashes. Then she made the mistake of looking lower.

He had a mouth that made her dream of spending hours kissing him. His lips were wide and captivating. Perhaps it was the effects the Red Eyes had on her that made her examine him with such longing.

But she had a suspicion that the stranger was always charming and fascinating. She had noticed it the first time. Only she had refused to acknowledge it. This instance, she couldn't help herself.

His gaze watched her as if he were waiting for her to come to a conclusion. Her stint in Edinburgh had proven that she couldn't trust anyone. Handsome or not, strangers were enemies.

"I'm trying to help," he said and took a step toward her.

Lexi had turned her head to the second man right before them. She was so wound up that she reacted before she thought twice about it and stabbed him.

"Dammit," he said between clenched teeth. His fingers tightened around her wrist. "Stop doing that."

Lexi blinked in confusion. He acted as if she had actually hit her target. That couldn't be right. He would've reacted with pain, not stood there as if nothing had happened.

She glanced down at her knife and felt as if she had been knocked flat on her back. There was blood on the blade. Her gaze jerked to his left side where she saw a dark, wet stain on his sweater.

Lexi took a step back, suddenly more afraid than she had been before. "Leave me alone," she said and held up the knife.

"I would, lass, if you would but come to your senses and stop following the Dark around."

Following the dark? What the hell was he talking about? He was insane and probably high on drugs. That was the explanation for him not reacting to being stabbed—twice.

She backed across the narrow street, keeping both men in sight. The second one had killed the Red Eye he had been fighting. For just a moment, Lexi thought about thanking him, then thought better of it.

When she reached the corner, she turned and ran, tucking her knife back up her sleeve. She was halfway home when the rain began to come down in a torrent.

Everywhere Lexi looked, she saw the Red Eyes. Her brain felt as if it were in a fog. She was so disoriented that she almost didn't notice the two Red Eyes stationed outside of her flat.

Lexi immediately turned the other way, mumbling a string of curses as she did. What rotten luck. It took everything she had to keep going when all she wanted to do was get out of the wet clothes and into a hot shower to warm up.

She had to get out of the rain and find shelter so she could stop the chills that seemed to have settled deep in her bones.

"Well, that didna go well," Darius said when Thorn came to stand beside him.

Thorn glanced down at his side. "You could say that."

"You let her stab you? Twice in one day?"

"I didna *let* her do anything." It was a lie, and both of them knew it.

Darius watched her run down the street. "She held her own with the Dark. The lass has gumption in spades."

"And no' much sense."

"You can no' blame her for wanting retribution."

Thorn shrugged. "We're assuming someone died."

"I think you're right. That's the only explanation for her risking her life so."

"She knows how close to death she came," Thorn said. "I saw it in her eyes just now. She was scared."

"Yet still stood against them. Brave girl."

She certainly was. Thorn looked up at the gray skies as the rain fell faster. It was the perfect time for them to fly, but neither he nor Darius would risk it with so many Dark looking for them.

"She appears dead on her feet," Darius said.

Thorn had noticed that as well. The dark circles under her bloodshot eyes were more pronounced than the day before. "Let's clean this up."

"I'll clean it up. You follow her."

Thorn nodded to Darius and started after the female. He wished he had thought to ask her name, but he doubted she would've given it to him. She didn't trust him, and she was right to question everyone and everything.

The Dark Fae had changed things by coming to Edinburgh. Great Britain had always been off-limits to them, but they were blatantly showing themselves. They wanted war, and they wanted the humans to know what they were.

The Dragon Kings, however, preferred to keep the humans in the dark on all things magic. Mainly because the Kings knew exactly what would happen if the humans learned of them.

They had been through that once. The result was the Kings sending all of their dragons to another realm to stop the war while they remained behind.

The Dark would keep pushing. The war they wanted had been accepted by the Kings. The only difference this time was that the rules had changed—at least for the Kings.

The Dark Fae couldn't care less who knew of their existence. They fed off humans.

The Kings might have taken a small lead, but soon they would have to decide to fight the Dark in their dragon forms, or give the realm over to them.

Neither possibility was a good one.

CHAPTER
SIX

Three hours later and Lexi couldn't shake the chills. The rain had yet to stop, and by the looks of the dark gray sky, it wasn't going to either. She went from store to store, anything to keep moving and stay warm. Though it didn't help when she went back out into the rain each time.

The soup she ate helped to warm her, as did the tea, but the moment she saw a Red Eyes in the pub, she hurried out, leaving half of her soup uneaten.

Her stomach rumbled. Everywhere she looked there were Red Eyes. It was as if they had taken over the world like the aliens did in the sci-fi movies.

If it was all a dream, she wished she would wake up. But she knew it was real. Every deadly, gut-wrenching, heart-stopping moment of it was genuine.

Lexi stopped beneath the overhang of a shop and looked around at the city. Edinburgh hadn't been on her wish list to see. It had been on Jessica's, but Lexi found Scotland to be different than what she'd expected.

Though now, she was beginning to hate the city. She just wanted to be warm and dry beneath dozens of blankets so she could sleep.

She didn't have the money to find another place to stay, but she couldn't return to her flat with the Red Eyes there. She couldn't sleep on the streets either.

Lexi bit back a sob. She was alone in a dangerous city full of killers. What had ever made her think she could do this on her own?

She wiped her sleeve across her face and huddled against the wind. God, she was so cold. She could no longer feel her toes, fingers, or her upper lip, and her nose was quickly following. Everything was numb—and wet.

A police vehicle drove by, and for just an instant Lexi thought about going to D.I. MacDonald. That thought was quickly forgotten since she knew MacDonald would just send her on her way or urge her to return home.

Lexi didn't think she would ever crave the South Carolina heat and humidity, but she was longing for it now—including the giant mosquitoes that came with living there.

She closed her eyes to help relieve some of the pain. Almost instantly she jerked, snapping her head up as it fell forward as she dozed off.

Blinking several times to help wake herself, Lexi looked around and noticed a Red Eyes watching her across the street. Fortune was on her side when three women came out of the store. Lexi spoke to one of them and started walking with them.

It took everything she had not to turn and look at him over her shoulder. She stayed with the women for another two blocks before she ducked into a pub and went to stand by the fire.

Thorn ignored the rain as he watched the female through the window of the pub. To make matters worse, he wasn't the only one. Dark Fae were everywhere and beginning to take notice of her.

He wanted to pull out his dagger and start killing the Fae, but in such a crowded place with so many humans, he couldn't. Then there was the female. Not to mention with so many Dark around, one would get away and alert the others as to which Dragon King was in the city.

It was better if Thorn remained hidden and watchful. He had seen the female fall asleep on her feet twice now. She looked much worse than she had earlier in the day. He wasn't sure how much longer she could go before her body simply gave out.

He felt a push in his head from Darius from the mental link shared by all Dragon Kings. He opened his mind to Darius and asked, *"Everything taken care of?"*

"Aye. As well as ten more kills between then and now."

"There are too many humans around for us to fight now."

"I know," Darius said, his voice dripping with annoyance. *"I thought the female would've returned home by now. She's no' tracking any Dark."*

"I followed her to her building, but there were Dark standing near the door. She took one look at them and turned around."

"Perhaps she's smarter than you realize."

Thorn twisted his lips. *"I never said she wasna smart. I said she'd be wise to leave well enough alone."*

"Would you?"

"Nay."

Darius chuckled. *"Me neither. She's drenched."*

"She's been walking the streets all day. Where are you?"

"Above you on the roof. There are Dark crawling everywhere. I think the female unintentionally led us to their main location."

Thorn had taken notice of all the Dark as soon as they entered the area. "*Aye.*"

"*I wonder how long until the woman notices?*"

"*No' soon enough.*"

"*She looks . . . awful.*"

Thorn drew in a deep breath. "*Exhaustion. And . . . sickness.*"

"*Damn.*"

Thorn felt the same way. He didn't think the woman even knew she was sick yet. If only she would leave the area, but the pub was warm and dry.

Just as he expected, she found a table and ordered food. He blinked through the rain dropping from his eyelashes, trying to mentally hurry the woman to leave.

"*It was a mistake to follow her,*" Thorn said to Darius. "*We're supposed to be killing Dark.*"

"*We're doing both. Besides, I'm no' leaving. It's going to take both of us to get the mortal out of this area.*"

"*She needs out of Edinburgh.*"

"*I'm in agreement, but she's no' going to leave on her own.*"

"*Darius,*" Thorn said when a Dark walked to the woman's table.

She didn't even look up at him, but concentrated on her food. Her head nodded to whatever he said, and then he walked off. Thorn released a breath.

"*What is it about her that draws their interest?*" Darius asked.

Thorn shook his head and smiled. "*Look around the pub. Look around the area. Anywhere there's Dark, whether they're wearing glamour or no', the humans can no' take their eyes off them.*"

"*And yet the female willna even look their way.*"

"*Exactly. They're narcissistic. Whoever doesna pay*

them the attention they think they deserve must be wrong somehow."

Darius was quiet for a moment. *"Thorn, all of the mates to the Dragon Kings act this way toward the Dark."*

Thorn frowned as he looked at the female. *"She's no' a mate."*

"All of us thought it was because the women were mated to Kings. What if it's more? What if it's something else?"

"She felt their pull this afternoon when she stabbed me. I saw it."

"But she fought it," Darius argued.

Thorn couldn't deny that. How much would the mortal have to endure before she could no longer withstand the Darks' seduction?

"We have to get her away from them. She needs to know who they are, Thorn."

"The more she knows, the more danger she's in."

"She's in it up to her arse already."

Thorn knew Darius was right. Though that didn't make anything better.

"We willna let her die. I give you my word."

"Doona. If it's her time, nothing can stop it."

Darius snorted. *"We're Dragon Kings. We can keep her safe."*

An image of the past flashed in Thorn's head. He instantly shoved it aside, refusing to dwell on such things.

"Thorn."

He bit back a growl. *"I hear you. I can no' just waltz into the pub. She'll probably try to stab me again."*

"Probably," Darius said, chuckling.

As soon as Thorn saw Darius, he was going to punch him. *"Next time, you stand there and take the blade."*

"For her? I think I just might."

Thorn found himself glaring, but he wasn't sure why.

Thankfully, the woman paid the bill and stood. *"Here she comes."*

"Stick to the streets. I'll watch your back."

Thorn crossed the street after she exited the pub and turned left. He was twenty steps behind her, keeping to the shadows.

They had gone six blocks and were almost out of the area. Thorn wouldn't breathe easy until she was away from so many Dark. Just as they reached the end of the block, three Dark turned the corner.

The woman's feet faltered for just a heartbeat, but it was enough that the Dark saw. They smiled at her, but she turned her head away.

Thorn withdrew his dagger and walked faster. He stepped into the streetlight and waited for the Dark to see him. Their attention diverted from the mortal to him, just as he intended.

"Stay with her," Darius said. *"I've got these wankers."*

Before Thorn could reach them, Darius landed in front of him, killing one Dark by ripping out his heart.

Thorn stayed with her, and a few seconds later, Darius let him know the three Fae were dead. The rain never let up, and neither did the mortal. She walked constantly, stopping occasionally when the rain got too heavy.

It was past midnight and the streets nearly deserted when the rain finally stopped. He could hear her coughing and the wheezing of her breathing.

He and Darius had piled bodies of Dark Fae all through the city. Thorn didn't think the mortal saw them any longer. Her focus seemed to be staying on her feet.

Darius caught up with him after another skirmish with the Dark. "I'd have thought she would've stopped by now."

Thorn slowed when he realized she was shuffling her feet. "More rain is coming. She needs to get dry. Why does she no' find a hotel?"

"Maybe she doesna have any money."

Why hadn't Thorn thought of that? That had to be the reason, because though the female might be reckless, she wasn't stupid.

"Thorn."

But he had already seen that the female had stopped and was weaving. He closed the distance between them, catching her as she fell over. He felt her fever as soon as she was in his arms. She was pale and her breath rattled each time she drew air.

"I know where we can take her," Thorn said.

Darius shrugged as he looked around. "Lead the way."

Thorn couldn't remember the last time he had walked so fast. Even then, he didn't outrun the rain. He found the building and waited for Darius to open the door. Thorn raced up the stairs, taking them three at a time.

"Where are we?" Darius asked.

Thorn stopped beside the door and waited for Darius to use his magic to unlock it. The door opened and Thorn stepped inside. "Darcy's flat."

Darius stood at the doorway and looked around. "This is the place Rhi warded against the Fae."

Thorn smiled as he made his way to the bedroom. "The verra one. The female will be safer here than anywhere else in the city."

CHAPTER SEVEN

Dreagan

Con calmly set his hands flat on the table and looked over the double row of monitors to Ryder. It took everything he had not to explode with fury. But control was what he was known for. It was his trademark, his tool used effectively against friends and foes alike.

When he wanted to bellow and smash the expensive new monitors, he merely took a deep breath and slowly released it before he asked in an even voice, "What do you mean, you lost him?"

Ryder set down his half-eaten jelly-filled donut and wiped the powder from his lips. "As I explained, Ulrik just disappeared."

"Impossible." None of the Dragon Kings had that ability. Even if Ulrik had his magic back, there was no way he could've picked up something new after thousands of millennia without magic.

Ryder shrugged, his hazel eyes never wavering from Con. "I can play the clip again, if you'd like."

"Nay. Have you located him?"

Ryder shook his head. "He could be anywhere."

"Or nowhere." Ulrik was proving to be impressively skilled at evading Con's watch. Con had made the mistake of thinking Ulrik's dragon magic would be bound for eternity.

He'd never expected Ulrik to find a Druid with enough power to handle dragon magic. It was the last mistake Con would make regarding his old friend. "What about Rhi?"

Ryder's blond brows rose. "Rhi? You've never asked to find her before. What's up?"

"Just tell me if you can find her."

"You won't find her," said a voice behind Con.

He straightened and turned to find Henry North standing in the doorway. Henry was a mortal who worked for MI5, but he had proven himself a trusted friend and ally to all at Dreagan.

The only issue was that Henry had fallen—hard—for the Light Fae despite everyone warning him to keep his distance from Rhi.

"The Dark are easy enough to track because they aren't keeping themselves hidden," Henry continued, his English accept clipped with frustration and a dose of anger.

Con should've realized Henry would've been trying to find Rhi while he tracked the Dark over the world. No wonder the mortal had been on edge of late. "You think Rhi is hiding?"

"Yes." Henry ran a hand through his short brown hair. "There's no sign of her or Balladyn anywhere, and my network of people don't miss anything."

Ryder finished typing on his keyboard and leaned back in his office chair. He stared intently at the rows of screens that made a semicircle around him.

Con walked around the desks to view them himself. He looked from screen to screen, hoping to find a hint of Ulrik or Rhi—or both.

He had a bad feeling that Ulrik had strengthened a bond with Rhi when he carried her out of Balladyn's fortress where she had been held captive. Rhi was more powerful than she realized. If she sided with Ulrik . . . Con didn't even want to finish the thought.

"You think Rhi and Ulrik are together," Henry said into the silence.

Con glanced at Henry and nodded.

"She wouldn't do that." Henry's brow furrowed deeply. "Did you hear me? Rhi wouldn't side with him. She knows Ulrik is the one out to destroy Dreagan."

"Ulrik is out to destroy me," Con corrected.

Henry waved away his words. "By coming at Dreagan and the Kings. Rhi has people she counts on here. She wouldn't turn against any of them."

"Rhi . . . hasna been the same since Balladyn tortured her. Doona put your faith in her, Henry."

"Everyone talks about how much you hate her," Henry said, his lip lifted in contempt. "You'll do anything to put her in a bad light and turn people against her."

Con opened his mouth to reply, but Ryder beat him to it.

"Henry, you've no' slept in thirty-two hours. Take a rest and eat," Ryder urged. "You'll feel better once you do."

Henry looked from Con to Ryder before he turned and stalked from the room.

"He's in love with Rhi," Ryder said as he looked up at Con. "Do us all a favor and try to remember that when you're doing your usual bashing of her."

Con ignored his words. "I want to know the moment you find Ulrik. It would be even better if we could discover who else is helping him. Ulrik is good, but he couldna do all of this on his own. He has people. Let's find them."

"Will do," Ryder replied.

Con started out of the room, but paused at the door. He

looked back at Ryder to find the Dragon King watching him. "I do remember Henry's feelings. It's why I didna tell him what I truly think about Rhi and Ulrik."

"You think she's turning Dark."

It wasn't a question, and Con didn't treat it as such. "When was the last time you saw her wear pink?"

Ryder shrugged. "I doona know."

"Before Balladyn kidnapped and tortured her. He kept her in his fortress for weeks, Ryder. He used the Chains of Mordare."

"She broke the unbreakable Chains of Mordare," Ryder stated with a grin.

Con still couldn't believe Rhi had broken them. Every Fae throughout eternity who had worn them had died horribly. And yet Rhi had shattered them. "That she did, but it doesna alter the fact that she is changed."

"So was Kellan after the Dark tortured him."

"Rhi is refusing to see the queen."

At this news, Ryder's eyes widened. "That can no' be right. Rhi's greatest achievement was being a Queen's Guard. She adores Usaeil."

"*Adored* would be the correct word. It doesna help that Usaeil was having her followed by another of the Queen's Guard."

"She's going to lose Rhi's trust."

Con lowered his gaze as he thought back to what he'd heard the last time he visited Usaeil. "She already has."

"You've certainly taken a keen interest recently with the Queen of the Light."

He'd wondered if anyone had tried to discover where he had been going. Now he knew. He was going to have to be more careful. "Update me as soon as you find anything."

Con walked back to his office. He was more worried than anyone knew, because they had yet to put the pieces together. Ulrik was dangerous and could bring down the Kings with the help of the Dark.

Rhi knew things about the Kings because of her lover, some of which she could use against them.

Put Ulrik and Rhi together, and Con wasn't sure if the Kings could win. *That's* what kept him up at night.

The latest with the Dark making themselves known in Scotland was infuriating and was something that needed to be handled immediately.

The only good thing was that the Dark's attempt to discover the weapon that could destroy the Dragon Kings had been put on hold. But for how long?

Every decision, every move he made was with the thought of the Kings' survival. He was thinking of every conceivable notion and attempting to prepare. The wrench in everything was Rhi.

Would the Light Fae turn against the Kings? Or would she continue to stand beside them?

He'd known the moment he first saw her all those centuries ago that she was trouble. Rhi had her own set of rules, and despite being a great fighter, she was stubborn to a fault and extremely dangerous when her temper was up.

And lately her temper was always up.

The same power that allowed her to revive a dying world could destroy one without even realizing it if she couldn't control her anger.

Con wouldn't change the past or what he had done or said to Rhi. Thankfully, there was a King who considered her a close friend. Now all Con had to do was convince Rhys.

Thorn stared down at the woman as a new day dawned. She was huddled beneath the blankets. Naked.

That part had been . . . difficult. He was a male, after

all. It was in his makeup to look at a woman. And he hated himself for wanting a peek of her when she was ill.

It had taken both him and Darius to get her out of her soaked clothing. Thorn shielded her as much as he could, which meant he was holding her while Darius cut off her clothes. Then Thorn had buried her under a mountain of blankets with the heat cranked up.

What worried him was that she had yet to stop shivering. Her fever was just as high as it had been when he carried her into the flat.

"We could ask Con to heal her," Darius said from the doorway.

Thorn shook his head. "He willna. Con will protect the humans as a race, but he willna risk coming here and the Dark seeing him to save one female."

"Her name is Lexi Crawford."

Thorn raised a brow as he looked at Darius. "You snooped."

"I got tired of calling her 'the female.' I found her identification in her jacket."

Thorn rubbed his eyes with his thumb and forefinger. "This place is safe enough to leave her, but she's too sick."

"She needs medicine."

"Aye, but what kind?" Thorn threw up his hands in defeat. "I doona know the first thing about treating a human illness."

Darius made a sound at the back of his throat. "Then are we no' lucky to have so many humans as mates to the Kings? Call one of them."

Thorn berated himself for not thinking of that sooner. He pulled out his phone and dialed Darcy. The Druid answered in the middle of the second ring.

"Hey, Thorn," she said cheerfully.

"Hello, Darcy."

"Oh," she said, her voice dipping low and her Scots accent deepening. "You don't sound good. Is everything going all right? I know Warrick wants to be there helping you."

Thorn looked down at Lexi. "He needs to be there with you."

"Then what's going on? I can tell by your voice that something is wrong."

"There's a sick woman."

There was a beat of silence before Darcy said, "Then ask her what's wrong."

"I can no'. She passed out hours ago and has yet to wake."

"Okay." Darcy blew out a breath. "Tell me her symptoms."

"She has a fever. When I touch her skin, it burns."

"Not good," Darcy mumbled. "What else?"

"She's shivering, her breathing is labored and wheezing." Thorn swallowed. "She was out in the rain all day yesterday."

"You were following her?"

Thorn didn't want to reveal too much or have Darcy read too much into things. "Darius and I spotted her several times following the Dark. I suspect one of them killed someone close to her, and she's out for revenge."

"Except," Darcy urged when he paused.

"They're on to her." Thorn closed his eyes. "She's no' quite immune to them, but they doona affect her as they do others."

Darcy grunted through the phone. "You mean how they affected me that first time."

"Aye. And, just so you know, I brought her to your flat."

"I was going to suggest that. It's the only place the Dark can't get to her in the city. You said she's been unconscious?"

"She has."

"Thorn, she needs medicine and a doctor. It could be nothing more than a simple cold, or it could be the flu. Either way, you can't let her fever continue. It has to be broken."

She was talking to him as if Thorn would know how to do something like that. "How do you break a fever?"

"Medicine, usually, but my mother put my sister in a bath filled with ice water once."

That he could do. "What else?"

"She needs fluids. She can't get dehydrated."

He frowned. That wasn't going to be as easy. "Anything else?"

"Find a doctor."

"You know we can no'."

"If the fever doesn't break, you won't have a choice unless you want her to die."

That was something Thorn wasn't going to allow.

CHAPTER
EIGHT

Thorn filled the tub with cold water. He didn't see how putting Lexi in cold water was going to break the fever that was caused by her being cold and wet the day before, but then again, he knew very little of the human body.

Thorn found a nightshirt in Darcy's wardrobe and slid it on Lexi. He gathered Lexi in his arms and walked to the bathroom where Darius waited.

"Are you sure about this?" Darius asked.

Thorn glanced down at Lexi's face, which was covered in sweat. "Nay."

He dropped down to one knee and lowered Lexi into the bath. Thorn set her against the back of the tub. Her head lolled to the side.

"She's no waking."

Thorn squeezed his eyes closed for a moment. "Did you expect her to feel the cold and come to?"

"Aye," Darius said grumpily. "She's no' so much as twitched."

Thorn had noticed. He hadn't bothered to ask Darcy how long to leave Lexi in the water. If only he could heal someone with a touch like Con could, but that wasn't Thorn's power.

The seconds ticked by slowly. After a few minutes, Thorn touched her forehead with the back of his hand and let out a sigh of relief. He swiveled his head to Darius. "She's no' as hot as before."

"That's good," Darius said, though he was frowning.

After another five minutes, there was no change. Once Lexi began to shiver, Thorn took her out of the tub. The nightshirt clung to her curves like a second skin.

He looked over to find Darius watching her. Thorn needed her out of the shirt quickly before she became more ill. He set her on the rug next to the tub.

"Need help?"

Thorn threw Darius a look. "I can handle this."

"You think I'm looking?"

"Nay."

"That's right. But you are."

"I'm no'," Thorn said angrily and wrapped a towel around Lexi.

"Doona bother lying to me." At that, Darius walked out of the bathroom.

Thorn drew in a deep breath and slowly released it. He wasn't looking at her.

He tossed the towel away and removed the nightshirt before he threw it in the sink where it landed with a sucking noise.

Thorn grabbed the towel and set about drying her. He tried to close his eyes when he got to her breasts, but they refused to obey him.

His gaze drank in the small, perky breasts and the pink tipped nipples. His hands slowed as he gently rubbed the towel along the indent of her waist and over her hips.

He shook himself, inwardly berating himself, as he hurriedly finished drying her. He wrapped her in the towel and carried her back to the bed and put her in another gown before tucking her back under the covers.

There he sat watching her, hoping that she would awaken and stab him again. He was supposed to save her, not observe her slowly dying before his very eyes.

Suddenly Thorn remembered Darcy's warning about dehydration. He jumped up and filled a glass with water. As he was searching for a way to get Lexi to drink, he spotted a bag of straws. He grabbed one and rushed back to the bedroom.

He sat on the bed and gently lifted Lexi's head. Using the straw, he slowly dripped water through her parted lips.

"That's it. Drink for me," he urged as she swallowed.

Thorn fed her the water until the entire glass was gone. He refilled it and continued through another glass as the minutes passed.

The day crawled at a snail's pace. Darius came and went often, taking the chance to kill any Dark he came across. The longer Lexi went without waking, the more anxious Thorn became.

He went to the kitchen to refill the glass with water. Upon his return he found Lexi had shoved the covers down to her waist.

Thorn felt her head and noticed the dampness of her skin. It wasn't long after that sweat beaded her skin and she was moving her head back and forth mumbling something about a Christina.

That got Thorn wondering. He opened the mental link and said Ryder's name. It didn't take his friend long to answer.

"*Thorn*," Ryder said, his voice smiling. "*How's it going?*"

"*We're killing Dark.*"

"*Then it's going well.*"

Thorn had to smile at that. "*Aye, it is. I need you to look something up for me.*"

"Sure."

"Can you search the murders in Edinburgh that have happened recently and tell me if any of them is named Christina? I also suspect she's American."

"Give me a sec, and I can tell you."

Thorn sat impatiently as he wiped Lexi's brow with a damp cloth.

It was just a few moments later when Ryder said, *"I found something. A Christina Butler from South Carolina who was visiting the city with three friends was killed a week ago. Her death was ruled a murder, but her killer hasna been caught."*

It was just what Thorn had suspected. What he wanted to know was where were the two other friends? *"Does it name the friends?"*

"Nay."

"Thanks, Ryder."

"Anything else?"

Thorn rung out the cloth and wiped Lexi's face. *"Nay."*

"You have no' happened to see Rhi, have you?"

Thorn twisted his lips. *"No' since she bailed on helping us get Darcy away from the Dark."*

"That's what I thought. Just wanted to check."

"Everything all right at Dreagan?"

Ryder released a long sigh. *"Nothing will be right until Ulrik is stopped, the Dark are wiped from this realm, and we find V."*

V. Thorn had forgotten that he had woken and left Dreagan without a word. No one knew where he was, and he refused to answer Con's mental call. They needed all hands on deck, so for any one King to leave without a word was not good news.

"Feel free to come and help us kill Dark," Thorn said.

"Doona tempt me. I could use a diversion. Talk soon."

The link was severed. Thorn looked down at Lexi. He

was learning more and more about her. Her name, where she was from, and what was driving her. If only she would wake.

Lexi was lost in a fog so thick she couldn't see her way out of it. She flung out her arms, calling out her friends' names hoping they would help her.

She stumbled through the mist that seemed to hold her back. Sweat covered her. She was so hot. No matter how many times she clawed at her clothing to remove it, she couldn't get any of it off.

Lexi shouted for her friends again, but only silence greeted her. Her foot hit something. She looked down and saw Christina lying upon the street, her eyes lifeless.

She knelt beside Christina and touched her short black hair. Then she cupped her face and tried to wake her. Lexi knew she was gone, but she couldn't stop calling Christina's name.

Her friend was dead because she hadn't acted on her feelings and warned her away. Worse, Lexi hadn't followed her immediately. It had taken her too long to find Christina. If only she had acted quicker, found her sooner, Christina might be alive.

Suddenly, the fog vanished. Though no one touched her, she had the feeling that strong arms were wrapped around her, soothing her fears and her sorrow.

Lexi closed her eyes and breathed easier. No longer was there the weight of being responsible for Christina's death on her shoulders. For the moment, it was gone. Lexi basked in the peace of it and didn't fight the sleep that claimed her.

Thorn held Lexi against him as he stroked her hair. He hadn't wanted to hold her in such a manner, but her thrashing and the hollowness of her voice as she repeatedly called Christina's name had been too much.

As soon as Thorn pulled her against him, she calmed. He held her, loathed to move away, even though he noticed that her gown and the sheets were soaked with sweat.

Thorn was still holding her when Darius returned. Darius didn't bat an eye when he came to the doorway and saw them.

"Her fever broke," Thorn said.

Darius nodded and left. He came back a moment later with a clean set of sheets. Thorn gathered Lexi in his arms while Darius stripped the bed. As soon as Darius had the new sheets on, Thorn laid her down and found another gown. He hastily changed her and covered her once more—peeking at her only twice.

"You didna look," Darius said.

Thorn wadded up the soaked gown and tossed it with the sheets. "She's ill."

"That wouldna stop most."

"I'm no' most."

Darius was silent for a long while before he said, "Nay, Thorn, you're no'."

Thorn looked at him. He wasn't surprised that Darius had answered Con's call for all Kings sleeping away the centuries to wake for battle. What Thorn was shocked at was Darius himself.

The last time he had seen Darius he had taken to his cave, intending never to wake again. Darius wasn't jesting when he said he had his demons. All the Kings did, but Darius had more than most.

"What?" Darius asked.

"I never asked. How are you?"

Darius's smile was tight, forced. "I'm killing Dark. I'm doing pretty good at the moment."

Thorn wondered how long that would last.

"I hear that my awakening was compared to Kellan's," Darius said. "Are you concerned?"

"A King takes to his mountain for many reasons. I'm no' concerned about you. I'm concerned *for* you."

Darius dropped his gaze to the ground. "I'll be fine."

"There's no need to lie. No' to me."

"You live long enough, you suffer every way imaginable. The mortals can no' grasp what we endure, what we can never forget."

Thorn nodded. "And yet some of us have found peace with their mates."

"I doona expect the same for myself. I'm . . . unable to . . ." Darius swallowed, his pause lengthening.

With a soft turn of his lips, Thorn waited for Darius to look at him. When he did, Thorn said, "I know."

Darius hastily looked away and then walked into the kitchen. Thorn turned his attention back to the bed and froze when he found Lexi's eyes open.

She stared at him a moment, and then softly closed her lids, drifting back to sleep. Thorn tucked the covers around her before he touched her cheek with the backs of his fingers.

Bora Bora

Rhi sipped on her tropical alcoholic beverage and soaked up the rays of the sun. She wiggled her toes as she reclined on the lounger, and then frowned when she saw the black nail polish.

Black. Why couldn't she seem to use another color? Oh, there was the gold, silver, white, and even blue as an accent, but only black as the base.

The darkness within her smiled.

Rhi rose off the lounger and walked to the edge of the turquoise water. The golden sand beneath her feet was as hot as the unforgiving sun. Despite only being there a few days, her skin had begun to bronze nicely.

She walked into the water until she was up to her thighs, then she dove in. The cool sea felt wonderful. She smiled as she watched fish swim below her.

Rhi broke the surface and treaded water as she looked back at the beach. It was a secluded place. She liked having the stunning scenery all to herself. Perhaps it was because she knew Balladyn was always trying to find her, to convince her to be his, but she knew she was being watched.

They were veiled. This was the third time in two weeks she had felt such a presence. It wasn't Balladyn. If he knew where she was, he would be trying to seduce her, not watching her.

It also wasn't Inen from the Queen's Guard. He was powerful, but not nearly powerful enough to keep veiled for so long. No one other than Usaeil herself—and Rhi, though no one else knew that—could stay veiled as long as they wanted. Usaeil was Queen of the Light. She wouldn't be spying on Rhi this way.

Rhi was intrigued. Who would want to follow her?

More importantly, why?

CHAPTER
NINE

Lexi opened her eyes to see she was in a bed. It was a woman's studio flat by the looks of it, but it wasn't hers.

Her throat hurt, and her mouth was dry. She desperately needed something to drink. She sat up, wondering why her body was so sore.

There was no one about that she could tell, and she really wished she could remember how she got there. Lexi slid her legs from beneath the covers and over the side of the bed. She stood, and her legs immediately buckled. She managed to grab hold of the bed to keep herself standing.

If she didn't know better, she would say she had been sick. She got her legs underneath her before she looked out the window. The sun was high in the sky, which meant she had slept. Since her eyes no longer hurt, she suspected she'd slept at least a good eight hours.

Lexi spotted a pile of sheets near the door. She saw her sweater sticking out. Suddenly, she realized she was naked expect for the pale yellow Victoria's Secret nightshirt she wore.

She slowly walked to the stack to get her clothes. Lexi bent and pushed the sheets away to reveal all of her clothes.

That should've made her happy, except that they were cut to pieces.

Just what the hell had happened?

And why couldn't she remember?

Lexi looked for her knife. It had to be around somewhere. It took her two tries before she could stand. A walk around the studio and she found her knife laying on an end table next to the sofa.

She hurried to it. Once she had the weapon in her hand, she felt a little calmer. She wouldn't be in control until she had on clothes and was back at her place.

If she could get past the Red Eyes.

"Good. You're up."

She knew that deep, silky smooth voice. Lexi didn't have to look to know it was the stranger, but she couldn't help herself. She turned and lost herself in his deep brown eyes.

His long dark hair was down once more. It was thick and straight, and sexy as sin. Damn him for being so good every time she saw him. He smiled then, looking charming and wicked all at once.

Despite a valiant attempt, Lexi took stock of his white tee, jeans, and boots.

"How do you feel?"

She felt like she had been dragged through Hell and back. "I'm fine."

Lexi winced at the croaking that was her voice. What had happened to her? She rubbed her throat and glanced into the kitchen.

Warily, she walked in a wide circle around him until she reached the kitchen. Using the counter as a crutch, she got a glass off the shelf and filled it with water. Lexi kept her eyes on him as she drank four glasses.

The stranger remained where he was, silently watching

her with his cool gaze. This was the third time she had encountered him. No longer could she call it coincidence.

She set the empty glass down and braced herself against
the counter. "Where am I?"

"This flat belongs to a friend named Darcy," he replied.

"How did I get here?"

His lips compressed for a heartbeat. "I brought you."

Lexi gripped her knife tighter.

He held up his hands, palms out. "I'll no' hurt you,
lass."

"What did you do to me?"

He lifted one shoulder in a shrug. "I caught you when
you fainted."

"I don't faint."

One dark brown brow lifted. "I beg to differ. You were
sick. I brought you here and nursed you."

She put her empty hand against her stomach. That
meant he'd been the one to undress her.

"You've been out for three days."

Her gaze snapped to him. Three days? She couldn't
have lost that time. She needed it to find Christina's killer.
Lexi looked at the wardrobe. Surely there was something
in there for her to wear. At least something that would do
for her to get to her flat and change.

"I know you want to leave, but you might want to
rethink that, Lexi."

She jerked at the sound of her name.

He pointed to her jacket. "I had to know who you were.
Your money is still there, by the way."

"Since you know my name, I think it's only fair I know
yours."

He glanced away, as if trying to come up with a reason
not to tell her. "It's Thorn."

Why did she look at his mouth when he spoke? She

couldn't deny there was something altogether alluring about his mouth.

Lexi mentally shook herself. What was wrong with her? She didn't have time to ogle a man, no matter how good-looking he was. She had a murderer to catch.

"I need clothes," she said.

He looked at the door, then slid his gaze back to her. "I wouldna advise leaving this flat just yet."

"I've already lost three days. I can't lose any more."

Lexi made her way to the wardrobe and threw open the door. She was looking through the clothes when she heard him come up behind her. She turned around to tell him to back up when her knife sank into his side.

Thorn sighed loudly and looked at the ceiling as if to ask for help. When he lowered his eyes to her, she was trapped in his gaze. His fingers gently wrapped around her wrist and pulled the blade out.

"That's the fourth time you've stabbed me," he said flatly.

Lexi couldn't believe he was so glib about it. Didn't he feel any pain? She looked at the wound to see how deep the knife went.

She felt light-headed when she found the wound and watched it close up. The knife clattered to the floor as it fell from her numb fingers.

"Easy," Thorn said as his hands gently took hold of her. "Look at me, Lexi. Look into my eyes."

Somehow, she dragged her gaze up to his face. Her brain couldn't process what she had just seen.

"I didna wish for you to see that." His face scrunched. "You've had a wee bit of bad luck recently, it seems. I would've spared you witnessing any more than you already have."

"You healed."

His face smoothed of all emotion. "Aye," he answered

firmly. "You sense evil when you're around what you call the Red Eyes. Do you feel that with me?"

Lexi felt the warmth of his hands on her arms, the strength within his fingers as he held her tenderly. If he had brought her to the flat, he'd had ample opportunity to harm her, and yet he hadn't.

"No," she answered.

He relaxed. "I'm glad to hear it, because I'm only trying to help."

Lexi felt her strength waning quickly as the room began to spin. She hated being sick, and now was the worst possible time. Perhaps a hot shower would do the trick. And clothes. She really needed more clothes on if Thorn was going to stand so near.

Thorn. Such an odd name. Was it short for something?

"Nay," he answered, a small smile playing about his lips. "It's just Thorn."

Could he read minds? That should bother her more, but she couldn't stop looking at his mouth. And it wasn't just his mouth. It was the entire package.

But his face . . . wow. His penetrating dark eyes hypnotized her. His brows were thick, slashing over his eyes in a hard line that went with his square chin. And that jawline. It looked as if it had been cut from granite.

Muscles bulged on his arms. His tight shirt formed over his wide chest and thick shoulders. Hard. He was hard everywhere.

Except his mouth. It simply wasn't fair for a gorgeous man to have such a tantalizing mouth. Almost too full for a man, but Lexi liked the look. She wanted to touch his lips.

No. She wanted to kiss his lips.

She grew concerned when she saw one side of his mouth lift in a smile so wicked and wanton that her stomach fluttered. Surely that wasn't right. That only happened in books. People's stomachs didn't flutter from a smile. Right?

Lexi lifted her gaze to Thorn's eyes. His smile was fading as he frowned. It took everything she had to stay on her feet. She was suddenly thankful that he was holding her because the room began to swim again and she couldn't keep her eyes open.

She needed to get back to bed. All of a sudden, she realized that her feet felt as if they were blocks of ice.

"Lexi?"

She licked her lips and tried to step out of his grasp. "I need to lie down."

The next instant she was in his arms. Lexi rested her head on his shoulder. She should demand that he set her down so she could walk. The problem with that was that Lexi didn't think she could make it to the bed on her own.

She fought to keep her eyes open when he returned her to the bed and covered her. It was wrong on so many levels that she was sick. She rarely got sick, but this one was a doozy.

Every inch of her ached. It was as if getting out of bed and learning she'd lost those days was all done on adrenaline. Once that faded, her body let her know quickly how bad it felt.

"Rest," Thorn ordered, though his deep brown eyes were filled with concern.

"I can't. I need to find . . ."

"Your friend's killer."

Lexi's muddled mind tried to sort out how Thorn knew, then she didn't care. "Yes. The Red Eyes need to be stopped."

"They've noticed you've been following them. They're tracking you now. You can no' go out there, and especially no' sick."

Lexi wanted to cry. She was failing.

"You're no' failing, lass. You've worn yourself out."

"Stop reading my mind."

He was grinning again. "I'm no'. You're talking."

Lexi wanted to argue the point, but it was taking too much energy to keep thinking, much less talking. She let her eyes close.

As she drifted off to sleep, she heard Thorn say, "The Dark Fae willna harm you. No' while I'm around."

Thorn checked Lexi's forehead to make sure the fever hadn't returned. Then he sat back in the chair and called to Darius.

Darius immediately answered. *"What's wrong?"*

"Lexi woke. Her fever might be gone, but the sickness isna. She's going to need a doctor."

"I'll see what I can do."

Thorn rose and walked to the window. A part of him wanted to rush out of the flat and kill the Dark he saw walking on the street, but another part of him, the part that spoke the loudest, urged him to remain with Lexi.

He was tasked with killing the Dark, but he had also taken a vow to protect humans. Thorn wasn't sure why Lexi had stuck out more than any of the others, but she had. Even though he knew history could very well repeat itself, he would do all that he could to keep death from finding her.

CHAPTER
TEN

Darcy drummed her fingers on the kitchen counter as she looked out the windows and toward the mountains. Dreagan wasn't just beautiful. It was serene, a place where she knew she was safe.

Then there was the magic. As a Druid, she could sense its power in every blade of grass and every rock of the sixty thousand acres.

She couldn't imagine being anywhere else but with Warrick, even as the number of enemies of the Dragon Kings continued to grow.

The ceremony to bind her and Warrick together had been scheduled for a week ago. They had put it off because of the war with the Dark Fae. It was tradition for every Dragon King to be there to witness their union, but Warrick didn't want to wait.

Only after the ceremony would she become immortal, living as long as Warrick did. Traditions were important to the Kings, and she wanted everything to be perfect. Especially since so much had gone awry in her getting to Dreagan.

Strong arms came around her from behind. Darcy

closed her eyes and smiled when Warrick kissed her cheek before resting his chin on her shoulder.

"Something is bothering you," he said.

Darcy loved how easily he could read her. As their love and bond grew, she was finding it just as easy to decipher him. "It's Thorn."

"Did he call again?"

She shook her head and turned in his arms to look up into Warrick's face. His cobalt gaze held hers. "Despite the unfathomable time you Kings have walked this earth, you know very little about humans."

"Ah," Warrick said with a nod of his blond head. "You doona think Thorn can care for the female?"

"I think that it would be better if he took her to a doctor. There could be a number of things wrong with her."

"Or nothing."

Darcy knew he was right. She lowered her gaze to his impressive chest and ran her hands over the thick muscles there. "I have an acquaintance in Edinburgh. She's a doctor."

"Darcy," Warrick began.

"I know," she hurried to say as she looked into his eyes. "You don't have to tell me how important it is that all of you remain secret, but there was something in Thorn's voice."

Warrick's eyes narrowed in concern. "What was it?"

"I don't know his past, but I got the feeling that it was important that the woman live."

Warrick's lips pinched into a flat line. He looked over Darcy's head and stared out the window for long moments. She didn't rush him. She also knew he wouldn't tell her what had happened in Thorn's past, and she didn't care to know.

Finally Warrick lowered his gaze to her. "Come with me."

They walked hand in hand from the kitchen, up the stairs to their bedroom. Warrick shut and locked the door, then he pulled out his phone and dialed a number.

To Darcy's surprise, he put it on speaker. She smiled at Warrick. Through eons of secrecy and shielding himself, he never stopping bringing her into his world and showing her his love.

"War," Darius said in answer.

"I've got you on speaker, and Darcy is here with me," Warrick said.

Darcy sat next to Warrick on the bed. "How is the woman you and Thorn found?"

"No' good," Darius answered. "Lexi's fever broke, but she's still sick. Thorn just asked me to find a doctor."

It was just as Darcy had feared. "I know someone who might help."

There was a beat of silence before Darius said, "You trust them?"

"She doesn't know about magic or that I'm a Druid. But she's good at what she does. It's not in Sophie's nature to turn away those in need. She'll help."

Darius sighed. "What's her name?"

"Sophie Martin. She works at the Royal Victoria Hospital in Edinburgh."

Warrick added, "I'll get Ryder to send over all her details."

"Did Thorn call you again?" Darius asked.

Darcy glanced at Warrick. "No. It was just something in the way he spoke of Lexi."

"Thank you," Darius said.

Warrick said Darius's name to keep him from ending the call. "What's the story with the woman?"

"She's an American visiting here, and one of her friends was killed by the Dark. Lexi set out to find the killer."

Darcy was so shocked she couldn't find the words. She'd

had her own run-in with the Dark. There's no way she would actively seek them out. Then she looked at Warrick and knew she would do anything for him, including facing a horde of Dark Fae.

Warrick whistled low. "Are you going to stop her?"

"What do you think Thorn will do?"

"I think he'll help her."

Darius chuckled. "I suspect you're right."

"How are things there?" Darcy asked.

"Bad. Verra bad," Darius answered in a grim tone. "There's been no sign of Ulrik."

Warrick said, "Ryder can no' find him anywhere either."

"He may be with the Dark."

Darcy still had mixed feelings about Ulrik. She had been the one to unbind his magic, and in doing so she got to see his past through his memories. There were things the others couldn't begin to fathom that he'd endured.

All because he had been betrayed by a human and retaliated in the only way he could—by killing them. All that got him was banishment from Dreagan and to walk the earth forever in human form.

Until he found her.

"I'll let you know about the doctor," Darius said.

The call ended, but Darcy was still thinking about Ulrik. She had truly thought him an ally.

Warrick's hand covered hers. "I hate him for nearly killing you."

She hated Ulrik for nearly being killed.

"But," Warrick said, "the Dark think you're dead. They're no longer looking for you."

Darcy shifted to face him. "I know. I keep wondering if Ulrik did it on purpose."

"I can no' figure it out myself. He had no reason to help you."

"Unless he's not as bad as everyone thinks."

Warrick raised a brow. "If Con or the Druids hadna been there, you would've died."

"But I didn't. I'm here. Let's think on that."

Warrick kissed her forehead as he pulled her against him. "Ulrik brought Lily back from the dead. Now there's a possibility that he helped you. Yet he's aligned with the Dark to bring us down. None of it makes sense."

"One moment I think Ulrik is a decent guy, and the next I think he's the Devil himself." Darcy held Warrick tighter, thankful that she had him in her life. "Trying to figure it out makes my head hurt."

"Aye, love, but if we choose wrong, it could be the end of us."

Darius stood at the back of the Royal Victoria Hospital. From what Ryder discovered, Dr. Sophie Martin was due to get off work in thirty minutes.

He had already been by her flat. On the way to the hospital, he'd cleared several streets of Dark Fae. It had taken him longer than he would've liked to cart the bodies to the warehouse and remain unseen.

Like Warrick, Darius didn't mind working alone. With Thorn occupied keeping Lexi alive, he couldn't see Darius battling his own demons. Just as Darius wanted.

His patience was running on empty when thirty minutes past the time the doctor was supposed to get off she walked out of the hospital.

He spotted her easily enough, despite her red hair pulled with some clip that kept it all together at the back of her head. She walked at a steady pace with her head up, a purse on her shoulder, and a black bag in hand.

Darius knew all about the doctor. She was from London and had attended Oxford. After a few years at a London hospital, Sophie Martin moved to Edinburgh where she had been for the past seven years.

She was single, which made things much easier for Darius. He wouldn't have to contend with a husband or boyfriend wondering where she was.

He also knew that she was known to pay house calls to those who either couldn't afford a doctor or who couldn't get to her. Darcy had been right. Sophie was the perfect one to help Lexi.

Since Darius knew her route home, he put himself in a place where she would have to walk past him. In order not to frighten her, he stepped out of the shadows that dusk provided.

"Dr. Martin," he said.

She halted instantly, her gaze on him. "And you are?"

"We have a mutual friend. Darcy Allen."

Sophie relaxed a fraction. "How is Darcy?"

"Doing well. She suggested that I find you. Darcy believes that you'll be willing to help me."

Sophie stood tall, her olive gaze direct. "What do you need help with?"

"I've a friend who is ill. She's being chased by some verra bad people, and we can no' risk bringing her to the hospital."

Sophie regarded him for long moments. "What type of man are you?"

"No' a nice kind."

"Yet you would stand here waiting to bring me to your friend?"

Darius eyed her. "You asked. I told you."

She adjusted the black bag in her hand. "I need your name."

"Darius."

"Darius what?"

"Just Darius," he replied, hiding his grin. He liked the way she held herself, the way she looked as if she could take on the world single-handedly. He held out a piece of paper. "Here's the address."

She looked at the paper and returned her gaze to him. "You're not coming with me?"

"As I explained, bad people are after her. I'm going to make sure they doona get close."

Darius turned and blended into the shadows. He waited to see what Sophie would do. He almost expected her to refuse, but she raised her hand to call for a taxi. A few moments later, she got into the car and drove off.

"I knew there were Dragon Kings in the city," came a voice behind him.

Darius smiled as he faced the three Dark he had seen circling the hospital. "I didna think you idiots would ever find me."

"What did you want with a doctor?" asked one.

Darius shrugged and widened his stance. "If you best me, I'll tell you. But you willna best me."

He lunged forward, ducking a blast of magic and slammed his fist into the abdomen of one of the Dark. The only time he felt . . . normal . . . was when he was killing the vermin.

Sophie had her mobile phone in her hand. She was about to call Darcy and see if she had sent Darius, but Sophie hesitated.

It had been Darius's admission of not being a nice guy that threw her off. Most lied, but he was deliberately honest. And that struck her as . . . odd.

Much to her dismay, it intrigued her as well. She didn't want to be intrigued. She had gone out of her way to keep all men at a distance for over seven years.

Sophie was exhausted after a fourteen-hour shift at the

hospital, but just as Darcy said, Sophie never refused someone in need.

When the taxi stopped, she quickly looked around the area. With all the murders each night, being careless was no longer an option.

She paid the taxi and stepped out of the car to find a tall man with long dark hair waiting for her. He smiled and held out his hand. On instinct, Sophie took it.

"I'm Thorn. Darius said you agreed to come. Thank you," the man said. He motioned to the door as he looked behind her. "We best get inside so you can see to Lexi."

Sophie watched Thorn carefully. He was vigilant, the kind of man who appeared calm and unobservant when he was anything but. He was the kind of man who knew when danger was coming before anyone else.

The same kind of man Darius was.

Sophie wondered if she should turn around and leave. She had the unwavering feeling that she was getting involved in something perilous. But something urged her onward.

"Lead the way," she told Thorn.

CHAPTER
ELEVEN

Thorn watched with his arms crossed over his chest from the end of the bed as Dr. Sophie Martin examined Lexi. After several minutes, Sophie sat back in the chair Thorn had used.

She opened her black bag and pulled out a syringe and a small bottle. "She has the flu. How long has she been ill?"

"About three days. I got her fever down, but that didna seem to help much."

Sophie glanced at him before she filled the syringe with liquid and then put the needle in Lexi's arm and drained it. "This will help. It's an antibiotic."

Thorn let his arms drop. "She's going to be all right?"

"Yes," Sophie said and smiled at him. "You've done a good job."

"She doesna make it easy," Thorn grumbled.

"Patients rarely do. Make sure she stays hydrated."

Thorn watched Sophie gather her things and stand. "So . . . that's it? Just a shot? That will make her well?"

"It should, yes. I would've preferred to talk to her, but I couldn't get her to wake up. I'd like to return tomorrow and check in on her."

Thorn readily agreed.

Sophie walked to the door. "Keep her out of the weather."

"You needn't worry about that. I doona intend to let her out of the door."

Sophie's olive gaze went to the bed once more as her smile faded. "Darius said she was in some danger."

"In truth, doctor, everyone in the city is if you read the papers."

She opened the door. "I also see the news."

"Steer clear of anyone with red eyes."

"No one has red eyes."

Thorn bowed his head. "As you say. Be careful out there, doc."

"And you," she said before she walked away, the door closing softly behind her.

Thorn sent a quick text to Warrick and Darcy to let them know that Sophie had visited and treated Lexi. All Thorn had to do now was wait for Lexi to wake up.

That he wasn't looking forward to. The only reason she hadn't left the flat earlier was because she was ill and weak. After the shot, she might well wake feeling better than before.

Then Thorn would have a hell of a time keeping her inside the flat. He had wanted to avoid telling her all the details of the Dark, but he had a sneaking suspicion he wasn't going to have a choice.

Ireland
Dark Fae Palace

Ulrik stood next to his uncle, Mikkel, as they waited for the king of the Dark Fae to finish his whispered conversation with Balladyn.

"I'd appreciate more of a heads-up before you have a Dark take me from my shop," Ulrik said in a low voice.

Mikkel chuckled. "Acting a little childish now, aren't you?"

"You know the Kings watch me. You're making things worse."

"As if I care," Mikkel stated in a harsh tone, the vocals coming out nasally as he used the British accent he had perfected. "You're here to get your revenge and ensure that none of the Kings realize I'm the one really pulling the strings."

Balladyn turned away from Taraeth, his gaze landing on Ulrik. It was clear to one and all that Balladyn was ready to make his attempt at the throne. Ulrik wondered if Taraeth knew.

He imagined that Taraeth thought himself above such things. Just as Mikkel assumed Ulrik would stand there and let him rule the Silvers.

Not. Going. To. Happen.

Ulrik had suffered more than any being on the planet with his Silvers just a few hours from him. Let Mikkel think what he would. The bastard was too self-assured to realize he was underestimating Ulrik.

Just as Con was.

"I would've loved to have been there to see Con's face when you killed the Druid," Mikkel said with a satisfied smile. "If they were no' going to kill you, they will now. I understand she was Warrick's mate."

At Taraeth's nod, Mikkel walked to the king of the Dark. Ulrik glared at his uncle's back. Just as he thought he might have a few minutes to himself, Balladyn came to stand beside him.

"Mikkel is making great headway against the Kings."

Ulrik clasped his hands behind his back and shifted his shoulders in the jacket of his charcoal gray suit jacket. "Enough of the shite. What do you want?"

"I want you to stay away from Rhi."

This surprised Ulrik. He turned his head to look at the Dark who was watching Taraeth and Mikkel. "You want to warn me away from her?"

"She's had enough dealings with the Kings. It's time she returned to her own."

"You're no' one of her own, or do I need to give you a mirror?"

Balladyn's nostrils flared as his head swiveled and he glared at Ulrik. "Rhi was always meant to be mine."

"Perhaps you should tell her that." At his silence, Ulrik smiled. "You have. Let me guess, Rhi didna take your offer."

"She just needs time."

"If you think she'll turn off her love for her King, then you doona know her at all."

Balladyn looked him up and down. His Irish accent was thick with anger when he said, "Then you know you don't stand a chance with her."

"Oh, I doona know about that," Ulrik said, agitating Balladyn further.

Balladyn's red eyes narrowed into slits. "What's that supposed to mean?"

"Who do you think carried her out of your fortress after you tortured her? Who do you think she visits when she needs to talk? She has an amazing mouth. If I'd known how delicious she tasted, I'd have kissed her centuries ago."

Balladyn growled and pulled back his hand. The only thing that stopped him from using magic was Taraeth calling his name.

Ulrik smiled. "Your chain has been yanked. Go to your master."

"You have one as well."

But not for long. Ulrik watched as Balladyn turned and walked out of the chamber. The Dark had it bad for Rhi. Balladyn was taking things slow for the moment, but when would he push her to make a decision?

Long, slender fingers slid over Ulrik's shoulder and then down and across his chest. The female Dark came around to stand in front of him in a dark silver silk chemise. Her black hair hung midway down her back with thick stripes of silver running through it.

"Taraeth has given me to you for the night," she whispered in a seductive Irish brogue.

Ulrik looked down at her tempting lips and wrapped an arm around her. He bent and put his mouth next to her ear. "Taraeth? Or Mikkel?"

She shrugged, kissing his neck. "Mikkel asked that you be occupied. Taraeth chose me."

Why would his uncle snatch him from his shop in Perth only to have him kept engaged while they were visiting Taraeth?

"What did Taraeth tell you?"

She laughed breathlessly up at him and wound her arms around his neck. "To do whatever you want."

Just what he'd hoped to hear. Ulrik didn't spare his uncle another glance as he walked from the chamber with his hand on the female's back.

Once they were in the corridor, he stopped and faced her. "Take me back to Perth."

"I . . . I can't. Mikkel wants you here," she said with a shake of her head.

"And your king, who you obey without question, told you to do whatever I want. I want to return to Perth."

She blinked her red eyes. When she hesitated, Ulrik pivoted and began to walk to the Fae doorway that would return him to his shop.

"Wait," she said and hurried after him.

"Do you know who I am?"

She nodded, having to jog to keep up with him. "Of course."

"I'll give you one warning, Dark. Doona cross me."

She took his hand and yanked him into a side room. He had his fingers around her throat in an instant, pinning her to the wall in the next heartbeat.

"My sister is the one sent to seduce Mikkel," she said while gasping for air.

Ulrik loosened his hold, a frown taking root. "Taraeth sent her."

The Dark jerked her head up and down. She didn't claw at his hands, but kept her arms by her sides. "The king trusts few."

"Did he pick you to come to me today?"

"Yes," she whispered.

Ulrik released her. "What does Mikkel really want you to do with me?"

She touched her throat with her hand and swallowed several times before she raised her eyes to him. "He wants to search your store."

"For what?"

"He wants to be sure you're not plotting against him."

So, the bastard wasn't as dumb as he looked. Ulrik took a step back from the female and released her. "What's your name?"

"Muriel."

"Well, Muriel, do I believe you or no'?"

She gawked at him. "I've no reason to lie. I hold no allegiance to Mikkel."

"And what if I do?"

She lifted her chin. "You don't."

Ulrik liked her spunk. "He's my uncle."

"And the one trying to usurp what is rightfully yours."

"What else do you know?" he asked, thoroughly captivated.

Her face softened. "I know that you're not a man to back down from what he wants."

He raised a brow.

"I know that you've been meeting with Taraeth for centuries. Long before your uncle."

It wasn't until that moment that Ulrik realized she was after something. "You've seen a lot, little Dark."

She shrugged indifferently.

"What do you want?" he asked.

Her gaze swept over him. "A night in your arms."

"Just a night?" he teased.

"As long as you'll have me."

She was flirting with him now. "What do you really want?" he asked.

"I want revenge."

No one understood the need for vengeance better than Ulrik. He had been planning his for Constantine for what seemed like an eternity. But he was closing in on his prize.

"Against?" he asked.

She cocked her head to the side. "You have your secrets. I have mine."

Ulrik's gut told him not to trust her. He didn't trust anyone. There was something about her that made him consider the option however. She saw a lot in Taraeth's court. She could tell him much about Mikkel's comings and goings.

Then again, she could be telling Mikkel his plans.

"I'll help you, Ulrik, King of Silvers, if you'll help me," she purred and ran her hand up his chest.

He grasped her wrist, halting her arm. Then he bent his head until their lips were nearly touching. "Shall we seal the deal with a kiss?"

"I thought you'd never ask," she said huskily right before she put her mouth to his.

CHAPTER
TWELVE

When Lexi next opened her eyes, she noticed how much better she felt. It was the noise that drew her attention. She raised her head and found Thorn in the kitchen making coffee with his back to her.

His dark hair was pulled back today. She rested her head on her arm to get a better look at him. His gray shirt once more hugged his impressive body. His long sleeves were pushed up past his elbows. His black jeans gripped his narrow hips, showing off his fine ass and his long legs.

Though he looked good in the clothes, she couldn't help but imagine him in something more . . . historical. Like a kilt, or even something piratey.

He took a drink of the coffee, then with mug in hand turned to face her with a smile. "Good afternoon."

Lexi groaned as she glanced out the window. There were clouds again, once more hiding the sun. She couldn't tell what time it was.

"How many days did I lose this time?"

"Just the one," he answered. "How do you feel?"

Lexi took stock of her body. It no longer felt as if she had been dragged behind a vehicle. "Better, actually."

"Good. You have the flu."

Wonderful. Just what she needed. "I don't feel like I have the flu."

He raised a dark brow, his gaze pinning her as he walked to the bed. "We had a doctor come see you last night. She gave you a shot. Her orders were that you stay inside."

"Impossible." Lexi sat up and rolled her head from one side to the other to stretch it. "I have things that need to be done."

"Like catching Christina's killer?"

She froze. Slowly, she slid her gaze to Thorn with her heart thumping in her chest. How had he known?

"You said a lot when the fever had you." He shrugged then and said, "After, I searched the names of the victims and found Christina's. It didna take much afterward to put two and two together."

Lexi leaned back against the wall with the pillows behind her back. "I had one week left. I've lost four days. Three won't be enough to find him."

"You willna have those three. If you leave this flat in this weather, you could relapse."

Lexi lowered her gaze to her hands clasped in her lap. "I promised I would find her murderer."

Thorn let out a long-suffering sigh. "There is much you doona know. You're no' the only one fighting them."

"You are?" she asked as her gaze went to him. She leaned forward, wondering if she'd really seen him heal, or if it had been a dream. "Tell me all you know. Please."

He hesitated, as if he couldn't make up his mind. A resigned expression came over his face. "What have you seen them do?"

"Change," she replied instantly. "I've seen them change the color of their eyes and hair. How do they do that? Is it some illusion?"

"Nay. It's magic."

It was on the tip of Lexi's tongue to tell him magic didn't exist, but by the seriousness of his gaze, she kept silent. "How?"

"Do you believe you're the only intelligent beings on this earth?"

She scrunched up her face. "Well, duh."

"You'd be wrong."

Her breath left her in a whoosh. "You're lying."

"I'm no'," he said softly. He leaned forward and put his forearms on his thighs, his gaze on the floor. "Lexi, I doona wish to tell you any of this. You're no' ready for it. But I also know that if I doona, you could get yourself killed. You need to understand the full extent of the danger."

"Then tell me." Lexi was proud of herself. Her voice was smooth, even if she was shaking on the inside, as if on another level, she knew she wasn't going to like what she heard.

"What you've seen are the Fae. The Dark Fae, to be precise. There are Light Fae, but it's the Dark who have the red eyes."

Lexi sank against the wall. She had heard him call them Dark. But Fae? Surely not. Beings like that only existed in fairy tales.

"You doona believe me."

She looked to find Thorn staring at her. "I . . . I don't know what to think. I know a man with red eyes killed Christina, though there wasn't a mark on her. I know that I've seen them change in ways that defy logic. Yet, if the Fae were real, wouldn't more people know of them?"

"They came to his realm millions of years ago. The Dark feed off souls. You didna find a mark on Christina because every time they had sex with her, they took parts of her soul until nothing was left."

Lexi was going to be sick. She clutched her stomach

wanting to tell Thorn to stop while at the same time silently begging him to tell her everything.

"There was a war. The Fae Wars. The Fae were stopped before they could take over this realm. They signed a treaty agreeing to stay away, but the earth is a large place and no' everywhere can be patrolled. They slipped in here and there, taking their victims."

"Who fought the Fae? Us?"

Thorn sat back in the chair. There was doubt in his eyes, as if he didn't want to tell her the answer.

Lexi wasn't going to give in so easily. "You began this. Tell me. Because if it was us, that's not something that would've been kept secret."

"Nay, it wasna humans."

Somehow Lexi already knew that's what his answer would be. "There are other beings here?"

He gave a single nod.

"Who? What?" she urged.

"They keep to themselves. You'll never see them."

"But you know them."

Thorn waved his hand. "I help them."

"I want to help. I want to fight the Fae."

"No' all Fae are bad," he said. "The Light Fae sided with the other beings and helped end the Fae War."

Lexi rolled her eyes in agitation. "Fine. I want to fight the Dark."

"You have no magic."

She laughed at this. "As if any human does." When he didn't so much as blink, she knew she was once more wrong. What the hell was happening to the world she knew? "There are those with magic?"

"Druids."

"Oh." What else could she say? There was so little history about the Druids. Now she began to see why. "I have to avenge Christina."

"The Dark seduce you with a look, a smile, a touch. No one can withstand their pull. Your body instinctively knows it'll receive unimaginable pleasure at their hands. You seek it, crave it—and unknowingly go willing to your death."

Lexi's stomach rolled. Poor Christina. She never stood a chance. "Is there a way to block what the Dark do?"

Thorn's head leaned to the side as he studied her. "I know a few who can. It's rare, however, I watched you shake off their attempt."

"What are you talking about?"

"The Dark use glamour to change their appearance and hide their red eyes. You then wouldna be able to tell if you were talking to a human or a Fae. You felt the desire they can flip on in a human like a switch, and yet you fought it and got away."

Lexi remembered that encounter on the street. She hadn't known that's what was happening, or that she had come that close to dying. "How did I do it?"

"I'd verra much like to know."

"I've seen others flock to the Re . . . Dark all over town. Why are their eyes red?"

Thorn rubbed his palms on his thighs. "All Fae are breathtakingly beautiful. They also all have black hair. It's a choice the Fae make to turn Dark. The first time they take a life, their eyes turn from silver to red. The more lives they take, the more silver runs through their hair."

Lexi thought back to the guy who had killed Christina. His hair was more silver than black. "Dear God."

"I can understand you wanting to avenge your friend's death, but if you get close to a Dark, it'll be your life you lose."

Lexi shook her head. "This can't be real. Please tell me this is all some kind of sick joke."

"I'm sorry, but I can no'."

"I didn't think so. It's just . . . how could all of this be happening and no one get that it's other beings doing it?"

Thorn smiled sadly. "Humans like to pretend they're the only ones here."

"Yeah." Lexi had wanted to know the truth, but it made things much more complicated. How could she ever trust anyone again? If a Dark was using glamour, she'd never know it.

"I have a friend who has been hunting the Dark with me. His name is Darius," Thorn said as he got to his feet. "He'll be here shortly. He went to your place and gathered your clothes."

Lexi took a deep breath to try to steady herself. "Where am I, by the way?"

"A friend's. Her name is Darcy Allen."

"That's right. You told me that." She blinked, because she now knew she hadn't dreamed he had healed before her very eyes.

"Her place was warded by a Light against all Fae. The Dark can no' get to you here."

"I saw you heal."

His dark eyes dropped to the floor as he sighed.

When he didn't reply, she said, "Say something."

"I'd hoped you had forgotten that."

"Forgotten?" she asked in surprise. "How could I possibly forget that I stabbed you and watched your skin mend on its own?"

He shrugged and lifted his gaze to her. "You were still ill."

"What are you to be able to do something like that? Is it magic?"

"Aye."

"Are you a Druid then?" Because he wasn't Fae. He was unimaginably good-looking, and though his hair was dark, it wasn't black.

"Nay." Thorn motioned to the kitchen. "If you're hungry, I can heat up some soup."

"That sounds good." Lexi scooted to the edge of the bed and let him change the subject. For now. "I'd also like a shower."

Thorn eyed her. "Are you strong enough for that?"

"Probably not, but I'm going to do it," she stated.

He smiled as he turned away. "I'll start your food then."

Lexi waited until he was in the kitchen before she gingerly climbed out of bed. The last time she had nearly fallen on her face. She didn't want a repeat.

She took her time walking to the bathroom. After she turned on the water to get it hot, she looked in the mirror and closed her eyes at what she saw. Her hair was sticking out everywhere. She was pale with ugly, dark circles beneath her eyes.

It wasn't like she wanted Thorn to ask her out on a date—*liar!*—but she didn't want to look awful either. Lexi turned away from the mirror and stripped out of the gown.

It wasn't until she stood beneath the spray of water that she remembered Thorn had seen her naked. He hadn't shown the least bit of interest.

"You've been ill," Lexi told herself.

She angrily shoved aside such thoughts and began to wash. As she did, her mind went over all that Thorn had told her.

Fae. There were Fae on Earth, as well as some other kind of being. Those others had saved humans from the Fae, but why would they want to remain secret?

Then again, with the history of what humans did to things they didn't understand, she could well comprehend their decision. Still, she wished she could thank them for helping.

How shocking and strange to learn humans weren't the only intelligent beings on the planet. It scared the shit out of her to the point that she wasn't sure she could ever walk the streets alone again.

Nothing would ever be the same for her. She could never look at a person again without wondering if they were human, and she couldn't even think about dating.

Perhaps Thorn was right. She should go home.

CHAPTER
THIRTEEN

Rhi stood atop a mountain looking at Dreagan. She was far enough away that none of the Dragon Kings would know she was there.

No matter how hard she tried, she always found herself back in Scotland. It was pathetic. Her King would never love her again.

It was something she told herself almost daily, but then she would remember the heart-stopping passion, the way he placed kisses over her body as if he were worshipping her, and the way he had once smiled whenever she walked into a room.

Those thoughts used to make her cry for the longing in her heart to have all of it again. But, oddly, there were no tears this time. Just . . . sorrow to have lost something so precious.

A love of the ages.

That's what he had called it. Rhi had been too wrapped up in the desire and him to fully comprehend everything. It wasn't until he turned his back on her that it hit her.

"Rhi? Can you hear me? Where are you?"

She had heard Henry's summons for weeks now. He

was handsome, and a wonderful kisser, but he was mortal. She had known it was wrong to kiss him. Rhi told herself she needed to feel something, but she was only going to hurt Henry.

It would've been better had she just told him the truth. Yet, she didn't want to wound him as she had been hurt. So she left.

Now he called to her daily.

"Forget about me, Henry," she said. "I'll only ruin things for you."

Rhi had been jumping from place to place in the hopes of finding some sort of peace and contentment. But it wasn't to be had.

She refused to return to Usaeil's court. The Queen of the Light had taken a Dragon King to her bed. Rhi had a suspicion that it was Con, but she couldn't prove it. Yet.

The fact that Usaeil had done everything in her power to break Rhi and her King apart was like a splinter she couldn't get out. It stung viciously that Usaeil would now have a relationship with a King.

Rhi also couldn't go to Dreagan anymore. How could she after she had refused to aid Warrick and Darcy? Rhi still didn't understand why she hadn't rushed to help as she always had.

Already she had gone to Ulrik too many times. And Balladyn . . . The Dark wanted her. He pursued her relentlessly, and what worried her was that she enjoyed it. It felt good to have someone want her so desperately.

Then there were his kisses.

It would be so easy to give in to Balladyn. He would shield her as her King had once done. Balladyn loved her. How had she not seen it before?

Rhi shook her head viciously and turned her back on Dreagan. She was so confused. She didn't know what to do anymore or where to turn.

Then she thought of the one place she could go, the one person who she knew would always be there for her.

In a blink, she teleported from the mountain to a cabin deep in the forest. She had taken only two steps to the porch when the door opened and Phelan appeared.

The Warrior's smile dimmed when he saw her. "Grab the whisky," he said over his shoulder to his wife and Druid, Aisley.

Phelan didn't say another word. He opened his arms and Rhi walked into them, burying her head in his chest. He held her tightly, rubbing his hands up and down her back.

"Do you want to talk?" he asked softly.

She shook her head. It felt good to be able to lean on someone. Phelan was the only one who didn't want something from her. He was the only one she could show weakness to and know he would never use it against her.

"It's been weeks, Rhi," the immortal Highlander said. "I've been worried."

Rhi still remembered the first time she had spoken to Phelan. As a Warrior, a man with a primeval god inside him, he had been torn about his feelings for Aisley.

Phelan's blood could heal anyone of any ailment. The only thing he couldn't do was bring someone back from the dead. He hadn't known why his blood had such power.

But Rhi had.

She had watched him for centuries before she finally told him that he was a prince of the Fae. His ancestor had bedded a Light Fae, who happened to be the queen's brother, which is how his blood was able to cure anything but death. He was of royal blood on both sides of his family, with his mortal side being the rulers of Saxony.

From the first time she and Phelan had spoken, there had been a bond that developed quick and strong. She had no more family, so she considered him a brother, and Aisley a sister.

"Can I help in any way?"

She smiled at Phelan's words, finding tears gathering in her eyes. "You already are."

Rhi shared almost everything with Phelan. The one thing he didn't know was who her Dragon King lover was. Because if he did . . . Phelan would go after him.

She stepped out of Phelan's arms and wiped away the tears that had fallen. With as much of a smile as she could muster in place, she met his blue gray gaze.

"Tell me his name," Phelan said tightly. "Tell me who the bastard is so I can knock some sense into him."

"I would love to see that."

"I'd do it for you."

Rhi sniffed, feeling better than she had in days. "I worried you'd be angry with me."

Phelan's gaze turned troubled as he led her inside the house. He ushered her to the two sofas where Aisley already sat with three glasses of whisky.

"Rhi," Aisley said and stood. She rushed to hug her.

It had taken Rhi the longest time to become comfortable with the affection Phelan and Aisley showed her. Until Rhi realized they were like family, and it was all right for her to love them as she did.

Phelan's frown made Rhi uneasy as she accepted the whisky and sat beside Aisley. "You are angry."

"Nay," Phelan said. "I'm worried."

"Why didn't you show up?" Aisley asked. "Did someone detain you?"

It was there, the out Rhi could use to cover her ass. They knew she was a Queen's Guard and was called away for duties all over. She could lie and everything could go back to the way it was.

But she couldn't lie. Not just because she would feel unimaginable pain—a trait she inherited from her mother—but because they were family.

"No." The word hung heavy in the air. "I wanted to. I intended to. Then . . . I couldn't."

Phelan set his untouched whisky on the coffee table between them and leaned forward. "Was it because Ulrik was there?"

They had no idea how she had helped him and how he had held her. They didn't have a clue of the shared kiss or how she found herself going to Ulrik again and again. And they wouldn't. "No."

"I don't understand." Aisley's troubled fawn-colored eyes looked from her to Phelan and back again.

Rhi swirled the amber liquid in her glass. "I don't really either. The one thing I do know is that ever since I was taken by the Dark and held by the Chains of Mordare, I feel . . . darkness within me."

"Nay," Phelan stated loudly. "You're no' Dark, Rhi."

She smiled at him. "I didn't say I was. I said I felt a darkness within."

"Fight it."

"Phelan," Aisley admonished. She looked at Rhi and asked, "Is it too strong to fight?"

Rhi shrugged. "Not exactly. It's more that I'm not sure I want to fight it."

"I can't lose you," Phelan said.

Rhi couldn't look into his eyes. She dropped her gaze.

Aisley's hand covered hers. "You might not have been in Edinburgh to fight the Dark, but you sent us to help. You didn't have to do that. You're fighting the darkness, Rhi. All you have to do is not give in."

That was easier said than done. If she took Balladyn's offer, she knew the darkness would claim her quickly. She who'd vowed to never become Dark.

"What can we do to help?" Phelan asked.

Rhi looked up at him. "You're doing it. This is the only place I can come and be able to be myself."

Phelan sat back with a sigh. "I've no' told the other Warriors yet, but a war has begun."

What? How could she not have known? "When?"

"In Edinburgh with Warrick and Darcy." Phelan ran a hand down his face. "There's much that has happened, Rhi. Ulrik stabbed Darcy."

Rhi shook her head, not able to process the information.

"We used our magic," Aisley said of the Druids. "Until Con could get there and heal Darcy."

Rhi tossed back the whisky. She set aside her empty glass and got to her feet to pace. Unable to process what they told her about Ulrik, she focused on what she could think about. "The first Fae Wars were horrendous. I lost my brother in that war. That was ages ago before there were so many mortals on this realm. We were able to hide the battles. We won't be able to hide them now."

"We?" Phelan asked. "You'll fight with the Kings?"

She halted and turned her head to him. There hadn't been any other thought. "Of course."

"So will the Warriors and Druids," Aisley said.

Rhi looked from one to the other. "No. You mustn't. The Dark are insidious. Many of the Druids from MacLeod Castle have children. No amount of Druid magic or the fact that the castle is hidden from mortals will stop the Dark."

Aisley's face paled, but she lifted her chin. "This is our world, Rhi. We have magic. We can't just stand by in this war."

"We willna," Phelan said as he got to his feet. "I'm a Warrior. My god demands I join this fight."

Rhi shook her head in frustration. "Why didn't you call to me? Why didn't you tell me before now?"

"Because you've no' been yourself," Phelan said softly. "You needed time."

"Tell me everything," she demanded as she once more took her seat.

As Phelan studied her, Rhi felt someone else's gaze on her. Her unseen follower. Everywhere she went, he was there. Without a doubt he was Fae. Light or Dark, she wasn't sure. To be able to remain veiled as long as he did, she suspected he was Dark.

Had Balladyn sent him? As soon as the question emerged, she pushed it aside. Balladyn wouldn't want anyone but himself to know what she did. It wouldn't be the king of the Dark, Taraeth. He had bigger things to concern himself with—like bringing down the Kings.

It wasn't Usaeil. The queen of the Light might be agitated with her, but she would never send a Dark after Rhi.

"Constantine has sent pairs of Kings all over England and Scotland to battle the Dark," Phelan said. "They've invaded Edinburgh, Inverness, London, and all the biggest cities. Even Ryder is being sent out to Glasgow."

Aisley nodded as he spoke. "Phelan and I were about to go to Dreagan to see if we could help. The Kings are stretched tight."

Just what the Dark wanted. Rhi had known another war would come eventually, but she hadn't expected it this soon. "Is the Light helping?"

"No' that I know," Phelan said.

"Well I know one that is," Rhi said as she got to her feet.

If Usaeil was too focused on her Dragon King lover to think of their people, then Rhi would do it for her.

Phelan's frown was filled with worry and apprehension. "Rhi, what are you thinking?"

"I'm a Queen's Guard. I can call the army in if I see they're needed. And I see they're needed."

CHAPTER
FOURTEEN

Lexi woke from dozing again. The light was dimming from the day. It didn't seem fair that she was beginning to feel better as the hours slipped through her fingers like sands in an hourglass.

She had dreamed of the Dark Fae, of glowing red eyes, and evil so cloying it suffocated her. She had also dreamed of desire, but it wasn't the Dark she saw. It was Thorn.

Lexi glanced around the studio. She heard him in the bathroom. The door was slightly ajar, but she couldn't see him.

"A pity," she whispered.

Because if Thorn looked good *in* clothes, she couldn't imagine what he looked like *out* of them. It made her smile just thinking about such a fine body. That is, if she could look away from his eyes. The man's gaze drew her in like a bee to nectar.

And once she looked into his sensual dark brown eyes, she was a goner. Completely, utterly lost. She had always heard of people who seemed to have old souls. Until Thorn, she hadn't understood what that meant.

Thorn might dress as if he were part of the modern

times, but she couldn't shake the feeling that he had seen—and been part of—so very much more.

She shifted on the bed. Her gaze was drawn to the wardrobe and the door that stood open with the mirror. That mirror showed directly inside the bathroom to Thorn.

Lexi's mouth parted as she let her gaze run over such a specimen. He faced the sink, shaving. It wasn't his thick sinew and two percent fat. It wasn't the way his shoulders tapered to a narrow waist or how the muscles bulged in his arms when he moved.

It was the tattoo.

She had never understood people's need to mark themselves with permanent ink. Though she could appreciate good art, not once had she seen a tat that remotely appealed to her.

Why then couldn't she take her eyes off the dragon? It covered Thorn's chest in a curious mixture of black and red ink. The dragon was in a standing position with its head turned to the side and lifted upward as if looking at Thorn. Its mouth was open on a roar, making the dragon appear fierce and vengeful. Its wings were spread wide like it wanted to take flight.

With such a huge tat, Lexi expected to find more of them on Thorn's body, and unless they were on his legs, hidden by his jeans, there were no more.

Lexi lifted her gaze to look at his face. He wiped off the rest of the shaving cream with a towel and ran a hand over his jaw. Thorn was putting on his shirt, covering the tat, when there was a knock at the door.

He exited the bathroom and glanced her way. Their gazes locked for a moment before he opened the door to let in a tall redhead.

Lexi sat up as Thorn and the woman said hello. Then both of their eyes were on her.

"You're awake. That's good," the woman said in an English accent.

Thorn walked behind the woman as they made their way to her. "Lexi, this is Dr. Sophie Martin. She's the one who tended to you last night."

"Thank you," Lexi told her.

Sophie sat down and released the black bag she carried. She put her hands in her lap and regarded Lexi. Lexi was doing her own looking. The woman wore a thick black coat that hung to mid-thigh. She unbelted it and began to slowly unbutton it before she shrugged out of it.

The fine doctor wore a white sweater, black pants, and black and white heels. The only color was her vibrant red hair that was gathered at the back of her head in a twist with a few strands falling around her face.

Sophie's pale complexion was flawless, and her olive eyes kind. "Tell me how you're feeling?"

Lexi was conscious of her bed hair, only made worse by falling back to sleep with it wet. She wore a nightshirt and nothing else. She didn't think she could feel any less attractive if she wore a potato sack. "Much better."

"Good, good." Sophie pulled out a stethoscope and listened to Lexi's breathing. "Your coloring is returning."

"I just can't stop falling asleep."

Sophie sat back after examining her eyes, throat, and ears. "It'll even out once your body feels that it's had enough."

"You told Thorn I couldn't leave the flat, but I must."

Sophie frowned and tilted her head to the side. "You do realize you were severely ill, right? You should've been admitted into the hospital. If you go out, you could relapse."

Lexi had hoped the doctor would allow her to leave, but she wasn't surprised at the answer. She couldn't decide whether to let Thorn and his unknown friends handle the Dark, or to continue with her promise to Christina that she would find her killer.

"You're on the mend, Lexi. As long as you remain inside, that is. I think my services are done," Dr. Martin said as she gathered her bag after she put on her coat.

"Thank you again," Lexi said.

Thorn put a hand on her back. "It's getting late. Darius is downstairs waiting for you. Perhaps you'll allow him to see you home safely."

Sophie paused at the door. "I'll be fine on my own."

Thorn stared after her a moment before he closed the door and turned to Lexi. "You healed quickly."

"If that was the case, I wouldn't have slept the day away."

"You went days without much sleep. That, combined with the weather and your weakened body, couldn't fight off the infection."

Lexi didn't bother to tell him that she hadn't eaten much during those days either. Surveillance wasn't like what they showed on TV. It was exhausting. There was very little time to empty her bladder, much less grab a bite to eat.

"You're still determined to go after the Dark despite all that I told you?" Thorn asked as he walked to her.

She pulled her knees up to her chest under the covers and shrugged. "Now that I know what they are, I can't believe they didn't see me. They're everywhere, and seemingly growing in number by the day."

"Aye." A vein jumped in his jaw as he stared at the wall.

"Why hasn't Darius come up?"

Thorn blinked and looked at her. "He's been out hunting the Dark. However, he was able to bring your luggage."

"You're not even going to let me return there?"

"The Dark are no longer interested in it because you've

no' been back, but I doona want to chance it. You have two more days here. Why no' remain where you're safe?"

It was a valid question. One a sane person would know how to answer, but she hadn't been in her right mind since she found Christina's body.

"Lexi?"

She nodded in response. "I just wanted to find the one responsible."

"They're all responsible."

"He laughed about her death," Lexi said, remembering. "When they came out of the alley, all four of them were laughing."

The bed sank as he sat on the edge. "I doona want to find your body."

Her gaze lowered to his chest where she recalled seeing the tattoo. How she wanted to run her hands over it and ask him why he had chosen that design.

"I want another shower and to wear clothes," she said, suddenly conscious of his nearness and the heat radiating off him. "Unless you want to tell me how you can heal from wounds?"

Thorn stood in a fluid motion. "The bathroom is all yours. Darius is picking up some food so you'll get to meet him soon."

"I can cook," she responded as her legs draped over the side of the bed. Lexi felt a warmth spread over her when Thorn's gaze dropped to her legs.

"I can no'," he hurried to say as he turned around. "Darius chooses no' to, so we'll have takeout tonight."

Lexi stood, happy that she felt stronger. "I'm so hungry, I could eat an entire cow."

Thorn laughed as she walked into the bathroom. She was closing the door when she looked up and saw him watching her. Something warm and erotic raced down her back at his look.

* * *

Thorn closed his eyes and groaned. No longer could he deny the desire for Lexi. It grew by the hour and every time he looked at her. Every moment spent with her only deepened the desire to a hunger.

It was time for Darius to stay in while he went hunting. He had been around Lexi too long, nursing her and watching over her. Seeing her.

He opened his eyes and stared at the bathroom door. Like a delusional fool, he told himself he hadn't looked at Lexi when he undressed her those times. It was a lie, a blatant lie he told himself because he stupidly thought he could get past his own desires.

But he knew her body. He hadn't touched it as a lover, but his gaze had.

Thorn swallowed. Had she removed the nightshirt yet? Did she stand naked beneath the shower, letting the water run over her peach-colored skin?

He fisted his hands as he thought about cupping her breasts. They were on the small side, but round and firm. Her nipples were a dusty pink, and begged to feel his tongue.

Thorn was used to need. He'd had his share of women, but there were few times in his eons of life that he was fully sated. He learned to live with such hungers. That's not what worried him.

It was the ache he felt to kiss Lexi, the yearning to hold her against him, the craving to sink between her legs. Those longings rocked him.

So many times he wanted to tell her about the Dragon Kings and what he really was, but he knew it would be folly. Lexi had suffered greatly while in Scotland. She needed to return home and heal properly.

Thorn made the decision then not to tell her about the Kings. She would be wary of the Dark, but she could

go on with her life. It would do her no good to learn of the
Dragon Kings and their involvement.

Why then was it hard not to tell her who he was? He
wanted her to know how he was able to heal. He wanted
to reassure her that he could—and was—killing the Dark
as fast as he could. That he was looking out for her and all
humans.

He turned his back on the bathroom and went to stand
at the windows looking down at the street. There was no
doubt he was relieved to have saved her from the Dark, but
it wasn't a permanent situation.

Thorn had no idea of the state of things in South Caro-
lina. He didn't know if their streets were overrun with
Dark or not, and with the rate of the things progressing in
Scotland, he wouldn't know.

The only way to ensure her safety was to either remain
by her side, or keep her in the flat. Thorn remembered what
Warrick had gone through to keep Darcy within the walls
of her store. He wasn't going to repeat that madness.

Already he itched to hunt and kill the Dark. For four
nights he had left that all up to Darius, but now it was time
for him to return to the streets and his duty.

He heard the water shut off. Thorn gripped the window-
sill and fought to remain where he was. Tonight he would
go out. Darius could stay and watch Lexi.

CHAPTER FIFTEEN

Lexi finished drying her hair and ran a brush through the length. She looked semi-presentable now, even without putting on any makeup. Though she was tempted.

It would seem as if she were trying too hard. Instead, she opted to look more like a healthy person rather than an invalid.

She stood back and looked in the mirror. Lexi had found her favorite white shirt. It was billowy and the neck was so wide it hung off her shoulder. The sleeves skimmed her arms nicely, stopping just past her elbows. She wore a white tank beneath, because she wasn't brave enough not to. Lexi then chose a pair of dark denim and two pairs of socks since she couldn't manage to keep her feet warm ever since she arrived in Scotland.

One more look at herself and Lexi closed her luggage and walked out of the bathroom. She came to a halt when she saw a man at the kitchen table pulling food out of a bag.

He nodded at her, though his eyes barely glanced her way. "It's good to see you up, lass. I'm Darius."

"Hi," she said and looked around the small studio for Thorn.

"Thorn will return. He had to go out for a wee bit."

Lexi walked to the table, her stomach rumbling at the smell of food. "I hope there's another bag of your food," she said as she unwrapped it to find the fish and chips.

Darius pulled out a chair so he could sit. "A lass with an appetite. I like that. Eat your fill. I can always get more for myself later."

She liked him instantly, despite the way he appeared to keep part of himself closed off. Lexi bit into the fish and closed her eyes as she savored the flavor.

After stuffing a chip—it was really a French fry, but when in Rome—in her mouth, Lexi eyed Darius. His hair was a little longer than Thorn's, and whereas Thorn's was nearly as dark as night, Darius's was blond.

"Thank you for bringing Dr. Martin for me," she said around a mouthful.

Darius tore off a piece of fish and shrugged as if it were nothing. "You needed help," he said before he popped the bite in his mouth.

"I hope you brought her home as Thorn said you would."

Darius's lips thinned for a moment. "She refused my aid, but I followed her nonetheless and made sure she arrived safe and sound."

"Everyone should know about the Dark."

Darius nodded in reply. He watched her as she ate. It would normally have made Lexi feel self-conscious, but she was too hungry to care.

"How do you kill one?" she asked offhandedly, hoping he would take the bait and tell her without thinking.

"Nice try, lass."

Lexi put down the chip she had been about to eat. Her stomach was suddenly too full to even look at the food. "I'm not going to go after them here, but what if they're in South Carolina? What if I walk out my door and there's one standing there?"

"Then you're in trouble."

"So I can't kill one?"

He set down his food and leaned back in the chair. "Nay. I saw you withstand their pull, but how long could you hold out? You would have to get close in order to kill one."

"And you don't think I can ignore their pull."

A thick blond brow rose in his forehead. "Have you seen a woman succumb to them?"

"No." And she didn't want to.

"I think if you did, you might rethink things."

Lexi rolled her eyes. "I'm just a fragile female, right?"

"I've seen women tougher than men," Darius said, his voice lowered with a hint of annoyance. "Your sex has nothing to do with your weakness. The Dark prey on humans for a reason. Your kind are drawn to them."

Your kind. What was that supposed to mean?

Before Lexi could ask, the door opened and Thorn filled the entrance. He halted when his gaze landed on her. She shifted in her seat and ran a hand over her hair to make sure nothing was sticking up.

Thorn's face was pulled tight, as if he were trying hard to control some emotion. He jerked his head away and closed the door.

"Better?" Darius asked him.

Thorn grunted in response.

Lexi frowned and rose to get something to drink. She checked the fridge and got a bottle of water as she considered Thorn's remark, or lack of one.

In all the time she had been alone with him he had been easygoing, his voice calm and even. Now he looked as if he were stretched thin, as if every nerve ending was on fire.

"What do you do back in South Carolina?" Darius asked her when the silence stretched for too long.

Lexi returned to her seat, putting her between Thorn and Darius at the round table. "I'm a masseuse. I work for a spa in Charleston near one of the B&Bs known for its romantic location. We get a lot of couples coming in for a massage."

"You make a good living?"

"I do. I'm one of the senior masseuses, so I can set my own hours. I have loyal clients who come in every couple weeks on a constant rotation."

Darius nodded in appreciation. "What brought you to Scotland?"

"Jessica," she replied with a smile. "We all had destinations in Europe that we wanted to see. We pooled our money together and took three weeks off."

"Sounds like fun. Tell me of your friends," Darius urged.

She really didn't think he was interested, but the more they talked, the more relaxed Thorn became. So Lexi kept talking. "Jessica's family is obscenely wealthy. She doesn't have to work, but to her mother's horror, she got a job at the spa with me doing facials." Lexi laughed as she remembered it. "Jessica is part of Charleston high society, so for her to be working for her mother's friends doing facials was shocking."

"I can imagine," Darius said, a hint of a smile poking through.

"Then there is Crystal, whose family is on the fringes of high society. They make really good money. Her father owns a construction company." Lexi paused for a moment, her smile dying as her thoughts turned to Christina. "Christina ran with the same crowd as Jessica and Crystal. Her parents are surgeons."

She drank her water and saw that both of the men were watching her. Lexi licked her lips and set aside her drink. "Crystal dreamed of seeing Paris. Christina wanted to see Venice."

"What did you want to see?" Thorn asked.

Lexi looked into his dark brown eyes and shrugged. "I was so happy to be getting out of Charleston that I didn't care. I chose London since it was close to Paris and not that far from Scotland. We had three amazing weeks in Europe. We were flying out of Edinburgh in just days."

Darius grabbed a handful of chips and ate them one by one. "How did you meet your friends?"

"I worked at the country club as a waitress my senior year of high school. I still don't know why Christina befriended me, but as soon as she began talking to me, so did Jessica and Crystal. We all went to college together and stayed in a house Crystal's parents owned."

Lexi ducked her head. "The only way I was able to afford college is because I didn't have to pay rent. Her parents took care of the utilities and kept the kitchen stocked with food. I wasn't part of their social class, but they all took me in as if I was. I owe them so much."

"Friends like that are rare," Darius said.

It didn't go unnoticed by Lexi that neither man asked about her family. She tore off a piece of fish and ate it. "I'm a fair hand at drawing. If I can draw Christina's killer, will you find him for me? I owe it to her and her family to have her murderer brought to justice."

Darius wiped his hands on a napkin. "It'll be our justice, Lexi, no' the authorities'."

"I'm just fine with that."

"We'll find him," Thorn said. "No matter how long it takes."

Lexi knew that he would. Thorn was that kind of man. The kind like back in history who when he gave his word, he wouldn't go back on it. Thorn had just given her his word, and she was able to breathe easier knowing it.

"Tell us about being a masseuse," Darius urged.

She looked from Thorn to Darius. "You both have gone out of your way not to ask about my family."

Darius lowered his gaze. Only Thorn kept eye contact.

"Do you already know?" she asked.

His chest expanded as he inhaled and then slowly released it. "Nay."

"Now you're lying."

Thorn clenched his jaw. "I know you doona have family. I doona know more than that."

"That's right. I don't have any family. It's been like that for so long that I've gotten used to it." *Now who's lying, Lexi?*

Thorn and Darius waited silently for her to tell them however much she wanted to divulge. Everyone who mattered in Charleston knew of it, so she never had to speak the words. In college, no one had been important enough to share such a thing with.

Why then was it different now?

Lexi sighed and leaned her head back against the chair. "I was an only child. My parents' marriage was rocky, at best. My father was a hardworking man who only wanted to give his family all that he could. My mother was an alcoholic. Despite that, my father stuck by her because he loved her deeply. I wish she could've seen his suffering."

An image of her parents filled her mind. "We were at a New Year's Eve party. It was my junior year, and I had turned seventeen two months before. My boyfriend dumped me before Christmas, so I was miserable. I didn't want to spend the holiday at home alone so my father talked me into going with them. I actually had a good time."

Thorn's lips softened into a smile when she glanced at him.

Lexi lifted her head and continued. "We thought we were watching how much Mom had to drink, but she was sneaking drinks when we weren't looking. As soon as we broke the New Year, we put her in the car and headed home."

She stopped, the pain of it still hurting after all these years.

Thorn put his hand atop hers and squeezed.

Lexi slid her gaze to him and drew in a shaky breath. "Dad had driven her home so many times. Even I had. She always sat in her seat singing or laughing. I don't know what made her reach over and jerk the steering wheel into oncoming traffic that night. I can still hear the crunch of metal."

Darius mumbled something as he shook his head. Thorn's look of regret was better than any words he could've spoken.

"You've been on your own ever since?" Darius asked.

"Yes," Lexi said. "In a way. In others, I had Crystal, Jessica, and Christina."

Thorn's thumb gently smoothed over her hand. "Now I know why you were so determined to find Christina's killer."

"I want to be able to tell them he's dead."

"You will," Thorn vowed.

CHAPTER
SIXTEEN

Lexi rose the next morning feeling more like herself than before. She showered and changed, only to find it was Darius once again with her.

"I thought I heard Thorn when I was in the shower," she said.

Darius nodded, flipping through the TV. "You did. He'll be back later."

The hours passed slowly as she and Darius watched movies. She kept waiting for Thorn to return, but he didn't.

"I'm going to go out for food," Darius said that evening. "Anything you want?"

"Whatever you'd like," she answered.

"Be back shortly," he said and left the flat.

Lexi jumped up and went to the window to look outside. Darius exited the building and turned right. He had gone only a block before she saw him cross the street and step in front of a man.

A moment later, Darius shoved him into the alley. Lexi held her breath as she tried to find an angle that would let her see into the alley, but nothing worked.

When she next saw Darius, he had blood on his shirt.

He looked both ways down the street. Just as he was about to duck back into the alley, two men ran toward him.

Lexi gasped when she saw the black and silver hair of one. "Dark," she whispered.

She watched as Darius took out a knife and began to fight them. Lexi stumbled back a step from the window when she saw a bubble about the size of a grapefruit appear in one of the Dark's hands. He then threw it at Darius.

Darius ducked, and the bubble glanced off him. Still, it seemed to impair him as Darius shook his head as if to clear it. The Dark advanced on him then.

Lexi screamed his name, pounding on the window. She started to turn to leave the flat when Thorn appeared on the rooftop across the street.

He jumped from the six-story building to land as light as a cat behind the two Dark. They spun around to fight him. That's when she spotted that he also used a knife. He was so quick in his movements that she couldn't keep up with him. The Dark continued to throw their bubbles, and it seemed that every one that hit Thorn only angered him more.

The fight was over in quick order with the Dark laying dead between Darius and Thorn. Lexi wished she knew what they were talking about standing there so casually. Anyone could come upon them and see the bodies.

She couldn't believe all of this happened so close to the flat. As soon as she saw Thorn start to turn around, she jumped to the side of the window, plastering herself against the wall.

Lexi counted to sixty before she peeked around the corner and saw that Thorn was already gone. Darius had two dead bodies draped over his shoulder.

She didn't think twice. She ran to the door, grabbing her coat as she did. Her jacket was on by the time she reached the door to the building. Lexi looked through the glass for any sign of Thorn or Darius—or Dark.

With the coast clear, she hurried out of the building and across the street. She ran to the alley, stopping as she reached it and slowly looking around the corner. Lexi caught a glimpse of Darius as he turned left.

Lexi was silent as she jogged after him, occasionally looking up to make sure Thorn wasn't watching her from above. She had to know who they were to jump from buildings and heal like Thorn did. Not to mention being hit with those bubbles by the Dark. Those bubbles were weapons, and she imagined they were magic.

Your kind. Darius's words replayed in her head as she followed him down one street to the next, staying far enough back that he wouldn't see her.

No human she knew could jump off buildings and land on their feet without breaking bones. And taking the bubbles of magic? She couldn't imagine that was easy.

Lexi lost Darius's trail when she came to a warehouse. She was about to retrace her steps to the last turn to see if he had gone another way when she climbed some grates to look into the warehouse.

She saw the numerous dead bodies of the Dark before she saw Thorn and Darius. Though she knew they hunted the Dark, it was different seeing the outcome of their work.

Then again, the Dark weren't of this world. They were aliens, beings who fed off humans. What did she care if they were killed and their bodies gathered in such a manner? She couldn't feel anything for them, because the Dark didn't feel anything for humans.

She pressed her face closer to the window when she saw Darius begin to undress. What could he possibly be doing?

As soon as he folded his shirt, he took a deep breath and changed. Into a dragon.

Lexi gasped in surprise and jerked back at seeing the purple dragon, toppling off the crates to land hard on the concrete. She scrunched her face as pain radiated through her.

"What a pretty thing," said a male voice with an Irish accent.

"Leading us straight to the Kings, too," said another.

Lexi opened her eyes and found three Dark standing before her. She tried to roll over and get away, but they roughly took hold of her.

She could feel the seduction they were pouring into her, but she refused to give in to it. Lexi wasn't going to end up like Christina. She knew what these beings were and what they wanted. She was strong. She could—no, she *would*—fight.

They dragged her to the door of the warehouse and barged in. Darius was once more in human form, though he was naked. She saw a dragon tat on his back before he whirled around, his lips lifted in a sneer when he spotted the Dark.

"Look what we found," said the Dark with a thick Irish accent who walked behind her. "She led us right to you. I had no idea she would deliver such a fine prize, but I'll not look a gift horse in the mouth."

Lexi looked at Thorn, but his gaze was on the three Fae. Anger rolled off him in thick waves. His eyes promised death. And pain.

"You've made a dreadful mistake," Thorn said in a dangerously low voice.

Chills rose up on Lexi's skin. She had seen Thorn smiling, had known his gentle side. This Thorn . . . well this Thorn was lethal.

The Dark returned to stand behind her. Thorn's nostrils flared in fury, his face set in hard lines. Lexi tried to swallow. She was getting a firsthand experience of battle and danger, and she didn't like it. In fact, she was frightened to such an extreme that she was shaking.

"Does the woman mean something to you?" the Dark asked Thorn as he touched her face.

Lexi jerked away and turned her head to glare at him. "Touch me again, asshole, and I'll cut your balls off. We'll see if you can fuck a human to death then."

The moment the Dark's smile turned to a sneer Lexi knew she might have overstepped things a little. More than a little by his furious glare.

"You dare to talk to me in such a way?" the Dark asked her.

All the anger over Christina's needless death that had kept Lexi going for days returned with a vengeance. It choked her it was so strong. Her vision turned red, and all rational thought vanished as she focused on killing a Dark—any Dark.

"You dare to come to my world and slaughter us as if we mean nothing?" she returned with a scathing look. Lexi looked him up and down and laughed. "I'll fight every one of you. I'll make it my goal to slice off every Dark Fae dick. I'll make sure that you can't harm another human again."

She was surprised Thorn and Darius hadn't told her to be quiet. In fact, she was astonished they stood silently, but she couldn't take the time to think of it. She was confronting a Dark, and even though he wasn't the one who had killed Christina, he was still an ass.

The two Dark holding her exchanged worried glances. Lexi let her lips curl into a smile. She had them worried now.

The Dark leader gripped her hair painfully, jerking her head backward. "You think the only way we kill is by fucking you?" He laughed. "Ask your Dragon Kings. Ask them what else we can do. Or perhaps I'll show you."

His hand came around her, palm out. Lexi looked down to see a bubble grow. It was perfectly round and clear except for the faint shimmer of iridescent color.

The Dark leaned close so that his mouth was next to her ear. "You may be able to withstand our appeal, but you won't be able to hold back your cry of pain when you feel this. Know that while the Kings are trying to protect you that I'll take great joy in killing them."

Lexi glanced at Darius who stood silently behind and to the right of Thorn. When she looked at Thorn she thought his look alone would slay the Dark where they stood.

There was a moment where everything was hushed, as if the world took a deep breath and held it. In the next instant, everything moved frantically.

The Dark turned his hand to push the bubble into her at the same instant Lexi saw Thorn change into a dragon with scales the color of wine, followed a heartbeat later by Darius.

Thorn roared, the sound deafening, and pulled in a breath. She saw fire swirl in his throat. His massive hand rose over Lexi. She could only stare in a mixture of terror and panic.

The two Darks holding her loosened their grip. She yanked her arms away and dove to the ground as the first of the flames flew from Thorn's mouth.

She huddled on the floor with her arms over her head. The heat never touched her as she'd expected. Lexi turned her head when she heard screaming and saw that something was over her, something with the same deep wine scales that she had seen on Thorn when he shifted.

Lexi remained where she was until the last of the screams died. Then Thorn's hand was gone. She still didn't move. Dragons. My God, Darius and Thorn were *dragons*!

The ground trembled when Thorn stepped away from

her, but Lexi still didn't have the nerve to lift her head. Fae and now dragons? What else was on her world?

"Lexi," Darius said, standing near her. "It's over, lass. You can lift your head." When she didn't move, Darius chuckled wryly. "This from a human who bravely trailed the Dark? You doona need to fear us."

"You're dragons," she mumbled.

"That we are."

It was said so matter-of-factly and without a hint of apology that Lexi lifted her head to see Thorn in human form standing twenty feet away with his back to her and his hands braced on a table.

A hand was held in front of her face. Lexi hesitated for just an instant before taking Darius's hand as he helped her to her feet.

He wore nothing but a pair of jeans, and with his close proximity she could see that his dragon tat went from his back to his front with his dragon's head looking over his right shoulder in the same black and red ink.

"Go to him," Darius urged in a whisper.

Lexi turned her gaze to Thorn. The man who had so tenderly held her was a fire-breathing dragon. A real-life dragon. Her brain was having an impossible time registering the facts.

She took a few half-steps toward him, slowly closing the distance. When Lexi looked behind her, it was to discover Darius gone and all that remained of the three Dark Fae were piles of ashes.

Lexi stopped when she was six feet from Thorn. He stood naked, his back expanding with every breath he took. She had known he would be heart-stoppingly gorgeous naked, and she had been right.

"Why didn't you tell me?" she asked in a soft voice.

"Because of this verra reaction."

CHAPTER
SEVENTEEN

Thorn's heart still raced at how close Lexi had come to death. He had been given the barest hint of hope when she had bravely stood against them.

Her defiant words appealed to him on a primal level, but her precarious position made his blood turn to ice. Thorn had been so enraged, so incensed that he had one thought—save Lexi.

It wasn't until it was over that Thorn realized what he had done. She had seen him shift. Lexi now knew the secret that everyone at Dreagan worked so tirelessly to protect.

"You're the other beings killing the Dark," she said.

He closed his eyes. "Aye."

"You're a dragon."

His chin dropped to his chest. There were many reasons he hadn't intended to tell her what he was, but the biggest was the way she was handling things now. She was in shock from all she had seen. When that shock gave way, she would be too frightened of him to even be in the same city.

"You're a damn dragon!" she yelled.

Thorn was going to have to have Guy wipe Lexi's memories of anything to do with him. It might even be better if she didn't remember the Dark either.

"Look at me," she demanded.

He whirled around and held out his arms. "What do you want me to say? Aye. I'm a dragon!"

"How?" She gave a small shake of her head, her voice breaking on the word.

"We've been here since the beginning of time."

"Impossible. We'd have found something."

Thorn lifted one shoulder. "We have some human allies who have helped to keep us hidden."

"This makes no sense." She looked around at the warehouse as if seeing it for the first time.

"None of this would be an issue if you'd remained in the flat as I told you."

Her gaze narrowed on him. "Told me? I'm not some dog to be ordered around."

"Nay, you're a human who has stepped into a war she has no business knowing about!"

"Maybe if more of us *humans* did know we wouldn't be dying by the dozens every day because of the Dark!"

Thorn took a step toward her. "You really think knowing of the Dark would stop the deaths?"

"It certainly couldn't hurt," she replied, moving toward him.

"That simple thinking is why the Fae came for you to begin with. You think in the entire universe that you're the only beings? Do you really think there are no' other planets with life on them?"

"I don't care about them, I—"

"Well you should care," he interrupted. He took another step. "Use your brain, Lexi. You're smart. Look around at your world. Do you really think cancer can no' be cured when your doctors have cured almost everything else? The Dark keep preventing it. They want you weak and stupid."

"I'm not stupid."

"I told you how dangerous it was out on the streets. I told you to remain inside the flat."

She rolled her eyes. "I had every intention of doing just that except I saw you jump off a six-story roof. Humans can't do that."

"That still doesna mean you should've followed us!"

They were so close he could see the black circles around her irises. Her gray eyes were stormy with anger, fear, and anxiety.

"I used my head," she retorted.

Thorn looked down at her and nearly groaned when he felt her breasts rub against his chest. To his horror, the fury in her gray eyes turned to desire.

No matter how hard he tried, he couldn't stop himself from yanking Lexi against him as he took her lips in a savage kiss.

He spun her around and pressed her up against a wall. Her hands delved into his hair as she answered his kiss with one just as fierce and violent.

Thorn came to his senses and lifted his head. He looked down at her swollen lips and his hard cock begged him to continue. Whatever thought he had vanished with his craving of her.

He touched her cheek before he slid his hand around to the back of her neck and held her head as he slowly kissed her, tasting the passion and need.

His hand slid between them intending to unbutton her coat when he heard her hiss. Thorn leaned back, concern filling him when he saw her look of pain.

"It's my left side," she said, breathing heavily.

Thorn knew he hadn't touched her with his talons. That meant it was . . . He couldn't finish the thought.

He walked her to the table and helped her to sit atop it while noticing for the first time the burn in her jacket. Then he carefully unbuttoned her coat and pushed it open. Thorn closed his eyes when he saw the wound.

"What is it?" Lexi asked while trying to look at it.

He hadn't moved quickly enough to save her. The Dark should never have been that close to her with its magic.

"Thorn?"

Her sweater was burned where the bubble of magic had grazed her.

"I don't feel so well," she said thickly.

Thorn caught her as she toppled to the side. "*Darius!*" he yelled through their mental link.

A second later Darius ran back into the warehouse. He took one look at Thorn holding Lexi and slid to a stop. "Is she . . . ?"

"No' yet," Thorn said and laid her down. He then rushed to find clothes they had stashed there as soon as they found the warehouse. "She was hit with the Dark's magic."

"Shite," Darius said and rushed to them. He peeled back her coat and saw the wound. "It's not as bad as it could be."

"It's bad enough." Thorn thought to never be in this position again. He'd vowed he never would, and yet where did he find himself?

Darius looked up at him. "We need Con."

Thorn was shaking his head before he finished. "We've been through this."

"He'll come for this."

Thorn gathered her in his arms and walked from the warehouse.

"Thorn, she needs medical attention."

"I know."

Darius was at his side. "What is your plan?"

"I willna chance Con refusing to help. Lexi is a human

who got in the way, and with the war, Con will say she's a casualty."

"Tell him she's your mate. That always gets him to help."

Thorn lengthened his strides as night began to fall. "I'll no' lie."

"She could be your mate."

"So could that woman to my left," he said, nodding to the old lady at the corner. "I'm no' going to lie to get Con here. He already thinks I've betrayed him."

Darius blew out a breath. "I suppose you have another plan?"

"I do."

Thorn was ever so glad to see Darcy's building come into view. He didn't breathe easy until they were inside and Lexi was on the bed.

He went to the kitchen counter where he had left his mobile phone. Thorn scrolled through the contact list and found the name he wanted. He hit dial and impatiently waited for them to answer.

"Hello?" said the male voice.

"Fallon, it's Thorn. I've got a problem."

There was a beat of silence. "Where are you?"

"Darcy's flat. A human has been hit with Dark magic."

"We'll be right there," Fallon said.

The call disconnected. Thorn turned around, unsure of what to do now.

Darius gave a nod of approval. "Quick thinking."

Both of them turned to the door when a knock sounded. Fallon was a Warrior who had the ability to teleport anywhere he wished, which was a great asset.

Thorn strode to it and yanked it open to reveal Fallon, his nephew Aiden, who was also a Druid, and Aiden's mother, Marcail.

"Where is she?" Marcail asked.

Thorn stepped aside as Aiden and Marcail went to the bed and began to look over Lexi. He closed the door behind Fallon. "Thank you."

"How many times did the Kings come to our aid? It's nice for you to call on us," Fallon said as he watched his sister-in-law and nephew. "What happened?"

Thorn walked to the table and took the chair that would give him the best place to watch Lexi. "Her friend was killed by the Dark. I saw her following them and attempted to stop her. She wouldna, and the Dark realized someone was tracking them. They're all over the city, Fallon."

"I didna think it had gotten so bad so quickly."

Darius joined them at the table. "We do as much as we can, but there's only so much the two of us can do against so many Dark."

"Let us help," Fallon said.

Thorn looked at him and smiled. "You are."

"So the Dark tried to kill her for following them?" Fallon asked.

Darius gave a shake of his head. "Today she followed us to a warehouse where we were taking some dead Fae to . . . dispose of them."

"Dispose meaning you burned them, I'm guessing," Fallon said as he leaned on the table.

"Aye. What Lexi didna know was that the Dark saw her and decided to follow. She led them right to us."

Fallon ran a hand down his face as he leaned back in the chair. "That's bad luck."

"The Dark threatened her," Thorn continued.

Darius's lips tightened. "Then we let loose dragon fire on their arses."

"I thought I got to Lexi quick enough, but I didna. She was hit with their magic." Thorn glanced at the bed to see the two Druids with their hands palm down over Lexi as they chanted.

Fallon jerked his chin to his family. "Their magic is strong. They'll find a way to save her. I would've thought you'd call Con."

Thorn looked away, not wanting to tell anyone who was not a King what was going on within their ranks. Darius, however, didn't have that problem.

"You know Con," Darius said. "He can be single-minded at the best of times. We're in the middle of war. He's no' going to stop to come to Edinburgh to save one human."

Fallon grunted in response.

The minutes slowly ticked by as Druid magic filled the flat. It seemed an eternity later before Marcail and Aiden lowered their hands. The two walked to the table where they both sat heavily in their chairs.

"That was . . . awful," Marcail said. She lifted turquoise eyes to Thorn. "It was just a glancing blow. Anything more could've killed her."

Aiden accepted a bottle of water from Darius and downed it quickly. He wiped the back of his hand across his mouth and sighed. "Is that what we've got to look forward to?"

Fallon leaned toward Thorn on the table. "Let us help. If the Kings fail, we'll be fighting them anyway. Our numbers could help swing the tide."

Thorn looked at Darius before they both nodded.

"Here we go again," Marcail said, a worried frown pulling at her lips.

CHAPTER
EIGHTEEN

Fallon arrived back at his home to find all the Warriors and Druids waiting for him, Marcail, and Aiden to return.

Marcail walked to Quinn and buried her head in his chest. Fallon nodded to his youngest brother. The Warriors had been talking amongst themselves for a while about helping the Dragon Kings kill the Dark Fae whether the Kings wanted them to or not.

Long, slim fingers intertwined with his. Fallon turned and smiled at his wife. Larena's smoky blue eyes searched his before she squared her shoulders. "We battled the worst of the *droughs*. We're more than ready for the Dark Fae."

Fallon smiled. Leave it to his wife to put it so eloquently. As the only female Warrior, Larena was uniquely suited for warfare since her power was being able to turn invisible.

Lucan, the middle MacLeod brother, kissed the back of Cara's hand and nodded to Fallon.

"Some of us have already fought these bastards,"

Hayden Campbell said. "Malcolm, Logan, and I know what to expect."

Ian stood from his spot at the long table where they all had gathered for many meals. "I spoke with Tristan yesterday. He and Dmitri are in Aberdeen fighting the Dark. He's worried."

The Dragon Kings and Warriors had a unique bond. Tristan was their newest King, having dropped from the sky a few years earlier. Before that Tristan was known as Duncan, Ian's twin, who unfortunately had been killed by one of the evil Druids they had fought. All were happy to learn that Duncan had returned, even if he didn't remember his brother.

"The Dark feed off humans," Charon stated. "We can no' leave our women alone."

"Or Aiden and Britt," Marcail said.

Charon nodded, repeating, "Or Aiden and Britt."

Ramsey ran a hand over his chin. "They'll come here."

Isla looked at him from next to Hayden. "Let them try."

"I second Isla," Tara said and elbowed Ramsey.

Fallon raised his hand for silence when everyone began talking at once. "We've been through a lot as a group. We've lost family," he said, glancing at Ian. "We've lost friends."

"That's what happens in war," Broc stated.

"That it does." Fallon took a deep breath. "We had a few years of peace. It was . . . refreshing. Many of us started families. There are now children to consider."

Larena looked at Fallon. "What my dear husband is trying to say is that each of you must decide to join this fight. No one is pushing another into this."

"Exactly. As Charon pointed out, the Dark feed off humans. Since we're immortal, I doona know how that changes anything. And as Ramsey said, the Dark will come here. We can no' leave the castle unprotected."

Malcolm chuckled. "Fallon, we're Warriors. We have primeval gods inside us who demand blood and death. I'm fighting."

"Damn straight," Evie said to her husband with a nod. "I don't want to have to worry about Dark Fae with little Malory."

Lucan and Cara shared a few whispered words before Lucan said, "I'm in."

"I'm in," Quinn stated.

Fallon had known his two brothers would be some of the first to agree. He wasn't surprised at Malcolm's response either.

"As if you have to ask," Hayden said when Fallon looked his way.

Galen nodded, as did Broc.

Logan made a face. "I'm hurt you'd even ask."

"You know my answer," Ian said as he put an arm around Dani.

Camdyn grinned. "Of course."

"I'm a mixture of Druid and Warrior. The Dark will get a surprise when they encounter me," Ramsey said when Fallon came to him.

Arran gave him a thumbs-up even as Ronnie wiped a tear from her face.

"We're in," Phelan said for both him and Charon.

Fallon had expected no less from his men. "We'll need a plan. What the Kings are doing by splitting up and staying hidden as they kill the Dark is working. I say we take their plan and use it."

"And what of us?" Reagan said. She glanced at Galen before looking around the table at the other Warriors. "You men don't expect us to just wait here for you."

Laura looked pointedly at Charon as she said, "I agree with Reagan. We've proved our magic is powerful enough to be used in battle."

"Aye, sweetheart," Charon said as he cupped her face and gave her a light kiss. "But you've no idea what would happen to me if I lost you."

"How do you think I'd feel?" she asked.

Larena poked Fallon. "We're a group. We're stronger together. We need to use everyone."

Fallon raised his voice and said to the great hall, "I know what it's like to fight alongside my wife. We're immortal, but we can be killed. She just reminded me how strong we are together. So, together we will remain."

"Let's go in shifts," Lucan said. "We'll rotate who stays here to look after the children and who fights."

Hayden nodded eagerly. "That sounds like a solid plan. It will give us a rest and allow everyone some downtime before we fight again."

"It'll also allow us to know what's working and what's not," Gwynn said.

Saffron then added, "That way we can quickly shift our attacks."

"And if someone is hurt?" Tara asked. "All of you know I'm a realist. We need to think of this."

"Isla willna be out there without me," Hayden stated.

Quinn looked at Marcail. "I think we're all in agreement to that when it comes to our wives."

"We'll go out in two pairs at a time," Fallon said. "Since the children will be here, this place has to be well fortified."

Phelan lifted a hand in the air. "Once the Druids are done adding more spells, I'll call in Rhi."

"We start tomorrow. Take the night. We meet here at dawn," Fallon said.

Ulrik entered the Fae doorway into Taraeth's palace. He was a regular in the king of the Darks' residence, so no one paid him any attention.

He strolled down the corridors until he came to a small alcove. It was tucked away at the end, hidden from the eyes of others, but gave him a great view of anyone who ventured down the hallway.

A smile formed when he saw bare legs. Muriel leaned forward and winked at him, her dress sagging at the front to give him an ample view of her breasts.

The night he'd spent in her arms had been nice, but he couldn't let himself relax. He still didn't trust the Dark. After what happened to him, trusting wasn't an option. Ever.

Then there was the fact Mikkel was looking through his place. Not that his uncle had a chance in Hell at finding anything. It was the point of it all that irked Ulrik.

"You're late," Muriel said.

Ulrik lifted a brow. "I'm right on time."

"I don't like to wait then."

"Then doona get here so early."

"I had to make sure no one was around." She sat back and patted the area beside her. "Sit, lover."

Ulrik unbuttoned his suit jacket and sat, shifting so that one arm rested on the back of the pillows as he half-faced her. "Tell me you have something for me."

"Oh, I do." She all but purred. "Mikkel plans to kill you."

"Tell me something I doona already know."

She blinked and looked affronted. "How would you know that? He just shared that with Taraeth last night."

"I know my uncle. He's a conniving, shrewd arse. He's dreamed of being a Dragon King. He'll do whatever it takes to see that it happens. It was simple deduction."

Muriel's face lost all of its fake seduction. "Ulrik, he has many allies."

"And many enemies."

"As do you."

He grinned at her logic. "I've had thousands upon thousands of years to think of every conceivable way to solve problems."

She looked down at her hands, a frown marring her features. "Taraeth agreed to help Mikkel."

"Mikkel doesna need any help. He wants to find out what side Taraeth is on. Besides, if Taraeth really was on my uncle's side, would your king have sent your sister to seduce Mikkel?"

Muriel shrugged one shoulder as she fiddled with the hem of her dress. "There's more."

"Oh?"

"Mikkel doesn't intend to let you kill Constantine. He'll let you fight Con right up until you're about to defeat him, then Mikkel will step in."

There were few things that could break his calm, but that was one of them. When it came to his revenge against Con, nothing was going to stand in his way.

That was one item he assumed Mikkel would keep to their pact. Mikkel might talk big, but he was afraid of Con. He didn't stand a chance going against the King of Kings.

"Let my uncle be that stupid."

"I've kept up my side of our arrangement," Muriel said, raising her red eyes to him. "Have I not?"

Ulrik stood and held out his hand. He saw someone approaching out of the corner of his eye. "That you have, lass. Where would you like to go?"

"I was think— "

"I see someone has caught your attention," Mikkel said as he walked up. "Why not bring her to my house, Ulrik? We'll all have dinner together."

Ulrik had been too intent on Muriel to see his uncle in time. He hated how Mikkel went out of his way to sound English instead of Scots. Ulrik used accents on regular occasions when doing business, but that was different. Mikkel was trying to pretend on multiple levels.

Ulrik faced Muriel and forced a smile. "It's up to you. Would you like to have dinner with my uncle and his . . . friend?"

"It would be an honor," Muriel said while batting her eyes at Mikkel.

Mikkel smiled and slapped Ulrik on the back. "Be there at seven."

Ulrik waited for him to walk away before he dropped his smile. He swung his gaze to Muriel. The Dark wasn't just a temptress, she was a good actress.

"I'm not playing you," she said while meeting his gaze. "I keep my word."

Ulrik had done his research on the Dark Fae. She and her sister were orphans, having lost their parents during the Fae Wars. Taraeth had taken them in, but only to work in the palace as nothing more than slaves.

Her sister, Sinny, found a knack for spying that Taraeth cultivated. As for Muriel, her petite frame and mouth-watering curves caught the eye of everyone who visited Taraeth. But neither of the women were free. Taraeth owned them.

"Before we go further, I want to know why you picked me to help you," he demanded.

Muriel's eyes crinkled as she smiled. "That's easy, lover. Look in the mirror."

"Muriel."

She ran a hand over his jaw. "Because you're hard and unforgiving. Because I knew that if anyone could help me, it was you."

Ulrik gave a bow of his head. It was enough. For now. He would want to know more later. "You were choosing a place to go?"

"Your bed."

CHAPTER
NINETEEN

Thorn rose from the table after Fallon and the Druids teleported back to MacLeod Castle.

"Con willna be happy we agreed to let the Warriors help," Darius said.

"Con can bite my arse."

Darius's gaze never wavered as he studied him. "What is it?"

"I can no' do this." Thorn turned his head to look at Lexi lying so still upon the bed. She had just gotten well, and now she was injured in a war she should know nothing about.

Darius followed his gaze. "Ah," he said slowly. "She's going to have questions when she wakes."

Thorn inwardly grimaced. He wanted nothing more than to see Lexi sit up and her gray eyes look his way. After their kiss—their scorching, soul-stealing kiss—he could only think of caressing her skin, of learning every curve . . . of making love to her.

It seemed that rarely did he wake from dragon sleep and there wasn't a war. Thorn was tired of it all, but most of all he was weary of having to hide who he was.

"Take care of her, will you?" Thorn asked as he faced Darius.

A frown married Darius's brow for a moment before he nodded. "You're leaving."

"Aye. I'm going to contact Guy. Lexi's mind needs to be wiped of everything involving us or the Dark."

"You should be here with her when Guy comes."

"I can no' do this again. When she wakes, take her to the airport. Guy will be there to erase us."

"I'll see it done," Darius promised.

Thorn took one last look at Lexi before he walked from the flat. By the time he exited the building, he was looking for Dark Fae. He was angry and frustrated and desolate. They were the perfect outlet.

Darius watched Thorn stride down the street. He had an idea of what Thorn was feeling, because it hadn't been that many centuries ago when Darius had searched for something to kill.

He almost felt sorry for any Dark who got in Thorn's way that night. None ever stood a chance before, but that night, they would die slowly. There would be lots of pain involved.

It had taken Darius a very long time to realize others' pain didn't dim his own. He hoped Thorn found that out earlier than he did.

Though with the war, it might not be a bad thing to have Thorn in that frame of mind. All the Dragon Kings were angry at the state the Dark had pushed them to, but Thorn's fury went to another level.

Darius didn't worry about Thorn. He might be working through things, but he wasn't a fool. Thorn knew his limits. Because even though Thorn had left, Darius knew Thorn would be watching Lexi from afar the next day.

When Thorn was out of sight, Darius turned to retrace

his steps to the table. He pulled out a deck of cards and began to play solitaire when he felt a push in his mind.

He opened up the link when he recognized Constantine's voice. "*Aye?*"

"*I need an update on the situation there.*"

"*It hasna improved. No matter how many we kill, more Dark arrive daily.*"

Con sighed. "*It's the same all over Scotland. Have the Dark discovered either of you?*"

"*Nay. The few that do doona live to tell it.*"

"*Good.*"

Darius snorted loudly. "*Ask the question you really contacted me for.*"

"*Thorn helped Ulrik, Darius. Even you should see how that put him in a bad light.*"

"*Warrick helped him as well,*" Darius pointed out.

"*Warrick was helping his mate.*"

"*And Thorn was doing what he could for Warrick.*"

There was a pregnant pause. "*Darius, this war could be the end of us. I need to know I have every King with me.*"

"*Then stop being an idiot. Thorn would never betray us.*"

"*You're sure?*"

"*Without a doubt.*"

"*Have you seen Ulrik?*"

Darius shuffled the cards. "*We've no'. Should we expect him?*"

"*Possibly. He disappeared and then showed back up at The Silver Dragon. Now he's gone again.*"

Now that got Darius's attention. "*He vanished? All the cameras you have up around his shop and you still couldna see where he went? Are you sure he's no' inside?*"

"*We're sure. He was exiting the shop by the back entrance when he simply vanished.*"

"You think he's with the Dark?" Darius asked.

"We know. They were quick enough so that many of the cameras didna catch them, but one of the new ones Ryder obtained was able to capture everything. We saw the Dark."

Darius began to set up another game of solitaire on the table. *"We've known he's worked with the Dark. Why is this news we should be concerned over?"*

"Because he was gone a long time, and now he's gone again."

"Or he's been back and you've no' known it. We doona have cameras inside his shop, remember."

Con all but growled, *"Doona remind me. Keep your eyes open for him either way."*

The link was severed, causing Darius to shake his head. He knew being King of Kings was a right only the strongest, the most powerful of them could have. However, Darius wouldn't take on Con's responsibilities for all the treasure in the world.

Ulrik was unpredictable, which made it nearly impossible for them to try to stay ahead of whatever he might do. It put the Kings on the defensive instead of offensive. That automatically put them on the losing side.

If only Ulrik hadn't gotten his magic unbound. Darius knew that taking Ulrik's dragon magic had been their only option. Now, after so many eons, Ulrik wasn't just coming for Con; he had his magic. Out of all the Kings, Ulrik was the only one who could challenge Con and possibly take over as King of Kings.

Darius was surprised Ulrik hadn't woken his Silvers. Just thinking of the dragons sleeping caged inside the mountain made him long to see his own dragons. To have the sun glint off their dark purple scales.

"Thorn," Lexi mumbled from the bed.

Darius shifted his attention to the mortal. She sat up,

shoving her long hair out of her face. He remained where he was until she looked over the entire flat.

"Where is Thorn?" she asked.

Darius had been dreading this part. "Out."

"By out, you mean he's left."

Darius briefly thought about lying, but he could see by the lift of her chin she had pieced it all together. "Aye."

Lexi stood and winced. She looked down at her side before she slid her gaze back to Darius. "What happened?"

"You were hit with Dark magic. Lucky for you, it merely glanced off your side."

"Lucky, huh?" she mumbled. She slowly made her way to her luggage where she found another sweater before going to the bathroom.

Darius gathered the cards together and set them aside. "You are lucky."

"Oh, yeah. Definitely," came her voice behind the closed door of the bathroom, dripping with sarcasm. "I'm such a lucky person that my parents die and leave me alone. I'm so lucky I lose one of my best friends here. I'm so lucky I got hit with Dark magic." The door opened and she leaned against the doorway. "I'm so lucky that Thorn left."

Darius wasn't sure what to say to her. He motioned for her to sit. "All Thorn wanted to do was protect you. He feels he failed."

"And our kiss?"

Kiss? A lightbulb went off in Darius's head. "I didna know of a kiss."

Lexi shrugged and walked to the table. She took the chair opposite him. "Well, there was a kiss. A kiss that was . . ." She trailed off and looked away.

"I see." Darius rested one arm on the table. "You mustn't be angry at Thorn for no' telling you about us. Everyone who knows finds themselves in extreme danger. We were shielding you and ourselves."

She nodded and gathered her light brown hair at the base of her neck and wound it around her finger as she once more met his gaze. "The more people that know, the more likely your secret is told."

"Aye." Darius was happy she could at least see that. "For thousands of years few knew that the Fae walked this realm."

"I don't ever want to meet another Fae."

"The Light are our allies. They do take humans to their beds, but only once and they doona take their souls."

Lexi rolled her eyes. "Oh, that makes me feel better."

Darius bit back a smile. "It should. The only ones wanting to kill your race are the Dark."

"I want to know everything there is to know of your race." She gave a slight shake of her head. "How can there be dragons so big around that no one sees?"

"We take to the skies at night. Few bother to look up anymore. Thunderstorms are also perfect times for flying."

She squared her shoulders. "Tell me more."

Since Darius knew Guy was going to wipe her memories there was no point in not telling her. "We've been here since the beginning of time. For millions of years dragons ruled. Then one day humans arrived."

"Arrived?" Lexi asked with a frown. "How? From spaceships?"

Darius chuckled. He rose and uncorked a bottle of wine. He poured himself a glass and looked at Lexi. At her nod, he poured her a glass as well. Then he returned with a wineglass in each hand, handing one to her. "Nothing so grand. Your kind just appeared out of nowhere. No' only was your race mortal, but you had no magic. You were defenseless."

"As we are now."

"No' all of you."

Lexi nodded in agreement. "That's right. The Druids."

"As soon as the humans appeared, every Dragon King shifted into human form to be able to communicate. From then on we were free to shift from dragon to human and back again."

"How many Dragon Kings are we talking about?"

"As many colors as you can imagine."

She leaned on the table. "Now I remember. When I saw you in dragon form you were purple." Her gaze went to her wine. "Thorn was the color of the wine. Deep burgundy."

"Just as you humans have different races, so did dragons. All sizes, all colors. The strongest dragon with the most magic was king of his race."

Lexi took a drink of wine before she raised a brow. "All kings? What, arc you prejudiced against females?"

"No' at all. I'm sure had things continued we would've seen a Dragon Queen, but at that time, there were none."

"What happened? Did you get tired of having us humans here?"

Darius swirled his wine as he looked at the claret color. "I'll admit that I wasna exactly happy to have the mortals around, but for several centuries things were fine. It started slowly. I doona think any of us Kings thought much about it."

"What started slowly?"

"The humans' jealousy of our magic and the power we had."

Lexi scrunched up her face. "That sounds like us. We always want to be the ones in charge."

"The humans began to hunt the smaller dragons. We were shocked, but left things alone. The humans had killed a dragon here or there for food, just as a dragon had killed a human here and there for food. The dragons had never been told there was a being on this realm that wasna to be eaten."

Lexi twisted her lips in revulsion.

"You eat nearly every animal on this planet, do you no'?"

"That's different."

"Hardly," he stated.

CHAPTER TWENTY

Lexi waved away his words. "What happened next?"

"We were betrayed."

"By who?" Lexi asked, surprised.

Darius merely looked at her.

Then her mouth formed an O as it dawned on her. "A woman."

"I doona think the other Kings have thought about it, but once we were able to shift, every King was drawn to mortals. Many of the Kings had women as lovers, but there was one of us who fell in love with one of you. His name was Ulrik. He was the type who never found someone he didna like, and everyone liked him in return."

"Christina was like that," Lexi mumbled.

"Ulrik's best friend was Constantine. Con is the King of Kings, the one who keeps us all together. He learned of the betrayal of Ulrik's woman and sent Ulrik away to keep him from having to deal with the situation. After Con told the rest of us, we found her and killed her."

Lexi swallowed into the silence. "What was her betrayal?"

"Ulrik didn't just have her as a lover. He brought her

into his home and protected her and her entire family. He was going to perform the mating ceremony with her, which would make her immortal and live as long as he did."

Lexi shifted in her chair. "I'm gathering that she didn't just cheat on him?"

"If only she had." Darius took a drink of the wine. "Nay, she was going to try and kill Ulrik."

She covered her mouth with her hand. What was wrong with people? This woman had it all. Why would she do something like that?

Darius smiled sadly at her response. "You're surprised?"

"Without a doubt," she said after she lowered her hand. "Why would she do that?"

"I told you. The mortals didna want to allow us to stay in power. What they didna know is that we can no' be killed by anything they possess."

"Nothing?"

"Nothing then and nothing now. No' even one of your bombs or missiles. The only thing that can kill a Dragon King is another Dragon King."

Lexi filed that information away. "That's incredible. I also guess it's something this woman didn't know."

"Ulrik had no reason to tell her. She assumed that he could be killed as easily as a dragon."

"What did Ulrik do when he returned?"

Darius's chocolate gaze looked away. "He went mad. He was furious that we had killed her, and blinded by his rage that she would betray him. He changed, seemingly over-night. His anger ruled him, and he turned it on the beings responsible."

"Humans," Lexi said.

Darius nodded and took another drink of wine. "Con tried to rein Ulrik in, but he was out of control. The more humans he killed, the more dragons the humans destroyed. The war was horrendous. There was death everywhere."

Lexi cringed at the image Darius was painting.

"Kings turned against Kings as sides were taken between Con and Ulrik. Constantine proved he was the King of Kings when he gradually talked each King into rejoining him. Ulrik didna care. He continued his carnage, intending to wipe the realm of every last human."

She drank her wine silently, loathe to interrupt Darius.

"Ulrik ignored every attempt by Con to stop, and with more dragons dying by the day, we had no choice but to take drastic action. We sent our dragons to another realm to save them. After the war, the humans couldna stand to see them. And we all knew that even if we found peace, the dragons would be in danger."

Lexi was saddened for Thorn, Darius, and all the Dragon Kings to have sent the dragons away.

"There were four of Ulrik's Silvers who wouldna leave his side. We Kings gathered our magic and bound Ulrik's. We stripped him of his ability to communicate with the Silvers, banished him from our land, and sentenced him to walk the earth for eternity as a human. We then put a spell on his Silvers to make them sleep and keep them caged in a mountain."

Lexi nearly dropped her glass. "There are still dragons here?"

"Aye. We ensure they doona wake."

"And if they do?"

Darius issued a small shrug and met her gaze. "With the dragons gone, the Silvers hidden, and Ulrik taken care of, we returned to our land and slept away a century or two. When we woke, we discovered we had turned into legend and myth."

"You've stayed hidden ever since?"

He nodded slowly. "It wasna easy during the first Fae War, and I worry that now will be impossible with as many humans as there are."

"The first Fae War," she repeated, remembering how Thorn had told her the Fae had come to take control of their planet. "When was that?"

"About eleven thousand years ago."

Lexi couldn't wrap her head around that amount of time. "The Dark are in the city. They kill every night, and with little thought to be caught."

"They want to be caught. They want you to know about them, the Light Fae, and the Dragon Kings."

"Why?" she asked in confusion. "What do they think that will accomplish? We'd find out quick enough what they want, and we would never side with them."

Darius's dark eyes hardened a fraction. "True, but then your race would be all too willing to try and kill a Dragon King. A Dark is scary, but he appears human except for his red eyes and his magic. A Dragon King is another matter entirely. We can fly, we breathe fire, we can shift, and we're massive."

"I see your point," she said, a little ill.

"We've protected your kind, even during the war between our races," Darius said. "It's a vow we all take seriously. The last thing we want is to be fighting the Fae and humans."

Lexi felt her hair fall loose. She wound it back up again to keep it out of her face. "No. That can't happen. How will you stop the Dark?"

"By continuing what Thorn and I were doing before. We'll keep hidden and kill every Dark that crosses our path. There are more Dragon Kings throughout each of the larger cities as well."

"Just how many are you?"

Darius grinned. "Less than there were originally, but more than you think."

"That's not an answer."

"It's the only one you'll get, lass."

She smiled, appreciating his need for secrecy. "Where do you hide? By the accents, I'd guess here in Scotland, which is pretty easy considering all the mountains."

"Aye, we're in Scotland. Dreagan is our home."

Lexi frowned. Dreagan. She knew that name, but she couldn't place where.

"Dreagan whisky," Darius supplied at her questioning look.

"Oh." Now she was duly impressed.

This brought a wide smile from Darius. "We've been making whisky far longer than anyone, and we're damned good at it."

"If you say so. I'm not a whisky drinker."

"Taste it, and you just might change your mind," he challenged.

Lexi laughed. "I might take you up on that." Her smile dropped as her mind turned to Thorn again, as it had during Darius's story. "Thorn isn't coming back, is he?"

Darius looked at her a long moment before he shook his head. "Nay, lass, he isna."

"Was it something I did? Is he angry that I followed you?"

"I know I am," Darius said with a serious look. Then he sighed and lowered his gaze to the table. "But the answer is nay. Thorn didna leave because of something you did, but rather because of what happened in his past."

Lexi's heart thumped with apprehension. "Was he in love?"

"Thorn never fancied a woman enough to want her as a mate, if that's what you're asking." Darius lifted his eyes to meet hers. "Our capital, so to speak, was always Dreagan, but each dragon race had a place they preferred all over the globe. For Thorn and his Clarets, it was the canyons. There was a village there that Thorn gave his protection to, even after the war between our races. He watched over them always, defending them against any-one who would do them harm."

She finished her wine and waited for him to continue.

"There was a family there who saw him shift into dragon form and fight off a group of Dark Fae. They brought him into their house and fed him. A friendship developed that progressed through the years. When the Fae Wars began, Thorn wasna able to go to them immediately. He wasna worried because they lived in such a remote area."

"And when he did go to them?" Lexi asked.

Darius ran a hand down his face. "By the time he got there, most of the family was already dead, including the father and two sons. The mother was alive enough to watch as the Dark took turns with her three daughters."

Lexi shrank into her chair. "How awful."

"Thorn descended upon the group of Dark and killed them, but it was too late for the daughters. He stayed with the mother until her last breath."

Yes, Lexi could see Thorn doing that. As gentle as he was with her, he would remain so no one would have to die alone.

Darius caught her gaze. "I doona tell you this lightly. It's no' in our way to share other's pasts."

"Then why did you tell me?"

"I'm no' sure. Maybe so you would understand Thorn. He felt as if he had failed the family he'd promised to protect. He made that same assurance to you, and you came close to dying. It doesna matter though. Your flight leaves tomorrow, and you'll put this place behind you."

Tomorrow. Was it really already time for her to leave? She wasn't sure she wanted to after seeing the Dark and the Dragon Kings in action.

"How do you feel?" Darius asked.

She knew he was changing the subject, and she let him.

Later she would mull over her thoughts and all she now knew of Thorn. "Better. The Dark have a powerful punch."

"What did it feel like?"

Lexi raised a brow. "Really? I saw you get hit by one of their bubbles."

"I know what it feels like for me. I want to know how bad it is for a mortal," he said.

"I was too shocked at first to even know I was hurt. Next I was arguing with Thorn, and then came that kiss." She licked her lips, remembering his amazing taste. "When it hit, the pain was awful. It felt like falling off my water skis and not letting go of the rope while being bounced along the water, trampled by a herd of cattle, and kicked in the chest by a horse all at once."

Darius rubbed his jaw. "So. I'm guessing verra painful."

Lexi slapped his arm as she stood when he grinned. She walked to the sink and rinsed out her glass. Her first thought upon waking was Thorn. It hurt, worse than the Dark magic, to discover he was gone.

After a kiss that literally curled her toes, Thorn walked out of her life without a word. For once, Lexi really wished luck would turn her way.

CHAPTER
TWENTY-ONE

West Ireland
Usaeil's Castle

Rhi stood outside the castle staring at the gray stones. The wind howled as it came off the sea. The castle sat high on the cliffs overlooking the deep blue water.

Was Usaeil with her lover? Doubtful, with the war starting. Rhi wouldn't catch whoever it was now. But soon.

"I'm glad you returned."

Rhi turned around to find her queen. She wanted to demand that Usaeil tell her who her lover was, but Rhi knew in order to get that information, she would have to make Usaeil think she didn't care.

"What is it?" Usaeil asked, concern clouding her face.

Every Fae—Dark or Light—was beautiful. It was both a curse and a blessing. Usaeil used her looks to make her way in the human world as a famous American actress. With her long black hair, silver eyes, and amazing body, it hadn't been difficult for her to catch everyone's attention.

"The Dark succeeded in starting a war," Rhi finally answered.

Usaeil sighed, a pained expression flashing in her gaze. "I know."

"Do you?" Rhi asked innocently.

Usaeil snapped her gaze to Rhi. "I am queen. Of course I know what's going on."

"What are you going to do about it?"

The queen's gaze sharpened. "I suppose you already think you know what I should do."

"Call the army."

"Absolutely not," Usaeil said, affronted. "Think, Rhi. It's bad enough the Dark walk the streets so freely all over the world now. If the humans saw us as well, it would be chaos."

"So leaving the Kings to fight this war alone is your desired option?" Rhi tried to hide the anger from her voice, but it came through nonetheless.

Usaeil shook her head, crossing her arms over her chest. Her hunter green maxi dress billowed in the fierce wind. "So you've been to Dreagan. Con would never ask you for help."

It took everything Rhi had not to slap Usaeil. The darkness within her growled, begging her to make her queen suffer as she had suffered for unnamable centuries. Somehow Rhi kept from giving in.

She smiled and lifted her face to the wind to let it cool her heated cheeks. "I wouldn't have the first clue what he did." She lowered her face and once more met Usaeil's gaze. "I've not been to Dreagan, but I don't need to go there to know what's happening."

"I'm not sending the army, and that's the end of it."

"And if the Kings lose?" Rhi demanded angrily.

"Con would never let that happen!"

She was taken aback by Usaeil's shout. "Since when do you have such faith in the Dragon Kings?"

Usaeil didn't seem to care that her hair was flying about

her with the increased wind. "The Kings protect this realm and the mortals. They've not failed before, and they won't this time."

"It's not just the Dark they're fighting. It's Ulrik as well."

"The Kings can handle it," Usaeil said tightly.

Rhi felt her watcher's eyes once more. How long had he been there? And why was he so interested in what she did? He was seriously getting on her nerves. If he didn't show himself soon, she wasn't going to give him a choice.

She turned and started to walk away when Usaeil called her name.

"Where are you going?" her queen asked in a surly tone.

Rhi shrugged and looked around. "I don't know."

"I need you here. We have our own problems."

"I have friends who need my help."

Usaeil's voice rumbled around her as she bellowed, "I'm your queen, Rhiannon! I demand that you remain and take your post as a Queen's Guard."

Rhi recalled how hard she'd worked to become a Queen's Guard. It was to honor her brother, but also an accomplishment she'd wanted for herself. How odd that she couldn't care less about the position now.

She looked at Usaeil as if seeing her for the first time. The queen's face was pulled tight, a frown of worry knotting her brow. At one time Rhi would've been the first to discover what troubled her queen.

Not any longer. Usaeil had lost her trust and her confidence.

"I resigned, remember?" Rhi said.

Usaeil's gaze hardened. "I didn't relieve you of your post."

"I don't need your permission to walk away. Besides, you don't want me as a guard. Not with all I've been through. Just one warning. Take care of our people."

Rhi teleported away before Usaeil could say more. She wasn't surprised when Usaeil used her magic to try and make her return. A surprised cry from Usaeil when she failed made Rhi smile.

Still, Rhi was intrigued. What could be going on at court that caused Usaeil to be so anxious? Rhi veiled herself and teleported into the queen's antechamber.

It was a place where everyone gathered to see who would visit the queen. It was also a place where the Queen's Guard stood as sentries.

"It's the Reapers," a man whispered.

The female next to him looked around nervously. "It's the only explanation."

The Reapers. That was the second time she had heard it spoken. There was one person Rhi knew she could go to for answers.

She thought of the desert and in the next instant found herself standing on a mountain of sand, the sun beating its penetrating rays upon her.

"Balladyn," she said.

Perth, Scotland
The Silver Dragon Antique Shop

Ulrik stood in the center of his store as images flashed in his mind of Mikkel's people, who had once more been in the store.

It was all Ulrik could do not to put up more magic to keep the buggers out, but that would only alert Mikkel. Nay, his uncle needed to keep thinking Ulrik was blindly doing his bidding.

Ulrik put to memory every face who had dared to enter his store for Mikkel. Those people would answer for their snooping in the not too distant future. For now, however, Ulrik pushed aside his rage.

It was a feat he'd learned to accomplish eons ago after he had gone stark raving mad. For that, and so many more things, Constantine would pay with his death.

Ulrik walked to the back of the shop and the hidden stairs that led up to the second floor. He bypassed the room he made others think was his and went to a panel in the wall. There he said a few words and the door slid open, revealing his bedroom.

He meticulously removed his suit and hung it back on the hanger before neatly putting his shoes back on the shelf. The rest went in the hamper for cleaning.

A quick shower later, he dried off and once more stood in front of his closet. Dinner with Mikkel. It was going to be anything but nice.

Ulrik chose a black suit and deep red dress shirt. Once he was dressed, he ran a hand through his damp hair and chose to leave the length loose.

He walked out of his secret room and back down the stairs to the store. With keys in hand, he exited the back of the shop and locked the door.

Ulrik looked directly at one of the cameras Con thought he had so cleverly hidden. He was going to his car when a Dark appeared next to him.

He clenched his teeth as he recognized one of the Fae who worked for his uncle. The Dark touched him and tele-ported him away.

Ulrik found himself standing in a foyer. He glanced up at the high ceilings painted with some cherubic scene that made him roll his eyes. A glance around the black and white tiled entry and dark wood walls holding priceless pieces of art showed that it was another residence of Mik-kel's he hadn't been to.

There was a blur of movement as Muriel was deposited beside him by the same Dark Fae.

"I could've just used the doorway, you know," she said to the Dark before he vanished.

Ulrik hid a smile at her irritation. He nodded in approval at her black chiffon dress that hit her thighs and dipped low in the front to reveal ample cleavage. The sleeves billowed from her shoulders to her wrists where they were gathered.

Her black and silver hair was left to fall down her back. With her metallic silver stilettos she made a striking figure.

"So you approve?" she asked with a smile.

He held out his arm. "Definitely."

"Where do we go?" she asked as she took his arm and they began to walk.

"To the open door." He pointed down the hallway to the door in front of them.

Neither he nor Muriel said another word. They walked into the room to find Mikkel bending over a chair and placing a kiss on Muriel's sister, Sinny.

The two sisters looked at each other and cordially nodded, as if they didn't know each other. Ulrik bowed his head to Sinny as his uncle stood and smiled brightly.

"Ulrik," he said and came over to slap him on the back.

Ulrik ground his teeth together. Muriel's hand tightened on his arm. He glanced down at her to find her red eyes on him.

Was that concern he saw there? The Dark Fae should know not to waste such emotions on him. He knew how to take care of himself.

"Let's sit," Mikkel said and pulled Sinny to her feet before walking her to a table already set for dinner, complete with lit candles.

Ulrik helped Muriel into her chair at the round table. He placed her across from her sister so Ulrik could keep an eye on his uncle.

"It's about time Ulrik found a companion," Mikkel said, his sly smile directed at Ulrik.

"I'm the lucky one," Muriel said.

Mikkel's gold eyes slid to her. "I expected you to keep him occupied for one night, but it seems you're good enough in bed to hook him."

"Mikkel," Ulrik warned.

Muriel placed a hand on Ulrik's knee under the table. "I am very good at what I do," she told Mikkel.

"So it would seem." Mikkel held her gaze for long moments. "Ulrik has never minded sharing."

It was obvious that his uncle was trying to bait him, but Ulrik had thousands of years of practice. It was going to take more than a reminder that one of his assets had been working for Mikkel. Losing Abby had been a blow, but it was the last time his uncle would put one over on him.

Muriel smiled pleasantly at Mikkel. "I share no one's bed but Ulrik's for as long as he wants me."

"Or as long as Taraeth allows it," Mikkel said and motioned to a servant to pour the wine.

Ulrik swirled the red liquid in his glass before he took a drink. "It was your idea to send Muriel to me, Mikkel. I suppose it was to make sure I didna find your people rummaging through my store."

Mikkel laughed out loud. "I was beginning to think you hadn't known."

"Twice now you've been there. Did you find what you were looking for?"

Mikkel set down his stemless wineglass and eyed Ulrik. "I wanted to make sure you weren't hiding anything from me."

Ulrik was hiding quite a lot, but Mikkel would never find it. "We made a deal."

"So we did."

The seconds of silence stretched as they stared at each

other. Ulrik could kill Mikkel right there. There were two reasons he let his uncle continue breathing. One, because eventually Con would learn about Mikkel, and it would keep him guessing as to who was attacking, him or Mikkel.

Two, he was going to crush Mikkel and slowly take away everything he craved—his money, his power, and his connections. It had already begun, though Mikkel didn't know it yet.

Nor would he until the very end.

"Shall we eat?" Sinny asked as she leaned up and touched Mikkel's arm.

His attention swiveled to the Dark using glamour. "Of course."

Ulrik had found another weakness of Mikkel's—Sinny. Not only did he not know he was being spied upon by one of Taraeth's assets, but he was well and truly smitten.

CHAPTER
TWENTY-TWO

The alarm on Lexi's phone woke her. She reached over and turned it off before she let out a sigh and flopped back on the bed.

She was leaving Scotland. Her last few hours would be all she had left of such a terrifying time. But not all of it had been terrible. There was Thorn.

And his kiss that set her soul ablaze.

That kiss was burned into her memory. It was a kiss she'd thought only existed in fantasies. The kind of kiss that changed her entire world and made her crave him as if he were the only thing that could keep her alive.

All night she had lain in bed hoping Thorn would return to the flat. The more time that passed and he didn't, the more the ache in her chest grew.

It was ridiculous, right? She'd just met Thorn. She knew next to nothing about him.

That part wasn't entirely true. She'd learned a great deal from Darius, but some of it she knew by Thorn's actions alone.

Christina used to say that everyone had someone out

there for them, and if Lexi wasn't careful, she wouldn't be paying attention well enough to see him.

"Well, I saw him, Christina," she whispered.

Lexi threw off the covers and rose. She spotted Darius standing by the windows overlooking the front of the building as he had done all night.

"Morning," she said.

He raised a hand, but didn't utter a sound. Lexi shook her head and went to take a shower. It didn't take her long to get ready and make sure all of her things were packed.

She zipped her suitcase and stood. Darius was watching her with a peculiar expression on his face when she exited the bathroom. "What?" she asked.

"I expected you to put up a fight about leaving."

Lexi grabbed the handle of her suitcase and rolled it behind her to the door. "I thought about it, but the truth is, I don't have the money to stay. I feel okay about leaving because Thorn gave me his word he would kill the Dark. I left the sketch I drew on the nightstand."

"You accept his word so easily?"

"I do. Why does that surprise you?"

Darius blew out a breath. "You surprise me, Lexi Crawford. That doesna happen often."

He took her suitcase and carried it down the stairs and set it on the sidewalk. Then he waved over a taxi. While Darius put the suitcase in the trunk, Lexi looked around for Thorn.

"To the airport, please," she told the driver after she got in the car.

Lexi was reaching over to close the door when Darius grabbed it. She had no choice but to move over when he climbed in beside her.

"What are you doing?" she asked.

Darius held out her purse. "You almost forgot this."

She had put it in her luggage, completely forgetting she was going to need her passport as well as her money. Her mind was so focused on Thorn that she was surprised she managed to get her jeans on the right way.

"Thanks," she said and took it. "But you still haven't told me what you're doing here."

"What does it look like?" he asked as he gazed out the window.

Lexi rolled her eyes. "Are you afraid I won't get on the plane?"

"I promised I would see you safely to the airport. That's what I'm doing."

Thorn. Thorn had made Darius promise to accompany her. Even when he wasn't with her, he was looking out for her. No one had done that except for her father and her mother—when she wasn't drunk.

They rode in silence to the airport. Every mile away from the city center meant she was farther and farther from Thorn.

By the time the cab stopped at the airport, it was all Lexi could do to keep a smile in place. Darius was a gentleman and got her luggage.

She tried to take it from him, but he gave her a look and paid for the taxi. There was a mixture of shock and surprise as she watched the cab drive off.

Lexi had to run to catch up with Darius when he walked off. "You didn't have to do any of this," she told him.

"We keep our promises."

We meaning the Dragon Kings. If she ever had any doubt, she didn't now. "Thank you."

He stood beside her in line as she got her boarding pass and checked her luggage. They walked slowly to the security line where she knew he couldn't go.

"It was nice meeting you, Darius."

He smiled as he put his hand on her back and ushered

her to the left where there was a small niche with chairs. There, a man with long honey brown hair and pale brown eyes stood.

"Guy," Darius said.

"Darius," he answered in return. Then Guy's gaze moved to her. "So this is Lexi. Nice to meet you."

It didn't take a brainiac to realize Guy was another Dragon King. That's not what concerned her. It was his presence.

"I'd like to say the same if I knew why you were here," she replied.

Guy's smile widened. "I came to meet you, of course."

"Because I'm the idiot who led the Dark right to Thorn and Darius?"

Guy's eyes narrowed a fraction as he sent a quick glance to Darius. "Is that right?"

"Look, you don't have to worry," she said to them. "I'm not going to tell anyone the things I've seen. The Dark are blatantly roaming the streets and the police thought I was nuts. Can you image what would happen if I mentioned dragons? I prefer to remain out of mental institutions, thank you very much."

Darius dropped his hand from her back. "Remember, no' all humans are without magic."

Right. "The Druids. Too bad I didn't get to meet them."

"They were at the flat after you were hit with Dark magic. They healed you."

Lexi raised her gaze to the ceiling in frustration. "Of course." She lowered her face and Guy's hands went on either side of her head.

His gaze was penetrating, seeking, and no matter what she did, she couldn't look away. His voice was steady and soft, lulling her to trust him even though she couldn't understand a word he was saying.

Then his words became clear. "Listen to me carefully,

Lexi. As soon as I release you, you're going to turn around and go through security and never look back. Close your eyes."

She did as he commanded and felt his hands fall away.

CHAPTER
TWENTY-THREE

Thorn saw Guy and Darius exit the airport. So it was done. Lexi was on her way home with no memories of the Dark, him, or their kiss.

It was for the best. He knew it even as inside he yelled for her.

Thorn remained where he was until Darius and Guy joined him. Darius gave him a single nod. That's all he needed to be assured that everything had gone to plan.

"She seemed nice," Guy said.

Thorn turned his back to the airport. If he remained, he might go to her. "She is."

"You do know that when I erase memories that I see them, aye?"

Of course Thorn knew that. He turned his head to Guy. "And your point?"

"She experienced a lot in a short time. She saw you and Darius in true form and didna run away. Then there was the kiss."

Thorn halted and whirled around to face Guy. "Never mention that again. I let her go for her safety."

Guy's expression said he thought Thorn a fool. "Was that wise?"

"Aye." Thorn didn't wait around for more questions. He had Dark to kill. He strode off, leaving the two of them behind.

Guy looked at Darius who was staring at the airport. "You didna agree with Thorn's request."

"In a way I did," Darius said. He swiveled his head to Guy. "The chemistry between them might have begun slow, but it heated fast. I think Thorn is scared that history might repeat itself."

"Is it that, or did he fear that she might verra well be his?"

Darius shrugged and said, "I guess we'll never know now, will we?"

"It's a shame. I think Lexi would fit in nicely at Dreagan."

"It's no' our decision. It's Thorn's, and he's let her go."

Guy held up his hands at Darius's harsh tone. "I'll no' say more. Good hunting."

"Same to you," Darius replied and walked away.

Guy turned to the terminal. He couldn't shake the feeling that Thorn had made a grave mistake. Guy didn't just see memories. If a feeling was strong enough, he felt it. And he certainly felt Lexi's hurt that Thorn hadn't said good-bye.

That emotion was almost as strong as the one that hungered for Thorn.

"Farewell, Lexi," Guy said.

Rhi saw Balladyn step from the Fae doorway. She had known he would come. The smile he bestowed was warm with hope shining in his eyes.

"You called," he said with a smile.

Rhi licked her lips and fidgeted under the heat of the

harsh sun. "I did. I knew if anyone could answer my question, it would be you."

"Now you have my curiosity piqued. What is it you wish to know?" he asked as he came to stand before her. His hand lifted and a finger grazed her arm.

"The Reapers."

Balladyn laughed, one side of his mouth quirking up in a grin. "A tale told to scare children."

"It also scares adults."

Balladyn waved away her words. "Yes, because they heard them as children."

"You studied our Fae history as much as my brother. Rolmir knew facts. I need to know facts."

Balladyn's smile dropped. A frown formed as he looked at her. "You're serious."

"Of course I am." Then she sighed and cut him a look. "You think I used that as a ruse to get you here?"

"The thought had crossed my mind," he stated in a flat tone.

Rhi met his red eyes. "I wouldn't do that."

He turned away from her and ran his hands through his black and silver hair that fell midway down his back. "All legends are based on myth."

"And myths are based on truth. I need the truth of the Reapers."

Balladyn looked at her for long moments. "The legend we were told said that if we didn't behave the Reapers would come for us in our sleep and steal us away."

"Then there was the part about doing Dark magic," she added.

"We know that part isn't true."

"Do we? Dark Fae come up missing all the time."

Balladyn made a face. "They were careless and got killed."

"That's the legend. Where do we go next?"

Balladyn stared at the sand. "I know I read something about the Reapers once, but I can't bring it to mind."

"Will you look?" she asked.

His gaze lifted to her. "Why do you want this information?"

"There is talk everywhere I go of the Reapers suddenly. I just . . . I have a feeling it's important."

"Then I'll see what I can find."

Rhi was beginning to smile when he added, "For a price."

She should've known. "What's the price?"

His hand cupped her face as his lips descended on hers. He kissed her hard, passionately, and pulled back before she could end it.

"That's half up front," Balladyn said with a wink before he vanished.

Lexi was glad of the security screening of the passengers, but it was a nightmare to get through. She was on the way to her gate when she saw the bar.

She climbed onto a padded stool and looked over the various bottles lining the glass shelves. It would be nice to have a drink before she boarded the plane and took the eight-hour flight—in coach—back home.

Since she didn't have her friends with her, she was likely to end up sitting next to a screaming kid. She was never lucky enough to sit next to a handsome, single guy.

"What can I get you?" asked the bartender with a friendly smile.

Lexi shrugged as she looked at him. "I'm in Scotland, so let's go with whisky."

"A fine choice." He motioned to the bottles of Scottish whisky, which proved to be more abundant than any other type of liquor. "Which would you like?"

She look askance at the number of bottles to choose from. "Give me the best you have."

"The best?" he asked, brows raised.

"The best."

A few seconds later she had a glass before her. He set the bottle to the side. "You're going to enjoy this brand. It is the finest Scotch whisky in the world. It's expensive though."

"I'm only here once." She handed him her credit card, and raised the glass to inhale the flavor.

Normally she couldn't stand the smell of whisky, but this had a nice aroma that made her think of mountains, heather, and lochs.

She took a small sip. To her surprise, it went down smooth with only a slight burn. Lexi had three more tastes by the time the bartender returned with her credit card.

"I'll leave the bottle for you to look at. There's a lot of history at the distillery that you can read about on the label."

Lexi thanked him as he walked off to tend to another customer. She wished now she had tried whisky when she first arrived in Scotland. She had balked about going to a distillery, but that had obviously been a mistake.

She put her wallet back in her purse and felt something hard in the lining. Lexi opened her purse wide and felt along the sides. It took her a minute to find the slit in the lining.

Shock reverberated through her when she saw the knife. It had a smooth handle made of what looked like black glass. The blade was silver and about as long as her hand.

Lexi had a vague memory of buying a knife in Edinburgh, but this wasn't it. Where had this come from, and what was it doing in her purse? Not to mention, she didn't know how she had gotten through security with it.

Her stomach was in knots as she took another drink of

the whisky. She felt . . . odd, as if she should remember something important.

She pushed that away and focused on what to do with the knife. It was pretty, but she wasn't going to bring it on the plane. With her bad luck they would end up finding it and charging her with something before sending her to jail. No, the knife had to stay in Scotland.

Yet, when she thought about putting it in the garbage or leaving it behind, it felt wrong.

Lexi tucked the knife back into the lining of her purse. She took another swallow, her gaze landing on the bottle.

"Dreagan," she said the name.

Then she saw the logo of double dragons.

The room spun and dots clouded her vision as she struggled to catch her breath. All of the memories returned with a roar, filling her mind with the Dark Fae, Christina's death, Thorn, Darius, and the fact they were dragons.

Lexi also recalled Guy. He had taken her memories. Thorn hadn't just left her, he wanted her out of Scotland without a single recollection of him.

Fury consumed her. How dare he take away what she'd learned of the Dark? To send her back to Charleston and not know what to do if a Dark showed up?

Lexi's vision cleared as anger settled like a stone in her stomach. She shoved aside the remaining whisky and stood. She stalked from the airport and got into the first taxi she found.

Thorn owed her answers, and she was going to make damn sure he gave them.

CHAPTER
TWENTY-FOUR

Thorn had a Dark Fae slumped over each of his shoulders as he carted them to the warehouse for destruction. The closer it got to Halloween, the more Dark there were. He had a bad feeling about the holiday the humans enjoyed to celebrate.

The day passed quickly as it always did when in battle. It was the only way Thorn could get through it all after seeing Lexi at the airport.

"It looks like you did a good thing inviting the Warriors and Druids to help with the way things are going today," Darius said from beside him. "We're going to need them."

Thorn slowed as he approached the warehouse to make sure no one was near. "I didna invite the Druids. The Warriors can hold their own against the Dark. The Druids can no'."

"I'll let you tell Laura and Dani that. Those women didna bat an eye as they fought today."

Lexi hadn't either, Thorn thought, his mind turning to her as it so often had since she left. He used his magic and opened the warehouse door as they approached. As he walked inside he said, "I welcome their help, but for everyone's sake, I hope the Dark doona try and take them. I know the War . . ."

His voice trailed off as a lamp clicked on and Lexi slid off the table where she had been sitting. Thorn couldn't decide if he was furious that she was still in Scotland, or elated that she was here.

"How dare you," she stated, her Southern accent thickening.

The minute she began walking to him, Thorn dropped the dead bodies. He blinked, confused. How was she here? More importantly, why did she remember him?

Anger pulsed around her as she strode to him. She halted before him and reared back her hand. Her palm connected with his cheek, sounding as if a shot had been fired as his head snapped to the side. It was so unexpected. Thorn hadn't imagined she would hit him.

He rubbed his left cheek and gave her a stern frown. She responded by raising a brow and giving him a look that could've scorched him where he stood.

"You didn't just leave without a word, you had my memories taken. What gives you the right to do such a thing?" she demanded.

Thorn opened his mouth to explain, but she spoke over him.

"You left me defenseless. I would've had no idea who the Dark were or how to fight them, because if you think they won't show up in South Carolina, you're off the mark, buddy."

Darius backed up a step. "Uh . . . I'm going to collect the other dead Fae."

Lexi didn't even look his way. Thorn had seen her scared, sick, and wounded. He had seen her frustrated, angry, and annoyed.

But he had never seen her enraged.

She was a sight to behold with her gray eyes glittering

violently and her chest heaving as she spoke rapidly. She gave no quarter, showed no mercy.

Before him stood a queen of war who would take no less than the absolute truth.

And heaven help him, but he craved her for it.

"You almost got away with it all." She gave a shake of her head and started past him.

Thorn reached out and grabbed her arm, halting her beside him. Her head whipped around, light brown hair flying around her as she met his gaze. "I had a verra good reason."

"My protection?" she asked with a snort. "I think I already covered that."

He looked down into her eyes that were as stormy as rain clouds and knew at that moment that he couldn't let her go twice. He'd tried that already.

No matter how many times he attempted to tell himself his feelings for Lexi would fade, they hadn't. "You were nearly killed."

She tried to pull away, but he held fast. "I wasn't," she said.

"What if you are the next time?"

Lexi made a face and threw up her other arm in irritation. "In all this time with humans have you learned nothing? I could be struck by lightning when I walk out of here. I could choke on a fish bone at dinner. Life is short."

Thorn lowered his gaze to her mouth. He hungered to taste her again, to feel the fire of her need, the burn of desire. Her lips tempted like nothing else. "No' for me."

Lexi's stomach quivered when she saw Thorn looking at her with such yearning. His mouth was inches from hers. They had already danced around their attraction once. She thought they were past that after their kiss, but for some reason Thorn was keeping his distance.

She softened her lips and leaned slightly toward him,

unable to do anything else. There was no sound other than their breathing.

Thorn lowered his head. Their lips were about to touch when he suddenly pulled back.

Lexi extracted her arm from his grasp and turned away. "I could forgive you anything but taking my memories. You stepped over the line."

She walked out of the warehouse hoping he would stop her, but that wasn't Thorn's style. He was a Dragon King, an immortal who had been alive for millions of years and seen so very much.

How silly to think that she, a nobody from Charleston, could catch his attention enough to have some sort of relationship.

Lexi didn't stop walking until she reached a road. She looked around, trying to determine what she was going to do. Her clothes were on their way back to the States. Now that she had checked in for her flight, but didn't get on the plane, there was no way she would be able to transfer the ticket. Even if they allowed it, the fee would be astronomical.

Her hand went to her purse where the knife was when she saw movement in the shadows to her right. With her fingers around the hilt, she relaxed when she saw it was Darius.

"Where are you going?" he asked indifferently.

Lexi shrugged. "I don't know. A cheap hotel."

"Stay at the flat. It's protected. And free."

She briefly closed her eyes, her throat clogging with emotion. Anger had kept her going, but now all she wanted to do was curl up in a ball and cry. "I'd be a fool to pass up anything free at this point."

"Shall I walk you?"

Lexi held up a hand to halt him. "I don't think so. You agreed to Thorn's plan."

"You know why. I told you last night, though you were no' supposed to remember," he finished with a frown.

She gawked at him, completely at a loss. "You only told me because you knew Guy was going to erase those memories."

"Aye. Thorn will be furious when he discovers what I've done."

Lexi snorted and shook her head in disgust. "I won't be telling him."

Darius slid his dark gaze to her. "Stick around long enough, and you'll get to meet the Druids and Warriors."

As quickly as he appeared, Darius faded into the shadows. Lexi adjusted her purse and continued walking. Night was falling fast, and she wished she had taken Darius up on his offer to go with her after she saw the many Dark on the street.

They were clumped in groups, some standing together, some walking. Women and men flocked to them in droves. It sickened Lexi how they fawned over the Dark.

She caught a glimpse of a female Dark. The woman had hair to her waist that was more silver than black. Her red eyes were accented with heavy makeup. She had a body anyone would envy and legs that went on for miles.

The Dark wore a pair of black jeans and a red satin shirt unbuttoned enough to show her black lace bra beneath. The men around her were so absorbed with trying to get her attention that they didn't notice the others.

Lexi kept her eyes straight and continued past them as fast as she could without drawing attention to herself. She glanced across the street and saw the first jack-o'-lantern. Surely it wasn't already the end of October.

She checked her phone and saw that it was in fact October thirtieth. Had she really been so focused on the Dark that she hadn't paid attention to the date?

Lexi tried not to walk faster when the building came

into view. She crossed the street and casually strolled up the front steps while covertly looking around her. Even then she didn't breathe a sigh of relief until she got to the flat.

She was reaching for the handle when the door opened. A woman with dark hair and moss green eyes smiled at her. She opened the door wider and waved Lexi inside.

"You must be Lexi. You're just as Thorn described," the Brit said when Lexi entered.

Before she could form a response a second woman came out of the bathroom. She had silver blond hair and beautiful emerald eyes.

"We were hoping to meet you before we went out again," said the blond with a strange accent that wasn't American or Scottish but a mixture.

Lexi looked from one to the other, thoroughly confused. "Hi."

The brunette laughed. "Forgive us. It's been a long day. We just had a little nap, and we're anxious for our husbands to return. I'm Laura, and that's Danielle."

"Call me Dani," she said.

Lexi set her purse on the table. "How did you know I would come?"

"Thorn," Laura explained as she held up her mobile. "He said you would be stopping by."

"Oh." That all made perfect sense. Lexi walked to the couch and sank onto a cushion.

Dani sat on the opposite end. She tucked her blond hair behind an ear. "We heard how you went after the Dark."

"Not very smart, I know," Lexi said.

Laura came around the couch and sat on the arm next to Dani. "I don't know. You knew they were evil when so many don't."

Lexi looked at them. "Are you Druids?"

"Yep," replied Dani.

"So they allow you to fight the Dark?"

Laura laughed and exchanged a look with Dani. "If you knew our husbands, you'd understand how we have the same argument with them each time until they relent and let us fight."

"How many times have you fought the Dark?" Lexi asked.

"This is our first time battling the Dark," Dani said. "Before that we battled Druids who used dark magic."

Laura added, "Otherwise known as *droughs*."

"You're lucky you have magic to fight."

Dani's smile dropped some. "Not so lucky that we always know what's going on and fight these villains. Unlike the Dragon Kings, we can be killed easily enough."

"As can our men," Laura said.

There were male voices a heartbeat before the door opened and two men strode into the flat. Lexi stood as she looked from the pale brown–haired one with brown eyes who walked to Dani with a smile to the other man with dark eyes and brunette hair who kissed Laura.

"Who's this?" Laura's husband asked.

Laura softly touched his cheek. "This is Lexi. Lexi, let me introduce my husband, Charon."

Lexi nodded a greeting.

Charon wore a charming smile that said he was self-assured and completely satisfied with life. "So you're the Lexi that Fallon and Marcail spoke about."

Dani walked over with her man then. She smiled up at him and said, "Lexi, this is Ian."

"Hello," Lexi said.

Ian wore a friendly smile. "I wish we could chat longer, but it's our turn to get back out there and kill some assholes."

"Honey," Dani said with a frown.

Laura laughed. "Oh, Dani. Ian's right. They are ass-holes."

They waved to Lexi as the four made their way out the door. When they departed, the flat seemed suddenly too quiet.

There was no one to talk to, leaving Lexi with her troubled thoughts that centered on one person—Thorn.

CHAPTER
TWENTY-FIVE

Thorn stood in the warehouse long after Lexi left. His mind was spinning with possibilities of how her memories had returned.

He put a hand on the wall, his chest constricting with the thought of Lexi in the city at such a dangerous time. Thorn shouted Guy's name through their mental link.

Guy answered instantly. *"What is it?"*

"Are you sure you took all of Lexi's memories?"

"Of course."

"You must have left something," Thorn insisted.

Guy sighed loudly through the link. *"I didna. I got all of them. Why? What's going on?"*

"Lexi. She's here. And she remembers everything."

"Impossible," Guy stated in confusion.

Thorn ran a hand down his face and looked to where he had seen her sitting on the table when he walked in. *"Ask Darius. He spoke with her as well."*

"No one has ever had their memories returned after I took them. I doona understand."

"I doona either. I wanted to make sure you didna do something so she would get them back."

"You asked for a favor, Thorn. I knew the reasons, and I'd never do such a thing to you."

Shite. He was in real trouble now.

"What are you going to do?" Guy asked.

"The only thing I can. I'll protect Lexi until I can get her out of the city once and for all."

"Is she angry?"

Thorn rubbed his face where her hand had connected with his cheek. *"You could say that."*

He severed the link and closed his eyes. The only way to ensure Lexi remained safe was to board her up at the flat and stand guard over her.

That wouldn't work for several reasons. The main one was that he couldn't leave Darius alone to fight the Dark. Even with the Warriors and Druids, he was needed. Then there was Lexi. She wouldn't appreciate being held captive for any reason.

Thorn slammed his hand into the wall. "Fuck!"

"She knows the threats out on the streets," Darius said as he walked into the warehouse carrying more dead Dark. "I followed her to make sure she arrived without incident."

Thorn nodded, feeling numb and frozen at the same time. "How did this happen?" When Darius didn't respond, Thorn turned to him, his hands clenched at his sides. "Did she tell you?"

"She doesna know," Darius said and tossed down the two bodies.

"But you do?"

Darius let out a slow breath. "I have my suspicions."

Thorn threw out his hands in agitation. "I'm all ears."

"I was there with Guy. He took her memories. Lexi walked away without having any idea who we were." Darius ran a hand down his face. "Perhaps she's meant to stay here. With you."

Thorn shook his head. "Nay. Nay! She can no'. If she

does, the chances of her getting caught in the middle of this war rise each day she's here."

"Something triggered her memories. It was strong enough to wipe away Guy's dragon magic, and we both know that's never happened before."

"She thinks I left her defenseless," Thorn said. "I would never do such a thing."

Darius crossed his arms over his chest. "What did you do?"

"I put a Fae knife in the lining of her purse so she would always have a weapon."

"That shouldna be enough to break through Guy's magic."

Thorn rubbed the back of his neck. "Nay, it shouldna."

"You should tell Lexi it was you."

Thorn wasn't sure it would do any good. She was too upset. "Scotland is the last place she should be now."

"So tell her that as well. Go to her. Whether she wants to admit it or not, she needs you. And I've got everything covered for the night." Darius pointed to the door and urged, "Go."

If Thorn went to her, he knew he would kiss her again. If he kissed her again, he would want so much more. And if he made love to Lexi?

Thorn wasn't sure he could even think of that right now. He'd known from the moment he first made contact with Lexi that she was dangerous to him.

If there was trouble, Darius would let him know. Thorn looked down at his torn shirt and jeans that were covered with blood. He quickly changed, and without another word to Darius, left the warehouse.

Lexi stood at the window, but it wasn't the city she saw. It was memories of Thorn. She ran her thumb over the hilt of the knife she found in her purse.

She had seen it used before by Thorn. Had he put it in her purse? It sounded like something he would do.

The darker the evening became, the more people filled the streets. She blinked and looked down when music grew louder. It was coming from a pub at the corner where people could be seen laughing and dancing.

More and more jack-o'-lanterns popped up all along the street. Even more troubling was the number of Dark Fae. Very few were now using glamour, and it seemed to only spur the humans to gravitate to them even faster.

The door to the flat opened and heat spread over her. Thorn. She saw him through the glass of the window, but she didn't turn around. Lexi didn't trust herself not to blurt out how happy she was he was there.

He came to stand behind her, silent and powerful as he gazed out the window. "Things are getting worse."

"Why can't they tell what the Dark are? We look like cattle being led to slaughter."

"It's their appeal," he murmured.

Lexi swallowed past her emotion. "I'm scared for what's to come."

"In all my years, there was only one time I felt fear. That's when I had to send my Clarets away. I never experienced it again. Until you."

She was so shocked at his words that she turned to him. Thorn scared? Surely she misheard him. A man like Thorn would never feel such an emotion.

"When I saw you'd been hit with Dark magic, it was like watching my dragons leave all over again."

Lexi couldn't hear such words. They made her want him even more, and he had made it clear that there could be nothing. Aside from that one kiss.

"You were no' meant to come back." His voice was barely above a whisper as his dark brown eyes searched her face. "I was prepared for that. I wasna prepared to see you again."

He was close enough she could feel the heat from him. His eyes looked haunted, as if he were trying to come to grips with something.

"When I walked into the warehouse and saw you, I was angry because I knew you were still in the thick of all the peril. But I've never been so happy to see you," he said softly.

Her gaze silently begged him to kiss her, to make her feel like she was being scorched from the inside out.

He slid his hand around the back of her neck and held her as he covered her mouth with his. His kiss stole her breath, seized her soul. Lexi clung to him as their passion collided. And burned. He held her tight, his kiss deepening as their desire mingled and came together in a tangle of need and yearning so great she was drowning in it.

Lexi jumped up, wrapping her legs around his waist as they continued their frantic, heated kissing. The next thing she knew, she was lying on the coffee table with Thorn's wonderful lips trailing kisses down her neck.

She sighed and ran her hands over his back. Thorn sat up long enough to unbuckle his pants. Lexi took the opportunity to throw off her sweater to have one less obstacle between her flesh and his.

He was leaning over her again. His head lowered as he brushed his nose against hers. "Tell me to stop. Please, Lexi, because I can no' do it on my own."

She put her hands on each side of his face. "Don't ever stop."

He issued a groan before he took her mouth again.

Guy walked into Con's office to find him poring over some files. Guy tapped his knuckles on the opened door. Con glanced up and waved him in as he wrote something on a paper and closed the file, setting it off to the side.

Con sat back in his chair and took one look at him. "You look worried. What is it?"

Guy closed the door and leaned back against it. "Perhaps nothing."

"Or something." Con tossed his Montblanc pen on the desk. "Tell me."

"I went to Edinburgh earlier."

Con nodded his head of blond hair. "Aye. Hal was looking for you. Elena told us where you went."

"Did she tell you why?" Guy asked.

"Nay."

Guy let out a deep breath. "Thorn asked me to come. There was an American woman who he and Darius saved from the Dark. She had been following the Dark after they killed her friend."

"And?" Con asked as he sat up, resting his arms on the desk.

"Thorn and Darius had to tell her of the Dark to let her realize the danger. However, she followed them to the warehouse and saw them dispose of the Dark."

"I'm guessing they wanted you to wipe her memories?"

Guy gave a small shake of his head. "While she followed Thorn and Darius, the Dark were trailing her. When she saw Darius shift, so did the Dark. They took her and tried to kill her. Thorn saved her."

"I know Thorn and Darius. There's no way those Dark lived," Con stated.

"Nay, they didna. Lexi was wounded with Dark magic though."

Con's forehead frowned. "Thorn didna ask for my help."

"He didna think you would give it."

Con's face lost all emotion. "Is that so?"

Guy gave him a hard look. It was never good when Con closed himself off in such a manner. "Do you blame him after the things you said?"

"Did the woman die?"

"The Druids healed her," Guy explained. "That's when Thorn asked me to erase her memories."

Con shrugged and once more reclined in his chair. "It was the smart thing to do."

"Except I'm no' sure it was." Guy rubbed his temple with his right hand. "You know I see the memories I'm erasing."

"Aye."

"I saw Thorn and Lexi kiss right before he realized she was injured by the Dark."

"So?"

Guy dropped his hand. "It was no mere kiss, Con. It affected Lexi deeply, and based on the fact that Thorn refused to bring her to the airport, it did him as well."

"You think she's his mate?" Con asked.

Guy began to pace. "It's a possibility. Or it could be just an attraction that willna be denied. I took her memories, even though I had a feeling it was the wrong thing to do."

"I doona see the problem," Con stated in a firm voice. "Thorn made the right call, and you did as he asked."

"Except Lexi's memories returned." Guy threw up his hands as he paced. "I've been over it and over it ever since Thorn told me. She has no magic. There was no magic preventing me from taking her memories or anything that would allow them to return." Guy stopped and turned to Con. "Something or someone returned her memories."

Con slowly rose to his feet. "That's impossible."

"Lexi was waiting for Thorn at the warehouse. She told him she remembered me taking her memories."

"Where is she now?"

"At Darcy's flat."

"I think it's time I paid her a visit," Con said, walking around his desk.

Guy blocked his way. "Ah . . . if I guess right, you might want to wait until morning."

CHAPTER
TWENTY-SIX

With every kiss, every sigh, Thorn was falling. It wasn't just desire. He knew the taste of desire. What he felt for Lexi was so much more. It's what had kept him from her for as long as he had been able.

His palms caressed down her sides. Her flesh was warm, soft, and inviting. The sound of her ragged breathing shattered his will to go slow.

He held himself over her with his arms while she tugged his shirt up and over his head. Need, sharp and true, burned through him, demanding he fill her body.

Lexi sat up with him when he straightened. Her hands roamed seductively over his chest as she kissed his stomach.

Thorn hissed in a breath when her fingers grazed the head of his cock. With his pants already unbuckled, she merely tugged them down his hips.

He looked at her, watching as she slowly kissed her way to his aching rod. She wrapped her hand around his arousal and slowly slid her lips over him.

Thorn grasped her head as his fingers sank into the cool

strands of her long hair. He held her there while she took him deep into her mouth.

Lexi let her hand trail down Thorn's magnificent chest and his tight abdomen. She wanted to look closer at his dragon tat. The ink wasn't just black. It had a mixture of red in it as well.

But her attention was pulled away by his thick member. He was impossibly hard. Lexi ran her hands up and down his length along with her mouth. She was normally never this brazen with a lover, but Thorn brought out something wanton in her, something primal and urgent.

She didn't fight it. That never entered her mind. All she wanted was to give him pleasure so he might know a little of how she felt when he kissed her.

Lexi glanced up at him to see his eyes closed with a look of utter joy visible for all to see. The muscles in his arms moved as he held her. She knew in that instant that she had made the right decision in following her heart—and her body.

If Thorn let her continue much longer, he would be past the point of no return. He fought to remain on his feet as her mouth worked its magic. When he opened his eyes and looked down, his breath was sucked from his lungs. She was exquisitely erotic, divinely carnal.

And she was his.

He pulled out of her mouth and touched her face. Her gray eyes had darkened with passion, and the sight of her orange lace bra made his balls tighten.

Thorn kicked off his boots and removed his jeans. Then he smiled in approval when Lexi grinned up at him and laid back. He unzipped and removed each of her boots. While he did, she unfastened her belt and jeans, making it easy for him to tug them off.

All that was left from seeing every bare inch of her was

the lace at her breasts and between her legs. It teased him, tempted him.

Unable to keep away, he was over her again, their lips meeting in a breathless kiss, both needing the feel of the other. That should scare him—and it did. But he couldn't stay away. He was inexplicably drawn to her in a way he couldn't begin to describe or ignore. All he knew was that he had to have her.

Lexi sighed in pleasure. Thorn's hands were masterful as he caressed her as if had found a precious object. He made her feel treasured, beautiful, and cherished.

It was a first for Lexi, and it moved her deeply. Her eyes filled with tears at the heady emotion he invoked by simply touching and kissing her.

Her back arched, a startled cry falling from her lips when his fingers grazed a nipple. Her breasts swelled instantly and desire tightened between her legs.

He whispered something she couldn't make out. She wanted to ask him to repeat it, but the thought was lost when he unhooked her bra and removed it.

Lexi watched as he looked at her breasts as if he had just found a feast. When his gaze met hers, he stilled as a tear leaked out of the corner of her eye and trailed across her temple.

He caught it with a fingertip before it reached her hairline. Thorn looked from the teardrop to Lexi. No words were needed between them. She could see in his deep brown eyes that he understood.

She brought his head down for another kiss. He consumed her with that kiss, leaving no question that whatever was happening between them was meant to be—that it had always been meant to be.

Thorn had been struck by that single tear. Mostly because he realized she had felt something so profound, so intense it formed a tear. It made him wonder how he could have ever thought to let her walk out of his life.

He moaned at the taste of her sweetly seductive kiss. His hands moved between them so he could cup her breasts. Then it was her turn to groan.

Thorn ran his thumb over her nipple before circling the tiny bud. He ended the kiss and shifted down so he could wrap his lips around the turgid peak and suck.

"Thorn," Lexi said thickly.

Her hands were in his hair, her hips rocking against him. She had no idea what a sensual picture she was and how it took everything he had not to fill her right then.

He moved to her other breast and teased that nipple until it was just as hard. Her breasts fit his palms perfectly. He massaged them, his cock jumping when he felt the wetness between her legs.

Thorn slid his hand down her stomach, over her hips to the trimmed curls. He lifted his head to look at her. Lexi's pale brown locks were scattered around her on the table, her lips were swollen, and her eyes were glazed with passion.

Nearly where he wanted her.

He held her gaze as he slowly slipped a finger inside her. Her breath caught as her fingers clutched the sides of the coffee table.

When he withdrew his finger and then leisurely circled her clit, her eyes closed as she moaned. He knelt at the edge of the table and spread her legs wide.

It was the cool air on her that made Lexi open her eyes. She raised her head to see Thorn kneeling between her legs. She wondered what he thought of her nearly bare sex, and then it didn't matter when he leaned forward and flicked his tongue over her clit.

She sighed loudly, the pleasure rolling through her body. His tongue teased and licked as he brought her closer and closer to orgasm.

Each time she thought she might reach it, he would pause and thrust a finger inside her or pinch her nipples. She didn't know how much more she could stand. Her body shook with the need to find release, a release Thorn kept just out of reach.

Lexi was delirious. Her nerves were stretched tight as her head rolled from side to side. Desire was spiraling out of control all because of Thorn. He tended to her body as if he were worshipping it, as if he had waited an eternity to pleasure her.

The orgasm took her by surprise. She opened her mouth to scream from the intensity of it, but there was no sound. She could only lay there, her body jerking from the ecstasy.

Thorn watched the pleasure wash over Lexi. It was a sight to behold, one he wanted to see every day. He rose over her and guided his cock to her entrance before sliding within her tight walls.

He held her hip with one hand, his other braced near her head as he slowly thrust in and out until he was fully sheathed. When he looked down, Lexi stared up at him as if he were a star she had plucked from the heavens. No one had ever gazed at him in such a way.

He put an arm beneath her back and stood as her legs tightened around his waist. Her gaze softened, a soft smile lifting her lips

Thorn turned and sat on the coffee table. He cupped her face and smoothed her hair back. "You're beautiful."

The first movement of her hips had him clutching her waist. She wound her arms around his neck and gradually moved faster.

Their eyes were locked, their bodies rocking together in a dance as old as time. As good as it felt, it wasn't enough.

He held her tight as he moved off the table and laid her

on the rug. Thorn kissed her hard, letting her know how much he craved her, how desperately he needed her.

Her nails scraped lightly down his back. He pulled out of her until just the head of him remained. Then he drove deep.

It was hard enough to scoot her back. Her nails sank into his skin as a harsh breath passed from her lips. Thorn braced his hands on either side of her and began to move. His thrusts were fast, hard, and deep.

Soon her moans filled the flat. Her legs gripped him tightly, urging him faster. His hunger pulsed violently. It didn't allow him to go softly or gently.

This was him at his most primal. He was taking her wildly and violently, but there was no way to pull back. The attraction he feared had turned into unrelenting, un-wavering yearning.

He now needed Lexi in a way that could never be al-tered. With every thrust, he was staking his claim.

It never entered his mind that she might not want him with the same desperate intensity, the same ferocious pas-sion. All Thorn knew was that he had been an utter, com-plete fool not to have taken her to his bed sooner.

"Thorn," she whispered.

He felt her clamp around his cock as another climax swept her. She looked up at him, a silent urging in her gaze.

As if he could ever deny her anything.

Thorn gave in and let the orgasm come. Their bodies pulsed together, bliss sweeping them into an abyss of light and decadence the likes of which he had never known before.

He held her, their limbs tangled as they slowly came down from such hedonism. His eyes were closed and his forehead rested on her shoulder when her hand softly grazed his cheek.

Thorn lifted his head to look at her. There were no tears

now, just a smile so stunning that it crushed the last threads of reservations he had.

"Wow," she whispered.

He smiled and pulled out of her. Then he gently lifted her in his arms. She was boneless, a contented sigh the only sound from her.

Thorn walked to the bed and laid her down. Once he climbed in beside her, Lexi rolled toward him to rest her head on his chest.

He looked at the ceiling as he held her. Good or bad, right or wrong, he had caved and let Lexi in. He didn't know what tomorrow would bring. Nor had he figured out how she'd gotten her memories returned. But what Thorn did know was that he would die before he let anything happen to her.

CHAPTER
TWENTY-SEVEN

"*Thorn.*"

Thorn's eyes flew open at Con's voice in his head. He glanced at Lexi to find her asleep after hours of love-making throughout the night. His body was curved around hers, his arm thrown over her waist.

He took his time getting out of the bed so as not to wake her. Thorn walked to the couch and put on his jeans. Then he gathered their clothes and tossed them on a chair near the bed.

Once he made sure Lexi was covered, he walked to the door and opened it. Con stood there with Guy. Thorn looked between the two and blocked their entrance with his hand on the door frame.

"You're no' going to let me in?" Con asked in an even tone.

Thorn wasn't fooled. Con might appear calm and cool to the world, but inside was a maelstrom of anger and fury that broke through occasionally.

"We can talk here," Thorn said.

Guy jerked his chin toward the inside of the flat. "I believe he doesna wish to wake Lexi, Con."

"I'm awake," Lexi said in a mumble from behind him.

Thorn glanced over his shoulder and bit back a groan when the sheet fell to reveal her amazing breasts.

"I think," Lexi added.

Thorn made sure Con couldn't see, though Guy had turned his back to the flat. "Lexi, you might want to get dressed."

From the sounds coming behind him, Thorn knew she was gathering her clothes and walking to the bathroom with the sheet around her. Her hurried footsteps told him she sensed the situation was important.

When Thorn heard the bathroom door close, he turned on his heel and walked to the kitchen counter, leaving the door open for Con and Guy to enter.

Thorn turned on the coffeepot and crossed his arms while leaning against the counter. He had known Guy would tell Con about Lexi's memories. It didn't bode well that Con was here.

No one said a word. Guy stood near the door while Con walked the flat looking around as if he was interested. It was fake. Everything about Con was fake. The Dragon Kings accepted it because it was a mantle the King of Kings had to take with the humans.

Except that act had become Con's mask that he never removed.

Ten minutes later, Lexi walked from the bathroom freshly showered. She wore her clothes from the day before and her hair was gathered at the back of her head in a messy twist of hair and elastic that she made look good.

Her gaze went to Con first. She turned toward Thorn and spotted Guy. Her entire body went taut at seeing him. Thorn walked to her with a mug of coffee in hand.

"Morning," he whispered and handed her the cup.

She dragged her gaze from Guy and tried to smile. It failed. "Morning."

This was not how Thorn wanted to start the day. He wanted to wake her making love. Instead, she was on the defensive.

"Hello, Lexi," Guy said with a smile.

She blew on her coffee. "Hi."

"It seems, Lexi Crawford, that you're all anyone can talk about," Con said. He had his back to them looking at a picture on Darcy's wall with his hands clasped behind his back. "No one has ever had their memories returned after they've been taken by Guy."

"I won't apologize for something he had no right to do. They're my memories," she said.

Thorn waited for Con's response, because though Lexi's words weren't meek, her tone hadn't been bitter or angry.

Con turned to her then. "We've existed for a long time with mortals. For a short period, they knew of us. I know you know the story, so I willna go into details." Con walked to them and took a seat at the table. He then motioned for Lexi to do the same. "The majority of that time, humans have had no inkling we've been here. It needs to remain that way."

Thorn took the chair that situated him between Con and Lexi. He had no idea where Con was going with his statements, but Thorn didn't have a good feeling about it.

"It's imperative that our existence stays secret," Guy said as he took the last chair. "It's the reason I agreed to do as Thorn asked with your memories."

Lexi looked at each one of them, a knot of uncertainty forming in her stomach. She had been woken by voices, and sat up before she thought twice about it. Now she wished she were back in bed pretending to sleep so she didn't have to face whoever this man was.

She focused on the man in the dark gray suit. He wore no tie with his crisp white dress shirt. She caught a glimpse of dragon-head cuff links at his wrist. If he hadn't been wearing a suit, she would think he was a beach bum with his shortish wavy blond hair that was longer on top.

Then again, with his piercing black eyes and controlled movements, there was no doubt he was a lethal predator. "Who are you?"

"Constantine."

Of course. She should've known. Still, the King of Kings sitting next to her. Should she curtsy or something?

Lexi sipped on the coffee, the caffeine in her empty stomach doing nothing to calm her. "You want to know how my memories returned?"

"I do," Con said.

Lexi set her mug on the table, but kept both her hands around it. She shrugged. "I don't know what to tell you. I was sitting at the airport bar. I remembered how my friends wanted to go to a distillery, but I hadn't been interested. I thought with it being my last hours in Scotland that I would try some whisky."

She glanced at Thorn to see him frowning. "I told the bartender that I knew nothing about Scotch and to give me the best he had. He poured it and left the bottle, telling me to read the label for some history.

"It was as I put my wallet back in that I found the knife in my purse. I didn't understand how it got there. It wasn't the one I bought. Then, I took a drink of the whisky as I looked at the bottle. The label had two dragons on it."

"Dreagan," Thorn murmured.

Lexi nodded. "Dreagan. I knew that name. It sounded so familiar, but I couldn't place it. It wasn't until I looked at the dragons again that it all came back in a violent rush. I got up, found a taxi, and returned to the city. That's all there is."

"Who was sitting beside you?" Guy asked.

She shook her head as she thought back. "No one. I sat on one end, and there were two men sitting on the other."

Con studied her, his gaze seeming to size her up. "Did they speak to you?"

"No one but the bartender spoke," Lexi answered.

"What was the first thing you remembered?"

Lexi couldn't hold Con's gaze. His black eyes were too sharp. They saw too much. She looked down at her coffee. Her pause lengthened, not because she couldn't recall, but because of how fiercely his name had bellowed through her head. "Thorn."

"Doona look at me," Thorn said to Con. "I was killing Dark."

Con gave a single nod. "As Darius said. You were going to let Lexi leave?"

"Aye."

"Why?"

This Lexi was dying to hear. She'd wanted to know since she woke from her injuries to find him gone. The story Darius told her was heartbreaking, and that did play a part. But after their lovemaking last night, it didn't make sense. Nothing made sense.

"I had to," Thorn bit out.

That seemed enough for both Con and Guy, but not nearly enough for her.

"That's it?" she asked Thorn. "You had to? If I hadn't remembered, I'd be back in Charleston."

"And away from the danger here," Thorn pointed out.

"And you."

A muscle ticked in his jaw. Finally he said, "Aye."

Did that mean he was going to walk away from her again? It was a possibility she had known the night before, but everything seemed so different in the light of day after heated hours in his arms.

He had held her so tenderly, loved her so thoroughly. Then been gentle and fierce in turns, and it made her stomach flutter every time she thought of it. The soreness between her legs helped to remind her that it hadn't been a dream.

Lexi dropped her head and pretended to get sleep out of the corner of her eye while she took that time to try and gather the pieces of her obliterated soul.

To be fair, Thorn had made no promises. There had been nothing said of feelings or what was to come. Only the ecstasy they found in each other's arms.

She wanted to stand and make him face what was between them. But how was that fair? There was a war going on, a war that she might not otherwise know about had Christina not died.

Yet she did know about the Dark Fae, Dragon Kings, and magic. There was no pretending. Thorn was needed. If she wanted to show him and the others that she understood, then she should support him. Though it was going to kill her to do it.

"You're right," she said as she lifted her head. "I shouldn't have to be reminded about the Dark." She slid her gaze to Con. "I have no answers for you."

"I believe I have what I came for," Con stated after a brief pause.

Lexi frowned, not sure what she could've said that satisfied him. Con's eyes didn't look away from her. She took a deep breath, waiting for Guy to grab her and take her memories again.

This time would be even worse, because she wouldn't be able to look back and think of her time in Thorn's arms.

"What will you do now?" Con asked her.

Lexi blinked in surprise. "I don't know."

At the same time, Thorn said, "I'm protecting her."

She swiveled her head to him. Did that mean they weren't going to wipe her memories? Or did that mean that Thorn was going to make sure she got on the plane this time?

"As I assumed," Con said to Thorn. His eyes returned to Lexi. "Did Darius tell you how we made sure never to fall for a human again?"

Lexi turned her mug around in her hand. "No." And she wasn't sure she wanted to know. "I know of Ulrik and the betrayal by his woman."

"After Ulrik's banishment, the Kings combined our magic and cast a spell to ensure that we would never be betrayed again."

It sounded as bad as she thought it might. It also answered her question about whether Thorn had any feelings for her.

"For thousands of years the spell remained in place," Con continued. "Until a few years ago. We didna know the reasoning at the time, but the spell was broken. The Kings began to find love with humans. They took these mortals as their mates."

Guy bowed his head at her. "I'm one of them."

Now Lexi was even more confused. So the Kings couldn't fall in love, but now they could?

Con smiled, as if he knew she was baffled, yet his smile didn't reach his eyes. "I'll be the first to tell anyone that I doona want my Kings to take mates. We've been lucky so far, but I know a betrayal will happen. I tell you all of this because we've noticed a trend."

She watched as Con got to his feet and stood behind the chair. He adjusted his sleeves and cuff links before he rested his hands on the back of the chair.

"What's that?" Lexi asked.

His hard gaze softened just a fraction, and she thought he might have given her a true smile—though it was small.

"Because those mates are immune to the Dark after coming in contact with their Dragon King."

Lexi sat back and shook her head. "You think that's why I'm immune to the Dark?"

Con's blond brows lifted in his forehead. "Are you now? Interesting."

"I'll be damned," Guy said with a smile. "That's how my magic was broken."

Lexi threw up her hands in frustration. "Will someone enlighten me?"

Guy chuckled. "The kiss you shared with Thorn. You held on to that tightly. It took me a lot to erase that memory."

Lexi was afraid to look at Thorn, afraid he might be appalled by what Con and Guy were saying. A mate? Her?

No, that couldn't be possible.

Did she lust after him? Did she want to jump on him and strip off his clothes? Did she want to curl up on the couch and watch a movie with him?

Hell yes.

Lexi turned her head to find Thorn staring at her, his expression closed.

Which pretty much said it all.

CHAPTER
TWENTY-EIGHT

Rhi stood in her small cottage in Italy. It had been awhile since she visited. The last time was when *he* had been there.

How long had he known of the house? Not that it mattered. It was her last time there. The cottage was once a sanctuary for her, a place she could go that no one knew about.

Yet now there were two who knew. Her love and Ulrik. And that was two too many.

One by one she took down the bottles of nail polish and put them in a box. She took the clothes from the closet and put them in another box. It wasn't until she turned to the bed that she saw the nail polish.

Rhi stared at it for a long time before she picked up the bottle. Why did he keep returning? If he wanted to talk to her, he knew how to find her. Or was he becoming interested because she was trying to stop loving him?

She turned the bottle upside down and read aloud, "Titanium."

It was a shimmery dark silver with black, grays, and whites. It would go perfectly with her choice of clothes lately. The fact she hadn't used the pink he left behind—and that he knew it—made her chest ache.

But at least this time she didn't fall into the fetal position and cry.

It was a step in the right direction.

Rhi tucked the nail polish into the front pocket of her jeans and teleported away with her boxes. She breathed in the fresh sea air at her new destination.

She was on a small island in the Caribbean without another soul for miles. It truly was a refuge now. No one could stumble upon her here without her knowing about it.

The hut was sparse, but perfect. Palm fronds were laid over the metal roof, and it didn't have a single wall. The bed was queen sized and hung suspended by rope as thick as her wrist from the beams above.

The shower was as sparse as the hut. It had a showerhead that was attached to a three-foot-wide wall of cut bamboo that rose up six feet. The kitchen was nonexistent, and besides a tiny table with two chairs, the only other furniture was a hammock, a chair and umbrella in the sand, and a chest for her clothes.

"Perfect," Rhi said and snapped her fingers, exchanging her jeans and shirt for a white bikini.

She left the unpacking for later and dove into the water. For hours, she swam with the fish and dolphins. Beneath the water she wasn't being bombarded with everything. She could focus on one thing at a time.

The Reapers were being looked into by Balladyn. She would worry about his "payment" when it came due, and if he told her anything of importance.

Her biggest issues were Usaeil and the war. Rhi knew the queen was making the wrong decision about not helping the Dragon Kings. She couldn't understand why Usaeil wouldn't align with them.

The Dark's deliberate attack on Scotland to rile the

Kings worked to perfection. The war the Dark craved was in motion.

Rhi wasn't sure her participation in helping the Kings would be welcome after not coming to Warrick and Darcy's aid.

The fact was, she liked Earth. She liked humans. She didn't want to see the realm razed by the Dark. Whether the Kings wanted her help or not, she was going to give it.

Rhi swam to shore and walked onto the sand. Her watcher had found her again. Sooner than she had expected.

"Who are you?" she demanded angrily. "Show yourself!"

She used her magic to try and make them appear, but it bounced back at her, knocking her backward a few steps. Rhi stared at the spot where she had thrown the magic.

"What do you want with me?" she asked.

There was no response, just more silence.

She didn't have time for that. She used magic again and changed from her bathing suit to black jeans, black spiked boots, and a black turtleneck.

Magic also dried her skin and hair. She braided her hair in two small braids on each side of her temple, then gathered the bulk of her hair into a bun at the back of her head.

She closed her eyes and held out her hand. With a few whispered words, her sword appeared. Rhi strapped the sheath across her upper body so the sword rested against her back.

With a thought, she was in Edinburgh.

Rhi barely had time to look around before a Dark came at her. She unsheathed her sword and beheaded him. Looks like she arrived just in time, she thought with a smile.

Two more Dark came at her, their red eyes glowing in the night. Rhi backed into an alley, her sword at the ready. In two swings of her sword they were dead.

* * *

The morning went by quickly for Lexi. Since all three Kings—Thorn, Guy, and Con—asked her to remain in the flat no matter what, she had agreed. Although, she had nowhere else to go.

It wasn't long before another two couples from MacLeod Castle arrived looking weary and exhausted. She cooked them brunch as they rested and changed clothes.

She had just begun to clean up when a man popped into the flat. He just appeared. Out of nowhere.

Lexi gaped at him, but he merely smiled.

"It's good to see you up this time, lass," he said in a deep Scottish brogue.

Lexi couldn't remember meeting him. Her gaze dropped from his green eyes to the gold torc around his neck.

"I'm Fallon MacLeod. The eldest of the MacLeod brothers."

"A Warrior," she said with a nod, piecing it together. Fallon was the one who could teleport. He was also the one who had brought Druids to help heal her the night she was hit with Dark magic.

He gave her a wink. "I'm here to take this lot back," he said, motioning to the four behind him.

Lexi watched as he walked to them and put his hands on the shoulders of two of them. When they were all touching, they vanished.

"Now that could definitely be something I'd use," Lexi said with a chuckle. "No more astronomical plane tickets to visit places. He could just pop me back home."

If she wanted to return to Charleston. Which she didn't. That hit her suddenly.

It wasn't that she didn't want to see her friends, but the idea of leaving Thorn seemed . . . preposterous. It wasn't as if she had known him for long. Yet it felt as if she were meant to be there—even in the middle of a magical war.

She stood there thinking about her night with Thorn.

A more magical, dreamy night she had never imagined. How she wanted a million more of them.

With a smile she gathered the dirty dishes and brought them to the sink. Lexi just finished washing the last of the dishes when there was a knock on the door and Darius entered. He held several bags of food that he put on the counter. Then with a wave, he was gone.

Lexi laughed at the closed door. She wiped her hands on a towel and went to inspect the bags. As she drew close she smelled the fish and chips, and her stomach immediately rumbled with hunger.

She eagerly dug into the food and ate until she couldn't put another bite in her mouth. Then she moved to the couch.

Lexi didn't mind having most of the day to herself. It gave her time to think, which only proved to give her more questions than answers.

The afternoon passed with no one arriving. She tried to watch some TV, but she couldn't concentrate. With nothing else to do, she began to cook. She had no idea if the Warriors and Druids would return or if Thorn and the others would be hungry.

She baked a cake and some scones while she considered how she felt about Thorn. Like appeared too soft of a word for how she felt, but she wasn't sure she could call it the other "L" word.

That word seemed so . . . intense.

But that's exactly how she would describe how she felt for Thorn—intense.

Passionate was another.

Then there was fierce and profound.

She also felt awoken. Yes, that was a great word for describing just one of her feelings. Thorn had pulled her out of a fog and shown her the light.

Lexi let the desserts cook and set about putting some

chicken in the oven. Then she peeled and boiled potatoes for garlic mashed potatoes. She would wait to do the steamed spinach until later.

While she waited on the chicken, she realized how precarious she was to thinking of that "L" word in regards to Thorn.

Love.

She actually thought it aloud in her head. The fact she didn't feel like the earth was crashing in around her was revealing.

Lexi had never had time to think of love. It wasn't that she hadn't dated, but she could never see a future with any of those men. Which is why none of those relationships lasted longer than a few weeks.

It was different with Thorn. She *could* see a future with him. It might be a dangerous one, but it was also one filled with light.

But to even think she might be falling for him? That was pushing things. She needed to get a hold of herself quickly. With a half-hearted attempt, she tried to say that Thorn was just someone she was attracted to, but it fell flat. It was so much more than that—and there was no use in pretending otherwise.

How could she see a future with him when he was immortal?

Immortal. He could never die. The idea didn't compute in her mind. Even though if a King took a human as a mate, the female lived as long as he did, she didn't consider that option.

Because while she might feel deeply for Thorn, she was unsure of where he stood.

Lexi stirred the potatoes and opened the oven to check on the rosemary chicken. When she straightened, she heard a noise behind her and turned to find Thorn.

Her heart jumped in excitement at seeing him. He was

covered in blood again. Their gazes met and held. As soon as his lips softened into a smile, she returned it.

"You're flushed," he said thickly.

Lexi pointed to the oven behind her. "Cooking."

"It smells delicious," Darius said as he came in.

Following close behind him was a man with long dark blond hair and cobalt eyes. "I'm starving."

"You're always hungry," replied a woman with auburn curly hair pulled back in a ponytail.

Thorn walked to Lexi and pointed to the man. "That's Galen, a Warrior. The woman behind him is his wife, Reagan."

Lexi nodded just as another couple came in. The woman had wavy brown hair streaked with blond. Her blue-green eyes were filled with pain as she limped.

The man holding her up looked like he was ready to rip someone's head off. His eyes were focused on the woman as he brought her to the kitchen table. Only then did he let out a breath and run a hand along his black hair pulled back in a queue.

"Ramsey and Tara," Thorn said. "Ramsey is part Druid, part Warrior."

She hadn't known that was even possible. "Is Tara hurt?"

"She'll be fine," Ramsey said as he frowned at his wife. "If she would've listened to me, she would've never twisted her ankle."

Tara rolled her eyes and looked at Lexi. "Many a time a man's mouth has gotten him in trouble."

Lexi laughed, but quickly stopped when she saw Thorn staring at her. "What?"

"It's the first time I've heard you laugh." He tucked her hair behind her ear and let his fingers caress her cheek as his hand dropped. "Are you all right?"

"I'm fine."

"Liar," he said with a grin.

Lexi had started to turn away when he pulled her against him. His head lowered so that their noses brushed. "Doona ever be afraid to tell me the truth."

"I don't know what I'm feeling. I'm scared and worried. I'm afraid that every time you walk out the door you won't return."

He cupped her face with both hands and tilted her head back so that she looked into his eyes. "I'll no' leave like that ever again. You have my word."

She was completely taken by his declaration. He infuriated her at one turn, and the next he made her heart mush.

It was no wonder she fell so hard for him.

CHAPTER
TWENTY-NINE

Ulrik finished reading the news coming out of Edinburgh on his iPad. The number of deaths every night now had an international spotlight on the city.

The country was trying to keep things calm by not allowing the death tolls in other U.K. cities to be reported. But it was only a matter of time before the information leaked.

This wasn't how he would've gone about things, but it would help him reach his end goal—which was all that mattered.

He closed his eyes and expanded his dragon magic to make sure his uncle didn't have anyone or anything near watching him. Ulrik did this several times a day, but it was necessary with a man like Mikkel who couldn't be trusted with anything.

Once he was sure no one was watching or listening, Ulrik opened his eyes and reached for the bottom right drawer of his desk. Inside there was nothing but files. He pushed them to one side and sent a small burst of his magic toward the bottom.

A Dragon King's magic was as singular as a fingerprint.

Even if someone found the hidden panel, they would never be able to open it.

A small wooden door popped up slightly. Ulrik lifted it and took out a black file folder. Centuries of looking over his shoulder had made him cautious.

Out of all the people within his organization, he was the only one who knew every pie he had his hand in, every person who worked for him, and every plan he had going.

This black file, however, was all about Mikkel. As soon as Ulrik discovered his uncle had been on the realm since the dragons were sent away, he began investigating. Ulrik had to be careful and not alert Mikkel to what was going on. Which is why Ulrik hired over a dozen people investigating—each with a specific goal.

Mikkel's arrival helped Ulrik in one instance, but Mikkel also screwed him in many regards. The fact Mikkel was keeping the Kings busy made Ulrik smile. For once Con wasn't in the lead. He was trailing—badly.

Ulrik pushed aside thoughts of Con for the moment. New information had arrived on Mikkel the night before. Since Ulrik had been with his uncle celebrating with Taraeth over the Dark's insurgence in Scotland, he hadn't been able to read it.

He opened his laptop and went to a special Web site he had created for just such instances. It appeared as an e-mail, but with the right code to decipher the message, it went from being an article on a seventeenth-century oil painting to the report on Mikkel.

In moments, the entire message was deciphered. Ulrik read over the report listing all the companies in Mikkel's name, as well as shell companies.

It was one more piece of information Ulrik had. He added it to the listings of cars and homes Mikkel owned. With the new software he designed, it created a map of everywhere Mikkel went.

Ulrik was looking over the map, noticing that while Mikkel went all over the world, his concentrated visits were in Scotland.

Of course it made sense. Mikkel intended to kill all the Kings and take over Dreagan, as well as everything else. All of that hinged on Ulrik, because though Muriel told him Mikkel had stated he was going to kill Con, Ulrik knew the truth.

Mikkel liked to talk big. He also wanted to see what would get back to Ulrik. Mikkel might like to think he was mighty enough to take on Con, but both of them knew he didn't stand a chance.

Ulrik leaned back in his chair with his hands behind his head. He and Mikkel were playing a game of deception with the other. Mikkel had laid all the cards out on the table, but Ulrik knew there was one or two hidden up his sleeve.

Just as he was hiding from his uncle the fact that he had all his magic returned. Ulrik could take on Con that day, though it wasn't yet time. Con needed to see his world crumbling around him before Ulrik issued a challenge.

The interesting part would be how Mikkel intended to kill him. Ulrik had come up with a couple of ideas, but one stuck out as something Mikkel would think he could carry out.

The timing would have to be perfect. Everything would have to fall in Mikkel's favor once Ulrik defeated Con. Because the battle with Con wouldn't be easy, Ulrik assumed he would be injured, leaving him in a weakened state.

Supposing Mikkel also thought of that scenario, it would be the perfect time for him to attack Ulrik. The only crimp in the plan was Ulrik's magic. Mikkel would realize within moments of the battle that Ulrik had all of his magic.

What steps would his uncle take once he realized that regardless of who won between him and Con, Mikkel would never be a Dragon King?

Already his uncle had put things into action that disturbed Ulrik. Hitting Rhys with dragon and Dark magic so that he couldn't shift was one of the biggest.

Ulrik knew exactly what Rhys had gone through. The only difference was that Rhys had those at Dreagan. Ulrik had been utterly alone.

He hadn't trusted the humans to help him. So he had gone into the mountains and—for a time—went bat shit crazy. Those were the darkest centuries of Ulrik's life, and ones he vowed never to repeat.

Ulrik closed the folder and pulled out another. This one wasn't just about Mikkel. It also had to do with Dreagan. Ever since he discovered Mikkel had a spy at Dreagan, Ulrik had been focused on uncovering who it was—and then turning them to his side.

He ran his hand over the file before he opened it. It was taking longer than he wanted, but he was getting close to learning who at Dreagan was working for Mikkel. The list had been trimmed to ten names. Tomorrow Ulrik would narrow it even more.

Suddenly an image of Rhi flashed in his head a second before she appeared in front of his desk. The best thing he ever did was cast the spell to alert him when someone entered his store and home. The only one who had gotten through was Mikkel, but even that had been remedied.

"Stop them," Rhi demanded, her chest heaving.

He raised a brow as he looked her over. She was dressed for battle in all black with spikes coming out of her heeled boots, but leave it to Rhi to look elegant and beautiful doing it. "I take it you mean the Dark in Scotland."

"I do. Stop them."

"I can no'," he said and closed the file before she saw anything. With one push of a button, the e-mail went back to its original form.

Rhi put her hands on her hips and glared. "You can."

"Apparently you believe I hold more sway with Taraeth than I do." Ulrik rose and walked around the desk to her. "You're joining the fight, I presume."

"I've already killed several."

"I think it's a mistake."

She looked at him as if she didn't know him, which she really didn't. "This is your home the Dark are taking over. Doesn't that matter to you?"

"This realm was the dragons' long before mortals came. Now they get to live freely while the dragons languish on some other realm? I've long wanted the humans gone."

"And the mates to the Kings?"

Ulrik shrugged and leaned a hip on his desk. "That's no' my worry."

"I thought . . ." she trailed off.

"Thought what?" he pressed.

Rhi's silver eyes were filled with doubt. "You helped Rhys. You brought Lily back from the dead."

"Are you sure I was helping Rhys?"

She took a step back. "It wasn't that long ago you assisted Warrick in protecting Darcy. Or so I thought. I heard you tried to kill her."

Ulrik smiled coldly even as a faint glow began to surround Rhi. "I stabbed her and left her for dead."

Rhi flew at him, the force of her magic knocking him in the chest. He tumbled head over heels backward and landed on his back with Rhi straddling him as light emanated from her, blinding him.

"Why?" she demanded in a voice filled with fury.

Rhi wanted to control her voice, but the word came out as a yell. She was rage, she was darkness.

Even though she knew she was glowing and that at any moment she could destroy the entire realm of Earth, she couldn't rein it in.

Did she even want to?

Was this her punishment for ignoring Warrick's call and sending in the Warriors and Druids? She was sick to her stomach for abandoning the Kings before, and the need to take it out on someone was strong. Too strong.

"The darkness within you has grown since the last time we spoke." Ulrik's voice was soft, calm.

She noticed then that he wasn't fighting her, but merely lying on the floor with his hands by his head waiting for her to do whatever she would.

His words penetrated her mind, and it was like a fire being doused with water. All the anger went right out of her.

Rhi turned her head away and climbed off Ulrik. She leaned her back against his desk, hating her new self. It was like she no longer had control of who she was becoming.

Worse, she wasn't sure she could determine when the darkness was taking over and making decisions. The Light inside her was dimming.

"Look at me."

She blinked and found Ulrik squatting before her. His face was set in hard lines, his gold eyes glittering with anger.

"Get your arse up," he ordered.

Rhi frowned, not sure why he was talking to her in such a way. "Why?"

"Now!"

She climbed to her feet. He stood before her with his long black hair falling to his shoulders. The sleeves of his tan sweater were pushed up to his elbows, and he was barefoot in his jeans.

"You're a Fae," Ulrik said as he stared at her as if she were gum on the bottom of his shoe. "Act like it. I've told you from the beginning that you have the ability to determine if the darkness remains or no'. Make the choice. Either accept it—as well as what you'll become—or cut it from you."

"You make it sound as if I haven't tried to get rid of it," she argued. Rhi tried to turn away, but he spun her back around.

His gold eyes pierced her. "You have no'. It's as simple as that."

"I don't want the darkness. I want it gone."

"Then let it go."

Rhi threw up her hands. "I'm trying!"

Ulrik's smile was cold, hard. "You forget, Rhi. I know how powerful you are. If you didna want that darkness, it would be gone in a blink. You doona want to let it go. Whether it's because it allows you to think and do things you wouldna normally do, or if there is some other reason, it doesna matter."

"No," she said, shaking her head as if that would make what Ulrik was saying a lie.

His eyes narrowed for a second. "Or are you holding on to the darkness because it gives you the strength to let him go?"

She turned away. Why did Ulrik have to bring up her lover?

"As I thought." Ulrik came up behind her. He didn't touch her as he lowered his mouth next to her ear and whispered, "You're strong enough to cut out the darkness and let him go."

"Am I?"

Rhi waited for him to respond. When he didn't she looked over her shoulder to find herself alone. If she didn't watch it, there wasn't going to be anywhere she belonged.

She teleported from the store back to Edinburgh. It was time to take out her anger on the Dark.

CHAPTER
THIRTY

Halloween dawned with Lexi doing whatever she could to help. She cooked, she washed, and felt as useless as mud.

The Warriors healed almost immediately, and the Druids were able to repair themselves of any injury with their magic. It proved to Lexi just how inept and inadequate she was in this war.

She kept them fed and gave them a place to rest, but that wasn't even hers. She was a squatter in the flat. That was never more apparent than when she was alone like now.

Thorn left not long after dinner the night before, and he hadn't been back. None of the Kings had, actually. It was through Thorn that she discovered Con and Guy remained in the city to help.

Lexi walked to the window, her arms wrapped around her. She had promised to stay in the flat, but she was tired of being in the same clothes.

There was only so much cooking, baking, and cleaning a person could do before they went crazy. Lexi was nearly at that point.

She had no idea what was going on out there. While the

others risked their lives, she was safe in the apartment watching the horrors below.

If only she could help somehow. But she wasn't immortal and she didn't have magic. She would only be a hindrance.

Lexi tried to dispel the anxiety that had gripped her in the middle of the night. She had sent off texts to Jessica and Crystal about steering clear of anyone with red eyes.

She should've called them, but she didn't want a lecture from them on returning home. But Crystal's response to the text with "LOL" proved that her friends weren't taking this as seriously as they should.

There was nothing she could do. All the warnings in the world couldn't make someone realize they were in danger if they didn't want to see it. She hadn't seen it until it had almost been too late.

Lexi's hand went to the glass when she spotted Thorn at the entrance to an alley. He looked up at her and nodded. A smile pulled at her lips. Seeing him had done wonders to help push away the ominous feeling.

Then she frowned. His shirt was gone. Blood and grime covered much of his bare chest, and his jeans had holes burned in them.

"Thorn!" she said through the glass.

With a wave, he was gone.

Lexi lowered her forehead to the glass and closed her eyes. She was going nuts not being able to help and not knowing about Thorn.

How long was she going to have to remain here? She turned and looked at her phone. She could call the spa and tell them she wasn't coming back, but what about her apartment? What about all her things?

And that was assuming Thorn wanted her to stay.

She could always get a job in the city—if the city

survived. Her faith was in Thorn and the Kings, but the Dark were many.

Then there was the fact that Thorn never told her he wanted her to stay. There hadn't been any time alone to talk of their night together and where they might be headed. If they were headed anywhere.

Lexi wished she had some semblance of answers to her questions. She couldn't remain here much longer. Not just because she was going nuts in the flat, but because she had a life in South Carolina.

Granted, it wasn't much of a life. She had work and her friends, and that was about it. They were the things she knew and understood.

She had a crash course in immortals, dragons, and Fae. There had been little time for her to process any of it, and now that she was alone, it wasn't exactly a good thing.

It was Thorn and that kiss that brought her back to the city. But with every hour that passed, it felt more and more like a mistake.

Lexi curled up on the couch and grabbed her cell phone. She played a couple of games of backgammon before she checked her e-mails. As soon as she saw one from her boss, her heart sank.

Her finger hesitated over the e-mail before she clicked it. Lexi scanned the message, not surprised to discover they were telling her all her vacation had been used and they were docking her pay for every day she wasn't there.

She immediately dialed her boss's cell phone. Becky answered with, "It's about time. Is everything all right?"

Lexi dropped her head back on the couch and closed her eyes. "No, everything is far from all right."

"I heard about Christina," Becky said. "It's been in the papers. I'm sorry, Lexi."

"I was with her." Lexi covered her eyes as she began to

cry. "I let her walk out of that pub with that guy, and she died."

Becky sighed. "It's not your fault."

"It is," she said with a sniff. "I knew there was something fishy about him. I should've stopped her."

"Christina was an adult. She made her own decisions. Now," Becky said in her most motherly voice. "When did you get back in town?"

This was the part Lexi had been dreading. She blinked, drying her tears as she was able to focus on something else. "I'm still in Scotland."

"What? Why? Jessica and Crystal are already back."

"I had to stay. I wanted to find the guy. I was the only one who could ID him." Lexi looked at the ceiling. "I owe it to my friend."

Becky made a sound over the phone. "You're one of my youngest masseuses, but you have seniority. I'll keep your position open for now."

"Thank you. It means a lot."

"When do you fly home?"

Lexi cringed. "Well, that's the thing. I was supposed to have been on the flight the day before yesterday. I checked in at the airline and everything, but I couldn't leave. My luggage should be there already."

"I don't like you there alone."

"I met some people. They're helping me." That's all Lexi would tell her. The less Becky—or anyone—knew, the better.

Becky said, "You know, I do watch the news. I know there's some bad stuff going on in Scotland. You don't belong there."

"I'm safe. Do me a favor. If you see anyone with red eyes, stay away from them."

"Red eyes?" Becky laughed. "Bless your heart, honey. There's no one here with red eyes."

Lexi really hoped it stayed that way. After another few minutes of assuring Becky she was fine, Lexi ended the call.

All of that took less than forty minutes. The day was going to pass at a very slow rate if this kept up.

Thorn slashed the back of a Dark's knee with his knife and flipped the Fae on his back. Then he drove the knife in the Dark's heart and moved on to the next. He managed to look in on Lexi, but that's all he had time for. At least she had been at the window as he had hoped.

It eased him to see her and know that she was away from the danger that seemed to swell and expand with every hour. No matter how many Dark were killed, they weren't fazed.

Even with the Warriors and Druids, as well as Con and Guy, nothing seemed to put a dent in them.

"Stay dead," Guy ground out as he kicked a Dark in the face who was trying to get up.

Thorn wiped the blood from his face with the back of his arm and looked around. The street they were on was completely deserted. The shops were closed and no cars ventured down. People avoided it at all costs.

All because at the entrance stood Tara and Reagan using their Druid magic to keep everyone out.

"We need to hurry," Galen said as he glanced at Reagan. "It's taking a toll on them."

Ramsey used his claws to cut off a Dark's head. He tamped down his god, the bronze color of his skin fading as well as his fangs and claws. "I'll help the girls."

"Let's get them moved," Darius said.

Con stood in the center of the street. The impeccably dressed King of Kings was as filthy as the rest of them. His suit jacket was long gone. His shirt was in tatters and barely hanging on his shoulders while his pants were better served in the trash.

Con removed his cuff links and put them in his pants pocket. Then he turned his head to look at Thorn. "Why did you no' tell me you and Darius needed help?"

"Because we had it," Thorn said. "Besides, Edinburgh wasna the only city being attacked. We couldna spread ourselves too thin."

"Too late for that," Guy mumbled.

Thorn picked up a Dark and was reaching for a third when Fallon appeared with Larena, Aisley, and Phelan.

"Fresh meat," Galen said.

Aisley immediately went to stand with Ramsey. Tara and Reagan were teleported out by Fallon, who returned a heartbeat later.

"I've got them," Fallon said as he took two Dark and disappeared.

In a matter of minutes, Fallon had all the Dark in the warehouse waiting to be turned to ash. Aisley and Ramsey lowered the spell that would allow everyone back down the street again.

Thorn looked to the sky. It was past one in the afternoon. It had been hours since he checked on Lexi, and he would be lucky to see her before dawn at the rate things were going.

"We need to split up," Thorn said as he walked to the corner and looked down the connecting street after Fallon teleported away with Ramsey.

Con said, "Agreed."

Fallon returned and they huddled together. "It's a large city," he said.

"There are eight of us," Darius pointed out.

Con nodded. "Four teams of two."

They all took sections of the city. Fallon teleported

those to their location that was far away. Thorn remained as near to Lexi as he could.

He wasn't sure how he ended up with Con, but it didn't matter who he fought with. They all had the same goal in the end.

"She'll be fine," Con said.

Thorn glanced at him with a frown. "I know she's fine."

"Then stop worrying."

"I'm no'."

Con grinned as they reached their destination to find over a dozen Fae. "I always thought you were a better liar."

Thorn rolled his shoulders. "I put her in the safest place in this city. Nothing can touch her there."

He dove to the side to avoid a blast of magic from a Dark and came up to his feet with his teeth bared. There were no Druids to keep the mortals from seeing what was going on.

Thorn waited for the screaming to start. He only belatedly realized that all the mortals around were under the Dark Fae spell and had no idea anyone was fighting to keep them alive.

CHAPTER
THIRTY-ONE

Rhi moved through the crowd near Edinburgh Castle, killing Dark Fae as she went. Her sword was coated with blood as she spun and brought her weapon down in a slicing arc.

She fell to one knee as a blast of magic hit her in the back. Rhi quickly rolled and spun around to face her attacker.

There were five Dark lined up before her, each promising death in their eyes. For as long as Rhi could remember, she had been fighting the Dark. Tonight was just another battle among thousands.

"You've some nerve showing up here," one of them told her.

Rhi made a face at him. "Really? That's all you got, you pale-faced Pop-Tart? And if you know who I am, then you know why I'm here."

"I know who you are," said another. He looked her up and down. "It's Rhi. She's a Queen's Guard."

The Dark on the end to the left rubbed his hands together. "I'm going to enjoy killing you."

Rhi rolled her eyes. "Don't count your chickens before the eggs hatch."

"What?" they replied in unison.

"For jerks who feed off humans, you know nothing about them."

One shrugged his shoulders. "They're food."

Rhi was tired of talking. She leapt across the space, her sword up and ready to fall. As soon as she landed, she decapitated one Dark and swung the sword in a wide circle.

She leaned backward, arching her back so that she could see the Dark behind her upside down. Rhi flipped over without putting her hands down and thrust her sword back into the gut of a Dark.

Two blasts of magic hit her in quick succession. Her left shoulder burned in pain, but she ignored it as she went after her next victim.

The three remaining Dark circled her. Rhi smiled to herself. There was nothing like a battle to remind her of what she enjoyed. Killing her enemy was at the top of her list.

She spun, her sword an extension of her. It cut through the air, slicing an arm off one Dark as it slashed through the middle of another's head.

Rhi stopped and plunged her sword into the second Dark. She faced the last of the group and paused. Every Dark Fae in the area was now focused on her.

Someone dropped down beside her. Rhi swung her sword, stopping it just before it reached his neck. She gaped at Phelan and Aisley.

Phelan smiled. "Want some help?"

"They're fast," she whispered.

Phelan flexed his fingers as his skin turned gold when he released his god. Long golden talons sprouted from his fingers. He looked at her with Warrior eyes that were metallic gold from corner to corner. "Let's see."

Rhi glanced at Aisley. The Druid stood with her feet apart glaring at the Dark.

At once, the Dark rushed them. It was all-out chaos. Rhi kept her eyes on both Phelan and Aisley in case things got too difficult, but both the Warrior and the Druid were holding their own. Aisley with her powerful Phoenix magic and Phelan tricking the Dark with his ability to manipulate reality so they had no idea where he or Aisley were.

Rhi had no idea how long they had been fighting. Dark littered the ground in piles while the humans stood there dazed. She had been hit many times by Dark magic. It burned through her skin and muscle into her bone, making her ache. Rhi refused to give in. She bellowed in rage and cut down two more Dark.

She turned when Phelan shouted her name. That's when Rhi saw a man standing above her in the shadows of the castle. Her watcher.

At least this time she could see him. Too bad she didn't have enough time to confront him.

"Rhi!" Phelan shouted again.

He was making his way to her. Rhi pivoted and went in his direction, meeting him halfway.

"What is it?" she asked.

Phelan spun her around and thrust his claws into the neck of a Dark before Phelan grabbed his spinal column and jerked it out. "It's Lexi."

"Lexi?" Rhi asked with a shake of her head.

"Thorn's woman. She's at Darcy's flat," Phelan said as he fought.

Rhi stopped a Dark in his tracks with her sword in his belly. "What about her?"

"The Dark have been noticing Darius and Thorn at the building. They think someone is there." Phelan paused and looked at her. "They're going after Lexi."

Lexi was looking at her hair, searching for dead ends, she was so bored, when the first tremors made her sit up on the couch. She went to the windows and looked down to see dozens of Dark facing the building. Large bubbles of magic appeared between their hands that they then threw at the building.

The second tremor had glasses falling off shelves. The third made pictures crash off the walls as the windows began to crack.

Thorn had said the flat was warded. The Dark couldn't get to her. But she hadn't thought to ask what would happen if the building crashed. Not that it would matter. Lexi wouldn't survive anyway.

She rushed to her purse and put the dagger up her left sleeve. This could be a tactic to get people out of the building. Lexi wasn't going to fall for that. She was staying put.

After her last encounter, she felt no need to go head-to-head with a Dark again.

The building shook and groaned with each crash of magic. Lexi stood in the doorway of the bathroom. It wasn't much, but it was all she had for protection in the studio flat.

There was a loud crack and a moan from the building. Windows shattered and suddenly the entire front of the building fell off. Lexi was hit with a blast of cold wind. Bricks and mortar continued to fall as exposed and torn electrical wires sparked.

This situation was quickly turning from bad to worse. Lexi looked to the door. She might make it. There was no telling how the stairwell would be, but if she remained, she would be crushed beneath the weight of the building.

Lexi took off toward the door. The building had broken off six feet from the door. Plenty of room for her to make it. She was nearly there when another volley of magic tore off an additional chunk of the building, including the doorway out of the flat.

She scrambled to catch hold of the kitchen counters as she began to slide with the rest of the structure. Somehow, Lexi managed to get a grip and pull herself out of danger.

With her chest heaving and adrenaline pumping through her veins, she turned and scrambled back on her hands and feet when she realized how close she had come to being taken out with this last part of the building.

Lexi looked around. There was nowhere for her to go, nowhere for her to hide. Despite all the protection and the wards, she was going to die anyway.

She got to her feet and looked down at the Dark. They were pointing at her and wearing smiles. In the middle of the day a group of Dark had destroyed a building, but the humans around them didn't care.

Lexi looked down the street. No help was coming in the form of police or Thorn. He would have no idea what was happening since he was fighting the Dark himself.

The Dark were preparing another round of magic when Fallon appeared beside her. He took hold of her hand. Lexi smiled, because she was going to get out of it. She couldn't believe her luck.

Fallon suddenly bellowed in pain. He flew back into the flat with such force that she couldn't hold onto him. The building moaned loudly as the floor beneath her feet began to tilt.

Lexi looked down the street to see Thorn running toward her. But he was too far away. She screamed his name as she lost her balance and was thrown, the air whooshing around her.

"Nay!" she heard Thorn roar.

At least the Dark wouldn't kill her. It was the last thought in her mind before she had the wind knocked out of her.

Lexi opened her eyes to see a woman holding her. She

had silver eyes and black hair pulled in a bun. She glanced down at Lexi.

"I've got you. Hold on."

Lexi struggled to get air back into her lungs as the city vanished. Her stomach turned, threatening to be sick. She closed her eyes, but that only made it worse.

"It's over," the woman said.

Lexi opened her eyes to find herself on a hillside. She sat up, and turned away as she emptied her stomach.

"Sorry about that," the woman said. "It happens to those who've never teleported before."

Lexi wiped her mouth and lay back on the cool ground. "What just happened?"

"The Dark were coming to kill you. They figured out there had to be something of importance there for the Dragon Kings to return again and again."

She put an arm beneath her head to look at the woman. "Is Fallon all right?"

"He will be. My name is Rhi, by the way."

Lexi saw the astonishing beauty of the woman, from her flawless complexion to her amazing figure, despite the burned holes in her black jeans and turtleneck. "You're Fae."

"Light Fae. I've brought you to Dreagan."

"Why did you save me?"

Rhi smiled, though it held a sadness Lexi didn't understand. "It's what I do. And because I've been told Thorn has taken an interest. Speaking of, I better return and let him know where you are before he gets all thorny and such."

Rhi laughed at her own joke. She turned and pointed to a path. "Follow it, and you'll see the distillery. Before you reach it, you'll come to a manor. They'll take you in."

Lexi opened her mouth to thank her, but Rhi was already gone.

* * *

"Lexiiiiiii!" Thorn bellowed.

Thorn cut a wide swath through the Dark as he fought to get to the building, using his dragon magic of sound manipulation to disorient the Dark. His heart had literally stopped when he saw Fallon take the hit and Lexi fall. One moment she was there, and the next she was gone.

He was a madman, his rage uncontrollable. All Thorn could think about was getting to the building and searching for Lexi.

Thorn was focused, everything falling away but the Dark and the overwhelming, vast need to annihilate every Fae he could find.

Not even blasts of their magic could stop him. He roared through the pain and continued his killing spree as he saw Lexi fall over and over in his mind.

Thorn cut down a Dark Fae and turned to look for another. Blood and sweat dripped in his eyes. He blinked and swung out at the presence he felt beside him.

"Easy."

He fought them, throwing them off. "Lexi!"

"Enough!" someone yelled.

Thorn shook his head, trying to clear his eyes. Suddenly his arm was held, the hold strong enough to keep him in place.

"Thorn," Con said. "Enough!"

Thorn paused at the sound of Con's voice. He blinked several times and found the King of Kings to his right and Darius to his left.

"She's no' here," Con told him.

Thorn looked around, seeing that every Dark who had been on the street was dead. That should've made him happy, but all he could think about was Lexi. He was getting ready to jump to the floor where Lexi had been when

Fallon appeared next to them holding his side that was already healing.

"I'm sorry, Thorn," Fallon said. "I had her. I almost got her away."

Thorn nodded and shrugged off Con and Darius's hold now that the bloodlust had diminished. "Thank you for trying. How did you know?"

"I heard the Dark talking about meeting up here. I had a bad feeling," Fallon explained.

Thorn glanced up at the flat as papers fluttered to the ground and furniture leaned haphazardly over the side. "Is she up there?"

Fallon looked from Thorn to Con and back again. "She fell."

"She's no' here," Con said.

"That's because I got to her in time."

Thorn whirled around at the sound of Rhi's voice. He was so happy to know that Lexi was alive that he went to Rhi and hugged her. "Thank you," he whispered, squeezing his eyes closed. "Thank you."

She patted his shoulder and pulled away. "You're messing up my clothes, handsome. She's at Dreagan so you can stop worrying."

"How did you know we needed help?" Fallon asked.

Rhi shrugged. "Phelan told me."

"Nice of you to show up this time," Con said.

Rhi gave him an icy smile and turned her back to him, flipping him off as she walked away. "Bite me, jerk."

CHAPTER
THIRTY-TWO

Now that Thorn's mind was clear and focused, knowing that Lexi was safe at Dreagan, the scene before him sank in. "Shite."

"We need to get them moved," Fallon said of the Dark.

Con nodded, a grim look on his face. "Quickly."

Thorn tossed four bodies at Fallon, who caught them and teleported away. A second later, Fallon was back gathering more. Thorn saw movement down the street and spotted Rhi. The Light Fae was also busy removing the bodies.

"We need to hurry," Con said.

Thorn threw another body at Fallon. "We are." When Con didn't respond, Thorn frowned at him as he continued to work. "What are you no' telling me?"

"Let's get this done first."

Thorn straightened and grabbed Con's shoulder, whirling him around. "Tell me now."

A muscle ticked in Con's temple. "Kellan told me two Dark were spotted on the outskirts of Dreagan an hour ago."

"It's just two of the buggers. Granted, I'm no' thrilled about it, but it could be like here," Thorn said and swept his arm wide.

Con's gaze was steady, even. It was a look he had perfected eons ago to hide his emotions.

That's when it hit Thorn. "There's more Dark now."

"A few."

"Lexi is safe as long as she stays on Dreagan."

Con gave a nod and went back to gathering the dead.

Thorn was relieved once more. Until he remembered
that there was a section of Dreagan that wasn't part
of the magical boundary keeping the Dark Fae out—the
distillery.

Lexi stared up at the sky as she lay on the grassy slope of
the hill. Her heart was still pounding in her chest. She sent
up a prayer of thanks that Rhi had been able to save her.

For a moment, Lexi had really thought her life was over.
There had been a second of clarity where she had seen
Thorn and heard his bellow.

In that flash of time, there was a world of regret that
went through her mind. Not talking to Jessica or Crystal
since they returned to the States, or calling Christina's
parents.

The biggest, however, was waiting for Thorn to make
the move with her. She had known he was interested, but
hesitant. Having been raised in the South, she was taught
it was always the guy's decision to make the move.

"Thorn," she whispered, an ache in her chest at not being able to feel his arms around her.

Lexi sat up when she saw the dark clouds coming her
way. She stood and looked to where Rhi had pointed. Lexi
had no desire to get caught in the rain again.

The trail was easy to follow at least, even if the land
seemed to stretch forever with the mountains all around her.
She hadn't gotten far when a blast of wind whipped around
her. Lexi wrapped her arms about her middle, the cold
making her shiver.

The rolling landscape might be pretty, but she just wanted to get inside somewhere to warm up. The farther she walked, the harsher the wind became. Then came the first spattering of rain.

"Great. It's Edinburgh all over again," she grumbled.

The Dark Fae eagerly looked across the invisible border of Dreagan. "It's nearly time," Gorul told his comrades.

"They'll know as soon as we cross over."

He smiled and pointed to the distillery. "Not there. Too many humans visit every day for there to be a barrier up."

Vaurin laughed. "Perfect."

"What would be perfect is getting our hands on a Dragon King. Or a mate," said the third.

Gorul glanced at the sky and the thick, fluffy clouds that were growing darker. "The Kings are up there, watching. We'll have limited time to get in and create some chaos. Remember. We need to get them out in the open. We want the world to start focusing on Dreagan."

"Mikkel's contact is still reliable?" asked Vaurin.

Gorul shrugged. "Even if the spy isn't, it doesn't matter. Mikkel is not our leader. Taraeth is. The orders came from Taraeth."

"From Mikkel's request."

Another Dark chuckled. "Taraeth only agreed to Mikkel's urging because it coincided with what Taraeth wanted. Don't you know that?"

"Of course," Vaurin stated angrily.

Anticipation grew as more cars pulled into Dreagan. Gorul couldn't wait to disrupt the unflappable Kings. "Get ready. And remember, keep your eyes on the sky."

Lexi saw the red roofs and walked faster. Her clothes were drenched and her hair was plastered to her head. The few drops had turned into a torrential rain within minutes.

"Sun. I want sun," she said with teeth chattering. "And heat. Heat would be really, really good right about now."

She could no longer feel her nose. It was completely numb, along with her toes. Between her teeth chattering, sloshing through the water pooling on the ground, and the rain, she could hear nothing else.

"I won't get sick again. I won't get sick again," she kept repeating over and over.

It was significantly colder in the mountains than it had been in Edinburgh. The hills she had walked turned into mountains that she had a hell of a time navigating. At any rate, the trail was easily seen. Without that, she'd have been lost.

She began to jog in order to reach the buildings faster, and because she needed to keep her blood moving. Thorn wouldn't be there this time to catch her if she passed out. No one even knew she was there, so they wouldn't be looking for her.

"Gee. This will be great," she mumbled. "I get to go in and introduce myself to strangers. What do I say? I'm Thorn's what? Lover?" She cringed at the word. "I'm not his girlfriend. Do the Dragon Kings even have such a thing? I mean, surely they date. Right?

"I don't know what I am to him. Perhaps it'll be better if I leave Thorn out of it altogether. That way it won't be so awkward."

Lexi blinked through the rain dripping from her eyelashes. "It's going to be awkward no matter what. How will they even know I'm telling them the truth? I mean, I could be demented for all they know."

She slowed when she saw the huge stone manor that Rhi had spoken of. That's where Rhi had told her to go, but Lexi looked at the buildings of the distillery.

If she went to the manor, she would have to tell them who she was. At the distillery, they would give her a blanket and let her warm up. She might even be able to stay there until Thorn returned.

"Right," she said as she halted. "Because Thorn is on his way now. As if that's going to happen," she told herself sarcastically. "There's no way he's leaving Edinburgh anytime soon with all the Dark there. And with it being Halloween, it could be days or weeks before I see him."

That didn't make Lexi feel any better. It also made her wary of going to the manor. What was she supposed to do? Stay there mooching off them until Thorn was able to return? And what would his return do for her?

Lexi never liked being a problem, and that's exactly what she was—a problem. She hadn't left the country as she was supposed to. Then there was the issue with her memories.

Con wouldn't want her going anywhere knowing everything that she did. She was relatively certain they wouldn't kill her. A missing person was too messy. But they could try and take her memories again.

Did she go to the manor and stay there, waiting on Thorn in the hopes that he felt something for her—with the possibility that they'd take her memories again?

Or did she go to the distillery?

"And do what?" she asked herself. "I have no money, no cell phone, no clothes. I have nothing."

But she couldn't stay out in the rain. Lexi began walking again. The path continued on, bringing her closer to both the manor and the distillery. Ahead, she could see the path split. Left would take her to the manor, and right to the distillery.

When she reached the fork, she still didn't know what to do. She was leaning toward going to the manor when she heard a voice.

"Miss?" said an older man with a gray beard that nearly reached to his chest. "Miss, are you lost?"

He reached her then and shrugged off his jacket to drape over her shoulders. "Come with me so we can get you warmed up."

Lexi let him guide her toward the distillery. He wasn't asking questions or forcing her to make a decision. He was taking control, and for the moment, it was too easy for Lexi to let him do it.

"A dram will warm you up quick enough," he said as he ushered her to the back door of one of the buildings. It was an office with a corner fire stove.

He brought her in front of it and gently pushed her down on a wooden chair. With a pat on her shoulder, he walked out of the office deeper into the building.

Lexi closed her eyes and let the heat of the fire begin to thaw her. Her eyes snapped open when the coat was taken from her shoulders and a wool blanket shoved in her hands.

"Fine Scottish wool from the sheep right here on Dreagan," he said proudly of the tartan print. His wrinkled face scrunched up as he grinned. "You need to get out of those clothes, lass. I'm going to step out and make sure none bother ye. Wrap yourself in that blanket and stay by the fire while I get you something to drink."

With a firm nod and a kind smile, he left again.

Lexi's hands were shaking as she rose and began to peel the drenched clothes from her body. She left them piled in front of the fire along with her boots as she quickly wrapped herself in the blanket.

The wool scratched her skin, but it was thick and warm. She gazed into the fire thinking some of the flames dancing looked like dragons taking flight.

A Claret dragon the color of red wine rose in her mind. His wings were outstretched and his teal eyes looked at her with a question.

"What?" she whispered sleepily.

CHAPTER
THIRTY-THREE

Balladyn closed the book and sat back in his chair, a kernel of worry taking root. The library he had begun collecting after turning Dark was the most extensive one in the entire Dark realm.

It had taken him longer than expected, as well as piecing things together from different books, but he had the answer Rhi sought about the Reapers.

He scooted back the chair and got to his feet. His mind was sifting through all the information on the Reapers. Most of it had been legend. But as Rhi said, every legend starts with truth.

The truth, however, wasn't one Balladyn wanted to know, much less share. If it were anyone but Rhi, he would lie. He had never been able to tell her no. On anything.

Balladyn walked to the tall double doors and pushed them open. He had to find her. Immediately. She had to know the truth, because if Rhi was asking about the Reapers, it was because of more than just rumors.

His strides lengthened. The love he had for Rhi burned within him. She belonged by his side. Always had. Soon, she would see he was the one for her.

Her Dragon King lover had had his shot. The bastard had blown it. It was Balladyn's turn now. His anger had eaten at him for long centuries, and Balladyn had nearly destroyed her.

Nearly.

His Rhi was much too strong for that. She proved it by breaking the Chains of Mordare. If that didn't demonstrate she was meant to be his queen, nothing would.

All he needed Rhi to do now was let go of her dragon. Once that happened, she would see the darkness he fanned to life during her torture gave her strength and power.

Balladyn saw the doorway that would take him to the desert. Rhi would meet him there once he summoned her. He wasn't keen on imparting what he had learned, but he was looking forward to the kiss she owed him.

He wouldn't collect it now. No, he had somewhere else in mind to collect his price. A place they wouldn't be interrupted. A place that would seal his seduction.

"Balladyn."

He halted at the sound of Taraeth's voice. The king was becoming a nuisance. Balladyn turned and bowed his head. "Sire."

"Where are you off to in such a hurry?" Taraeth asked as he slowly closed the distance between them.

"I was coming to see you. I wanted to know the status of our attacks," Balladyn lied easily.

Taraeth raised a black and silver brow. "Did you? I would've thought you'd have been by my side from the start."

"I was doing some research." With Taraeth—or any insane ruler—it was always better to stick as close to the truth as possible.

"What could be more important today? We struck a great blow to the Dragon Kings this day, and it isn't nearly over yet."

Balladyn clasped his hands behind his back. "There has been something rattling the Fae of late, sire."

"What is that?"

Balladyn watched as Taraeth unconsciously rubbed his upper arm, all that was left after his arm had been severed by a mate of a Dragon King. "The Reapers."

Taraeth laughed as he walked around Balladyn. "Silly nonsense. They're not real, Balladyn."

"I know that. I wanted to gather evidence in my library to present it to those who were using that as fear not to do their jobs."

Taraeth stopped in front of him. "You using logic? You're my right hand because of your vicious skills. If I wanted logic, I'd ask myself a question."

Balladyn lowered his eyes, lest the king see the hatred and anger he couldn't hide.

"Kill the cowards," Taraeth said as he turned and started walking away. "I don't want weaklings in my army. Come along, Balladyn. If you want to keep your place as my right hand, then I suggest you get there."

Balladyn looked over his shoulder to the doorway. Rhi would have to wait.

It was the screams that startled Lexi. She jerked awake, thinking it was just a nightmare after the battle she had witnessed in Edinburgh. Then another scream sounded.

Lexi jumped up, holding onto the blanket tightly, and rushed to the door of the office. She peered through the window. No one could be seen. She didn't know how long she had been sitting there since the old man left her, but she was sure he hadn't returned.

She grasped the handle and slowly turned it until it opened. Lexi stepped out of the office, leaving the door ajar just enough in case she had to rush back inside.

Huge copper vessels filled the building. The heat was

oppressive as steam rose from the stills. The concrete was cool beneath her bare feet, but the machines made it difficult to hear anything.

Lexi walked the length of the building, looking behind her often. There wasn't a soul in the place. The screams had stopped as well, making everything eerily quiet.

She spotted a door and rushed to it while holding the blanket in place. A glance through the glass showed that the rain was still coming down. By pressing her face against the glass, she could see there was a structure across from her and one on either side.

Lexi walked out of the building but stayed beneath the overhang of the door. In the States there would be concrete everywhere, but not here. In order for her to go anywhere, she was going to have to walk on rocks.

An inner clock pressed her, urged her to hurry. There was no time to go back and get her shoes or put on her wet clothes.

Lexi looked at the buildings around her. She would need to choose one. Hopefully she would find someone who could help her.

She decided to go right and was halfway to the building when there was a scream cut short. Lexi whirled around, cutting her foot on a rock. It wasn't like she went looking for danger. Well, that wasn't exactly true. She did when she followed the Dark.

There was a part of her that told her to run and hide. But another part of her, the part that had seen Thorn risk his life for her and others, insisted she help whoever was in need.

Lexi adjusted the blanket so that it covered both of her shoulders. The water beaded on the wool and rolled off. She stayed close to the building and retraced her steps before continuing on.

The more she walked, the more she could hear moans

and crying. She reached the last building and looked around the corner to see yet another structure. It was much smaller with lots of windows.

There was a sign that labeled it a shop. As Lexi looked at it, a window suddenly exploded. She instinctively turned her head away. When she chanced another peek, she saw a body lying on its side away from her, unmoving.

The laughter that came from inside the shop chilled her. She knew that sound. It was Dark Fae.

A hand grasped her above her elbow, squeezing hard. She whipped her head around and found herself staring into Dark Fae eyes.

"Come join the party," he said in his thick Irish accent and yanked her after him.

Pain lanced through Lexi as she had to run to keep up with him. The rocks jabbed her tender feet, and his hold pinched her arm.

He opened the glass door to the shop and threw her inside. Lexi lost her balance while trying to keep the blanket around her and fell to the floor, sliding on something slick.

She sat up and saw the dark stain on the floor. Lexi turned her hand over and saw it was covered in blood.

"I found another, Gorul," the Dark said.

Lexi wiped her hand on the blanket and got to her feet to get away from the blood. It was everywhere. She saw the two dead people and tried to get away, only to find another.

She glanced around and saw a group huddled in the back crying in fear and moaning from desire while looking at the Dark as if they hoped they were chosen next. Whisky bottles were smashed everywhere, with the golden liquid dripping to the floor from the shelves.

Lexi spotted three women who weren't acting like the others. They watched the Dark as if they knew exactly what they were. One of the women met her gaze. Lexi looked into her coffee brown eyes. Her auburn hair was straight and cut to her chin.

"I recognize you."

The Irish accent brought her attention back to the Dark. As soon as Lexi looked at him, rage bubbled inside her. She knew his face. She had seen it over and over again whenever she thought of Christina.

The one who had brought her in chuckled. "She looks right angry."

Gorul smiled. "So she does. How do I know your face?"

Lexi wished she had the knife Thorn had given her. How she longed to plunge it in his heart. But it was with her clothes.

"There's death in her eyes," said a third Dark, who kicked one of the dead on the floor as he passed.

Gorul walked to her. He tapped a finger on his chin as he stopped directly in front of her before walking around her. His shoulder touched hers, and she quickly jerked away.

"You should be on your knees by now," he said, his red eyes narrowing.

Lexi rolled her eyes and looked away. His fingers gripped her chin and jerked her head back to him. He snarled as he leaned his head close.

"Sucks when things don't go your way, doesn't it?" she asked sarcastically.

He blinked and suddenly released her, smiling as he took a step back. "I knew it would come to me. You were one of the American girls in the pub. I chose the other one."

"Chose?" Lexi asked, her voice rising. "You didn't choose her, you insane freak. You killed her!"

Gorul's smile grew. "She begged me for it. She couldn't get her clothes off fast enough. After I had her a few times,

I turned her over to my friends," he said and motioned to the two men on either side of him.

It was bad enough to think one Dark had killed Christina, but to know that multiple Fae had taken her made Lexi want to be sick.

"I'm going to kill you," she promised Gorul. She looked at the other two. "All of you."

"A human?" the third Dark asked with a snort. "Not likely."

Gorul looked her up and down. "She's immune to us."

"Impossible," said the Dark who brought her in.

"Look at her," Gorul ordered.

Lexi gave them her most disgusted look. "You dare to come to this planet and think you can take it over. You dare to make us crave you, using us for food. You lost a war here once. You're going to lose again."

Gorul didn't frown as she had hoped. Instead, he looked like he had just won the lottery. He clapped his hands. "Do you know what we have in front of us, lads? We have a prize of the first order."

"Because she knows what we are?" asked the third one.

Gorul grabbed the back of her hair and yanked down until Lexi had no choice but to go to her knees. She refused to cry out. She poured as much hate into her gaze as she could and stared at the bastard.

"We have a mate of a Dragon King," Gorul said.

CHAPTER
THIRTY-FOUR

Thorn carried the last of the dead Dark off the street just as the emergency officials arrived. He went to the warehouse and dumped the body where Darius was already in dragon form burning the remains. Thorn then walked outside to join the others.

"What a day," Phelan said.

Aisley leaned back against the warehouse and nodded. "I thought we'd have made some sort of dent."

"Rest while you can, because it'll get worse tonight," Con said.

Larena sat on a crate. "I didn't realize there were so many Dark."

"We must have killed several thousand," Fallon said with a shake of his head. "Why do I feel like we didn't even make them blink?"

"Because we didna," Thorn said.

Guy clapped him on the shoulder as he walked past. "She's fine, my friend. She's on Dreagan."

"Who's there?" Thorn asked Con.

Con put on a T-shirt Guy handed him. "Kellan, of course. Cain, Arian, Roman, Anson, and Dmitri."

So few. Con was King of Kings. He made decisions that he thought best for their race. But he had spread them too thin, especially knowing that the Dark had been seen outside of Dreagan.

"We would be there as well," Guy added. "I'm glad we came though. You needed our help."

"I'm no' denying that." Thorn ran a hand through his hair. If only he could talk to Lexi and know that she was all right.

"Rhi," Phelan suddenly said.

They all turned and found the Light Fae sitting on a stack of crates with one leg crossed over the other. The hilt of her sword could be seen sticking up behind her right shoulder. She swung her leg casually and rested her hands on either side of her legs on the crate. It didn't seem to faze her that her shirt was riddled with holes from Dark magic. "Hello, lovelies." She then cut her eyes to Con. "And asshole."

Con turned his back to her. Thorn watched as Con pulled his cuff links out of his pocket and held them in his hand, rotating them in his palm.

"I hope you've all rested, because a storm is coming," Rhi said and pointed upward.

"If only we could take to the skies," Thorn said. "We could end this battle quickly."

Guy frowned as he stared at the clouds and darkening sky. "Aye, but we can no'."

"Why not?" Aisley asked. "The mortals are too busy either running or throwing themselves at the Dark. Use that to your advantage."

"She has a point." Con turned to face them as Darius walked out of the warehouse fastening a new pair of jeans. "It'll be dark as well."

"And raining," Guy said, excitement showing in his pale brown eyes.

Darius raised a brow. "Lots of cloud cover."

"The Dark would never expect it," Thorn said, smiling for the first time in hours.

Con put the cuff links back in his pocket. "Thorn, you and I will take to the skies. Guy, you and Darius remain here fighting."

"What about us?" Fallon asked.

Con replied, "How do you want to use your people, Fallon?"

Thorn bit back a smile. For all of Con's faults, he recognized Fallon was a leader, a king, if you will, of the Warriors. He was letting Fallon make the decision on where to place his people. Not everyone would have been so gracious.

"Will he ever stop surprising me?" Darius asked in a whisper.

Thorn gave a shake of his head. "Likely no'."

"Never," Guy agreed.

Fallon gave a nod of appreciation. "Splitting up worked earlier. We'll stick to that."

Thorn noticed Rhi hadn't said a word. She was looking to a spot off to her left with an expression of annoyance.

"What about Rhi?" Phelan asked.

Con shrugged, as if he couldn't care less.

Rhi looked at Phelan and winked. "Oh, don't worry, stud. I'll find a group to fight."

"You shouldn't be by yourself," Larena said.

Rhi smiled brightly. "That's sweet. Really. But I'm a . . . was . . . a Queen's Guard. They don't stand a chance."

Thorn glanced from Rhi to Con at Rhi's news. If Con was as shocked as the rest of them, he hid it well.

"What does 'was' mean?" Guy asked.

Rhi jumped down off the crates, landing as gracefully as a cat wearing four-inch heels. "Exactly what I said, gorgeous."

"Why did you leave the queen's service?" Darius asked.

Rhi's smile faltered. "I got tired of it. It's time for a new chapter."

Every King there knew it was a lie. The greatest achievement of Rhi's life had been her service to the queen.

It was unheard of for a Fae to leave the Queen's Guard. It was just as rare for the queen to dismiss someone as her Guard.

Rhi licked her lips and looked around at them. "The Dark are vain. Aisley, if you and Larena are up for it, I've got a plan we three could execute."

"Name it," Larena said.

Aisley smiled. "Count me in."

"Wait," Phelan said, but Aisley put a hand up to quiet him.

Thorn could well imagine Lexi doing the same to him.

"We each find a group of Dark and pretend to be just as enamored with them as the humans. Once we're close enough, we kill them."

Aisley nodded sharply. "I like it."

"I doona," Phelan stated with a look of dread.

Rhi walked up to him and patted his face as she looked at Fallon. "The best part is when you and Fallon jump in and start killing."

"Now *that* I like," Fallon said.

Thorn noticed how Con watched Rhi as she spoke. He couldn't tell if Con liked her plan or not since it looked as if he'd eaten an entire plate of prunes.

"Let's get in place then," Con said.

Thorn walked to Rhi before she could disappear. He touched her arm to get her attention. She swung her head to him. "I wanted to thank you again for being there to help Lexi."

"It's my pleasure, gorgeous," she said. Then her gaze softened a fraction. "She's pretty."

"Aye."

"Am I to assume by your interest that Lexi is yours?"

Thorn looked at the sky as he thought of their night together. "I doona know."

"That's answer enough."

"Is it?" Thorn lowered his gaze back to Rhi. "When it comes to Lexi I know the best thing to do would be to let her go and have her memories wiped again. But the thought of her gone is . . . devastating."

Rhi's silver eyes widened. "You've already wiped her memories?"

"She got them back."

Rhi gaped at him for long moments. "What?"

"I know. That's what brought Con here."

The Light Fae's gaze slid to Con who was talking with Fallon. "What did he do?"

"Nothing."

Rhi made a face. "Nothing? Are you sure we're talking about the same jerk?"

Thorn smiled as he nodded. "The verra one."

"Look, stud, I know none of this is my business, but if you've had Guy take her memories and she got them back, that's telling you something." She started to turn away and stopped. Rhi looked back at him and gave an exasperated shake of her head. "Perhaps I'm not the one to give advice. I've always said to follow your heart, and that has gotten me nowhere. Maybe I should say protect yourself at all costs."

"Rhi," Thorn said, not liking the way she was talking. It was almost as if she were saying she was giving up on her Dragon King. No. That just couldn't be possible.

"If you hunger for her more than you want to be in the sky as a dragon, and if you crave her on a level that goes so deep it physically hurts, then that's a warning, Thorn. For a select few, they get their happily ever after." Rhi blinked rapidly.

Thorn could only stare at the vibrant Fae who was being torn in two. It made him want to punch the King into the next century for being such a prick to let something so precious as Rhi and their love go.

"There are some who never experience it. The worst, the absolute saddest, get a taste of that wonderful life only to have it ripped so viciously from our grasp." Her smile was sad and pitiful. "You want to know a secret? You want to know how I survived Balladyn's torture and the Chains of Mordare?"

Thorn nodded slowly, knowing in his gut that he wasn't going to like what he heard.

"None of it came close to the pain I've been living with for all these centuries." Rhi laughed and lowered her head. Then she whispered, "It's killing me."

In a blink, she was gone. Thorn could only stare at the place she had been. They had all been such fools to think that Rhi was soldiering on always waiting for her King to remember why they had fallen in love.

But Rhi knew something none of them had accepted yet—her King had already given up on her.

"You know who the bastard is," Phelan said as he walked up. "Do you no'?"

Thorn didn't pretend not to know what the Warrior referred to. "I do."

"Tell me his name."

Thorn faced him to look into Phelan's blue gray eyes. "If Rhi willna tell you, then neither will I."

Phelan took a deep breath and slowly released it. "Rhi is my family. I know all the Light are supposed to be, but it's really only Rhi. She's been there for me and Aisley during the most difficult times. I need to help her."

"You are. She knows she can come to you. Doona pressure her, Phelan. Everyone else is. And trust me, you doona want to know who it is. It makes everything worse."

"If you had a sister, would you no' do everything in your power to make her sadness go away? Would you no' want to hurt the man responsible for breaking her heart?"

It felt as if someone had slammed their fist in Thorn's chest. Memories he hadn't allowed to surface in millions of years began to shift and move. "I did have a sister."

Phelan glanced away. "I didna know."

"You couldna have. Believe it or no', I do understand. I sent my sister and my family away to protect them. I have to trust that they're all right. I had to push thoughts of them aside and focus on my duties as King, because if I didna, I'd have gone daft with worry."

"But Rhi is here."

"Aye. She lost her family and her King in short order. It almost killed her, Phelan. It wasn't long after that her world crumbled again when Balladyn disappeared. You're her family now. Be the shoulder she needs. When the time comes, she'll tell you who it is."

Phelan closed his eyes as he shook his head, battling with what he wanted and what he knew he should do. He opened his eyes and looked at Thorn. "Tell me if I've met him."

Thorn clapped him on the shoulder as he walked off. Some things were better off not said.

CHAPTER
THIRTY-FIVE

Dmitri growled when Kellan dove from above him, his wings clipping Dmitri's.

"*What the hell, Kellan?*" Dmitri said through their mental link.

"*Listen,*" Kellan yelled.

Dmitri soared through the clouds over Dreagan. He listened past the rain and wind, past the beat of dragon wings and the animals in the Dragonwood.

There. He caught it. It was faint, so faint he wouldn't have heard it had he not been listening. A scream.

He dipped a wing and turned, following Kellan's path that took them over the distillery. Dmitri glanced to his left to see deep turquoise scales. Arian had heard it too. That must mean . . . Dmitri's heart skipped a beat. The mates.

Kellan's voice boomed through their link. "*Kings, be at the ready. Keep to your posts and your eyes open. Arian and I are going to make a pass over the distillery. Dmitri, take a look at the border near there.*"

"*Four more Dark have shown up at the northwest side,*" Anson said.

Cain growled low in his throat. "*Another two on the east.*"

"*Six more on the west,*" Roman stated in an irritated voice.

Dmitri saw Arian flying faster. He and Kellan each had mates. Knowing Arian's woman, Grace, she was in the manor writing. But Denae was another matter entirely.

It wasn't just those two women either. There were eight other mates on the grounds. It was the duty of every King on Dreagan to protect them as fiercely as they protected Dreagan and their secret.

Dmitri shifted slightly to give himself a direct path to fly over the border near the distillery. He flapped his wings to climb, using the fast moving clouds to keep him hidden.

His first pass brought him around quickly again. Dmitri tilted his wings so that he hovered over the driveway leading from the main road onto Dreagan. He saw nothing that would cause alarm there. Yet, the idea of Dark beginning to arrive on Dreagan didn't bode well for anyone.

Dmitri soared above the long, winding driveway leading to the distillery and shop. To his surprise, there were many cars still in the parking lot when it should have been deserted. It was the last day the distillery was open to the public until spring.

"*We have a problem,*" Kellan's voice rang out through their link. "*There are Dark Fae in the shop.*"

Dmitri fisted his hands, his talons itching to slice some Dark Fae in half. "*How many mates are in the shop?*"

"*Three. Jane, Shara, and Cassie.*"

"*I'm heading to the manor,*" Arian said.

Dmitri circled around the distillery. He could see Kellan's bronze tail disappear into the clouds below.

"*Keep them there, Arian. The Dark doona get into the manor no matter what,*" Kellan ordered. "*Anson, doona

*get far from Con's mountain. If you see a Dark, kill him.
If you see anyone—mortal or no'—near the mountain, kill
them."*

"Gladly," Anson replied.

Lexi laughed in Gorul's face, though inside she was frozen with fear. Not for herself, but for Thorn and everyone
on Dreagan. If she had only kept her mouth shut, but she
hadn't and she needed to think fast.

"Mate? What are you going on about?" she asked, derision in every syllable.

Gorul ran a finger along her cheek. He laughed when
she jerked her head away from him. "Who else but a mate
to a Dragon King would know such things about us?"

"Fine," Lexi said with a bored expression. She might
have failed theatre in school, but she was about to put on
the performance of a lifetime. "I'll tell you what you want to
know."

Gorul got so close their noses were touching. "Then get
to talking."

"I've known it was you who killed Christina. I saw all the
others with red eyes and began following them around the
city. I figured one would lead me to you eventually."

Gorul's expression darkened. "Humans really are pa-
thetically stupid."

"So stupid that I had a map showing your movements
and where you liked to congregate?"

"That's when a Dragon King found you," he guessed.

"After what I saw you do to my friend, do you really
think I would trust a man?" Lexi made a sound at the back
of her throat. "What I did learn was that I wasn't the only
one following your kind. There were two other men. I saw
them easily kill your people."

"The Kings," Gorul said between clenched teeth.

Lexi held her blanket tighter. "I don't know who they

were, but I learned a lot from them. That's how I discovered you were Dark Fae. I went to a pub where they were and eavesdropped on their conversation. It's how I know of the war and everything else."

"A likely story." Gorul gripped her face and turned it to the side. He licked her neck up to her jaw. "It doesn't explain how you're here now, does it?"

She was repulsed by his touch. Lexi tried to pull away from him, but he held her tighter. In his red eyes she saw the confidence that stole whatever courage she had.

"Let her talk," came a deep voice behind Gorul.

Gorul's face went slack. He dropped his hand and spun around, going to his knee. "My king."

Lexi's day kept going from bad to worse. The king of the Dark now stood in front of her. His black and silver hair hung midway down his back, and he was missing his left arm from above the elbow. He wore solid black from head to toe.

Next to the king was a tall Fae who looked as if he couldn't care less to be there. His black hair hung well past the middle of his back, and it was liberally streaked with silver. He also wore all black, but the inside collar of his silk button-down was dark silver.

There were a few other Dark Fae with them, but Lexi knew those two were the ones with the most power.

She was in deep shit now.

The king waved Gorul away, his focus locked on Lexi. Why did all the Fae have to be so damned gorgeous? She might not be begging them for sex, but she couldn't deny the effect the king and the man with him had on her. If she let herself, she could give in.

Then she thought of Thorn and was able to look the king in the eye.

He smiled slowly. "Some of my people love when

humans are meek and weak. For me, I crave the spirited ones. Like you, my dear."

Lexi refused to move when he touched her. She would show him nothing. The more defiant she was with him, the more he would want her. And that was one place Lexi didn't want to find herself.

"You were telling a very curious story." His Irish accent was defined, but not guttural. "I'm curious to hear how you came to be here."

"I ran," she said. "I saw more and more of your kind flooding the streets, and I knew I had to get out of the city."

"With no car?" asked the Dark with the king.

The king smiled. "That's Balladyn, my dear. He's my right hand, my enforcer. He's very adept at picking through lies."

"Then he'll have a hard time with me because I'm not lying."

Balladyn crowded her left side. Lexi kept her gaze on the king, pretending that she didn't want to shove past both of them and run screaming from the room.

"You ran from the city and just happened to find your way here?" Balladyn asked in a voice so soft and cold that Lexi couldn't hold back a shiver.

She slid her gaze to him. "If you didn't hear it in my accent, I'm not from here. No, I didn't take a car from the city. They were piled up all through the streets. I left on foot. I stayed off the roads in an attempt to keep away from you." She swallowed, keeping an image of Thorn fighting the Dark as if he had been born to it in her mind.

If he could be strong against dozens attacking him, then she would be strong against the ones she faced now. Because any other choice would be a catastrophe.

Thorn.

Just saying his name gave her strength. Lexi returned

her gaze to the king. "I've been on the move since last night. I got caught in the weather. I was completely lost when a man found me and brought me here."

Balladyn's red eyes narrowed. He leaned close and inhaled deeply.

Was it her imagination or had he just flinched, surprise flickering in his eyes?

"Then?" the king asked.

Lexi gripped the blanket tighter in an effort not to scoot away from the both of them. "I heard screams. I walked out and saw that maniac," she said with a jerk of her chin to Gorul, "and his friends killing people. But I didn't get away in time. They saw me and brought me in here."

The king took her hand that was clasped on the outside of the blanket and ran his thumb across her fingers. "Your hands are cold."

"I was caught in the rain. It's freaking cold here."

The king smiled. "You're naked beneath."

"Not entirely." She did still have on her bra and panties.

"I'm Taraeth, king of these maniacs," he said with a smile and cold, cold red eyes. He leaned his head to the side and motioned to the group of people. "Do you see those over there?"

Lexi nodded.

"Those humans are crying because of the slaughter my men wrought. Yet, they haven't run. Look at them, my dear."

"No."

Taraeth grabbed her chin and forced her face around to look at the group. She glanced at the ones moaning, their hands running over their bodies as they waited for the Dark to take them.

Lexi's gaze clashed with brown ones from earlier. The other two women she had spotted who weren't acting like the others were near her. All three were half hidden by the mass of people trying to get to the Dark. How long would they remain that way?

"That's how you should be acting toward us," Taraeth whispered in her ear. "You should have dropped that blanket and begged me to take you. Why haven't you?"

How had she not seen the anger in his eyes? Lexi's hand began to shake in his hold. She slowly turned her head to look at him. "I don't know."

Taraeth kept ahold of her hand and took a step back. "I've seen this once before. It was a mate of a Dragon King who was immune to us. She didn't want me to touch her, but I still made her climax. With Kellan watching as I did."

The fear she had felt from falling and the Dark tracking her were nothing compared to standing before Taraeth and listening to what he obviously had planned for her.

"Who is your Dragon King?" Taraeth asked.

Lexi shook her head. She was so scared that it took her two tries to say, "I d-don't know what you're talking about."

"Lying is going to make things so much worse, my dear," he said with a smile and death in his eyes. "I can bring you unimaginable pleasure while I'm slowly killing you. Or I can bring you pain. It matters not to me. Make it easy on yourself and give me a name. I want to know which of the arrogant Kings I'll have the enjoyment of hurting by killing you."

Lexi glanced at Balladyn to find him watching her intently. Before she could say anything, she doubled over. It wasn't from pain. It was from desire so intense and strong that she couldn't breathe.

Her sex pulsed, throbbing with need. The wool blanket scraped across her breasts as she tried to turn away. Her nipples hardened against her bra from the contact.

Lexi held back the moan as long as she could before she fell to her knees. Taraeth kept ahold of her hand, his thumb still stroking her.

"That need I just forced on you comes from being near us," Taraeth said. He laughed. "How long do you think you can go on like that before you try to give yourself relief?"

That thought had already crossed Lexi's mind. She glared up at him. "What a coward you are to violate me in such a way when there are hundreds of others who want you."

"Ah," Taraeth whispered as he sent more need pumping through her. "But that's what makes you so appealing. Soon, you'll be begging me to give you release. You'll forget everything and everyone but me."

He dropped her hand and turned away. Lexi wrapped her arms around her middle and groaned again. The desire was overwhelming. She pictured Thorn in her head and kept him there.

"Bring her, Balladyn," Taraeth said as he started to turn away. He paused and looked at the group of humans. "Another surprise. Bring the traitor, Shara, as well." Taraeth stopped beside Gorul and said, "Kill the rest."

A moan left Lexi when Balladyn lifted her in his arms. She was supposed to have been safe on Dreagan. What happened?

"Fighting it will only make it worse, woman," Balladyn murmured.

Fighting? She had no choice, because Lexi wasn't going to die like Christina had.

Thorn!

CHAPTER
THIRTY-SIX

Thorn removed his clothes and stood on top of the warehouse surveying all his enhanced eyesight could see—and it wasn't a pretty picture.

The once beautiful ancient city had taken a battering from the Dark. After the building Lexi had been in was destroyed, the Dark moved to other areas of the city and began to ravage it.

The rain was coming faster, hitting his skin like pellets. Wind whipped around him, as if urging him to shift and take to the sky. He glanced about for humans. How many times had they taken precautions so that the mortals wouldn't see them?

How many times had they not been able to shift because the humans were too close?

Now, not one of the mortals was paying attention. Con was already flying over the city. Thorn could see a hint of gold scales through the clouds.

Thorn could finally focus on the task at hand like he had before he saw Lexi the first time. It was a relief that she was completely out of danger at Dreagan. Finally, she was well and truly safe.

He jumped and shifted at the same time. His wings unfurled and caught the wind. It took him straight up to the clouds.

"*Ready?*" Con asked.

Thorn circled the warehouse to make sure no one had seen him. "*Been ready.*"

The two of them stayed in the clouds until they found a group of Dark. He and Con came at them from opposite sides. Thorn went first, blasting them with magic and pushing the Dark right toward Con.

Thorn dipped his wing to turn and flew off when Con came in and released dragon fire on the Fae. When they were done, no Dark was left alive.

With their victory, they moved on to the next section. It proved more difficult since there were numerous humans mixed in with the Dark.

Thorn tucked his wings and dove straight down from the clouds. Since he was unable to spread his wings fully between the buildings, he managed to spread them enough to halt his descent and even him out. He grabbed a Dark in each hand, crushing them.

Con dove down behind him, catching three Dark in his mouth and using his teeth to tear them to shreds before tossing them away.

Again and again they found their prey and unleashed hell.

Their attacks were enough to get the Dark to begin fleeing, but then there were the combined attacks of Rhi, Guy and Darius, as well as Fallon, Larena, Phelan, and Aisley.

Thorn flew back up to the clouds, content with their attack and the outcome. Con spotted another group that they were headed toward when Kellan's voice shouted in their heads.

"*Dark attack at Dreagan!*"

Thorn roared and dipped his wing as he quickly turned

and headed toward Dreagan. How had the Dark gotten in? There were precautions in place.

Then he remembered—the distillery.

Thorn roared again in fury—and fear. He flew swiftly, his heart sick that Lexi might be hurt. Or worse—captured.

It was as if the Dark knew where she was going to be every time he thought she was safe.

Rhi remained on the same street as Phelan and Aisley. She stayed closer to the Druid, because the Dark would like nothing better than to get their hands on her.

Though she kept an eye on Phelan as well. If the Dark ever discovered he was a Fae prince . . . she didn't even want to think about what would become of him.

She swung her sword around her, bending backward to get the two attacking behind her. Rhi straightened and kicked out her leg, her heel sinking into the Dark's throat.

Rhi.

She looked around for Con. There was urgency in his voice that she hadn't heard before. She glanced up when she felt a gust of wind go over her.

Then he was standing in the middle of the street naked. A Dark ran up to him. Con grabbed him around the throat and squeezed. The Dark clawed at Con, but it did no good. The King of Kings had a hold of him, slowly squeezing the life from the Fae with black eyes full of fury.

Con's head swung to her. "Dark are attacking Dreagan. Thorn has gone. All of this," he said as he tossed aside the dead Dark and motioned to the city, "was set up to divert our attention from Dreagan."

Dreagan. Under attack. By Dark. It couldn't be possible. But all she had to do was look into Con's eyes and see the lethal rage rolling off him to know it wasn't a joke.

She teleported out before she thought to ask Con why he assumed she would help. But she didn't go to Dreagan.

Instead, Rhi found Fallon and appeared next to the Warrior as he stood using his claws to tear through the Dark.

"I need you to get Malcolm to Dreagan immediately."

Fallon's black Warrior eyes looked at her. His black claws dripped with blood, and his gold torc looked stark against the black skin of his god. "What?"

"The Dark are attacking Dreagan. This was a setup."

She didn't say any more as she teleported to Dreagan.

Kellan dove toward the shop, rolling and shifting into human form. He landed on one knee with his hands upon the ground. His head lifted when he saw Taraeth and Balladyn in the shop talking to a woman.

He listened to their conversation as he made his way into the building. The fact Taraeth hadn't posted anyone near the doors told Kellan that the king of the Dark didn't care if the Dragon Kings came in or not.

Then Kellan heard the humans. No wonder the Dark weren't worried. No Dragon King could go in there with humans watching.

He saw Arian and motioned for him to go around front. Then Kellan snuck into the shop. Broken glass sliced into his feet, but he paid it no attention.

"*Taraeth and Balladyn are here,*" Kellan told the other Kings. Everyone needed to be prepared.

"Bring her," Taraeth told Balladyn.

After he ordered one of the Dark to kill everyone, Taraeth stopped and turned around.

"And bring the traitor, Shara."

Kellan waited until the Dark with Shara was even with the door to the hallway where he hid before he rushed them. Shara was taken down with them, but she sent a blast of magic toward Taraeth as she did. Kellan snapped the Dark's neck who had a hold of Shara and jumped up.

Arian crashed through the front glass doors and went

after the Dark standing there. Kellan motioned for Cassie and Jane to get the humans out, but the mortals wouldn't leave. The girls began to drag them out of the shop one by one.

Kellan took the blasts of magic aimed for Cassie and Jane. His leg gave out, sending him down to one knee. Kellan got back up with a grimace and braced himself for the Dark who came at him.

Then they were in hand-to-hand combat. It wouldn't have been a fair fight had Kellan been at full strength, but the Dark magic was taking a toll.

There was a loud roar that Kellan recognized as Thorn. The next instant, Thorn stalked into the shop naked and furious and grabbed the first Dark he saw, ripping his heart out without so much as a glance.

Thorn was looking around the shop as if searching for someone.

Kellan elbowed the Dark he was fighting in the throat and snapped his neck. The rest of the Dark vanished from the store in the next second.

Thorn stood in the middle of the shop shaking his head. "Nay. Lexi was safe here."

Arian's chest heaved, anger contorting his face. His champagne-colored eyes blazed with unadulterated fury. "I tried to reach them, but they teleported out before I could."

There was murder in Thorn's dark eyes. "They attacked the cities to take us away from Dreagan."

"Aye," Kellan said. "But why just the distillery? I thought they'd go after the weapon again."

"More Dark coming your way!" Dmitri shouted.

Kellan, Thorn, and Arian ran out of the shop and shifted into dragons. Kellan remained near Shara while Thorn and Arian flew to the skies and took their assault from above.

Rhi stood in the middle of the parking lot with her

sword raised, ready as Dark ran at her. A moment later and Fallon deposited Malcolm in the middle of the fray before teleporting away again.

"No' fair to start the action without me," Malcolm said. His skin turned maroon as he released his god and raised a hand to the sky as lightning forked from his fingers, sending bolts in every direction.

The sound covered the roars of the dragons, and the display would keep any humans from venturing out into the storm.

Kellan turned and beheaded a Dark with his wing who had been going after Malcolm. The rain continued to come in a downpour.

Thorn roared and dove right at the group of oncoming Dark. He flattened dozens of them before others began to hurl magic at him.

He was trying to fly back up to the sky when a huge bubble of magic hit him, instantly shifting him back into his human form.

Kellan took out the Dark responsible. Another flood of Dark Fae came at them, swarming the parking lot like ants.

"Kellan!" Rhi shouted from his left.

She was pointing to the ground where Thorn lay unmoving after hitting the ground hard. After what had happened with Rhys where dragon magic was mixed with Dark that nearly killed him, Kellan refused to take any chances. He stood over Thorn so no Dark could get to him.

Rhi was doing major damage to the Dark with her sword and quick movements while Shara used her Fae magic. Roars from Arian sounded around them as he continued to swoop down from the sky raining dragon fire on them. There were sudden shouts and war cries as more Warriors arrived.

"Another attack at the north border!" Roman said.

* * *

Lexi was meditating on Thorn. He was the only thing keeping her from begging someone to ease the desire building just as Taraeth had promised she would.

Someone said her name. She ignored it. She couldn't lose concentration. A hand connected with her face sharply, sending pain radiating through her.

"Are you sure?" asked a male voice.

Lexi moaned at the need clawing at her. She would not give in. She would *not* give in.

"I'm sure," Taraeth said.

Balladyn said, "She could've been speaking the truth. If she was a mate, she would've known to wait for the Kings to rescue her."

Lexi lifted her head and opened her eyes. She was in an office or library. It was obviously a place of someone with money, based on the furnishings and the opulence of the room itself along with all the books.

"Why bring her to me?"

Lexi focused on the man who spoke. He had black hair kept long and gold eyes. And he was strikingly handsome.

"A present," Taraeth said. He motioned to Lexi. "I already have her prepared for you. She'll remain in that state for several days no matter how many times you take her."

Lexi lifted her chin and looked back at the men staring at her. She glowered at them. "Cowards. You're all cowards."

CHAPTER
THIRTY-SEVEN

Thorn jerked awake and jumped to his feet. He blinked, recognizing he was deep in the mountain behind the manor. His head swiveled to the left where he heard a noise and spotted Kellan.

"What a clusterfuck of a night," Kellan murmured from his spot on a rock.

"Where is Lexi?"

Kellan rose from the seat wearing nothing but jeans. "How do you feel? We didna find any injuries, but I wanted to make sure you were no' hit with dragon magic."

Thorn shook his head. "I'm fine. Where is Lexi?"

"It's been a hell of a night." Kellan ran a hand down his face. "Con and Darius are still in Edinburgh trying to contain the city. They've pushed the Dark back and should be here soon. As should the others around the U.K."

Thorn fisted his hands at his sides. "Where. Is. Lexi?"

Kellan glanced away, and it was all the confirmation Thorn needed to know why his gut was tied in knots. A breath rushed from him in a puff.

"Dreagan was supposed to be safe. She was supposed to be safe," Thorn said more to himself than Kellan.

Kellan walked to him and put a hand on his shoulder and squeezed. "I didna know she was here. None of us did."

"Tell me everything." A mixture of ire and anxiety settled like a stone in his stomach.

Kellan dropped his hand. "I wasna there. A few of the mates were. Get dressed. They're waiting to talk to you."

Thorn didn't move for long seconds after Kellan walked away. Then he stormed out of the cavern to the stash of jeans. He jammed his legs in them and fastened them as he strode barefoot and shirtless down the corridor that led to the manor.

As he reached the door from the mountain into the manor, Thorn could hear voices coming from within. He opened the door and stepped inside the manor.

He followed the voices to the front room. As soon as they saw him, the conversation stopped. Thorn was hanging on by a thread. If Lexi was dead, he knew he wouldn't be able to handle it. Why was it everyone he gave his protection to died viciously?

He had known to stay away from Lexi, to let Darius protect her. And yet he had stepped in. For what? To get close to her and have her ripped from his arms?

Shara rose from a chair by the fireplace. Her face was smudged with dirt and her shirt and pants had burn holes in them from the blasts of magic. Her silver gaze met his. "She's strong, Thorn."

Those words hit him in the chest like a wrecking ball. He briefly closed his eyes and took in a steadying breath. "What happened?"

"We didn't know who she was," Cassie said fretfully.

Jane was holding her hand palm up in her lap so that the lacerations on it didn't touch anything. "It all happened so fast."

Kellan leaned a hand against the mantel. "Just tell him."

"We knew Dark were on the border," Shara said. "We were trying to get the last tour out so we could close up and get to the manor. The rain kept the tourists in the shop long after we should've closed."

Cassie rubbed her hands up and down her arms. "I saw the Dark coming. I shouted a warning of danger, but all it did was stop everyone in their tracks. They wouldn't move. They were like deer staring into headlights."

Jane nodded her head, looking down at her lap.

"They busted in. Cassie tried to get out without them seeing her to alert someone, but they came in the back as well. We huddled with the tourists in the hopes that they wouldn't recognize us," Shara explained. "They began to kill humans when a Dark walked in with Lexi."

Cassie licked her lips. "The Dark recognized her. He said he had killed her friend."

Thorn clenched his teeth. The bastard Lexi had been looking for accidentally found her. What were the odds?

"They wanted to know which one of you she was mated to." Shara's smile was sad. "She made up a story about following you and Darius and overhearing you talk of the Dark."

Thorn closed his eyes as he dropped his chin to his chest. "She had to deal with them alone."

"She held her own," Cassie said. "It was impressive. I don't think I could have."

Kellan blew out a breath. "When did Taraeth get here?"

"While the Dark questioned her," Shara said.

Thorn lifted his head and looked at the Fae. "Did he know she lied?"

"He suspected. She was convincing though." Shara tossed back a drink of whisky and took a deep breath. "She tried to tell them that she ran from the city after seeing all the Dark and cut across country."

Kellan's lips twisted. "Let me guess, Taraeth didna believe it was a coincidence she ended up on Dreagan."

Shara slowly shook her head. "More than anything, it was the fact she didn't throw herself at him." Shara's silver eyes slid to Thorn. "He . . . he forced desire on her."

Thorn let out a growl. He turned and swiped everything off the table near him, but it did nothing to ease the turmoil within him.

"He didn't have his way with her," Shara hurried to say. "He had Balladyn bring her."

Kellan said, "That's when I came in and stopped them from taking Shara."

Taking one mate was bad enough, but if the Dark had gotten their hands on two of them?

Thorn frowned as he glanced from Shara to Cassie to Jane. "Did he no' realize Cassie and Jane were immune to the Dark as well?"

Kellan shrugged and they looked to the women for an answer.

"They didn't pay us much attention," Shara said.

Cassie nodded in agreement. "They were focused on Lexi."

Thorn turned his head to Kellan. "They could've walked out of here with four mates. Why did they no' search the group of humans for the mates?"

"A verra good question," Kellan stated. "It doesna make sense."

"Nothing about any of this has. They've been walking the streets of the cities for days. They kill at will, with everything building up to this night. Then they attack here, but doona try to take one of us or more mates."

Shara crossed her arms over her stomach. "Lexi was a surprise for them. They didn't come for her."

"So why did they come?" Kellan asked.

Thorn slashed a hand through the air. "We'll figure that out soon enough. I have to find Lexi."

"I'm not sure you should try," Shara said in a soft voice.

Thorn pinned her with a look. "Would you expect Kiril no' to look for you? Would Kellan let the Dark have Denae again?"

"Nay," Kellan said. "I'd walk through that place every day for eternity for my woman."

Shara bowed her head. "Thorn, you need to be prepared for what you find. *If* you find her."

"I'm going to find her." He had no other choice.

Kellan squeezed the bridge of his nose with this thumb and forefinger. "This is what the Dark wanted. We're divided. Scattered."

"The best thing Con can do is bring everyone back to Dreagan."

Kellan's head snapped up. "And leave the cities?"

"Darius and I were there for weeks. Do you have any idea how many Dark we killed daily? It didna matter. The Dark kept coming. There's only one way to fight them to make an impact, and if we can no' do that, then why spread us so thin?"

Kellan stared at him for a long silent moment. "And you?"

"I'm going after Lexi."

Kellan's forehead puckered in a frown. "Alone?"

"Alone," Thorn said with a nod.

Shara gaped at him. "You can't be serious. First, you don't know where to go."

"That's where you come in," he told the Fae. "Tell me where Taraeth would take her."

Kellan shook his head. "I understand wanting to go after Lexi, but you can no' go alone. I was there with Rhi and Phelan as we got Denae out, and it still wasna enough."

"I go in alone," Thorn repeated. He looked at Shara then. "You can help by telling me where to go. If you doona want to, it willna change my mind about going."

Shara sank back down in the chair and numbly nodded. "All right."

Thorn glanced at Jane who was still staring at the floor while Cassie watched him. He gave a nod to Kellan and turned around.

He drew up short when he saw Con. Thorn had no idea how long the King of Kings had been standing there, and it didn't matter.

"We have a mess," Con said.

Thorn looked into his black eyes trying to figure out what Con was thinking, but as usual, Thorn came up empty. "On several levels."

"Your thoughts?"

Since when did Con care what he thought was going on? Thorn eyed Con warily. "It was all a setup for something. The weapon, perhaps."

Con shook his head. "They didna cross any of our borders except at the distillery. It's our weakest point to allow the tourists to visit."

"Why just the distillery?" Kellan asked. "They didna take anything. I think they would've left empty-handed except they found Lexi."

A burning need to kill Dark filled Thorn every time someone mentioned Lexi being taken. He was in control now, but once he found the Dark, Thorn was going to rain down hell upon them.

"And the cities," Thorn said. "They wanted us away from Dreagan."

Con nodded as he crossed his arms over his chest. "Why take us away if they were no' going to try to get on Dreagan again?"

"I think I know the answer to that," Ryder said as he walked down the stairs and came to stand in the foyer. His face was grim. "It's bad."

Con raised a blond brow. "Well? What is it?"

Ryder looked at each of them and ran a hand down his face. "You're right. It was all staged. Every last minute of it. It's a good thing I got in from Glasgow last night so I could contain this now."

"Just tell us," Thorn said in a low voice.

Ryder looked like he was about to be sick. "There was someone on the hill above the distillery. They filmed it all."

There was utter silence for a full minute as each of them took in what this meant for Dreagan and their way of life.

"How much did it show?" Con asked in a soft voice.

Ryder scrunched up his face in regret. "All of it. It shows Kellan and Arian flying as well as both shifting to human form. It also shows Thorn arriving and all the way to the Dark hitting Thorn with magic so that he shifted to human form and fell from the sky. It shows the Warriors, as well as Malcolm's use of lightning."

"Oh my God," Cassie murmured.

"The video has gone viral, Con," Ryder said with a shake of his head. "It's everywhere."

Thorn couldn't believe millions of years of secrets had gone up in smoke in one night. The last time Thorn felt this powerless was when they had to send their dragons away.

Con turned on his heel and walked upstairs without a word.

CHAPTER
THIRTY-EIGHT

Balladyn walked through the Fae doorway with Taraeth back to the palace. The night had gone exactly as they had planned. Why then did he have a feeling something was about to go awry?

"The Kings have thwarted us for so long," Taraeth said with a smile as they walked to his chamber. "It feels good to have a win."

"Shara got away."

Taraeth shrugged. "It doesn't matter. Soon, she'll be on her knees before me begging for forgiveness. I won't give it to her, but I'll enjoy allowing her to think that I will."

"Nothing kills quite so deeply as smashing someone's hope," Balladyn said with a grin.

Taraeth entered the king's chamber and faced Balladyn. "The Kings won't know which way is up by the time it all comes crashing down around them."

"We still haven't found the weapon."

"All in due time," Taraeth said. "Mikkel is confident he can get Ulrik to hand it over."

Balladyn wasn't so sure. "It's a dangerous game to work with both of them, sire."

"I've been doing it for centuries." Taraeth reclined on his throne. "Ulrik knows what I'm doing. Mikkel does not."

"You trust Ulrik more?"

Taraeth laughed. "Absolutely not. Ulrik is smarter, though. He sees things Mikkel does not. Whoever wins between those two will give me the weapon."

"To use against them?"

Taraeth's red eyes hardened. "You don't think I can make them hand it over?"

Balladyn bowed his head in a show of meekness that wouldn't last much longer. "I think they'll say whatever they need to in order to have the Dark army aid them."

"Ulrik hasn't asked for my army."

Now that Balladyn hadn't known. "Why not?"

"Ulrik intends to take Con down himself. Mikkel thinks he can do it without Ulrik, but that won't be possible. The only one who can take down Con is Ulrik."

Balladyn clasped his hands behind his back. "The odds of Ulrik beating Con and handing everything over to Mikkel are nonexistent."

"Exactly." Taraeth grinned. "Mikkel has made some brash moves that might get him the seat of power, but Ulrik is a wild card. He has a need for revenge that goes even deeper than mine. A man with that kind of demand is rarely foiled."

"Ulrik won't give you the sole weapon that is able to destroy the Dragon Kings," Balladyn said.

Taraeth shrugged. "Ulrik hates the humans. They're the ones who betrayed him and made him lose everything. Do you really think we're going to need to destroy the Kings with Ulrik in charge?"

"You believe he'll let us have the humans?"

"I know," Taraeth said as he leaned forward. "He wants

the humans gone so he can bring back the dragons. We'll be able to gorge ourselves on the mortals."

Balladyn smiled and nodded. "A fine plan indeed. You surprised me, though. Why leave the mortal with Mikkel? If she is a mate, her King will come looking for her."

"He can try." Taraeth leaned back. "The Kings don't know of Mikkel. They still think it's all Ulrik. I'll have them chasing their tails on so many levels that they won't know who to trust or what step to take next. And if they do find her, it'll be Mikkel's problem. Now, go. I wish to be alone."

Balladyn turned and walked out of the chamber. As soon as the doors closed behind him, he found a Fae doorway and went to the desert.

"Rhi," he called.

A moment later, she stepped through the doorway with sword in hand. Rhi was always beautiful, but she never looked more magnificent or fierce than when she was in the middle of battle.

Even dirty and wounded like she was now, he wanted to rip off her clothes and sink within her.

"I hear you were at Dreagan."

There was something in her soft, serene voice that set off warning bells. "Taraeth ordered me with him."

"You knew all of this was going down. Why didn't you tell me?"

Balladyn couldn't determine if she was angry or not. "You're not Dark, pet. I can't tell you anything."

She walked to him until she stood before him. "Is that so?"

"I smelled you on her," Balladyn said.

It was the wrong thing to say. Rhi's eyes flashed in anger. "I saved her and brought her to Dreagan, promising that she would be safe."

"You shouldn't promise such things." Balladyn tried to reach out and touch her, but she stepped away. He held out his hands and spoke in a low voice, "Easy."

"Did you call me here to rub it in my face that you took someone I helped?" she demanded, her grip tightening on the hilt of her sword.

Balladyn glanced down at her sword. She was quick enough that she could get the blade up and in the neck of an unsuspecting Dark. But Balladyn had helped train her. He knew her tricks. Or most of them.

"I called you because I have the information you seek on the Reapers."

Rhi's head whipped to the side as she stared at a sand dune.

Balladyn followed her gaze but saw nothing. "Rhi?"

"Tell me," she demanded without looking at him.

"It took some digging, as well as piecing things together to find the original story, but I learned the truth."

"How do you know it's original?" she asked, still staring at the dune.

Balladyn rubbed his jaw. "There was a hidden number sequence in the texts. If someone didn't know what they were looking for, they could easily think there was a mistake in the book."

"Go on."

"I found all but one of the pieces. I've exhausted all of my books. The final piece must be hidden somewhere."

She swiveled her head back to him with a frown. "I know the library you had at the queen's court."

"What I have now is three times that size. I have a copy of every book there is. I've looked through each of them twice. Someone has hidden the last piece of this puzzle."

Rhi lifted her chin. "Tell me what you do know."

"The Reapers are real. They are a group of Fae with immense power."

"How much power?"

"More than Usaeil and Taraeth combined. More than even you, I think."

A small pucker formed in her forehead. "What is their purpose?"

"They are judge, jury, and executioner."

"Why can't we see them?"

Balladyn shrugged. "It didn't say. There was a warning that they are not to be messed with. If they come after a Fae, it's over."

"Why haven't they come for Taraeth? Or you?" she asked with a smirk.

Balladyn would never let her know just how much her words hurt him. She had held his heart for so long, and she hadn't even known it. Nor did she realize he would do anything for her.

"You'll have to ask them," Balladyn said.

Her sneer faded. "Why do they come for us?"

"Something about the law and balance. It was in the old language, Rhi, and some of the lines were so faded I couldn't make them out. If people are whispering about Reapers, it's because they're back."

"Back? Where have they been?"

"I don't know or care."

She shifted feet and glanced at the sand dune. "Do they follow us? Can they remain veiled indefinitely?"

Balladyn looked at the sand dune and then back at Rhi. "It didn't say. You think someone is following you?"

"Yes. They have been for some time. I thought it was you."

"I can't stay veiled that long. When did it begin?"

She looked away from his gaze. "A few weeks. Whoever it is can track me anywhere."

"Are they here now?"

She looked up into his face, a frown of worry lining her face. "Yes."

"Have you spoken to them?"

"I tried." Rhi swallowed and gave a little shake of her head. "They won't show themselves or tell me what they want. My every action is being watched."

Worry, heavy and copious, swarmed him. "Has anything drastic happened lately?"

She gave him a dark look. "You mean like a trusted friend who I thought was dead but was actually turned Dark who kidnapped and tortured me while making me wear the Chains of Mordare? Is that the kind of drastic you were referring to?"

"Yes. You also left out how you shattered the chains and escaped, leveling my compound. Your power has increased, pet."

"And I have you to thank for that?"

Balladyn snorted in laughter. "Me? It was always within you. You held it back. I just helped you free it."

She took a step away from him, as if she thought he might try to take her again. Balladyn wanted her, but it wouldn't be by force. She would come willingly to his bed. No matter how long it took, he would woo her.

"Anything else?" he asked. He always held out hope that she would sever ties with the Dragon Kings, but it was a long shot.

When she quickly looked away, his smile died. Something had happened. "What is it? What happened?"

"I quit the Queen's Guard."

Balladyn was too shocked to speak. From the day both he and her brother, Rolmir, were chosen for the Queen's Guard, Rhi had worked to achieve the same status.

"Why?" was all he could get out.

Rhi threw up her hands, the point of her sword landing

in the sand when her arms fell back by her sides. "I don't know. It's just a feeling that Usaeil is failing the Light. She's more concerned with her career in the human world instead of seeing what is happening with what you're doing to the Kings."

Balladyn knew Rhi considered him her enemy. But he had never hungered to taste the enemy's kisses before now. Nor had he ever cared for one so much.

In his mind, Rhi was as far from his enemy as possible. She couldn't see that yet, but the fact she was talking to him as they once did before he was Dark was a start.

"There's something else," he guessed after seeing her loathing every time she spoke of the queen.

Rhi hesitated. She looked hurt and vulnerable in that moment, and Balladyn wanted to kill whoever had put her in such a position.

He closed the distance between them and gently put his hands on her arms. Balladyn was surprised she let him near. She had been so skittish since her arrival.

"Rhi," he said softly.

Her silver eyes lifted to his. "I believe the queen is having an affair with a King."

No other words were needed. Now Balladyn knew why Rhi left the queen. After the turmoil Usaeil had put Rhi through for her affair, it was completely wrong for Usaeil to go down that same road.

And it made Balladyn want to kill the queen for it.

CHAPTER
THIRTY-NINE

Lexi opened her eyes, her brain foggy. She blinked several times and looked around the room again, noticing more. It was large, spacious, and too lavish for her tastes.

Whoever lived here had money. And they wanted to make sure everyone knew it.

It was still dark outside. She brought her hand to her head. It ached terribly. What she wouldn't give for an aspirin.

"Finally awake, I see," said a male voice laced with humor in a refined British accent.

Lexi stiffened and tightened her hands on the blanket. She sat up, the leather couch creaking as she made sure she was covered. Flames danced in the fireplace as a man in a dark suit sat in the leather chair opposite her. He had a glass of liquor in one hand that rested on the arm of the chair. She looked into his face that appeared red and gold from the firelight to find him watching her.

She swallowed, remembering how someone had held her as they poured much of it down her throat. There had to have been something else in it because she had passed out.

Whatever they did, it stopped what Taraeth had been doing to her. Lexi almost thanked them. But this man couldn't be a friend of the Kings if he knew Taraeth well enough to have been brought a "present."

"I hear you have spirit. Did you use it all on Taraeth and his men?" the man asked with a chuckle.

Lexi sat back on the couch. "Will you let me go?"

"Heavens, no," he said. "Why would I do that?"

"Because I'm no one's property."

He leaned forward and smiled like a wolf about to devour a lamb. His gold eyes crinkled in the corners, as if he had been waiting for her to say just those words. "Oh, but you are now. Taraeth took you. The Dark don't easily hand such a prize over. Especially not with a mate of a Dragon King."

"As I told Taraeth, I have no idea what you're talking about, Dragon King." She snorted and rolled her eyes. "There's no such thing as dragons. Now, Fae? Obviously that's a different kettle of fish altogether."

He cocked his head to the side. "How do you know of the Fae?"

"They killed my friend." Lexi shrugged. The act had nearly gotten her free the first time and might work now. "I wanted revenge."

"Revenge, hmm?" He sat back in the chair and regarded her. "We know something about that, don't we?"

"Aye."

Lexi's gaze jerked to a dark place over her host's left shoulder. Someone was there and she hadn't even known it. She searched the shadows, but she couldn't make out anything about the man.

The man before her motioned with his hand with the drink in it. "Please. Go on. I'm dying to hear the rest."

Lexi pulled her gaze away from the shadow. "I saw two men fighting the Red Eyes. That's what I called them before I knew. These two men were killing the Dark, so I started following them as well."

"And they didna know it?" asked the shadow.

Lexi shook her head. "No. I did that for several days before I overheard them talking about the Fae and how this was a second war with them. The men seemed confident of winning."

"I bet they did," the man in the chair said with an evil smile.

"After that, I noticed that more and more Dark were popping up all over the place. I missed my flight back to the States, and the roads were clogged with cars. So I ran out of the city. I kept off the roads and stuck to going across country."

"Where were you headed?" the man asked.

Lexi lifted one shoulder in a half-shrug. "Anywhere that was away from Edinburgh. I thought if I could get somewhere safe I could call the authorities. Then I got caught in the rain."

"And you just happened to be on Dreagan?" he asked with brows raised, his starkly handsome face half lit by the fire.

It was really sad to see someone so good-looking be wicked. He might not have hurt her, but she could see it in his eyes. The man was malicious. He delighted in crushing the weak, savored in defeating the vulnerable.

"I had no map. I ran as far as I could, then I walked and ran some more." It was time to sprinkle in some truth, Lexi decided. "I saw firsthand what the Dark could do. I wanted no part in it. As for where I ended up, I was thankful someone found me and gave me a place to get out of the rain."

She looked down at the blanket around her. "As you can see, I removed my clothes to dry. The man gave me a blanket to warm up with."

"Oh, that I know to be true."

Now that confused Lexi. How would he know one thing but not others? Nothing about this entire experience made sense.

"The Dark found me and asked me the same questions you have," she finished.

The man smiled as he lifted the glass to his wide lips and took a drink. She noticed the hint of gray at his temples. "That is an amazing tale. You're going to stick with the story that you're not a mate to a Dragon King, I suppose."

"Dragons don't exist."

The shadow snorted. "And Fae doona either."

Lexi wasn't sure what to do or say. She was backed into a corner now, and there was nowhere for her to go.

The man rose from his seat and walked to a desk. He grabbed an open laptop and set it on the large wooden coffee table in front of her. He turned it toward her and motioned with his head. "Watch it."

Intrigued, Lexi scooted to the edge of the sofa. She poked an arm out of the blanket and hit play on the video that was on the screen.

Shock reverberated through her as she saw dragons flying and shifting into men before shifting back again. Her mouth fell open when she saw the claret dragon.

Thorn.

He shifted and ran into the shop where she had been. Lexi put a hand over her mouth. He had come for her. She hadn't expected him to, but he had come.

When the video ended, Lexi raised her gaze to the man who stood watching her as she dropped her arm to her lap. It was time for another Oscar performance. "I'm supposed to believe that is real?"

"You should," he said. "It's Dreagan. You were taken from that very spot."

"Whoever did this is very good with computer graphics. It looks almost real."

The man smiled and glanced at the shadow. "It's very real."

Lexi looked down at the screen that showed a picture of Thorn in dragon form. His mouth was open, and she could imagine his deafening roar.

She had seen him before, but now she got an uninterrupted view of his deep wine scales. There were short brow horns and another horn atop his nose. His tail was equipped with a stinger on the end that looked like a scorpion tail.

The sheer size of him was awesome and frightening. She had seen him up close, looked into his teal dragon eyes. Lexi was taken aback. How had she not remembered the color of his eyes in dragon form before?

She tore her gaze away from the screen. "What are you going to do with me?"

"Your Dragon King will be looking for you. He'll search the world over, but he'll never find you." The man chuckled and lifted the glass to his lips again. "I find that infinitely humorous."

"How many times do I need to tell you? I don't have a Dragon King. This video proves nothing. Things like this are faked all the time."

The man took a drink. "To him, you'll have just disappeared. I think it'll be fun to make him think you betrayed him."

Like what happened with Ulrik. Lexi looked at him with new eyes. Was she sitting before the banished Dragon King?

"You're going to keep me prisoner here?" she asked, appalled.

He nodded and sat down as he set aside his empty glass. "Yes, I am. You're lucky that I have a lover at the moment. I'm sure there will come a time when I'll take you. And I'll warn you, mortal, I like it rough."

"You have no right to keep me here."

He stood up in a rush. "I have every right!"

His face was contorted red with rage. He slowly un-clenched his hands and adjusted his suit jacket before he buttoned one button.

"You should kill me now," she said.

He paused as he began to walk off. His gaze was curi-ous as he looked back at her. "Why?"

"Because there will come a time when you have your guard down. That's when I'll kill you."

"Good luck with that." He walked around the coffee ta-ble and leaned down so that his face was inches from hers. "You see, I can't die. Nothing you can do to me will kill me."

"Everything can be killed."

Everything but a Dragon King. Lexi had her confirma-tion. This had to be Ulrik.

She got to her feet as he straightened and walked away. "I have friends and family who will search for me," she hollered after him as he walked from the room.

A thick arm came around her, pinning her back against a hard chest. In her anger she had forgotten the man in the shadows.

"There's no use in yelling," he said.

Lexi shook her head. "He can't do this. This can't be happening."

"You're a mate." His voice was flat, devoid of emotion. "It was a nice try lying, but I saw your face in the video. You recognized one of them. He thought it was shock. But I saw the truth."

Lexi wanted to cry she was so frustrated. How could everything be going so wrong? Thorn had warned her. He'd told her to get away, but she had fought the memory wipe. And look where she ended up.

"Who is it?" the shadow asked.

Lexi lifted her chin, refusing to speak.

"There are only a few dragons shown. One I know is already mated. It's easy to narrow it down. If I send word to the others that we have you, which one will come? Because he will. Nothing will be able to stop him."

Lexi closed her eyes. She wanted to stop his words, to block them out. Yet they had already been heard and lodged in her brain.

"Do you really want to know what we'll do with him?" the shadow asked. "It willna be pretty. You know he can no' be killed except by another Dragon King. But you already knew that, did you no'?"

"I don't know what you mean."

The words were there, but they didn't carry the conviction she'd hoped to convey. She had no control over her fear for herself and Thorn.

"You do," the shadow said. "We're no' the only ones who would be delighted to have a Dragon King. The Dark want another. They have a way of torturing the Kings until they lose their minds. The Kings go utterly mad. That's when the Dark release them and these demented Kings begin killing other Kings."

"Why are you doing this?" she demanded as she opened her eyes, turning her head to try and see him. All she saw was long black hair.

He leaned his mouth next to her ear. "Revenge."

"Please release me. I just want to go home."

"You should've run faster, Lexi. You should've stayed far away from the Dark. But most of all, you should never have fallen for your Dragon King. It'll only bring you misery and death. Humans and Kings were never meant to mix."

CHAPTER
FORTY

"Rhi!" Thorn shouted as he stood outside of the manor.

She was his only chance for getting to Taraeth's palace. Since only the Fae could see the doorways, he had to have her.

"You've been calling to her for half an hour," Kellan said as he walked up to stand against the fence. "She's no' coming."

"She has to." Thorn gripped the fence tightly.

They stood shoulder to shoulder in the night. "Perhaps you might want to think about what Shara said."

"Would you give up on Denae?" Thorn demanded as he jerked his head to Kellan.

Kellan looked down at the ground for a moment. "You know I wouldna. Thorn, are you sure she's your mate?"

"Aye, though I doona know if she'll have me. That matters no'. I gave her my protection. I promised her that she would be safe with me."

Kellan nodded slowly. "She was smart to try and make them believe it was by coincidence that she was here. It might work. If they doona think she's a mate, then there's a chance they willna take her quickly."

The thick board snapped in Thorn's hold as he imagined Taraeth—or any Dark—touching Lexi.

"If Rhi willna come, there's another way," Kellan said. He looked over his shoulder to where Fallon stood leaning against the side of the manor.

The tightening around Thorn's chest eased a fraction. "Of course. Phelan."

They were walking to Fallon when Rhi appeared in front of them. She put her hand on Thorn's chest to halt him, her silver eyes flashing dangerously.

"You'll leave Phelan out of this. The Dark don't know he's half-Fae, and it's going to remain that way," she said in a voice thick with anger.

Thorn gently took her hand and removed it from his chest. "I must find Lexi."

The Light Fae swallowed, a frown marking her brow. "I can find out where she's being held."

Thorn wasn't a fool. There was some kind of price involved. "How much is this going to cost you?"

"I can handle it."

Thorn grabbed her arm and looked into her eyes. "Nay. Just lead me to the doorway. I'll find Lexi."

Rhi smiled sadly. "You could be searching Taraeth's palace for weeks and never find her. Not to mention the Dark guarding the doorways. You would do Lexi no good if they capture you."

"Rhi, you doona understand. I—"

"I do," she interrupted him. "I understand perfectly. They took Lexi on the off chance she was a mate. They're planning on you coming for her."

"It's a trap," Kellan said.

Rhi glanced at him and nodded. "We've been lucky in getting Kellan, Tristan, and Kiril out of the Darks' grasp. Do you really want to attempt a fourth try?"

"I doona know what to do. I just need her back." Thorn released Rhi and turned away. He stared up at the sky.

Things used to be simple. All he'd cared about was keeping his Clarets in line and spending as much time as he could in the sky. There was nothing as wonderful as feeling the sun on his scales as he soared.

"I'll find where she's being kept," Rhi promised.

He didn't need to look behind him to know she was gone. Thorn didn't like putting Rhi in that position, but he had to get to Lexi.

Once Lexi was back in his arms Thorn would help Rhi with whatever she needed.

Rhi returned to the desert and whispered Balladyn's name. She stood with her back to the Fae doorway, unsure how she felt about talking to Balladyn again so soon after their last encounter.

"Rhi."

Her name was a caress falling from his lips. She closed her eyes, a mixture of feelings she was unsure of swirling through her as rapidly as a tornado.

It had been so long since anyone looked at her like Balladyn did. He didn't try to hide his craving. It was the love she still held for her King that kept her from him.

But Balladyn was whittling away at the wall around her heart.

He came up behind her and moved her hair over one shoulder. Her flesh tingled at his soft touch. Then his breath brushed against her bare neck.

How wonderful it would be to lean back against him, to lay her head upon his shoulder and feel his arms around her. She was a Fae who longed to be loved and held.

A woman who hungered to be needed.

To be desired.

His hands came to rest on her arms, caressing down to her hands. Her senses were in a riot as he leaned his head against hers.

She shivered when his lips brushed against her ear. A rush of breath fell from her mouth. No one had touched her as tenderly since . . . since her King.

It had been eons of time. She needed to be touched, to be reminded that she was a woman. The temptation to give herself to Balladyn was so strong. To have someone caress her body and bring her release was as enticing as Balladyn's seduction.

He placed a kiss against the side of her neck just beneath and behind her ear. "I dream of you," he whispered. "Every night I dream of us together."

This had to stop. She couldn't let him go on. Because if she did . . . she would give in.

If she let him take her, Balladyn would never be satisfied with just one night. He wanted it all.

She wanted . . . Rhi didn't know what she wanted anymore. The longer Balladyn touched her, the more clouded her thoughts became.

Rhi stepped away and turned to look at him. His red eyes blazed with desire, a need so deep and palpable that it made it difficult for her to breathe.

One side of his mouth lifted in a satisfied smile. "You're not immune to me then. Why fight this? You know we would be amazing together."

"Stop," she said and closed her eyes as she turned her head away.

"You called me, pet. You let me touch you. I can sense the need within you. Let me ease your body."

She shook her head. "Balladyn. Please."

If he pushed, she would give in. She was that close to the edge. Her loneliness and solitude had gone on too long.

All these centuries she shunned everyone as she waited for her King.

And what had it gotten her?

Heartache. Despair.

Hopelessness.

"What is it, Rhi?" Balladyn pressed in a voice filled with tenderness and tinged with worry.

She nearly broke down in tears when his seductive voice was gone. The kindness she heard meant that he saw how she teetered, but he didn't take advantage. It was the perfect opportunity for him. Why didn't he swoop in for the kill?

Rhi looked at him in confusion.

Balladyn took a step to her and touched her cheek. "I want you with a desperation that saps my very breath. I've waited thousands of years for us to be together. I want you to come to *me*, sweet Rhi. It's your decision." He wiped at the corner of her eye and the tear that gathered. "No more tears. Tell me why you called me."

Ever since Balladyn had told her he loved her, she wondered how she had ever missed it. It was there in every action, every look. Every word.

No wonder he had hated her so fiercely when he turned Dark. That love turned to hate, and somehow, back to love again.

If she continued to think about Balladyn and his claim of love, she would forget why she called him. Rhi pushed aside her tumultuous feelings and focused on the task at hand.

"You said you would do anything to have me, right?" Rhi asked. If she was going to get her answers, she had to use his feelings against him.

Balladyn lowered his hand to his side. "I would."

"What if I was taken by someone?"

His face went hard, rage barely leashed shone in his eyes. "Are you talking about the Reapers?"

"What if I was? Would you come after me?"

"Nothing would stop me from finding you," he stated angrily.

She glanced at the ground, feeling her follower's eyes on her again. Was he enjoying all that he saw? "Then you can understand what a King is going through looking for Lexi."

Balladyn blinked, his face going blank in a heartbeat. He took a step back as he looked at her in confusion. "You want me to betray my king?"

"I want you to help me," she implored. "You were at Dreagan. I was told you carried Lexi out. You know where she is."

For long moments, Balladyn stood staring at her. Finally, he released a breath. "It's a place a King would never expect to look."

Rhi felt the tension ease from her shoulders. "I should've known Taraeth wouldn't bring her to his palace. It's too obvious."

"Why do you continue to help the Kings, pet?"

She shrugged, wondering why there was no heat in his words. Rhi knew how deep his hatred of them went. "Probably the same reason I know I can come to you for help."

"I'm Dark, pet. Or have you forgotten?"

Rhi looked into the face that had been a major part of her life. She walked to him and rested her hand on his cheek as she met his gaze. It wasn't hard to look past the red eyes and remember the Fae who had stood by her side for so many years.

She needed to remember the monster he had become in order to keep from throwing her arms around him. "How can I ever forget? You tortured me. You tried to take my Light."

"Is this why you let me touch you? You were using me to get information?" he asked furiously.

Rhi dropped her hand and shook her head as she turned away. She took a few steps and stopped, wrapping her arms around herself. "No. I intended to ask you first thing, but then . . . you touched me."

"I can't tell you where the mortal is being held. Even if I wanted to."

"I know." It had been a long shot, but she thought maybe Balladyn could help.

"Taraeth would know it was me. We're the only two who went there. He'd kill me."

Rhi nodded. "I understand. There's someone else I can ask who will find her."

Balladyn was suddenly in front of her. His grip was tight on her upper arms as he looked at her as if he couldn't decide whether to kiss her or strangle her. "You've always twisted me about."

His head lowered and he placed a hard kiss against her lips. He held her there, breathing in deep, before he released her and stepped back.

"The mortal was a gift to a Dragon King," he said. He touched her face with such longing that it took her breath away.

Then he was gone.

Rhi whirled around looking for him. She clutched her stomach, more confused than ever before. He had given her the information, but she wouldn't allow him to die because of it.

She teleported back to Dreagan Manor and appeared in the foyer where Fallon was talking to Larena. When the leader of the Warriors noticed her, Rhi said, "I need Broc."

Without a word, Fallon was gone. Rhi looked up as she heard a crash above her. She took a moment and glanced around the manor. It was quiet, as if everyone was afraid to breathe. The tension in the manor was off the charts.

Rhi walked toward the kitchen and peeked inside to see the females sitting around the table talking in whispers. The strain on their faces spoke volumes.

She veiled herself and teleported to Con's office. He stood staring out the windows appearing as calm as he usually did. His office, on the other hand, was a different matter entirely.

The crash she heard was him. Papers littered the floor. His sword lay on his desk after he'd cleaved a chair in two. The crystal decanter and glasses were shattered.

"I know you're here," he said.

Rhi unveiled herself. The sarcastic remark she had been about to make died on her tongue. "What happened?"

"You must be the only one who hasna seen it."

"Seen what?"

Con pointed to the laptop on its side on the floor without turning around. Rhi picked it up and set it on his desk. She saw a video filling the entire screen.

"Play it," he urged.

Rhi hit the play button. In moments, she saw Kellan flying around Dreagan. It just got worse from there as she saw herself, Malcolm, Shara, and more Dragon Kings. By the time the video ended, she couldn't find words.

"Everything I've done to protect us erased in a single night." Con's voice held a barely restrained fury. "Every eye in the world is trained on Dreagan now. I had to pull the Kings off patrol because there are planes and helicopters flying over us since our restricted airspace has been revoked."

Rhi closed the laptop softly. So this is what the Dark had been about. "What are you going to do?"

"I've two choices." Con turned to look at her. "We can leave. Or we can fight."

Rhi walked to stand before him and lifted a brow. "Fight. This is your realm."

He studied her a moment, his face giving nothing away. "And the attention on us?"

Rhi rolled her eyes. "Always so dramatic. You might have enemies, King of Kings, but you also have allies. I shouldn't have to remind you to use them. Now, pull your head from between your ass cheeks, and get moving."

She didn't wait for him to speak, but teleported back to the foyer where Fallon waited with Broc.

CHAPTER
FORTY-ONE

Lexi sat on the bed against the headboard with her knees tucked. The room had everything she needed. Except her freedom.

The shadow had brought her up here before giving her a shove inside. Lexi spun around to get a look at his face, but the door closed, lock turning, before she got that chance.

As soon as she spotted the windows, she ran to them and looked down. She was on the third floor. From her view, she could see miles of open land before her. All she had to do was get free.

Lexi prepared to jump from the window. Only when she attempted to open it, it wouldn't budge. She even threw a stool at it in order to break the glass, but the stool didn't put a dent in it. It was the same for the small window in the bathroom.

She was well and truly locked away.

With nothing more to do, Lexi took a long shower. When she got out, there were clothes and a tray of food on the bed.

She briefly thought of refusing the food, but if there was

ever a chance of escape, she was going to need her strength. She devoured everything while she began to plot.

Thorn stood outside the manor and stared at the sky as dawn broke over Dreagan. They were grounded. Every Dragon King was prohibited from shifting and taking to the skies.

It happened once before during the war with the mortals. The Kings had taken to their mountains and slept. All of them except Con. He had remained awake and protected Dreagan.

Of all the Kings, he was the only one who had never slept. Thorn wasn't sure how Con got through the years. Sleeping away centuries was the only way Thorn had been able to deal with everything.

Millions of years later, they were right back in that same scenario. The difference was that this time there were billions of humans, and they had the technology to catch them in dragon form.

Dreagan would be under a microscope as the world waited to see if they were indeed dragons. All they could hope for was that the authorities didn't come onto Dreagan.

MI5 tried it once before and used Denae to do it. At least the Kings would be prepared for it this time. It was easy enough to conceal the caves and anything else they didn't want to be found with their magic.

But for how long would they have to endure being grounded? It would take decades before Dreagan stopped being watched—if they were lucky.

"Thorn," Rhi said.

He turned to find Broc and Fallon following her. Thorn hurried to them, hope springing anew. "Did you find where Lexi is?"

"I did," she said. "Taraeth doesn't have her. None of the Dark do. She was given to a Dragon King as a gift."

Thorn shook his head, unable to believe it. "Ulrik? They gave her to Ulrik?"

"It appears so," Rhi said and turned to Broc. "I hoped I wouldn't have to involve the Warriors, but I've no choice. Can you find Lexi?"

Broc turned his dark gaze to Thorn. "Of course."

Thorn watched as the Warrior closed his eyes and used his power. Broc was able to find anyone, anywhere. As they waited, Thorn slid his gaze to Rhi.

Who had she spoken with to discover that Lexi had been taken to Ulrik? A bad feeling swirled that it was Balladyn. And if Rhi was going to Balladyn, did that mean she had given up on her King? If Balladyn told her Lexi was with Ulrik, why hadn't he also told Rhi exactly where that was?

Rhi felt his stare and turned her head to him. "Don't ask," she said in a low voice. "It doesn't matter who I got the information from."

"It does if it puts you in danger."

"I'm not in any sort," she said. Her gaze skated away as if she were thinking of someone. "They won't hurt me."

Thorn's lips flattened. It was Balladyn. If the Dark managed to get Rhi's affections then it changed everything.

Thorn leaned down and whispered, "Be careful."

"I'm always careful," she said flippantly.

Thorn turned her to face him. He started to warn her against staying away from Balladyn. Then he remembered it was Rhi he was talking to. Nothing could break her love for her King.

"I know what I'm doing," Rhi said before he could speak.

Thorn dropped his hands. "If Rhys were here, he'd know what to say."

"Maybe. Maybe not."

"What the bloody hell are you two going on about?" Fallon asked with a deeply furrowed brow.

Rhi turned away from Thorn and hastily replied, "Nothing."

Thorn looked at Broc to find the Warrior straining, as if he were fighting against something. "Broc?"

"There's magic," the Warrior said through clenched teeth, his hands fisted at his sides and his muscles bunched. "They're trying to hide her from me."

"They?" Fallon asked worriedly.

Broc winced visibly. His skin turned indigo and huge, leathery wings sprouted from his back. He took a deep breath and released it along with a low growl.

"Shite," Fallon whispered.

Thorn grabbed Broc and tossed him against the manor behind a tall screen of bushes in case there were humans watching, hoping to catch some paranormal event. The Warrior never opened his eyes. He was too busy fighting the magic blocking Lexi to notice they were dragging him inside the manor.

"Dragon magic," Broc murmured hoarsely.

Thorn glanced at Rhi. He put his hands on Broc's shoulders. "Hold on. I doona know how this is going to work."

Then Thorn pushed his magic into Broc.

The Warrior bellowed long and loud in agony before he fell to his knees. Thorn looked up as a door flew open and others rushed to them.

Rhi stopped them, even as Con came down the stairs. Thorn met Con's gaze, waiting for Con to order him to stop. Not that Thorn would.

Con merely closed the distance and asked, "What's blocking Broc's power?"

"Dragon magic," Thorn answered.

Con nodded and stood next to Broc. "How much more can you handle?"

Broc lifted his head and opened his eyes to look from Con to Thorn. "I'm almost through."

To Thorn's surprise, Con put a hand on Broc and used his own magic. Broc's face contorted with pain, but he pushed through it, even as his body shook.

"Aberdeen!" Broc yelled.

Thorn and Con immediately released him. Thorn caught Broc as he began to fall over.

The Warrior sat back on his haunches and raised his head to Thorn. "She's in Aberdeen. Harkan Manor."

"Thank you." Thorn clapped him on the back.

Broc gave him a weary smile. "Just doona ever do that to me again."

Thorn straightened and looked at Con. "I'm going after her."

"I expected nothing less. However, I'm coming with you."

"No," Rhi said. Everyone in the room looked at her. "It's a trap." Her gaze moved from Thorn to Con. "For you. They know you'll help any of your Kings."

Thorn sighed as his eyes skated to Con. "She may be right."

Con's black eyes went hard and emotionless. "I willna remain here hiding. If they want me, they can try and get me."

"Ulrik wants to kill you," Thorn reminded him.

Con snorted in derision. "He's welcome to try. You willna be going after Lexi alone. Ulrik has already done enough damage with his little stunt with Rhys. I'll no' have another of my Kings harmed."

"Then it doesna matter who goes," Fallon said as he helped Broc to his feet. "Ulrik will try to kill or capture whoever it is. It's better if you doona go unaccompanied, Thorn."

With that, Fallon teleported Broc back to MacLeod Castle.

"Thorn won't be going alone," Rhi stated.

Con's gaze swiveled to Rhi. "No' a good idea."

"I'm not asking permission. You aren't my king," she said with a cutting glance. Rhi then turned to Thorn. "Ready?"

"All three of us are going," Con declared in a cool voice.

Thorn pulled out the Fae knife at his waist. "The more the better."

Rhi rolled her eyes and touched both of them. In the next blink, they were in a cluster of woods atop a hill looking down at a house.

"I'd like some warning next time," Con said and shrugged off her hand as he turned his head away.

Rhi smiled and said in a high-pitched baby voice, "Aw. What's the matter with the big, bad dragon? Is his tummy yucky?"

"Rhi," Thorn said, shaking his head while biting back a smile.

The Light Fae rolled her eyes. "If I'd waited, every King there would've wanted to come. We needed to leave right then."

Con turned and gave her a glacial stare. "You're no' in charge."

"Keep thinking you are if it makes you feel better," she said with a flip of her hair.

Thorn whirled on both of them. "Enough," he ground out. "I'm here for Lexi. If you want to help, great. If no', then shut the fuck up and leave."

Both Con and Rhi stared silently at him.

Thorn let out a breath. "While both of you were arguing, I counted six Dark along the perimeter."

"Seven," Con said and motioned to the house with his head.

Thorn looked at the manor and saw another on the

roof that he had missed. "Seven then. We need to take them out one at a time."

"That won't be easy," Rhi said. She pointed to the back of the house with a jagged fingernail. "See how they stay within eyesight of each other?"

Thorn ran a hand down his face. "As much as I want to fight Ulrik, I'd rather get Lexi in and out without him even knowing we are here."

"If anyone is fighting him, it's me," Con announced. "But it willna be here. We'll get Lexi. I'll have my day with Ulrik soon enough."

Thorn's gaze was on the manor. "Hold on, Lexi. I'm coming."

CHAPTER
FORTY-TWO

Lexi paced the room. The food had been delicious, and she ate every bite. Exhaustion was wearing on her, however. Fear kept her stress levels high, knotting her shoulder muscles so she couldn't relax.

She replayed the shadow's words to her over and over in her head. Dragons and humans weren't meant to mix. If that were true, why did Dragon Kings mate with humans?

The door was thrown open to reveal a young twenty-something man with dark hair. His eyes were filled with hatred, as if he couldn't stand to look at her. He might have been considered attractive except for the blatant loathing.

"I can't believe our luck," he said in an English accent dripping with callousness. "The Dark gifted us with a mate."

Lexi rolled her eyes. "How many times do I have to say that I'm not a mate?"

The man folded his arms over his chest and filled the doorway. "I knew a mate. She was a bitch of the first order. I helped kill her." He laughed, the sound cruel and icy. "She was my sister."

Lexi thought she might be sick, her stomach rolled so viciously. She knew there were people like this out in the world, but to come face-to-face with one was beyond disturbing. It made her want to get as far from him as she could.

He walked into the room, tracking her as she backed up until her legs hit the bed. He loomed over her with a smirk she was dying to wipe from his face.

Lexi was boxed in, his tall frame coming in contact with hers. She slapped his hand away when he tried to touch her cheek. Then he grabbed a handful of her hair and yanked backward hard enough to wring a cry from her.

"I hear the dragons are good lovers," he said with his face breaths from hers. "I'm not going to be kind or gentle. I'm going to take you rough and hard, and I'm going to make it last for hours."

He yanked her sweater off her arm, ripping it at the seam so that it hung open, showing her breast. The man smiled wickedly.

"Even if somehow your King found you, by the time I'm finished with you, you'll never let him touch you again."

Lexi clawed at him, kicking and punching even as he held her at such an awkward position. She landed a couple of hits, which only made her throw more. The sick bastard had another thing coming if he thought she was going to meekly allow him to rape her.

Her knee came close to connecting with his balls. So close that he released his hold on her hair before backhanding her. "Bitch," he growled.

Lexi hit the floor, her cheek feeling as if her bone had been shattered. She looked up at him, prepared to claw his eyes out if necessary.

"Leave, Kyle," came a voice from the shadows.

Her shadow was back. Lexi didn't think she would ever think she felt safe with him, but he was better than Kyle any day.

"He said I could have some fun," Kyle said as he glanced over his shoulder. "Bedding a mate sounds more than fun."

Lexi scooted away and got to her feet to put some distance between her and the psycho. She'd thought it was treacherous on the streets of Edinburgh with the Dark, but she was coming to realize just what Thorn had meant when he said that anyone who knew of the Dragon Kings was in grave peril.

"You'll no' touch her."

The shadow's voice had gone low, threatening. Dangerous. It even caused Lexi to shiver.

Kyle shifted so he could look into the shadows. "I don't answer to you."

The looming silence that followed was menacing.

Finally, Kyle lost his nerve. He sneered at her. "I wouldn't want to sully myself with anyone who has let a dragon touch them."

He pivoted and stalked out of the room, leaving the door open. Lexi hesitated for a moment before she decided to take a chance and make a run for it. She barely took one step before the shadow's voice stopped her cold.

"Doona even try."

Lexi glared into the darkness where he hid. "Why did you stop Kyle?"

"It's wasna out of the goodness of my heart, I can assure you."

"Then why?" she pressed.

"Perhaps I want to save you for myself."

Lexi swallowed as she heard the callousness of his voice. "Let me see your face."

"You appear brave, human, but I think it's all a show. Besides, you doona want to see me."

"Why?"

"Because if you do, I'll have to kill you."

She decided not to press any further. "I'll get free. I'm going to—"

"What?" he interrupted with a dry chuckle. "Kill us? Kyle has already died. The Dragon Kings killed him. He was brought back from the dead."

"That's impossible," she said with a frown.

"You've seen magic. You know it's far from impossible."

"He's evil."

There was a smile in the shadow's voice as he said, "That he is."

"I don't sense that in you."

"Then you're an even bigger fool than I first thought. I'm worse than Kyle. Much worse," he said with his voice dipping low.

Lexi couldn't give up on getting free. She thought of Thorn and his claret scales. He was powerful and deadly. He came for her at Dreagan.

But he had no idea where she was now.

"Hope is dying within you," the shadow said. "You'd be better off to let it die a quick death, mortal. No Dragon King will come for you. Because this is one place they would never think to look."

"Go away," Lexi said and turned her back to him.

None of this would be happening if she had gotten on the plane and returned to Charleston. But she hadn't been able to leave Thorn. Even now in her dire predicament, she thought of him, hoping he might find her.

She heard the door close and lock. Lexi squared her shoulders and lifted her chin. She was a modern woman. She had lived on her own for many years not waiting on anyone to save her.

Though she was lacking in the magic department, there

was always a way to get away. She would find it herself, no matter how long it took or what she had to endure.

Then she would find Thorn and throw her arms around him.

Balladyn stood looking over Mikkel's Aberdeen estate from the cover of trees. Dark Fae were visible as they patrolled the manor from the flat roof and ground.

It sickened him to have his race at the beck and call of Mikkel. As much as he hated Ulrik, the King of the Silvers had never asked for such assistance. Taraeth had a plan, and Balladyn suspected it was one that was going to get many of the Dark killed.

What concerned Balladyn now was the fact Rhi was near. Mikkel was a vicious bastard. He would delight in capturing Rhi. It wasn't that Balladyn worried about her being hurt. Rhi had enough power within her to rip Mikkel to shreds a dozen times over.

The problem was that Rhi didn't always use her magic as she should.

Lexi was at the estate, which meant Rhi wouldn't use the very thing that could prevent Mikkel catching her.

Balladyn blew out a long breath. "Rhi. Why couldn't you stay away?"

But it wasn't in her nature. She saved. It was part of who she was, her very essence. It was what drew him to her from the very beginning.

Just once he would like her to let the Kings fight their own battles. As long as she continued to help them, it proved she was still very much in love with her King.

Balladyn wasn't giving up on her though. Once she was able to stop hanging on to a love that no longer existed, then she would begin listening to her body and accept him.

She wanted him. He had sensed it the last few times he was with her. When she allowed him to touch her, to place a soft kiss on her neck, Balladyn had known things were shifting his way.

"Did your master send you, dog?"

Balladyn jerked, a low growl rumbling in his chest as he turned his head to find Ulrik leaning nonchalantly against a tree with his hands in the pockets of his slacks. "I figured Mikkel would've had you on a tight leash."

"I could say the same about you." Ulrik's gold eyes narrowed a fraction. "Unless Taraeth didn't send you."

"I do my own thing, Dragon. More than I can say for you."

Ulrik pushed away from the tree and removed his hands from his pockets. "You're no' here because of the mortal."

"As if I care that the human is a mate to a King or not."

"But you and I both know she is. Do you know who?"

Balladyn shook his head, finding no reason to lie.

Ulrik studied him a long moment. "That leaves only one other reason you'd be here. Rhi."

Damn the bastard. Balladyn hadn't expected anyone to see him. He was only there to make sure Mikkel stayed away from Rhi.

"Is that no' interesting." Ulrik looked at the house. "Did you tell her where the mortal was?"

"Never," Balladyn stated firmly.

"You know how powerful Rhi is. She doesna need you looking out for her."

Balladyn ground his teeth together. "Mind your own business."

"She came to me asking me to stop the Dark from attacking the humans."

Balladyn fisted his hands, refusing to let Ulrik know how much that bothered him. "Rhi has a soft spot for them."

"They ruined my life."

Balladyn heard the fury in Ulrik's voice. "I'll win Rhi."

Ulrik shrugged. "Perhaps. Whichever side Rhi picks is sure to win."

"That's not why I want her."

Ulrik looked at him with a bored expression. "Did Rhi come alone?"

Balladyn shook his head. "You know she didna."

"How many Kings?"

Balladyn smiled then. "This isn't my fight, Dragon."

Ulrik's entire demeanor changed. Gone was the relaxed, uncaring man. In his place was a warrior, one who was ready—and *very* willing—to kill.

Balladyn saw why Ulrik had been King of the Silvers. Mikkel had no idea what he was messing with. For the first time, Balladyn hoped he was around to see the battle between uncle and nephew, because it was sure to be vicious.

Ulrik's gold gaze shifted to him. "Taraeth will think you gave away the location. You'd best get to his side. *Irish.*"

"If I'm there, he'll assume I was a part of it. Why do you care anyway?"

Ulrik started toward the manor as he said, "Because you're going to be the next king of the Dark."

Balladyn remained where he was long after Ulrik left. The air around the manor had shifted. It was charged, waiting for the battle to begin.

The Dark patrolling sensed something was amiss, but they didn't know what was about to come at them. Balladyn expected Ulrik to warn them, but by the quiet of the manor, not even the banished King had informed Mikkel.

Balladyn found that he wanted to join Rhi in battle. She was amazing to behold. There hadn't been a single Fae—Light or Dark—that he wanted to fight beside except for her. With Rhi, he always knew she had his back.

They trained for so long together that each knew what

the other was thinking without putting voice to words. It was a special bond that meant everything to him.

"I'll not give up on you, Rhi," he whispered.

She had no idea it was while he held her in his compound and she fought against his torture that she reminded him of everything that he had lost when he became Dark.

After she was his, he would tell her how stupid it had been for him to think that he wanted to hurt her. He had lived with evil and hate for so long that he hadn't realized all he wanted was her.

And her love.

Soon he would tell her all that and more.

CHAPTER
FORTY-THREE

Thorn yearned to shift into a dragon and bellow his fury. Thanks to the Dark and Ulrik, that was no longer possible.

He was still more than capable of freeing Lexi in human form. That was little comfort at the moment. Knowing she had been taken by the Dark, and then given to Ulrik, made his gut burn with anger.

"We need to time it just right," Rhi said.

Thorn only wanted the battle to start, because it meant he was that much closer to Lexi.

"It willna take long for Ulrik to know we've attacked," Con said. "He'll go straight for Lexi and use her as a shield."

"Ulrik doesn't need a mortal as a shield," Rhi said.

Con's head slowly turned to the Fae. "How would you know?"

"Would you?" she retorted saucily.

A muscle ticked in Con's jaw. "Nay."

"Con has a point," Thorn said. "Ulrik is likely to hurt Lexi."

Rhi was shaking her head even before he finished. "He won't."

"What is it you know that we don't?" Con demanded.

Rhi shrugged, but wouldn't meet their gazes.

"We know it was Ulrik who brought Lily back from the dead," Thorn said. "But we can no' understand why he then tried to kill Darcy."

Rhi visibly swallowed. "You're talking as if I know."

"Do you?" Con laced those two words with acid.

"I know as much as you." Rhi held out her hand and her sword appeared.

"Whose side are you on?" Con's black eyes were pinned on her. "Before we go down there, I think Thorn and I have a right to know."

Rhi finally looked at Con. Her gaze was filled with disdain and contempt. "Everyone knows I think as highly of you as I do the mud on my boots."

"You've been there for us many times," Thorn intervened. He didn't want to accuse Rhi of anything, but Con had a point. "No one is denying that fact. But Ulrik carried you out of Balladyn's stronghold. Balladyn is the one who told you Lexi wasn't with the Dark."

Rhi's silver eyes went hard. "If I ever align with Balladyn, you'll know it because my eyes will be red."

"And Ulrik?" Con pressed.

Rhi's smile was mocking as she said, "I never knew he was such a great kisser."

"You kissed him? Figures," Con stated coolly.

Thorn turned his back on Con and caught Rhi's eyes. "If you tell me you're with me on this, then I believe you. Lexi's life is at stake. I can't lose her."

"You won't." Rhi's face softened as she inhaled deeply. "I use the tools given to me to gain information. For myself," she said to Con as she leaned to the side and shot him a look. She then straightened and focused on Thorn. "Let's go get Lexi."

Thorn smiled at Rhi. The Light Fae had sacrificed so

much for the Kings. She had been a true friend and ally to them in the past, but she was changing rapidly.

Balladyn was chasing her, and it now appeared that Ulrik was as well. If her King didn't step up and set things right, Rhi would be lost to them forever. Because it didn't matter if she chose Ulrik or Balladyn, either choice went against the Kings.

"I'll deposit Con on the ground. You and I'll take the roof," she said.

Con looked at the flat-topped roof and the patrols. "There's more Dark on the roof. If Thorn goes with you, he'll be fighting Dark instead of looking for Lexi."

"Fine. I'll take Con," she said, heaving a loud sigh.

"Ulrik is crafty," Con warned Thorn. "Be ready for anything."

Thorn stared at the estate. "Understood."

Then he withdrew his dagger and nodded to Rhi. In the next instant Thorn was at the back of the manor facing a Dark. He plunged his dagger in the Fae's neck and let him fall as Thorn spun and lunged to the next Dark that came running.

When that one collapsed, he found a door and opened it. Thorn had gotten only a few steps inside before two Dark came at him.

In the narrow hallway, he was limited to what he could do, but it also hindered the Dark. Thorn thrust the dagger upward through a Dark's chin.

He yanked his blade out and pushed the now dead Dark against the other. Thorn leapt over the lifeless Fae and reached for the other's chest to take out his heart.

Instead, he was hit with a double whammy of magic from the Fae with such force that he went flying backward. The pain was agonizing as the magic burned through his skin and into muscle and bone. Thorn gritted his teeth and got to his feet before he tore off his ruined shirt.

His chest was healing rapidly, but the poison in the magic would stay in his body for many hours to come. The next time the Fae threw magic, Thorn dodged it, but took the sound of the bubble and used his dragon magic to amplify it a hundred times over. Then he focused it directly at the Fae.

The Dark fell to his knees holding his ears as blood ran from them. Thorn drove the blade of his knife in the dark's temple and twisted.

He kicked the Fae off his blade and stepped over him. There was an opening ahead. Thorn reached it and stepped into the foyer as five Dark appeared.

As always, Balladyn was in awe watching Rhi with her sword. She moved fluidly, sinuously. Almost erotically. Her body was supple, her movements both beautiful and deadly.

For long moments, he stared at her before he noticed who fought beside her. Constantine.

Balladyn was about to teleport to Rhi before he thought better of it. Rhi would assume he was fighting against her instead of with her. All he could do was watch her beside the King of Kings.

"Bastard," he murmured.

Con's day was coming. Balladyn had no doubt Ulrik would win. Vengeance and hate were powerful tools that could overcome insurmountable odds.

Balladyn took a step toward the estate as Rhi was hit with Dark magic. She stayed on her feet and ducked another blast. But a third shot of magic hit her square in the chest and knocked her off the roof.

Just before she hit the ground, she vanished. Balladyn released the breath he had been holding. A second later, she was next to Con again, albeit moving slower than before.

Her wound didn't heal as quickly as the Dragon Kings, but it didn't diminish her sword arm in the least. In minutes, she and Con dispatched the Dark they were fighting.

As soon as the last Dark fell, they headed to the entrance that led inside the house. Rhi was running ahead of Con when the door opened and a massive bubble of magic came hurtling out of the shadows.

Balladyn yelled Rhi's name as the magic barreled into her. She once more flew backward, landing hard upon the roof. He waited for her to get up and shake it off as she had before. But she didn't.

"No."

Balladyn couldn't breathe, couldn't move.

"Rhi!" Con yelled as he dodged more magic coming from the doorway.

Balladyn tried to see who was responsible, but it was too dark within the doorway.

Constantine used his own magic to deflect the bubbles coming at him. He made his way to Rhi and checked her, only to leave her lying there as if she were dead.

"No. No, no, no, no, no," Balladyn murmured in disbelief.

CHAPTER
FORTY-FOUR

Lexi stood against the wall and listened to the sounds of battle. She knew those sounds well. The grunts of pain, the gurgles of the dying.

They were forever imbedded in her mind after her encounters in Edinburgh.

Her gaze was on the door, waiting to see if anyone would burst in. Seconds turned to minutes as no one came. She didn't know if it was Thorn or someone else attacking. Truth be told, she didn't want to wait around to find out.

With the way her luck had been unfolding, it was going to be someone much worse than the Dark Fae or her new captor, Ulrik.

Lexi made her way to the door and tried the knob. It held fast. She turned the handle with both hands, squeezing her eyes shut as she gave it everything she had. When it didn't budge, she beat her hands against the wood and screamed in frustration.

Through it, she heard a slight click.

Lexi quieted and looked down at the knob. Had someone just unlocked it? What if it was Kyle on the other side? What if it was Ulrik? Worse, what if it was the shadow?

A chance at freedom stood before her, or she could remain in the room waiting for something to come for her.

She grabbed the knob and turned. The door opened. Without a second thought, she flung it wide and rushed out of the room.

Lexi tried to ignore the dimly lit hallway and the numerous shadows throughout—or who might be hiding in them. She ran down the corridor searching for stairs.

Suddenly, she was grabbed and thrown to the floor. Her head slammed against the wood, dazing her. It took her a moment to get her bearings. That's when she realized something heavy was on her, preventing her arms from moving.

Her eyes came into focus again. That's when she found herself looking up at Kyle's face.

"Just how did you get out?" he asked in a condescending tone, his lips twisted in annoyance.

Lexi tried to shove him off her, but he was too strong. "Get off me, jackass."

He leaned down until his face was next to hers. She turned her head to the side.

"Better get used to it. I'm going to be on top of you for a while."

She was not going to be raped. Lexi made her body go limp. It was the hardest thing she had ever done, but the only chance she had was to catch Kyle by surprise.

A chuckle rumbled Kyle's chest. "By the time I'm done with you, you'll be praying for death."

Every instinct clamored for her to fight, to struggle against his hold. But Kyle wanted to dominate her. He wanted to prove his strength and that he was somehow better than she was.

"He's not here to stop me now," Kyle continued as he pulled her arms above her head and held them with one hand.

Lexi bit her tongue to keep from screaming in revulsion when he cupped her breast and squeezed. She kept her focus on a marble statue of a lion.

Thorn held his left side as pain radiated from the repeated hits of Dark magic. He leaned against the wall and looked at the dead Fae around him as he breathed heavily. A glance up the stairs showed that no more were coming, but he had no idea how many more were in the manor.

The sounds of battle continued to come from above on the roof. He hoped Con and Rhi had already made their way inside the house.

Thorn pushed away from the wall and ran up the stairs cautiously. He reached the second floor without incident. He looked both ways and decided to go to the right.

Every minute that passed without finding Lexi, his anxiety grew. With each room he looked into and found empty, a pit of despair began to knot painfully in his gut.

He finished his search of the second floor and went to the third. Thorn looked up and saw a Dark waiting for him on the landing.

Thorn jerked to the side to miss a blast of magic. Thorn bared his teeth and barreled into the Dark, crashing them through a door.

Lexi didn't know how many minutes passed as she lay there limply and let Kyle rub and grind on her. She bit her tongue to keep from gagging, blood filling her mouth.

His grip on her hands hadn't loosened in all that time, and his other hand was getting bolder. Already he had shoved her shirt up her stomach.

It was the crash that jerked his attention away. Lexi used his diverted attention to rise up and head-butt him at the same time she brought her knee up into his balls.

He cried out in pain and rolled off her, holding his nuts. Lexi jumped to her feet and ran to the marble lion sitting on an accent table. She hefted it up and turned to see Kyle on his knees trying to stand and come for her.

Lexi slammed the statue down on his head. He fell to the side, a huge gash spilling blood onto the wood floor.

Thorn had his hand blasted with Dark magic, knocking his knife out of his grip. He gritted his teeth and peeled back his lips in a growl as he slammed his other hand into the Dark's chest and yanked out his heart.

He tossed the heart aside and climbed off the Fae so he could grab his knife. His head whipped around when he heard Lexi's scream. Thorn rushed from the room and saw her across the hall standing over Lily's brother, Kyle.

The son of a bitch was supposed to be dead, and the only way Kyle was alive was because of Ulrik. Just one more reason for Thorn to hate Ulrik. The bastard did one good deed. Then in the next breath did something foul and evil like bring Kyle back from the dead.

After what Thorn witnessed with Rhys and Lily, he wasn't going to allow Kyle to live another moment.

"Lexi," he called and ran to her.

She turned her head to him and dropped the statue as she rushed into his arms. Thorn held her tight, unable to believe that she was with him once more.

He glanced at Kyle to see him unmoving. With the amount of blood filling the floor, Thorn was sure that Lexi had killed him.

"Are you hurt?" he asked thickly. He was shaking at having her back in his arms again, proving just how much she meant to him.

She shook her head. "I want to leave. Now."

Thorn took her hand and looked around for a way to the roof. He didn't want to go back downstairs and chance running into Ulrik. A bad feeling plagued him the longer he was in the house without seeing Ulrik.

"Con and Rhi are on the roof," he told Lexi as he pulled her out of the room. Thorn then spotted an open door and stairs beyond.

He was at the door before he realized he no longer heard any sounds from above. Since he had yet to see either Con or Rhi, that meant it was bad news.

"Stay behind me," he whispered to Lexi. He handed her the knife and nodded.

She returned his nod and gripped the weapon tightly.

Thorn slowly walked up the steps, glancing behind him often to make sure no one snuck up on them. The door to the roof was ajar, giving him just enough of a view to see Rhi on her back, unmoving.

A bellow of pain filled the air. Thorn gradually pushed the door open until he could see the six Dark standing over Con throwing magic at him in a constant rotation.

"Soon he'll be too weak to fight us," said one of the Dark with a mocking sneer.

Another smiled. "We'll have the King of Kings as a prisoner. Taraeth will be pleased."

"I wonder how long it'll take him to go mad so we can send him back to Dreagan to kill all the others?" asked another.

The Dark all laughed at the comment while they continued to toss magic at Con, pinning him down as he writhed in pain.

Thorn couldn't imagine the amount of agony Con was enduring. Thorn then spotted Rhi's sword next to her outstretched arm. He dove from the doorway toward it.

Thorn caught hold of the hilt as he rolled and came to his feet. He spared Lexi a glance. She gave a nod of encouragement. Thorn turned his attention to the Dark and launched himself at them, beheading two at once as he landed.

The other four turned to him, but it was too late. Thorn moved with lightning speed to quickly stab three more before he pierced the final Dark through the chest.

Lexi was standing beside him then. "Oh my God," she murmured, her eyes on Con.

Thorn lowered his gaze and inwardly cringed. Con's entire upper body was burned. He was healing rapidly, but not fast enough for Thorn.

Lexi rushed to Rhi and touched her cheek. "Thorn, she's cold."

"Shite," he said.

The longer they remained on the roof, the more likely that Ulrik would appear. He had to get Lexi away, but he couldn't leave Con or Rhi.

If it was night he would chance shifting and taking them all away, but it was still light. Con groaned as he opened his eyes. His breath was ragged and pain was etched into every hollow of his face.

Con rose up on one elbow. "We need to get out of here."

"Tell me something I doona know," Thorn answered tersely.

Con climbed to his feet, wincing, and took a step toward Rhi. "I'll carry her."

"Nay," Thorn said. He walked to Lexi and pulled her against him with one arm. "Hold on."

Her arms instantly went around his neck. Thorn heard her quick intake of air as he jumped off the roof to the ground.

A moment later Con landed shakily next to them. "I've got her," Con said of Lexi.

Thorn gave a nod and released Lexi to jump back to the roof for Rhi. He gathered the Fae in his arms and looked at the door leading into the house. Then he leaped to the ground.

"Is she going to be all right?" Lexi asked of Rhi.

Thorn glanced at the Light Fae grimly. "Let's worry about us getting away first."

"Did you see Ulrik?" Con asked.

Thorn shook his head. "Nay, and that worries me."

"No' half as much as it worries me."

Thorn moved his gaze to Lexi. "Take Con's hand. We're going to run fast and hard."

Lexi lifted her chin as she put her hand in Con's. "I'm ready."

After a glance at Con, they started running.

"It was the perfect time to kill him," Mikkel said sharply from behind Ulrik.

Ulrik waited until the group made it across the lawn to the shrubs and disappeared into the wooded area before he responded. "It wasna the time."

"We had Con weakened."

"I'll no' fight him in that state."

"I don't have a problem with it," Mikkel said angrily.

Ulrik turned and faced his uncle. "Then you should've taken your chance. Con hasna sunk as low as I want him to. And when I fight him, he'll be at a hundred percent."

"You're a fool." Mikkel's lip was lifted in distaste.

"Do you think I'll lose?"

Mikkel looked at him and grunted. "You should take every advantage that comes your way. You've always thought yourself so noble. It's why you were banished and your magic taken. You should've fought Con and taken over as King of Kings eons ago."

His uncle was looking for a fight, and though Ulrik was more than ready to give it to him, it wasn't time for that yet either. Mikkel liked to tout his plans, but Ulrik had plans of his own that had been in motion for thousands of years.

Mikkel sneered and turned on his heel.

Ulrik watched his uncle stalk away. Ulrik then exited the room and went across the hall to where Kyle lay dead. The stupid bugger had gone after Lexi. Kyle should've listened to his warning to stay away from her. The mortal got what he deserved.

He brought Kyle back from the dead once. There wouldn't be a second time. Not because he couldn't— though that's what he would tell Mikkel—but because he hadn't wanted to retrieve Kyle's soul to begin with.

Ulrik wasn't surprised when Balladyn appeared next to him. He looked at the Dark Fae and saw the worry in his red eyes.

"It was Mikkel," he told Balladyn, guessing what the Dark's question would be. "He was aiming for Con, thinking he could take down Con now. Then the Dark stepped in, and Mikkel didna have the balls to try and take Con from them."

"How bad is Rhi's wound?" Balladyn asked.

Ulrik was just as furious as Balladyn that Rhi had been hurt. "Verra. He mixed his dragon magic with that of the Dark again."

"She needs me."

Ulrik put a hand on the Dark to still him. "Her best bet is with Con. He can heal her."

Balladyn closed his eyes for a moment. Then he nodded and was gone.

CHAPTER
FORTY-FIVE

Lexi was wheezing by the time Thorn and Con slowed. There was a pain in her side, and she couldn't draw in a breath big enough. She had no idea how long they had been running, but at least they had gotten away.

Thorn slowed when another house came into view. He stopped next to some trees and handed Rhi to Con before he took off again.

Lexi watched him race to the car parked in front of the house. He got inside and hotwired it before driving it away.

"Come on," Con said as Thorn approached.

Lexi held her side as they once more ran to where Thorn waited alongside the road. Con got in the back with Rhi still in his arms, and Lexi climbed in front. The door wasn't shut behind her before Thorn gunned the little car.

"How is she?" Thorn asked as he glanced in the rear-view mirror to Con.

"There's no response."

Lexi looked behind her to Con and Rhi. It was odd to see Rhi so pale and lifeless. There was a large hole in her black shirt where the magic had hit her in the chest. Burn marks were still visible. "What happened?"

"Dragon and Dark magic," Con answered.

Lexi looked at Thorn to see lines of worry bracketing his mouth. "I gather that's bad."

"Extremely," Thorn said as he glanced at her. "Ulrik used it against one of us recently. It prevented Rhys from shifting, making him choose between living a life as a dragon or a human."

Lexi looked at Con, but his gaze was straight ahead on the road before them. "What happens when that kind of mix hits a Fae?"

"I doona know." Thorn shook his head. "It's no' good that she's no' waking."

Lexi faced forward and looked at the dashboard to see that Thorn was driving a hundred miles per hour. "How far to Dreagan?"

"Over two hours," Con bit out.

Lexi fastened her seat belt. They were far from out of danger, but at least she was with Thorn again. That in itself was enough to let her breathe easier.

She caught Thorn glancing at her every few seconds. Lexi smiled and leaned her head against the seat as she looked at him. "It wasn't a bed of roses, but I'm all right."

"You killed Kyle."

"Kyle?" Con asked.

Thorn nodded. "Kyle was there."

"The jerk was trying to force himself on me." Lexi shivered, thinking of his hands on her. "He said he killed his sister, who is a mate."

Thorn took a curve and laughed. "He has no idea Lily is very much alive. I can no' believe Ulrik brought him back from the dead to begin with. Perhaps it's better if Lily doesna know what Ulrik did."

"Agreed. Lexi," Con said. "We're going to need to sit down with you and go over every detail of your time with Ulrik."

"Of course, though there wasn't much that happened. He did show me the video. He took great joy in that," she said.

Thorn's hands tightened on the steering wheel. "Ulrik has a lot to answer for."

"His time is coming," Con said.

Thorn was never so glad to see Dreagan as when it came into view. He took the back roads onto their property and drove straight to the garage.

Kellan and Rhys were there to meet them. Rhys opened the back door and took Rhi from Con. Thorn got out of the car and looked to Lexi.

"It could've gone verra badly," Kellan told Con.

Kellan was Keeper of the History, so he saw in his mind major events to record for Dreagan.

Con walked past them. "The car needs to be returned immediately."

Thorn exchanged a look with Kellan before he motioned for Lexi to follow them into the manor. Once inside, the house was in a state of chaos with everyone worrying how their new predicament would affect them.

"He doesna look good," Kellan said of Con.

Thorn watched the King of Kings ascend the stairs. "They were going to take him."

"I know. It was quick thinking on your part." Kellan turned to the sitting room where Rhys had laid Rhi on the sofa. "Did Con attempt to heal her?"

Thorn shrugged a shoulder. "If he did, I didna know it."

"We're going to need him."

"I know." Thorn glanced at Lexi. He wanted to take her aside and talk to her, but now wasn't the time.

Kellan leaned closer and said, "We have something being held in the caverns that will interest you and Lexi."

Thorn frowned as he looked at Kellan. "You know I can no' bring her down there."

"For this, you'll want to break the rules. And based on what I learned from Darius as well as Shara, Lexi needs this."

"I gave a promise to Lexi. Tell me I can fulfill that promise," Thorn said.

Kellan gave a small smile. "He's waiting for you whenever you want to take her."

Con reached his bedroom and barely got the door shut before his knees gave out. He landed hard, his lungs seizing from the Dark magic.

The pain was debilitating. It swirled through him, reaching every muscle, every bone. It burned, sizzling within him as if it were trying to eat at him from the inside out.

It had been everything he could do on the return trip to Dreagan to act as if he wasn't in pain. He attempted to heal Rhi once, but it had been too much for him, and he nearly passed out.

Never before had he experienced this kind of weakness. And if scared the hell out of him.

Not because he feared Ulrik would use it again, but because it would put the others at a disadvantage. Con was going to have to start thinking ahead. Whether he remained King of Kings or not, Dreagan, the Dragon Kings, and even the weapon hidden in his mountain needed to be protected.

Con sat on his haunches, his hands on his thighs as he took control of the pain—or as much as he could. The wound on his chest had healed externally, but it was what the Dark magic was doing internally that worried him.

He sat there for several seconds before he struggled to

climb to his feet. No one could see him like this. It was important that all the Kings see him as strong and resilient.

Too much had happened recently. If they witnessed him in this state, they would think he couldn't take care of them as he always had.

Con walked to his closet as he kicked off his shoes and pants. Then he opened the bottom drawer and pulled out a black tee before grabbing a pair of jeans. He put on the clothes and a pair of boots.

He then looked in the mirror. After a long examination of himself, he turned on his heel and exited his room, pain pounding through him with every movement. He made his way downstairs to the front sitting room where everyone gathered.

"No Fae has ever been struck with such a mixture of magic," Shara said.

Con saw that Lexi and Thorn stood apart from the rest. By the look of the couple, they wanted some time alone to talk.

A look around at all the women in the manor made Con inwardly cringe. The Kings had been lucky so far. None of the women had attempted to betray them, but Con knew it was inevitable.

The first betrayal had been a vicious blow to the Kings and lost him a friend. What would a second betrayal do?

Con ignored the looks of the others as he walked around to the front of the sofa and sat on the edge. The room spun as agony filled him. It hurt to breathe, much less move.

Even now he wasn't sure his magic would do any good.

He looked at Rhi's face. No cheeky remarks fell from her lips. No cutting looks from her silver eyes. It was strange to find her so still. The last time he had seen her like this was when her magic exploded Balladyn's fortress.

Con drew in a breath, and then put his hand on Rhi's.

He tried to use his magic. His muscles seized from the pain, and he barely kept the pain from showing on his face.

He focused past the anguish to the place he always went to for comfort—a place deep within his mind that didn't allow anything else in.

Con exhaled and pushed his magic into her, urging Rhi's wounds to heal. The pain was manageable this time, allowing him to use his magic as he needed. Almost instantly, the burn marks disappeared. Con kept his magic going a little longer just to make sure all of her injuries were mended.

When his hand fell away, he was expecting her to open her eyes and demand that he get away from her. But Rhi slept on.

"She needs time, is all," Rhys said into the silence.

Con watched as Lily threaded her fingers with Rhys's. "Aye. Time," Con agreed.

Kellan said, "Rhys, take Rhi to one of the spare bedrooms so she can rest."

Con moved so Rhys could lift the Fae and carry her out. One by one, the others filed out of the sitting room, leaving only Kellan, Ryder, and Dmitri.

"Update," Con said to Ryder.

Ryder's lips twisted. "There are now dozens of Web sites popping up claiming to have dragon videos. Dragons are all anyone can talk about on every news channel around the world. They dominate YouTube, blogs, and newspapers."

So it was as bad as Con had feared it might be. "Are you taking the sites down?"

"Aye," Ryder said. "I've got Gwynn and Evie from MacLeod Castle helping me as well."

"Good."

Kellan crossed his arms over his chest. "Con, you need to rest."

"I'm fine. We have work to do."

Dmitri rubbed the back of his neck as he glanced at the floor. "The police came by about an hour ago. They wanted to see if the shop was damaged."

The shop. Con had completely forgotten to have that cleaned up for just such a visit. He couldn't forget something so simple as that. All it would take was one small mistake to crumble their now very fragile existence.

"We took care of it," Kellan said.

Dmitri nodded. "Aye. Nothing out of place. It had them scratching their heads."

"That's one spot of good news," Con said, more relieved than the other two would ever know. "Good work."

Dmitri threw a thumb over his shoulder. "What of Thorn and Lexi?"

Con's gaze slid to the doorway, but there was no sign of the couple. "We'll know soon enough, I'm sure."

"Thorn is taking her to the mountain," Kellan said. "We caught the Dark who led the attack here. He's the same one who killed Lexi's friend."

Con lowered his gaze to the floor and inhaled deeply. "She deserves her revenge. If she can no' kill the Dark, Thorn will."

Lexi didn't think there was ever a time she was more nervous. When Thorn beckoned her to go with him after Con healed Rhi, she quickly followed.

When they reached a door, Thorn held it open for her. She walked through it, stunned to find herself in a tall, but narrow, tunnel inside a mountain.

Cool air brushed over her skin. She glanced behind her at Thorn who closed the door and stepped around her.

"This way," he said as he started walking.

Lexi followed him while she took in everything. Right at the entrance, and appearing about every ten feet, was a sconce in the mountain throwing off light so she could see where she was going.

Never was she more grateful than when she saw the carvings and etchings of dragons along the walls. Everywhere she looked there were dragons. The carvings were so spectacular that she was having a hard time following Thorn and not stopping to run her hands over the artwork.

Lexi hurried to catch up to Thorn and belatedly realized the floor was pitched downward. The farther down they went, the more she saw of doorways from the cave that branched off.

She wanted to explore them. Especially when she glanced inside a cavern and saw a massive dragon carved along an entire wall breathing fire.

She was completely enthralled until she walked a little farther and saw another cavern—with four large silver dragons sleeping in a cage.

"Those are dragons," she said in awe, stopping.

Thorn halted and turned his head to look to the dragons. "Those are Ulrik's Silvers. They wouldna stop following his orders or leave with the others, so we had no choice but to use our magic so they would sleep."

"And if Ulrik wakes them?" she asked.

Thorn looked at her over his shoulders. "We willna allow them to hurt any humans."

Which was all fine and dandy as long as Thorn and the other Kings were around. What if Ulrik won against Con? He would then be King of Kings and making the decisions.

Lexi gazed at the Silvers, the color fading from a deep silver at the base of their necks and along the spines to pale silver under their stomachs.

These weren't Dragon Kings that shifted, but real dragons who cared not about puny humans. It made Lexi wonder what her world would have been like had there not been a war between their two species. Would magic be a way of life? Would seeing dragons or hearing their roars be as common as the sound of a jet?

"Do you want a closer look?"

Lexi shook her head and looked at Thorn.

He faced forward and continued on. "Just a little farther."

By the look on Thorn's face, she knew she had done the wrong thing. "I'm not afraid of them," she said as she followed. "It's just that after seeing you, nothing else compares."

He slowed, allowing her to catch him. There was a smile on his face as he looked down at her.

They came to a halt then with Thorn turning her toward an entrance. She looked in and couldn't believe her eyes. There in the middle of the small room was Gorul. The very Dark who had killed Christina.

The Dark was surrounded by four Dragon Kings. Whatever they were doing kept the Dark from teleporting away. Gorul was turning in a circle looking at the Kings with contempt. Then he spotted her.

He looked her up and down and sneered. "You should be dead."

Thorn moved behind her and whispered, "They've been holding him for you."

If there wasn't such a surge of anger at seeing the Dark, she might have cried for what the Kings—and Thorn—were doing for her.

She glanced at Thorn and touched his hand as she walked into the cavern. Her gaze then turned to Gorul. "Taraeth didn't keep me for himself."

"As if I believe that," Gorul said.

Lexi shrugged and stopped in front of him, her arms crossed over her chest. "I don't give a damn what you believe. But I'm here. What does that tell you?"

"That you're going to get what your friend got."

For the first time in . . . days . . . Lexi wasn't afraid. She knew the Kings were powerful. She knew they wouldn't allow Gorul to do anything to her. Then there was the fact she had been through so much, as well as having killed a man.

She would have to deal with the ramifications of taking a life later, but for now Gorul didn't scare her as he once had.

"You're not going to lay a finger on me," Lexi said. She felt Thorn move up beside her.

Gorul looked at Thorn before the Dark's gaze slid to her. "You got yourself a Dragon King. It won't matter. Not in the end."

Con came in from another entrance that Lexi hadn't seen. He stood opposite her behind Gorul. The Dark Fae swung around and began laughing when he saw Con.

"Your days are numbered, Constantine."

Con stared at Gorul with soulless black eyes. With some unspoken command, Darius and the other three Kings guarding Gorul stepped back.

Lexi didn't move. She was waiting to see who was going to kill the Dark. Watching the life fade from his eyes would finally give Christina justice.

"You attacked Dreagan," Con's voice rang clear and strong in the cavern. "You attacked and killed mortals on our land. You were part of a plan that took Lexi away from safety and attempted to take Shara."

"She's a traitor," Gorul said of Shara. "She was Dark."

"Was," Con said softly.

"Taraeth has put a price on her head. They'll be coming for her."

"Let them try," said a deep voice to Lexi's right.

She turned her head to see a man with wheat-colored hair and shamrock green eyes blazing with a warning. He must be Shara's King.

Lexi wondered what it would feel like to have Thorn come to her defense like that. She knew what it felt like to be in his arms and to witness his power. But to be the center of his world? It's what she longed for.

How did she tell him she loved him? Thorn wasn't like other men. Nothing they had done had been normal. How did she even know if there was anything more for them?

Gorul lunged at Con. Lexi expected him to be drawn up short from magic that kept him in the cavern, but there was nothing. Right before he reached Con, Thorn was there, holding Gorul's arms behind his back.

"The almighty Constantine can't fight his own battles?" Gorul asked.

"I willna be killing you," Con stated.

Lexi was shocked when Thorn turned around with Gorul. He leaned close to the Dark's ear and said, "She's going to do it."

Lexi didn't hesitate in taking the blade Darius held out for her. All she kept seeing was Christina's lifeless eyes, her cold, naked body laying so awkwardly on the wet cobblestones. Lexi took the few steps separating them and plunged the dagger into Gorul's heart.

"You won't be hurting anyone ever again," she said before twisting the blade.

His face went gray as shock and surprise filled his red eyes. He struggled to draw in a breath before his eyes rolled back in his head, and he slumped in Thorn's arms.

Lexi stared down at the Dark Fae who had taken something precious from the world in Christina. Now Lexi could call her parents and tell them the bastard had gotten his due.

She inhaled and looked around the room. The Kings each gave her a nod of approval before they walked from the room. When she tried to hand the dagger back to Darius, he gave a shake of his head with a little smile.

Con was the last to leave the cavern. He bent and hefted Gorul's body over his shoulder before he too departed.

"Thank you," she told Thorn.

"I promised he would be dealt with."

"And I knew you would keep that promise. You could've killed him, and then shown me the body."

Thorn's gaze was penetrating. "I knew you needed to do this."

She eyed Thorn, wondering why he looked as if he might be sick at any moment.

"I spoke to Ulrik," she said to break the silence.

Thorn's look grew even grimmer. "None of us can shift or fly now. I doona know how long it'll last either. Did Ulrik hurt you in any way?"

"No, though I don't know what his plans were. There was another man. He kept to the shadows, but he frightened me more than Ulrik. Then there was Kyle."

Thorn ran a hand down his face. "You got free of him on your own. You're a survivor."

"They kept telling me you would never find me."

"Nothing was going to keep me from you."

If only he knew how her knees shook. She didn't know if this was the end of her time with Thorn, and it made her heart break to think that it was.

Thorn swallowed and slowly walked to her. "I'm not good at this."

"At what?"

Why did she have to be so damn beautiful? She had been through hell and back, and she stood there as if she could take on the Dark all by herself.

He was in awe of her.

She made him weak and strong, vulnerable and fierce all at the same time.

"This," he said and motioned between the two of them. "I've never been here before."

Her gray eyes held his, waiting for him to continue.

"I thought what I was feeling would go away. Then I kissed you. I'm drowning, Lexi, and I don't know what to do."

Her lips lifted in a soft smile. She reached out for his hand, and said, "Then we'll drown together."

Thorn hadn't realized how much he feared that she would want to get far away from him until she spoke. He yanked her against him, kissing her deeply.

He pulled back, but cupped her face with his hands. "You know every secret I have. I want you in my life now and forever, Lexi Crawford. I want you as my mate."

Her smile was radiant as she gazed up at him. "I've been yours from the very beginning. I'll always be yours."

"I love you."

"And I, my Dragon King, love you."

They were laughing through their kisses as they took their clothes off. Then Thorn lifted her so that her legs wrapped around his waist.

He turned them so her back was to the wall. She slowly slid down his cock, a sigh escaping her lips. Her nails dug into his back as he began to rock his hips.

Even as his life was turned upside down, there was one calm in the storm—Lexi. She was his, and he was hers.

For now and always.

EPILOGUE

Three days later . . .

Another couple wanting the mating ceremony. Con hadn't been surprised after seeing the smiles Thorn and Lexi wore when they finally returned to the manor. And with the Kings' enemies closing in, none of the couples wanted to wait any longer.

Con shut all four black velvet boxes. Then he rose and put on his suit jacket. He adjusted the gold dragon-head cuff links and grabbed the boxes.

His first stop was Iona's room. She opened the door with a smile. Her blond hair was piled at the back of her head with long strands falling about her face.

Her black dress was lace at the bodice with a high neck and long lace sleeves. The back dipped into a V to her waist where the dress then fell in several layers of black tulle.

"This is from me welcoming you into our family," Con said and handed her a box.

Iona took the box and opened it, her mouth falling open. She picked up the necklace where a large black pearl hung with a diamond atop it. "It's gorgeous. Thank you."

Con bowed his head and smiled. "I'll see you below."

He closed the door behind him and walked down the corridor to Darcy's room. Con rapped his knuckles on the door. As soon as he heard Darcy bid him enter, he opened the door.

Darcy turned from the mirror and held out her hands. "Do you think Warrick will like it?"

Con smiled as he looked at the strapless jade dress that came to mid-thigh at the front but dropped down to her ankles in the back. Around Darcy's waist were crystals that matched her strappy stilettos. "I doona think Warrick will care what you wear. He's going to be thinking of getting you out of it."

Darcy looked down at herself. "I hope so. Is it time?"

"Almost. I came to give you this," he said and handed her the box.

She took it, a frown marring her brow as she opened it. "Oh, my," she murmured.

Con watched as she touched the five jade beads attached to the gold bracelet. She looked up at him in such surprise that he smiled.

"Let me," he said and put it on her right wrist.

"Thank you. It's perfect."

Con winked at her and backed out of the room to go to the third mate—Grace.

Grace had come onto Dreagan to get past her writer's block and finish her book. In the end, she found the love of Arian, who couldn't live without her.

Con knocked on her door.

"Come in," Grace's muffled voice came through the door.

He opened the door and found her rushing about the room. There were a pair of silver stilettos waiting to be put on while Grace rushed about the room barefoot.

She wore a turquoise beaded gown that looked as if it

came right out of the 1920s. The sleeveless, long-waisted dress flattered her thin frame and short blond hair. The front dipped low, showing ample cleavage while the bottom hem was scalloped.

"Grace," Con said to get her attention.

"Give me a sec. I can't find the headband I bought. Ah, ha!" she cried as she found it and hurried to the mirror.

She placed the band across her forehead, the turquoise matching the dress to perfection. Her gaze met Con's in the mirror before she turned to face him.

"I'm here to give you this," he said and held out the box.

Grace eyed it before she hesitantly took it. "I heard you do this for all the mates."

"And yet you thought I wouldna with you?"

"It did cross my mind."

Con stood there while she opened the box and merely stared without saying a word or giving any emotion away on her face.

He was normally good at picking out the right pieces for the mates, but he must have gotten it wrong this time.

"I would ask that you wear it now, but after the ceremony, you can pick out whatever you'd like."

She lifted her dark blue eyes to him. "Why would I want to do that?"

"You doona like it."

"I love it," she said.

That's when he saw how her eyes were filled with tears.

"It's perfect." Grace sniffed as she took the anklet and sat to put it on.

After it was clasped on her right ankle, she ran her hands over the rose gold links to the heart in pure turquoise.

Grace looked up at him, smiling widely. "Thank you."

"My pleasure. I'll see you downstairs shortly," he said before he left.

Con paused outside of the room of his last visit. He hadn't wanted to like Lexi, but he hadn't been able to help it from the first time they met. She had spunk and spirit—all the mates did—but there was something about Lexi that he recognized immediately.

Perhaps it was because she reminded him of someone from his past.

Con knocked. A few seconds later Lexi opened the door, her brow knotted in a frown. "What's the matter?" he asked worriedly.

Surely he hadn't been wrong about her. She couldn't back out now. Thorn would be devastated.

She rolled her eyes and walked away. "I should've chosen a more traditional dress. He's going to hate it."

Con walked into the room and closed the door behind him. Then he took Lexi by the shoulders and turned her so that she faced the floor-length mirror.

They looked at her dress together. The claret velvet skimmed her body enticingly on the bodice. The neckline had scalloped edging that dipped to her breasts. The sleeves were long and narrow with black lace inserts from her shoulders down to upper thighs.

The dress was belted with black leather. Adding to the look was a six-inch drop of leather studded with silver above her right leg before the gown fell open in a slit to show the lining of black in the flowing skirts.

Her hair was pulled over one shoulder, and she had on black velvet booties.

"I think you look like you. In other words, you look perfect. There is no right or wrong way to dress for this. Each mate chooses the gown that best fits them."

Her shoulders sagged in relief as she briefly closed her eyes. "I love the dress, but as soon as I saw Iona, I began to question my choice."

"Doona," Con urged. "Thorn is going to love it."

Lexi smiled at him through the mirror. "I needed to hear all of that. Thank you."

"My pleasure." He stepped to the side and held out the black velvet box.

She accepted it with curiosity. Her gasp was loud when she opened the lid then covered her mouth with her hand. Tears misted her eyes when she looked up at him.

"It's my duty to give a gift. I hope you like them."

"I've always loved garnets," she said as she took one of the earrings out and put it in.

The curving French wire made it appear as if the five-carat multifaceted rectangle garnet was floating beneath her ear.

Once she had both in, he nodded. "The others are waiting for us below. Shall we go?"

Lexi set aside the velvet box and took his arm. They walked down the stairs and out the back entrance of the manor into the mountain.

Con paused to leave Lexi with the other three. "Count to twenty, then follow me," he told them.

He walked deeper into the mountain and spotted Laith, Warrick, Arian, and Thorn standing together as they waited for the mating ceremony to begin and their women to walk into the cavern.

He exhaled a long breath as the Kings took their places and Iona came into view first. Laith went to meet her and bring her to the front. Warrick followed suit with Darcy, and Arian did the same with Grace.

When Lexi appeared, Thorn simply stood there looking at her.

"Thorn," Con said, when the King didn't go to get her.

"I'm just taking the moment in," Thorn said with a smile, never moving his gaze from Lexi.

Her smile was wide when Thorn finally approached and

whistled in approval. Con winked at her when Lexi gave him a thumbs-up.

In a few moments, there would be four more humans mated to his Kings.

Did that make them stronger—or weaker? Only time would tell. But for the moment, Con approved of each mortal binding themselves to his Kings.

Daire left Dreagan and teleported to Edinburgh. There he found Cael standing outside a pub looking through the window at a Dark who had targeted two humans.

"Well?" Cael asked.

Daire shrugged and looked at the mortals on the street. "Rhi is just as we thought. I've been tracking her for weeks, and she's unpredictable to be sure. She goes from Dreagan to Balladyn to Ulrik with no rhyme or reason."

"What of her meeting with Usaeil?"

Daire leaned back against the window and crossed his arms over his chest. "Rhi is a wild card. Usaeil made a mistake that others have yet to see. Rhi, however, knows it. I'm still unsure of what Rhi's plans are regarding the queen."

"Where is Rhi now?"

"At Dreagan. The battle with the Dark left her wounded."

Cael's head snapped to him. "Should we be worried?"

"Con healed her, but she's still not woken."

"I want you there when she does. We need every detail."

Daire pushed away from the glass. "And if she doesn't wake?"

"We'll deal with that when the time comes. We have our orders. The others will be here shortly. We'll begin to exact justice on the Dark, starting in Edinburgh. I need you to remain with Rhi. She is—"

Daire nodded and interrupted him to say, "Important. I know. Balladyn could win her over."

Cael drew in a deep breath and slowly released it. "We've been too long away from this realm. We've turned into legend. The Fae are about to learn they must answer for their crimes. Including Balladyn."

"I think we should wait before dealing with him," Daire cautioned. "You don't know what it might do to Rhi."

Cael cut his silver eyes to Daire. "You may be right."

"She knows I'm following her."

"I would expect nothing less from Rhiannon."

V used the thick fog as cover and landed atop the mountain. It felt good to let the wind slide over his wings, to take the current up high and then dive through the clouds.

He shifted into his human form and stood looking down at the village below. A gasp behind him had him turning around. He saw the young woman and smiled. Her wind-blown blond hair fell half on her face, but it couldn't hide her bright blue eyes.

"You're naked," she said in Italian. When he didn't answer, she said in English with an Italian accent, "You're naked."

"So I am."

He faced her when her eyes drifted down his body. She smiled when she saw his arousal. Her blue eyes lifted to his. "My home is just there," she said, pointing behind her.

V walked to her and wrapped one arm around her waist, bringing her against his cock. "Do you really need a bed?"

"No," she said breathlessly, her arms coming around his neck.

He kissed her while hurriedly removing her clothes. He needed inside her—immediately.

Darius stood at the back during the mating ceremonies. He hadn't been able to endure listening to the words, but he had to be there.

As soon as the ceremonies were over, he told Con he was going back to Edinburgh to check on the Dark—and kill more if needed. Darius had gotten into the Lotus Evora in a stunning Nightfall Blue and driven to the city.

He parked near Darcy's destroyed building and began to make his way around the city. Several times he saw Dark drop dead as they were walking.

Darius didn't see the reason for the deaths until a Light Fae appeared before a group of Dark gathered outside a pub and killed all seven of them with a single word.

The Light Fae looked his way and vanished. Darius certainly wasn't upset to find that the Light were helping them clean the streets, but he had a suspicion that the man wasn't just any Fae.

To Darius's surprise, he found himself outside the Royal Victoria Hospital. He intended to walk out, but something held him back.

He waited for an hour before he saw the tall, willowy form of Sophie Martin twenty feet in front of him. Her red hair was down, falling about her shoulders in a thick wave.

She walked past him without looking in his direction. Two steps later she halted. Then she slowly turned to him. There were no words, no exchange of pleasantries.

Darius pushed away from the building and strode to her. He slid one hand around the back of her neck and the other around her waist as he kissed her.

She responded immediately with a fire that he had sensed within her. Their kiss turned frantic, scorching. He backed her into an alley and pushed her against a building. She dropped her purse and black bag and wound her arms around his neck.

Darius told himself to be worried about a woman who brought that much need and hunger to his surface, but he was too busy kissing her.

She reached between them and unbuckled his pants

while he yanked up her dress and tore her panties. Then he lifted her and thrust into her tight, wet sheath.

Darius closed his eyes as her ankles locked around his waist. Just this once. He would give in to his body with Sophie just this once.

Read on for an excerpt from the next book by
Donna Grant

SMOLDERING HUNGER

**Coming soon from
St. Martin's Paperbacks!**

It was his eyes.

Yes, his eyes. Those deep orbs the color of rich, dark chocolate. He hadn't tried to be glib or charming. He simply was.

Was that what drew her? Was it because he told her the truth, uncaring what she thought of him? She hadn't known men were capable of such things.

He hadn't flirted with her or tried to be charismatic. In fact, he had said very little the first time and nothing at all the second.

Instead, his large hand had cupped the back of her head and held it while he kissed her mindless. Her senses had been assaulted with his taste, his heat, his desire, and his smell. Even now she had only to think of sandalwood and chills raced over her skin.

Sophie blinked and found herself staring at her reflection through the small mirror in her locker. Her eyes were dilated, her lips parted, and her chest heaved.

Her sex ached to feel Darius's length slide inside her once more, to have him thrust hard and fast. Her breasts swelled and moisture soaked her panties.

My God. What was wrong with her?

He rode you good.

Sophie slammed her locker shut and turned on her heel. It was past midnight, and she wanted a few hours of sleep before she was back at the hospital for her next shift.

On her way out, she stopped by to check on the woman whose husband had beat her. The woman refused to press charges or to realize that if she didn't take some kind of action, she could end up dead.

Sophie paused by the door when she heard voices within. She peered around the corner to see a man with her. He was crying, swearing he would never do it again.

How many times had he said those same words? By the woman's medical records and all her broken bones, it had been many, many times.

Sophie had done her part. She gave the woman the same advice they gave every victim of domestic violence. The ball was in the woman's court. Sophie could only pray that she took a stand and got her life back.

As she walked out of the hospital, Sophie felt the wind hit her face with a blast of cold air. A light snow had fallen two days ago, and more was on the way. Even after seven years, she still wasn't accustomed to the harsh Scotland winters.

Still flushed from her thinking of Darius, she didn't bother to button her coat. Her heels clicked on the cobblestones as she made her way to the street.

Unable to help herself, she glanced to the spot where she and Darius had given in to their passion. The shadows hid the location, but she didn't need lights to know where it was.

For a short time, Sophie had forgotten her past and the betrayals that had shaped her into who she was. For a brief space she had just been Sophie. A woman who craved Darius's touch like she needed air.

And it had felt so good to give in to that.

She looked at the ground and swallowed. Damn Darius for showing up again. And damn her own mind for not being able to forget about him.

When she raised her head, her eyes clashed with chocolate ones. Sophie halted inches from running into Darius. She gripped her purse in one hand and her bag in the other while she wondered what to do.

"Walk around me," Darius said.

She frowned, anger cutting through her. Hadn't he been the one to come to the hospital, her place of work? Wasn't he the one in front of her now?

"Keep walking, Sophie. I'll find you later and explain," he said in a low voice.

She rolled her eyes and walked past him, making sure she ran into him hard enough to throw him off balance. Why had she romanticized their dalliance? Why had she once more found herself making a man into something he wasn't?

Darius had told her he wasn't a good man. Yet she had gone and made him out that way in her mind. All those nights dreaming of him, of the passion and desire, had created a man in her head who couldn't possibly exist.

After this run-in with Darius, Sophie was sure he would be well and truly out of her mind for good. She didn't have the time or inclination for men like him.

She opted to walk home instead of taking her usual cab. The air was brisk, and with the snow coming, it might be her last chance for a while. The walk felt good despite her feet hurting from two back-to-back shifts.

Sophie was beyond exhausted by the time she entered her flat. She tossed down her keys, purse, and bag at the entryway table. Then she hung up her coat and kicked off her shoes on the way to the bathroom.

She was unbuttoning her shirt when she paused to turn

on the water for the bathtub. After her clothes were in the hamper, she walked naked to the tub and poured a large portion of bubble bath in before lighting the candles set all around the claw-foot tub.

While the water filled, she turned on some music and shut off the lights. Her newest favorite was the soundtrack to *Outlander*. She climbed into the tub with the haunting melody playing in the background.

Sophie sighed as she leaned back and let the water and bubbles surround her. When the water was high enough, she turned it off with her foot.

Her eyes were closed as she relaxed. Slowly the tension and stress began to ease from her muscles. Her head lolled to the side. She was so tired she could fall asleep right there. The only thing that would've made everything perfect was wine.

And Darius.

With the music playing, Sophie couldn't help but think of Darius. She had come across a few Highlanders while in Edinburgh, but none of them compared to Darius. She hadn't even had to ask him if he was a Highlander.

It was in the way he held himself, the way he spoke. It was a look upon them that couldn't be faked or copied. Whatever made a man a Highlander was in his blood, in his very soul.

Movies and romance books loved to have Highlanders as heroes. Truth be told, Sophie had always found herself drawn to such men. Highlanders valued loyalty, honesty, and family. The alphas who would give their very lives for those they loved.

At one time she had dreamed of finding such a man for herself. She hadn't actually thought it would be a Highlander, however. She had been content with finding her man closer to home.

That's what she got for thinking men were like those

portrayed in film and books. Those were characters written by those who crafted them. They weren't real people.

Darius was the closest she had ever come to finding those heroes she used to read about. Then he proved he was as flawed as she was. Which was a good thing. She needed that so she didn't find herself wanting him in her life.

She didn't need anyone. Hadn't needed anyone in seven years, and that wasn't going to change. She lived her life the way she wanted without having to answer to anyone or take their bullshit.

It was just the way she wanted it.

Liar.

Sophie silenced her subconscious with a vicious kick. She knew exactly what she wanted, and though a quick tumble with Darius had done wonders for her mentally and physically, she knew better than to think of more.

She shifted in the tub and saw the candles flicker through her closed eyelids. Sophie opened her eyes, her mouth falling open when she saw Darius leaning against her sink watching her.

"What . . . ? How . . . ? There's no . . ." she began, only to find her brain had shut off.

His gaze blazed with unreserved longing while his hands gripped the sink tightly. Despite his lounging, his body was strung as tight as a bow.

How long had he been in her bathroom? How had she not heard him come in? And what did he want?

Regardless of the questions running through her head, none made it past her lips. Sophie fought against the tide of desire that swept over her. It didn't help, by the way, Darius looked at her as if he were about to throw her over his shoulder and take her to the bed to make love to her.

Sophie's sex throbbed just thinking about it. There was no way she would be able to carry on a conversation if she didn't get her body under control. And there had to be a conversation, followed by Darius leaving quickly after.

There would be no sex.

Ummm. Did you say something?

Shit. She was in trouble. The kind that would have her waking up in the morning groaning from—

Soreness?

—bad decisions. And Darius was definitely a bad decision.

His gaze dropped from her face to the water. A harsh breath left him. Her eyes traveled down his chest to his waist and lower, where she watched the outline of his cock lengthen and grow hard right before her eyes.

Her nipples tightened in response. When Darius murmured something beneath his breath in a gravelly tone, she jerked her gaze back to his face.

That's when she realized her nipples had broken the water's surface and the bubbles had drifted around her breasts. Sophie sank further beneath the water.

Darius closed his eyes briefly and drew in a ragged breath. When he looked back at her, he was once more in control.

Too bad she wasn't.

For long minutes they simply stared at each other. Sophie mentally undressed him, thinking how she would run her hands over his body and feel his heat and hardness.

"What are you doing here?" she finally managed to ask.

As if her words were a punch, he turned his head away for a moment and said, "You're in danger. If you ever see me, pretend you doona care. Make sure that anyone who is around thinks you would rather see anyone else but me."

"I can do that."

Had he winced? She was sure he winced. Now that was a shock. Since when did her words ever hurt anyone?

"I only came to tell you that," he said.

Sophie was suddenly sad that he might be going. She didn't want him there, but since he was, she didn't want him to leave. "Thank you."

He released the sink and pushed away from it. Darius walked to the tub and leaned down. "Be safe, doc."

His lips briefly touched hers. A moan left him the same time her hand snaked out of the water to wrap around his neck.